Dare to Au Pair

Dare to Au Pair

MAIA CORRELL

CamCat
Books

CamCat Publishing, LLC
Fort Collins, Colorado 80524
camcatpublishing.com

Paperback ISBN 9780744310320
Large-Print Paperback ISBN 9780744311686
eBook ISBN 9780744310344
Audiobook ISBN 9780744310375

Library of Congress Control Number: 2023950718

Book and cover design by Maryann Appel
Interior artwork by CSA-Archive, Deepika Praveen, VoinSveta

5   3   1   2   4

To Jill.
My best friend and soul sister.
May our adventures continue to bring us joy, laughter, and
divinely timed lifelong lessons.

CHAPTER ONE

*W*ell, this is craptastic.

Yes. *Craptastic.* How else do I describe chucking all my post-graduation eggs into a Dublin law firm's marketing coordinator position? And spoiler alert, only to *not* get the job I'm way over-qualified for but desperately need to give my resume a distinguished glow-up to launch my career into corporate America's high-flier travel industry.

What a world we live in. Where fully packed resumes, sporting flying colors in academic achievement and esteemed summer internships still don't carry enough *va va voom*. And rosy as my references may be, the cutthroat reality is that foreign work experience is a necessity to even get me to Continental Air's doormat—better known as the company I've been LinkedIn-stalking since I was twelve.

I should've taken that Santander job when I studied a semester in Sevilla. In my defense, Spanish Culture 301 feat. Food and Film was a bit more enticing than donning the ever-alluring and wrinkle-prone bank teller button-up in the Iberian Peninsula. At the time, I'd figured I'd be a shoo-in for the next opportunity that came around—wrong. I guess being 20 percent Irish doesn't mean much these days. How could my people do this to me!

Still, if I'd chosen the latter option in Spain, I probably would've avoided this floundering situation: splayed out on my childhood bed, analyzing my overconfidence when it comes to job applications, while my bichpoo, Zelda, casts me a sleepy-eyed glance to signal it's dinnertime. I stare up at the glow-in-the-dark stars covering the ceiling, and it temporarily distracts from the hauntingly dichotomous belongings collecting along the room's perimeter. Like the plastic bins that've gobbled my college dorm's contents. One Direction cardboard cutouts from my middle school heydays. Frayed stuffed animals that I refuse to part ways with no matter how hard Mom tries to pry them from my hands.

And as much as I'd like to indulge in yet another evening of scouring the online job boards, blasting a '90s rom-com or Planet Earth documentary in the background to keep me sane, I've got to make myself presentable for this—sigh—date. Yes, *the* Kat McLauren is going on a date. It's been twenty-two years, so better late than never, right?

I'd be lying if I said it wasn't on my mind all week. Like my brain had been marinating in a deliciously potent cocktail dishing up buzzing delight and cloying dread. Love that for me.

So, even though my back wants to glue itself to my third-grade butterfly sheets for eternity, come hell or New England beach traffic, I'm not gonna show up a sniveling mess. Besides, the ride there and back will give me ample time to course-correct this barely budding career of mine. That's the secret to ten-year plans: failure is *not* an option, especially for this summa cum laude destined for a corner office with a view of the country's most prestigious airline.

—*—*—*—

SHOWING UP TWENTY minutes early for this devilishly normalized form of mate selection comes with its perks. Relaxing into a weather-worn bench on the lawn beside the town's yacht club, I drink in the sight.

The shipyard is peaceful tonight. Melting into an electric orange horizon, the sun casts its last rays across a sailboat-studded cove. Twilight's cool air blows off the Atlantic as the water's gentle rippling hints of winds beyond the herd of boats bobbing around Hyannis Port.

For a moment, my focus cascades into the evening's serenity, capturing the scene in my memory—only mildly cursing for leaving my Canon at home.

Families, lovers, and friends stretch out on wooden decks, admiring the coral sky from their boats. How easy it must be for them to sink into their private bliss. I wish I could join them in their calm, diving in and rinsing off the worries of the world. Except my incessant foot tapping would have another thing to say about it.

Seriously, Kat.

I watch my foot bounce up and down, taking notice of my unpainted toes. Shit. Of all the footwear at my disposal, I had picked sandals. The one option that highlights my gloriously dull, unadorned toenails. Hopefully he doesn't think unpainted toes are uncouth, gross, or lame.

He, being Conor, whose profile I stumbled across last week on the dating app I swore I'd never use. But after many lonely nights I don't care to count, my friend Tiff not so subtly snatched my phone and downloaded it, insisting that it was my turn to finally "get some."

His profile isn't bad. I mean, he's objectively attractive, yes. Dusty blond hair. Probably hits the gym six days a week after a morning protein shake and might even sprinkle a few CrossFit sessions in there too. Definitely a lifeguard.

And our obligatory prescreening text chat isn't too mind-numbing. If discussing the newest fad to practice yoga while goats climb on our backs doesn't scream sexy, I don't know what does.

Really though, how else am I supposed to break the awkward tension when messaging a stranger who could turn out to be obsessive, psychopathic, or worse . . . nice. It would be great if I had prior roman-tic experience to pull from. But I don't. While everyone else my age was out having their sexual awakenings, I was burying myself in school and barely surmountable course loads. On the one hand, I've kept my clean-as-a-whistle academic record on its pedestal for all to see—Con-tinental Air most especially. On the other, the art of the French kiss is vitally missing from my life's report card.

I figured once I hit the first tailgate at UConn, shotgunned a Mill-er Lite, and wowed all the boys with some forced extroverted charm, it'd be smooth sailing from there. Yet, as much as I idolized the idea of *lady in the streets but a freak in the sheets*, I found myself watching from the sidelines too often to count. My roommates would make out with strangers at a New Haven nightclub or go skinny dipping without a second thought.

And there I was, propped up in bed preferring to watch *Little Women* or *Sleepless in Seattle* for the thirtieth time. In my defense, my choice was a tad more appealing than slugging vodka shots until 3 a.m. just for a guy drenched in cologne and back sweat to stick his slobbery tongue down my throat. And thus began the self-fulling prophecy for a dating dry spell.

Back to Conor. I wish I didn't have to use a blurry picture of a guy from his first frat party to gauge my attraction toward him. Why can't we have it like our parents did? Walk into a bar one night and find your mystery person hunched over a pool table. Better yet, what about the Jane Austen era? Walk downstairs and you oh-so-casually have company over to call on you. It's always some bogus connection like a friend of a friend of a cousin's old governess. Then, suddenly, the surrounding world collapses as your eyes meet theirs. From that moment on, whenever your paths cross, there's a fire lit beneath you, a shortness in your breath—and no, it's not the corset.

Wouldn't that be nice. Sometimes I think Jane should be shelved in fantasy. There's nothing general about that fiction.

Don't get me wrong, my life goal isn't marriage and triplets by twenty-three. But when you've still never even had a first kiss, you can only wonder if you'll be a bachelorette for life. Seriously, why is it that I can deliver the keynote at my graduation ceremony without a whisper of nerves, but the second I have to interact with the opposite sex, I'm a fumbling mess who doesn't know left from right? It's like all my intelligence, wit, and charm—if I have any—gets vacuumed from my body.

I flick up my phone.

7:37.

He was supposed to be here seven minutes ago. By now, the sun has almost fully sunk into the horizon, and the briny breeze reeking of low tide wanders to places where my chiffon dress isn't thick enough to block out the chilling air. Late May in Massachusetts really only brings warmth between the hours of ten and two.

I shift on the bench, nearly splintering the back of my bare thigh. Finally, my phone dings. I whip it up, my disappointment fleeing as quickly as I read his text.

Hey. So sorry to do this, but do you think we can reschedule? I popped a tire this afternoon.

Thank the heavens. After the superficial niceties of making sure he was okay, I let the whole date slide right off my back. The way I see it, I showed up, I did my part. I'm hoping his version of "rescheduling" is the same as mine, i.e., say it to be polite but no hard feelings if we both just let it fizzle out.

My stomach howls, and now that I have my night back, I know exactly how I want to spend it: plowing through enchiladas from the best Mexican restaurant in the Northeast while watching copious amounts of *Gilmore Girls* on my laptop.

I bolt to my car after picking up my order and sputtering out a few shaky sentences in Spanish to the hostess. Sure, I may have gotten a biliterate stamp on my high school diploma and minored in the language in college, but every time I have to use it, my brain likes to pretend it's washed all the built-up knowledge down the drain.

As if on cue, Tiff calls on my drive home.

"Yes?" I say to the dashboard speaker.

"How did it go?"

I give her the details, scant as they are.

"Kat, I'm so sorry."

"It's fine, really. I've got better plans." The warm tortilla chips taunt me in the passenger seat. "Wait, that came out wrong. I'm sure he's nice and all—"

"Why do you keep avoiding going out with someone?" Tiff blurts out.

Easy for her to say when she's had guys fawning over her since the seventh grade when she invested in a push-up bra.

"I'm not avoiding it, I just have—"

"Other things to focus on?"

"Well, yeah." I'm getting defensive now. She knows how important Continental Air is to me. I've been wanting to apply to their Young Soarers program since I first found out about it. It's only been within my top three talking points for the last decade.

"I just want you to be happy," she says.

"I don't need a guy to be happy. I need the fruits of my frickin' labor to start showing up."

Tiff's silence catches me off guard. I look at the dashboard illuminating my face. It's the only light gracing my body, save for the stoplights and neon street signs shining through the windshield. Kind of weird to think that once the big light bulb in the sky shuts off for the day, we're humbled to our small but mighty presence. We're left with ourselves and what we've created, good and bad.

Damn, I'm on a roll tonight.

But that's the problem I keep running into: I've got the one-liners—loglines in the making—but nothing to tie them together. No story. And I don't have the time to try and figure it out, at least not right now. If I wanted to be a filmmaker, I wouldn't have majored in Marketing, right? At the time, it seemed like the most creative of the "regular" degree paths. But, nonetheless, I'll get to the entertainment industry eventually. Once I've got my platform, fulfilled my tenure in corporate America, and figured out what the heck I'd make in the first place.

It's not for lack of trying. May I present the dozens of filmmaking competitions I've entered from second to seventh grade. Pardon my French, but screw the Massachusetts Junior Creatives board who said my work lacked "vigor, originality, and vulnerability." We try not to think about that. Besides, I'm sure the *eventual* patrons of "An Ode to the Lobsterwoman" would have thought differently.

It's the worst itch I've ever faced: a yearning to play in a different world but no clear entryway. I'm just a business school misfit with a pesky spark.

Nonetheless, I still have space for content brainstorming sessions on my calendar to keep my creative juices refreshed. I've had to move it around a few times, but it's there. I'll get to it.

But mark my words, Kat Nieve McLauren *will* be a filmmaker. She'll direct. She'll produce. She'll write. She'll run the gamut regardless of the genre she settles on. There's no pigeonholing this phoenix even if she doesn't know the route to her dreams . . . yet.

There's a clatter coming through the speaker. "Tiff, you there?"

"Mm-hmm. Sorry, we're cleaning up from dinner. Our au pair came today. She's from France." Tiff, being the oldest of five brothers and sisters, used to be the go-to babysitter when we were in high school and her two lawyer parents were tied up in court. When she and I went to UConn, her mom learned of an au pair program that hires anyone eighteen to twenty-eight from around the world and sticks them with a family to handle their kids.

"France," I say, sighing. "Sounds nice."

"How's your practice Young Soarers application coming by the way?"

"Fine." Of course I don't really believe that, but like hell I'm gonna let Tiff know. We may be best friends but I don't want her to hear me squirm. It's bad enough she gets to live with her boyfriend in New York while they work at their cushy accounting firm. I don't need to openly admit that I'm freaking out over previous years' essay prompts that I'm only using as prep for when the real application drops this summer.

Let me explain.

The Young Soarers program has to be the most coveted, the most prestigious, the most determinant of future success that the travel industry has ever seen. Reinforcing its hard-to-reach reputation, Continental Air only opens the hallowed admissions gates to new applicants every six years. And it just so happens that this year—my graduation year—intersects with the next induction window.

To be a Young Soarer is to be among a revered class of finance whizzes, top-tier marketers, and eloquent public relations professionals. I've had my sights set on it since I was still losing baby teeth and making Excel sheets outlining the most illustrious companies and their top-earning positions.

Now, as a fresh college graduate with a business degree hot off the overpriced textbooks, I *will* be among the fifteen Young Soarers selected, continuing en route to fulfill my vision board's timeline. First: Complete the Young Soarers three-year rotational program with stints in Accounting, Marketing and PR, and Pricing. Second: Schmooze through the corporate matrix with my plan to serve a lengthy term as the airline's international content editor—a.k.a. travel blogger, but with dental. I have to. It's only meant to be, given that I've been manifesting it for over a decade. Ever since I watched my first episode of *Globetrotter* and started making Pinterest boards chock-full of sculpted architectural masterpieces and turquoise waters. If I can't be a full-time movie-maker just yet, then I'll gladly settle for a country-hopping journalist in the meantime. Ideally, if I could somehow pair my future filmmaking career with world travel, *that* would be the dream. But the dream has to wait. There's no telling how many books on the law of attraction I've impulse bought after listening to the respective authors speak on podcasts. Okay, fine. Seven.

I don't take such an intensive plan lightly. Oh no. I'm putting in the hours. I *have* put in the hours. All those countless weekends when I had opted to plow through essays and miscellaneous assignments so I'd have ample time to review them before their deadlines, consequently forgoing spontaneous beach days and ski trips. All to ensure high marks, while filling my "free time" with campus club meetings. After all, a Young Soarer is "a leader who keeps their visions in sight, navigating their way through storms and maneuvering with gravitas."

Check, check, and check.

Unfortunately, however, I'm missing one vital check: sufficient work experience abroad. And no, my semester in Sevilla doesn't count. Studying in a foreign country for six months is apparently *too* mainstream these days.

Muddled conversation and clanging silverware pounds through the speaker. I almost forgot Tiff and I were on the phone.

"Hey, do you want me to send the au pair website your way?" she asks.

"Why?" I grip the steering wheel tightly, my knuckles getting whiter.

"You need the experience, right?" Her voice teeters on a matter-of-fact and polite suggestion seesaw.

My jaw clenches as the law firm's rejection swarms my frontal lobe.

"I don't know if that qualifies," I grumble.

"It should. You know my brothers. What our au pair will be putting up with can probably guarantee her a seat in the CIA."

Stomping on the car break, my torso lunges into my seat belt. Narrowly avoiding a deer darting across the road and into my headlight, the brown lunch bag holding my precious tortillas goes flying toward the glove compartment before spilling out on the sand-caked floor mat.

Lovely.

And by the time I pull into the driveway, my spicy rice bowl is getting lukewarm enough where it'll need the microwave to zap it back to life; the perfect segue to cut this conversation loose before I have to endure any more embarrassing pity.

—*—*—*—

I DON'T KNOW what made me do it.

Okay, false.

Pinot noir. That's the culprit.

Seriously, the one night I let myself go wild. What can I say? One and a half glasses later, and I'm a different woman.

I had just finished my spicy chicken, extra guac burrito bowl when the notification popped up on my phone. Tiff sent a picture of her family and the au pair from their earlier dinner. Next to pasta-sauce-smeared plates, their wine glasses hold only a few drops. It'd probably been one of those long dinners, where they've lost track of time and eaten so much but still have room to shovel in a few spoonfuls of Häagen-Dazs.

Must be nice. I take a long sip from my own glass.

"Don't waste me!" the red wine screams. I reason it'll start tasting funky tomorrow. Plus, I'm not *too* tipsy . . . yet.

As if my fingers have a mind and motive of their own, they tap away at my laptop's keyboard. I've interrupted my reality dating show and intermittent Instagram scrolls for this very important career-hinging research. It leaves me staring at the words "au pair jobs" sitting in the search bar. Hey, I *have to* indulge myself. If I can finagle an international job overnight, then only two months stand between me and submitting my perfectly pristine Young Soarers application. And when I'm *obviously* inducted—seriously, how many candidates have dedicated two-thirds of their lives to whetting their marketable skills and curating an immaculate academic record?—it'll at long last be the satiating culmination to a nearly fifteen-year-long effort. An odyssey, more like.

I tighten the grip on my phone, scanning Tiff's photo. Then I scour the search results on my laptop and am drawn to the first company that pops up. *Dare to Au Pair.* The name taunts me a little. I click on the website link, and gigs posted from the Pacific Islands to India confetti the screen. My eyes examine the postings as my hand attempts to pour the last few drops from the bottle. The wine has obviously impaired my dexterity, my hand magnetically repelling itself from the glass as I struggle to get the cherry red liquid into the cup. A few droplets splash on the Continental Air brochures strewn along the counter, right across CEO Howard Gupta's face, staining his plump cheeks. His quote bubble snags my attention.

"We treasure your trip, big or small. Whether you're flying from Chicago to Sydney or London to Florence."

Mmm, Florence. Italy. Pasta. I could roll with that. But after thirty minutes of trying to find any open au pair positions around Florence, I am realizing I am a little late to the game. Italy must be a hot commodity for au pair hopefuls. I bet it's a bunch of eighteen-year-olds who want to take a gap year, fly to Europe, fall in love, and eat the best food of their lives.

And maybe they will, good for them. But I'm not into wishful thinking. It's never resulted in anything I can rely on.

Combing through the last remaining European positions, I stumble on one that was only posted fourteen hours prior. The site doesn't give much detail on the family for privacy reasons. The only information I can see is three kids, ages eight to eleven. Èze, France.

A quick Google Maps search tells me it's on the French Riviera near Cannes and Nice.

So maybe it's not Italy. But it's on the Mediterranean. And I do love a good baguette. Besides, when I studied abroad in Spain, I hardly touched France, except for one hurried weekend trip to Paris. Maybe Èze would be a good fit. Plus, the man ringing me out at a souvenir shop back in Charles de Gaulle airport had even told me I looked French. I still don't know what he meant by that. Maybe it's my brunette hair or the way I purse my lips when perusing a store. Could be my freckled skin or curvy hips or the fact that I can just barely skate by on basic French thanks to some affinity for language learning.

Thank goodness Mom's at choir rehearsal, unable to hear me drunkenly converse with myself as I rationalize this application and browse plane tickets. Normally, I'd sleuth through "pros and cons" and "liked, didn't like" videos on YouTube to help make my decisions. But tonight, the pinot dictates. And I don't care if it is the wine talking; my gut is telling me this'll be good. How can it not be? Dips in the glittering Mediterranean Sea, fresh-baked croissants, and I just have to watch some kids a few days a week. I mean, I've babysat before, in much less glamorous settings. And this *does* sound more attractive than the internship I didn't even get: filing paperwork and arranging a tax attorney's schedule in Dublin. I'll probably have spare afternoons to get some writing in—screenplay treatments, documentary outlines, the like. Maybe I'll embellish my creative portfolio, snapping some pictures and establishing video shots. A deep breath fills my lungs and swiftly escapes me as my email dings.

It's from the Welcome Team at Dare to Au Pair.

That was fast.

The subject line reads, "Félicitations et Bienvenue!"

I didn't think this far ahead.

Holy craptastic crapperoni.

CHAPTER TWO

*T*ruly, I wasn't expecting unicorns to start line dancing across the floor while the New England Patriots sprayed champagne on me. But I thought I would feel something a bit more special than the heartburn swirling in my chest. Those fleeting seconds of relief after reading the congratulatory email came and went, leaving me right where I started—lying on my living room couch, no one around to divulge the news to.

Is this how all my classmates felt? The ones that got their jobs pregraduation? What did they do after the momentary little joy ride from uploading their "thrilled to announce . . ." posts on LinkedIn?

Something about "So grateful to have graduated from one of the top business schools in the country, and now I'm gonna be a European nanny, but don't worry because it's just a dues-paying means to an end" just doesn't sit right.

I'd rather keep my feed blank and save it for something worthwhile.

Mom took the news as best as she could. I wasn't fortunate enough to escape her blank stare that had drawn out for what felt like eternity. She followed up with her slew of questions that I couldn't answer because the au pair coordinators didn't tell me jack.

"Is it safe? How do you know? Are they paying you? What about food? What will Continental think?"

That last one irked me most of all. Why would *they* care? It's not like this type of work is beneath them. Besides, why can't I make a decision for myself without feeling like I need the world's thumbs-up?

Anyway, it'll be the breath of fresh air I need from living at home. Don't get me wrong, Mom is a wonderful human. She makes the best pot roast and gladly joins me for ocean swims, even when the water temperature dips below sixty degrees. Aside from that, we're two very different people. Exhibit A: She dutifully attends weekly vestry meetings, and I go to church on my yoga mat surrounded by quartz crystals. Do I need an Exhibit B?

We respect our differences, but the air is getting stale. And working abroad as a last-ditch effort to bolster my Young Soarers application sounds a bit more enticing than sitting around the house waiting for her to tell me for the nineteenth time this eon to clean out my closet. All while I go on another string of failed dates. No thanks.

The morning after I applied to my summer soiree, a hefty hangover loomed in my forehead—what I get for going with the nine dollar, bottom-shelf bottle of red. I tried for about two hours to undo my application, but in my drunken state, it looks like I had signed the binding e-contract after the coordinator sent me my acceptance email. And I wasn't really looking to drop $500 on the withdrawal fee.

It all happened so fast. I didn't even have time to regret it, because my flight to France would take off thirty-six hours after my acceptance email came through, and I had to pack two months' worth of clothes into one suitcase.

When I told Tiff the news, she cackled until my silence clued her in that I wasn't joking, and yes, I was *actually* doing it. We promised to FaceTime, but we're reluctant to admit that it's just a nicety meant to make ourselves feel better. These days, text is our norm, even when we live four miles away from each other. This time, I think we both know what'll end up happening. She'll be free when I'm busy and vice versa. The five hour time difference is just an added hindrance.

Our friendship clinging to childhood memories, it's like my best friend is slipping through my fingers. Like our chapter together is closing for now. Then who will I have? My social life has shriveled up like a raisin in the sun. Once the corporate era starts, Tiff will be living it up in New York with her boyfriend, Trey, and I'll probably coop up in some dingy Boston apartment alone. All our other college friends have moved out of state to bigger and better things, or so they say. But at least I'll be in my dream job with Continental Air once this joke of a summer is through. I hope.

—*—*—*

THE PLANE RIDE, rather vainly I thought, would be productive.

"I'll have so much time to brainstorm," I said to myself. Maybe I'd finally finish my documentary outline on Icelandic orca pods or the memoir from study abroad that's nagging for my attention.

Sometimes I appease the Capricorn in me with the productive butterflies that come from thinking about the work, as if the act of planning it is equally as exciting as doing it. But the leather-bound journal and my favorite ballpoint pen sit in my backpack underneath the seat in front of me. And I don't bother moving an inch to retrieve them.

Instead, a twisting knot swells in my stomach. It's an all-too-familiar feeling. I felt this same out-of-body confusion watching my classmates walk across the graduation stage. Each of them wearing ear-to-ear smiles and the same not-so-flattering cap and gown. The promise of new adventures brimming in their eyes. A gilded vision of the future. An illusion. Seriously, did they really shake President Cawley's hand thinking, "Goodbye shotgunning beers outside the football stadium. Hello cube farm at insurance firm. This is where the real fun begins." Who am I to assume? Maybe they're stoked, and I'm glad for them. But I can't be the only one who didn't want anything to do with that. Or they just have immaculate poker faces.

Still, it doesn't change where I'm at now. It's not like I can redo college. I don't know which direction I'd choose if I even had the chance. Filmmaker of sorts, yes. But when a career lives on a project-to-project basis with no guarantee of stability, income, or health insurance, it's hard to even think about taking the leap. Or, at least, that's what my divorced mother has drilled into me.

Plus, it's hard to admit to friends, family, and even strangers my dream to be a full-time creative if I'm not already a world-renowned Octavia Butler or Steven Spielberg. Like until you've won an Oscar or have taken home a National Book Award, don't even bother classifying yourself a creator of any caliber. It's a baseless and wildly false extrapolation, I know. But tell that to my clenching throat whenever someone asks about my real career aspirations.

My education is invaluable, I know it. Outside the major, it got me to think critically, to ask questions and learn from unique angles. I just wonder if my diploma read something different, what path it might have opened up for me.

But I can't daydream any more could-have, should-have, or would-have scenarios. Because if my plan of becoming a Young Soar-er inductee comes to fruition, I'll be well on my way to living out the timeline on my vision board's collage of magazine clippings.

Kat McLauren, travel writer extraordinaire with the nest egg to dive into the world of entertainment. A clear vision at my ship's helm . . . hopefully. Sure, there may be some residual impatience for not throwing the ten-year plan aside and taking life by the horns now. But I'm not willing to chance sitting in a two-hundred-square-foot apartment eating Cup Noodles for the ninth night in a row, wondering why I threw my common sense down the drain. Fact is, the uncertainty of it all would chew me up and never spit me out.

On top of all of this swirling in a constant loop around my head, I can't possibly write even half a sentence on this circus of a flight. Across the aisle are two women who apparently hadn't read the unofficial rules to pipe down after dinner was served on the red-eye.

Nope, they go right on with their conversation, so by the time we've reached the middle of the Atlantic, everyone on board, including the pilot, can tell how upset woman #1 is with her daughter becoming a yoga instructor in Bali and how woman #2 can't fathom where the younger generation's work ethic has gone.

It completely interrupts my perusal of the sparse documents the Dare to Au Pair company had sent about the kids I've been assigned. An eleven-year-old girl and two eight-year-olds, a boy and a girl. No names listed. All that's provided is an image of a rustic cottage, an address, a list of French emergency services numbers, and a brochure highlighting must-see attractions in the French Riviera.

The plane gabbers continue on with their gossip, so I cue the noise-canceling headphones.

Ah, that's better. The first dollop of quiet on this trip settles in, bringing with it a tingling in my stomach. I don't have enough evidence or Wi-Fi signal to consult Google for which of my chakras is getting all fired up. Then I begin to feel something else. Down my back this time. Not tingly. Wet. Cold and wet.

What the—

I leap forward as the chill sends shivers up and down my spine. Turning around, I meet the menace. It's a three year old who spilled his juice bottle. I smile at him and then his father who desperately apologizes in French. I open my mouth but realize I have no clue how to say this in his language. So I go with what I know that's closest.

"It's okay. Está bien." My aggressive head nods communicate more than my words.

He's cute. The kid, I mean. Well, the dad's not too bad looking himself. Forget age. He looks like he could be in a Giorgio Armani commercial. But as much as I can hope for a drop of vain attention, I'm delusional if I think he'd ever flirt with me. Without makeup, I can pass as a high school sophomore.

I wave to the little boy. At first he playfully grins, biting one of his fingers and giggling intermittently. But that ends without warning. Not two seconds later, his juice bottle goes flying and smacks me right in the forehead. His laughter explodes as the orange juice drips down my jawline. Other passengers offer napkins and empathetic glances that make me want to hurl.

Instead, I scurry to the bathroom at the rear of the plane and comply with the faucet's weak water pressure. The hairs framing my face are still sticky as I coat them with a damp paper towel. The coolness gives me pause, and I stare at myself in the reflection.

What am I doing?

I've exceedingly succeeded in having the most dreadful start-of-a-journey flight. Maybe this'll be the only bad juju for the trip. There's a hiccup in every travel story, right? I've just gotten it out of the way early on. I'm fine with that. So long as it's not foreshadowing my life for the next two months. I thought babysitting would be easy.

After I return to my seat and give the father and his kid a polite *it's-not-okay-but-I'll-pretend-like-it-is* nod, I grip the plastic armrests for the next three hours as my worries torment my brain.

What if I just quit while I'm ahead?

No, I can't do that. My hopefully soon-to-be Continental Air co-workers will think I have the work ethic of a fruit fly. But maybe I can find an excuse that would let me go home. Something socially acceptable that wouldn't stab my integrity or conscience. In the meantime, I just hope I can wrangle these kids better than I can the toddler kicking my seat.

CHAPTER THREE

*O*f course, *these* are my options. After dashing off the plane and toward the nearest souvenir shop in the terminal to replace the juice-stained T-shirt clinging to my lower back, I came upon the only remaining tops in my size—because I wasn't going to be one of those people flinging open my suitcase in the middle of an airport, giving every passenger, pilot, and air steward the pleasure of gawking at my pink zebra print underwear. (Don't judge. They're comfy!) Hence, why I'll either have to sport a France national team soccer jersey with a cobalt rooster or a see-through white tank with a big old croissant etched over the chest. I choose the former.

After collecting the rest of my luggage from baggage claim, I rather efficiently field a swarm of texts from Mom, answering in the shortest sentences possible now that I've reclaimed service.

I take a moment to drink in the scene. It's funny. Back in Boston, people's foreheads would be frozen in strain as they quicken their pace from the parking lot to the Dunkin line to their gate.

Here, a lackadaisical calm washes over most travelers, more interested in laughing while consuming café au laits at the bistro than they are in retrieving their bags. It's a symphony of sorts. The clinking of espresso cups, each couple or trio in their own conversation vacuum, completely indifferent to time. Bathing my ears in the French chitter-chatter passing by, I take momentary respite in the lyrical rhythm of the Romance language, dropping my shoulders to take full advantage of the soccer jersey's airy, moisture-wicking material.

Sticking with this might not be so bad after all.

But let's hope to high heavens I didn't just jinx the crap out of myself.

At the exit, floor-to-ceiling glass walls herald in the bright summer light. And though a kiosk selling fresh boules and pastries attempts to steal my attention, my buzzing phone alerts me that my Uber will leave in two minutes if I don't get a move on.

Outside, the sunshine paints my cheeks as a salty ocean breeze brushes against regal palm trees lining the street before kissing my bare neck. It's like an elixir. Like the place warps time and space completely. The air, balmy and soft, coats every inch of my skin like a waterless bath. In my daze, I locate my driver's license plate among the line of rideshare pickups and greet him with a head nod and a *bonjour* as he loads my luggage into the trunk of the Porsche. Not too shabby, huh?

His eyes go to crescents as he opens the side door and gestures for me to slide in.

I can tell by the way he's arranged a plethora of guide maps in the back seat pockets that he's one of those that panders to visitors. His wide belly and plump, round face are as welcoming and gentle as the sunshine. But the second he starts the car and the engine rumbles, my calm is broken. He, along with the other French drivers, floors it out of the airport car park. My palms grow increasingly sweaty. My left hand grips the seat belt, and the right takes hold of the paper map.

We ascend rolling green hills peppered with charming villas to the left and an oceanside cliff to the right. If he took a hard break, we'd surely go flying off the road and down hundreds of feet. Hard to appreciate the cobalt waters when they could be my gravesite at any second. But his driving eases as we take to a more residential route.

I peel the map off my hand, glued on by sweat.

The driver looks through the rearview mirror.

"Français?" he asks.

"N-no."

His smile is gentle. A few crease lines decorate his forehead, no doubt enhanced by years spent in a place like this, where the beaming sun and alluring seaside beckon the coastal residents outside every second of the day. He seems nice enough, but that doesn't stop me from hovering my thumb over the "track my ride" button. Precautions have to be taken.

I fumble around in my backpack for my Canon and snap a few wide shots of the transfixing landscape before us.

"Photographe? Photo taker?" The half-balding driver makes an imaginary camera with his hands, but I wish he'd put them back on the wheel.

I shrug. "Sort of. Not really."

Who am I to say without a credit to my name? My stomach tenses as I look at my camera.

"Américaine?" he asks.

I only nod. He doesn't need to know more than that.

"Summer vacation?" His accent is thick as peanut butter, but it's understandable.

"Something like that."

"No better place than Côte d'Azur."

I examine the paper map once. In the twenty-five minutes it takes to complete the nineteen kilometer trek to Èze, we transition from a mini highway tucked in the shrub-covered mountains to more residential lanes overlooking the city of Nice and the verdant Saint-Jean-Cap-Ferrat peninsula.

The driver points to various locales to our right. I feel the blood drain from my face as I see his gaze stray from the curving road in front of us. A two-foot stone wall separates us from impending doom, but as if he has eyes around his entire head, he spins the wheel at the perfect moment to keep in his lane.

A deep sigh departs from my upper body, my shoulders slumping back into the seat. I figure I might as well try to relax. I feel like Mom, always on pins and needles.

I shake my head, as if brushing off the bad juju I'm lugging around. Out the window and down the hill, one side of Nice is packed with apartment buildings, where locals decorate balconies with potted plants and the blue, white, and red-striped French flag. The other side of town is just as dense, but the sun-baked, weather-beaten terra-cotta roofs echo a longer history. Most buildings take on a washed yellow hue, almost glittering in the sun. There is an energy, a liveliness, one can feel even from hundreds of kilometers above. The entirety of the view is breathtaking, captivating. It's imperceptible where sky ends and ocean begins.

The roads we drive along are no less hypnotizing. Traditional brown stone cottages with lavender shutters dot the green ridges to my left alongside modern stucco French villas. Stacked stone walls hug the narrowing road like bookends, keeping the hills upright.

In the last twenty minutes, my once-tense body has loosened. My palms, once sweaty, have dried. It doesn't bother me—as much—that Antoine, the driver, barely evades dinging the motorcycles parked along the skinnying roads as he unfolds almost his entire family's history. How his parents, aunts, and uncles owned a vineyard a few miles north of Nice before Antoine's immediate family relocated to Èze where he and his wife opened a wine store.

La Cave. In English, The Cellar. Pronounced like *cah-ve* as Antoine instructs.

He offers to stop and show me, promising a few samples. I shake my head and politely decline. The family would be expecting me soon and—the family! I must've thrown all common sense of cordiality out the window. A gift. I didn't bring a gift. Do I need to bring a gift? Even if it's a terrible one, isn't it the thought that counts? I allow Antoine to take the detour, hoping he'll be able to guide my decision as to what's appropriate and what's not.

Soon, we make it to the main village in Èze a few miles north of the beaches, and it's so unlike what I've seen thus far. Here, flowering vines coat stone buildings sandwiched between tight and narrow cobblestone paths. It's quieter than Nice, but no less lively. It harkens to a place where toddlers take their first steps in the same spots as their great-great-great-grandmothers. The brochure highlights its medieval roots, but that's not to say the population is without the modern conveniences of pharmacies and real estate offices.

Antoine pulls to the side of the road, where a cluster of cars are parked.

Wind bouncing off the ocean cascades up the foothills and intoxicates my being. It's like it could lift me up and let me float for a little while.

He points up an inclined pedestrian street lined with shops displaying anything from fresh-picked citrus to handmade jewelry. Each of the doors is only a foot taller than my 5'2" stature. Conversations mull at the quaint outdoor cafés, where the paths widen just enough to fit six square tables. The crunch and savory scent of crusty bread makes my mouth water and my stomach rumble. I follow my guide past an ice cream shop selling hand-spun gelato and novelty dessert. While the pistachio cream and its biscotti crumble topping tempts me, the shop to the right wrangles my attention.

Peering through its window latticed with iron rods, I notice it's the only darkened store in the lane. The paint on the sign above the doorway is faded and chipped. Once bright dandelion-yellow letters signal a *librairie*. I'm guessing bookstore, given that *librería* in Spanish means the same. I squint a bit harder through the clouded glass. Empty ivory bookshelves line the walls. Tables in the center host cardboard boxes full of books collecting dust.

Do people not read anymore?

A red sign with white lettering plastered across the wooden door reads *a vendre*. I glance through the windows once more, imagining what must have once been a homely enterprise, a local's favorite. But I soon realize, someone's in there. A petite woman with frizzy brown hair lugs a few more boxes out of a back room. She heaves them on a central table, sighs, then sees me staring right at her, her forehead wrinkling.

Antoine mumbles something to me, pointing to a few doors up the street, and I break my stare with the woman in the bookstore. He holds his belly as he ducks into La Cave.

Hardly any sunshine sneaks in through the windowless storefront. The warm orange light painting the wooden bottle racks and stacked stone walls makes it seem like it's perpetually 8 p.m. Antoine greets his family with boisterous shouts, hugs, and cheek kisses. He introduces me to his wife Marie and their daughter Emilie—Emi.

"Tu rentres tôt," Marie claims, adjusting her oval glasses.

"Oui, Papa. You said you wouldn't be back until dinner," Emi adds, carrying a wooden crate with clinking wine bottles.

Antoine gestures to me standing in the doorway. "Ah, but we have a *spéciale* request." He says something in his wife's ear who immediately casts an endearing, honest smile and officially welcomes me inside.

While Antoine's and Marie's accents are thick like pea soup, Emi, who happens to be my age, speaks English as clearly as if she grew up in the States. And it turns out, she did. Well, from ninth through twelfth grade, she tells me. Turns out her mother wanted her to have wide-open options and that having English—much as she wanted Emi to keep her French heritage at the forefront—would put more opportunities on her path. Thoughtful.

Emi takes my arm and walks with me around the shop like she's known me her whole life.

"So what do you think?" Her accent hasn't escaped completely.

I wriggle my brow.

Emi expounds. "France, the Riviera, Èze?"

"Oh, it's beautiful." I stop myself from saying bonita or preciosa. "How do you say it in—"

"*Magnifique*." She smiles. Her bobbing auburn ponytail mirrors the bounciness in her voice. "Come, you have to try." Emi gestures to the twelve-foot-tall racks along the wall. My eyes trail to the deep cherry-red cabernet sauvignon from Bordeaux to the dusty pink rosé from Provence. But then I realize it's 10 a.m., and I'm meeting the host family in under an hour.

Shaking my head, I profess, "Oh no, I couldn't. I can't."

"But you wouldn't know if it's good or absolute *merde*."

I scratch my temple. "I didn't think you'd sell err . . . merde . . . here."

"Well, what's merde to me might be *orgasmique* to someone else. That's why you have to try it."

She's got me there.

Antoine chats up his wife while Emi pours me more than a hefty sample for me, then her. A pinot noir from Burgundy. I follow her lead as she swirls her glass and sticks her nose to the wine, inhaling aggressively before taking a sip. Silky, delicate, light-bodied, not too sweet.

Emi places a few pieces of dark chocolate, nuts, and cheese cubes on the counter and urges me to pair it with the wine. The flavors explode on my tongue, the accoutrements unmasking notes imperceptible on the first sip.

"You like?"

I nod, and we chat about our school history. Me, a marketing graduate. She, finishing her teaching degree in the next year. She fills me in on Èze's top boulangerie and what time to get there for the best selection. Her aunt and uncle on her mother's side are florists with a storefront two doors down. They have the very best selection of pink carnations and tulips.

I tell her briefly about my time in Spain. My tone doesn't venture beyond frank in my recollection. Not all study abroad semesters are coated in whimsy when you spend eighty percent of the time in text-books instead of backpacking the European Union.

Emi tilts her head. "So who are you staying with? Friends? Friends of your family?"

"I'm an au pair." A heavy weight drops in my stomach. The fact hasn't yet sunk in.

When I ask Emi about the closed bookshop I had passed just moments before, she swats her hand as if it's pointless to inquire. She hesitates saying more, and just as I am about to press her further on it, Antoine's voice bellows from the other side of the shop, bounding around the echoey stone walls.

Turning around to see what's causing the commotion, my eyes land on *him*.

The words "future husband" flash inside my brain while an explosive hormonal supernova crashes through my body.

For anyone who's ever denied instant attraction, they're either virgins of it or resentful liars. I don't know what it is about this guy. Sure, he's objectively—and most definitely subjectively—attractive. I do have a thing for tall, averagely muscular men wearing crewnecks and not-too-tight joggers. And his sun-kissed, wavy hair wrapped in a low bun only bolsters his grounded aura. He opens his suntanned arms wide, greeting Antoine and his wife as if he's known them all his life.

Emi catches me mid-stare, and she nudges my elbow. I can't help it. Nor can I help my palms going a bit sweaty and the giddy vibrations trembling in my throat.

It's the same feeling I've gotten while making eye contact with some guy at the gym and spending the entire forty-five minutes of my workout wondering if he's looking back at me. It's like a pop song. He likes me. No he doesn't. Yes he does. But it only ends in mystery as we hop off the treadmills and go about our daily lives. If I was a more experienced flirt, maybe some of these exchanges would have turned into a string of dates. But, alas, I haven't dedicated as many hours to flirting practice as I have to becoming a straight-A student. I don't know what's worse, my lack of romantic experience or the fact that I'll have to admit that to someone at almost twenty-three years of age.

The heat in my cheeks spreads to my neck and collarbone as Emi pulls me over to him.

"Bonjour, *cousine*," Emi says to him.

He reciprocates her greeting, and they kiss each other's cheeks.

Cousin? Did she say cousin?

As he peels his face back, his eyes trail to mine. In case the light in here isn't dim enough to hide the crimson skin splotches burning along my chest and up my cheeks, I twist my in-need-of-a-good-shower fish-tail braid down my chest.

"Bonjour," he says to me. His smooth voice scalds my skin.

Get it together, Kat.

I clear my throat and stick out my hand, awaiting his. "Kat Mc-Lauren."

He and Emi sneak a smile to each other.

"Kat," Emi says. "You're in France. Give Jamie a kiss."

I take a sharp breath. "A . . . uh . . ."

Jamie's smile diffuses to a chuckle.

"It's okay, Em." When he drops the French, his accent doesn't match Emi's. He's English. Of course. The kryptonite of all accents. "Jamie Chessley, pleasure to meet you." He shakes my hand.

Hope you like sweaty palms, Jamie.

"So who's your pick? Griezmann? Giroud?"

He notices my scrunched brow and points to the—unintentional—conversation starter I'm wearing. I look down at the jersey.

"Kat's going to be an au pair," Emi says proudly, latching her arm in mine.

Jamie raises his eyebrows. Is that good? Bad? I can't tell.

"I wonder if it's the Savoy family or the Blanchets." Emi taps her chin.

Jamie looks at me. "You don't know?"

I shake my head and pull out the picture of the little cottage the company provided. I pepper in some details like length of stay—two months—and number of kids—three.

Examining the photo, neither Emi nor Jamie seem to recognize the house surrounded by grasslands and deduce it be farther out from the coast, possibly closer to La Turbie or Peillon.

I'm about to show them that the address line still says Èze, but I become distracted by Jamie's sudden proximity. His forearm rests close to mine as he examines the sparse au pair reference materials. Antoine catches my attention, nodding toward the entrance. His parking meter is almost up, meaning I have a few moments to pick out a wine for the family I know nothing about, but Jamie avails to help as Emi greets incoming customers.

"Looking for anything in particular?" Jamie asks as we peruse the stacks of bottles arranged by region.

"Something that says I'm not cheap but I also won't be a kiss-up and spend a fortune on something you're probably gonna cook with anyway."

He smiles and points to a few options. His hands look to be stained by something red, like strawberry juice.

"Why are you in France?" I realize this comes out blunt and abrupt, but his brimming smile tells me he doesn't mind. "I mean, you don't sound like you're from here. What brings you to Èze?"

"Family. This is where we holiday. Every summer ever since I was a lad . . . My mum loves this one." Jamie picks up a 2015 pinot noir. "So why did you decide to give up your summer to babysit?"

"Wow, right for the jugular, huh?" I smile playfully and relay my postponed career start.

The more we talk, the calmer I feel, my nerves melting away, unwinding the knots in my shoulders.

"I take it back," he says. "That's genius."

"What about you? What do you do?"

"Hmm, how do I know you're not some reporter incognito?"

"Oh, so you're *that* important?" The corners of my mouth rise with my lifted brows.

Either I'm reading way too far into this or there is definitely a vibe here.

Jamie's reciprocated and pearly smile makes my diaphragm swell. "Baker by night and sometimes day. But don't tell my parents."

"I know what you mean," I say, brushing my fingers against the cool glass bottles, thinking of the half-finished documentaries on Cape Cod summers and New England epicureanism sitting in my Google Drive that I don't dare share with Mom again.

I've been down that road before. And it only ended with her warning I'd be a "starving artist" and me slamming my bedroom door in her face.

"Seriously." The enthusiasm drains from his cheeks.

Marie waves to Jamie, gathering his attention. "Prends cette caisse," she says, pointing to a wood pallet crate housing at least fifty pounds of wine sitting in crinkle-cut packing paper. A tag tied with twine to the handle reads "Chateau Vigne d'Argent."

Jamie lifts the crate and nods to the doorway. "C'mon," he says to me. "I'll walk you out if you'd like."

After gesturing to the bottle in my hands, I scurry around my purse for the euros I'd collected before leaving the states. "I just have to . . ."

"Don't worry about it," Jamie says.

Does he have a running tab with this place? What gives him such special treatment, besides being Emi's cousin? Marie waves us off as she attends to the customers talking her daughter's ear off. Emi prances over to the door just as Jamie and I are about to leave.

"Come back as much as you like," she says to me. "I *desperately* need a friend who hasn't run off for the summer."

Jamie and I make our way out of the musky wine cellar and into the narrow, winding cobblestone streets. Not a hint of sunlight brushes our skin until we make it to the overlook at the end of the road. The view seizes my attention. It looks like half the world is before me with a sapphire-blue ocean stretching from east to west. Sailboats dot the rugged yet lush coastline. Though inhabited, nature still exerts its domain here.

"You didn't have to do that," I say, holding up the bottle.

"I didn't." I straighten my spine at his response. "Your first bottle's free now that you're basically a family friend. Antoine must've liked something about you to bring you in."

I feel Jamie's eyes on me as I examine my feet scuffing the pavement.

"So, Kat from Boston. If you're not too busy at that cottage with the kids—"

"Emi is just a hop, skip, and a jump away. Yup, I got that." I smile while one tugs at his own lips. The warmth encroaches again. This time, starting in my lower back.

"And when you're done visiting Emi, I work up there," Jamie says, nodding his head. "In the restaurant. Chateau Vigne d'Argent."

I look over my shoulder. Up a stone staircase on the edge of the slopes sits a hotel made of the same medieval rock in the street, save for the terra-cotta roofing. Square windows decorated with pastel blue shutters give way to the cascading overlook. A terrace with tables and umbrellas closest to the slopes' edge enjoys the brilliant view as well.

"I'm usually the third-shift pastry chef, but I've been picking up some day shifts."

"Lucky we ran into each other then," I say, my neck and face warming.

"Sure is. Like fate." He grins. "Come by for some coffee and dessert anytime."

I hope to goodness the sun masks my tomato-red cheeks. He probably doesn't mean it to be anything more than good manners. Like the wine. It's customary. I force myself to look into his electric emerald eyes for more than two milliseconds and give him a polite smile. If I've learned anything from four years at business school, it's how to maintain eye contact and give a firm handshake, even when every insecurity inside me is screaming not to give away something so precious, so vulnerable.

The luminosity in his eyes fades when I tell him, "Maybe. If time allows," in the most procedurally formal voice I can drum up. Pushing his mouth into a half smile, he nods and waves *bonjour* to me as I spin around and make my way to meet Antoine in the car park.

I doubt I'll actually ever see Jamie again this summer. How can I when I'll be chin-deep in au pairing three children in a foreign country without knowing a single person besides my new acquaintances Emi and Antoine? My jam-packed resume still desperately *needs* this summer to go well if I'm going to guarantee myself a spot in the Young Soarers with Continental Air. I won't get distracted just because I have the hots for someone. Besides, Jamie would find out eventually what a fraud I am. What would he think once he knows I'm essentially Drew Barrymore in *Never Been Kissed*? For now, it's better to focus on what I know best: relentlessly brownnosing my newest employer.

CHAPTER FOUR

*M*y fingertips vibrate with nerves, and I force a painful swallow down my dry throat. At first, the porpoising car exacerbates the discomfort, but the bumpy cobblestone road begins to smooth out, and I catch glimpses of ocean in between the line of tall cypresses decorating the paved asphalt.

When Antoine makes a wide turn to the right, he punches in a special code at a ten-foot-tall wooden gate. The digital padlock goes green, and the gate fans its two doors open. I drop my jaw at the sight before me.

"Bienvenue," Antoine says. The gravel car park crinkles as he pulls to the front of the house, or should I say mansion.

"Antoine, are you sure this is right?" I ask, hastily pulling out the reference photo in my paperwork. Where's the squat little brown stone cottage nestled among prairie grass?

He chuckles a bit but doesn't explain himself.

Before me is a peach plaster chateau boasting two long rows of windows decorated with polished wooden shutters. The walkway to the front entrance forks to a connecting marble terrace wrapping around the house, and I suspect this is only a taste of what to expect inside. As I continue gawking, Antoine finishes unloading my suitcase from the trunk. He returns to the driver's seat after a long line of texts pepper his phone display. He sighs before waving to me.

"Mademoiselle Kat, c'était un plaisir. We'll see each other soon, I'm sure."

Wait, what? I step toward the car, but he's already in reverse.

"Angela's waiting for you," he yells out the window.

Who the hell is Angela? And how does Antoine know her?

He zooms past the entry gate and speeds off down the drive.

And just like that, I'm stranded in front of a gorgeous mansion that doesn't match the already sparse details I was given about my arrangements from Dare to Au Pair. I spend a few seconds scolding Kat from that buzzed May evening. *She* should've vetted this company more, especially with a name like that.

I drag my bags across the gravel, craning my neck to gander at the estate. A pang of embarrassment stirs in my stomach. My scuffed ruby-red Keds don't exactly match the palatial paradise vibe.

Every detail that might improve the residents' quality of living has been meticulously implemented. Even down to the wire basket wrapping around a towering leafy green tree. It holds mounds of chestnuts ready to be consumed. But I doubt any person that resides here has actually collected the tree's droppings.

I tidy up the side bangs falling out of my braid and convince myself that the deodorant I applied seven hours ago will hold up. Hopefully whoever answers the door won't notice any notes of fresh B.O.

Oh, but of course there's no doorbell. Maybe the two brass lion door knockers, one on each caramel-glazed door, aren't just decoration.

Except when I go to lift one of the rings, it doesn't budge, no matter how hard I strain. One of my suitcases slams against the stone porch, snapping off its handle into a million plastic shards. I scramble to recover the unstable bag, but as soon as I release my grip on the other, it too smacks the ground.

These people will surely have a hearty laugh waiting for them on their security footage.

I shake my head and lean the bags against the house's exterior—the few feet where there aren't any flourishing rose bushes or lavender plants.

Supposing my only other option besides jumping up and down and shouting is trying the terrace, I make my way west of the main door, but not before catching glimpses of a rolling field stretching past the right of the house.

Without a voice to be heard, I allow myself to frolic in the manor's fairy tale-like allure. The trellis-covered walkway to the terrace renders a shady, aromatic path with climbing vines of jasmine and orange blossoms overtop. It precludes a stunning oceanside view, complete with the Saint-Jean-Cap-Ferrat peninsula. No part of Èze's town center can be seen from up here, just the treetops along the sweeping mountainside.

My hand travels along the marble railing, warmed by the midday sun, and I drink in the sunshine. No one populates the wicker seating area, so I wander through the open glass doors connecting the terrace to a living room. Once my eyes adjust from the brightness outside, I set my sights on the interior. It's an immaculate blend of the building's history with modern comforts. Oil paintings surround plump sofas, and tapestry rugs rest over faded terra-cotta flooring.

"Hello? Bonjour?" My voice echoes down the sunshine-filled hall.

I find myself in the kitchen. Reclaimed cabinetry, a soft seafoam green. Wood beams stretching across the ceiling. Potted plants dotting the perimeter. Sunlight bleeding through, though not a speck of dust rests on the quartz island and countertops. Stainless steel appliances and a farmer's sink add a touch of modern glory next to the vintage brass pots and pans that hang over the stove.

An empty picnic basket sits on one of the island's padded stool chairs. My gaze trails to the round breakfast table where loaves of bread wrapped in paper and twine, fresh berry bushels, cheese wheels, and glass bottles of lemonade are spread along the knotted wooden surface.

The click of heels hitting tile crescendos too quickly for me to recollect the introduction speech I'd prepared on the plane. My legs cement themselves to the ground, and my arms lock to my sides. All sense of logic and proper human interaction escape me as soon as I hear *that* voice.

Commanding, feminine, and impatient.

"Te voilà. Et tu es Kat?"

I spin around. A woman at least a foot taller than me strides into the kitchen wearing a gorgeous houndstooth tweed pantsuit. She holds her chin high, looking down her nose at me as I sputter out "ums." It's an uphill battle to remember my name, place of origin, favorite kombucha flavor. It's only exacerbated as the woman starts tapping her foot and glancing at her watch like she has more important places to be.

"Yes. I'm Kat. Nice to meet you." An awkward half smile appears on my face. I feel my toes curl and shoulders rise the longer she goes without speaking.

"Hmm," the woman says, squinting her beady eyes. Her gold bracelets clink together as she crosses her arms. "Oui. Votre français?" She understands my English, so why she insists on French is beyond me. A sigh and a few eloquent foreign curses escape her mouth before muttering, "Your French? Is it any good?"

"My Spanish is better."

"Hmm," she says. "We'll have to fix that. Angela Lavergne," she says, sticking her hand toward me as if it pains her to do so.

"Have you had au pairs from the States before?" My voice begins returning to its normal pitch.

"No."

"Oh." Pitch up again.

"Follow me," Angela says, strutting out of the kitchen. "You're late. Let's not make that a habit."

I look at the time on my phone. Late? It's only three minutes past the time Dare to Au Pair sent me. Cheeks steaming, I hustle to catch up as Angela disappears down the hall.

"I prefer interviewing my au pair candidates starting in March, but my fashion line's autumn spread took precedence this year. Normally, I wouldn't use such a website for sourcing my employees."

Great, so I guess I'm the chopped liver of hired help.

"Our last worked for George and Amal," Angela name-drops. "But she only made it to July. We're accustomed to high standards in this house. I hope you'll be able to meet them." Angela doesn't look back at me once. Good thing too. It gives me a few seconds to rein in my bugged-out eyes.

We swiftly pass a few first-floor rooms I'd rather like to explore. A library lined in floor-to-ceiling bookcases and lounge chairs. The dining room with skylight windows and a long farmhouse table. Nearly every square inch of the house has been immaculately thought through. The furniture pristine, greenery or flowers at every turn, sunlight cascading in.

Angela breaks through my reverie with a stern warning. "The house is yours to use when you're not engaged with the kids. But under no conditions should there be any uninvited guests unless I myself approve them. We enjoy our privacy."

Angela spins around and takes a few steps in my direction; each heel click to the tile sends my heartbeat flying.

"Lastly, there is to be no, how you Americans say, funny business with my eldest son."

Eldest son? I rifle through the mental rolodex I filed away on the host family, trying to think of who she could be referring to. If I'm remembering correctly, Angela's three children are all very, very much too young to even be near my dating pool, let alone be in it.

"No exceptions. Should I catch you breaking this rule, you can say au revoir to ever working in France, or Europe for that matter, ever again."

I gulp, thinking about Continental Air's headquarters in Britain.

"I know what la Côte d'Azur can do," she examines me head to toe, "to *les hormones*."

Ah, zee French bluntness.

"You don't have to worry about these hormones. I promise."

"Bien." Angela sticks her chin up again. "He doesn't need any distractions. I know it's tempting for girls of your age."

I balk, taking another glance at the wealth oozing off every square inch of her home. What the heck is she talking about? From what I read in the information packet, the eldest son is only eight years old. What would I distract him from? Maybe rich people raise their kids to take over the family business from a young age? Or there's another son in the picture that Dare to Au Pair hadn't mentioned. And if there is, it's presumptuous for Angela to assume I'd get sent into a tizzy before I've laid eyes on him.

"Are my rules clear?"

"Crystal." I quickly follow up with, "understood," when Angela's furrowed brow tells me she doesn't get the American colloquialism.

"I'm always watching," she says, holding my stare for much longer than necessary.

We arrive in the foyer, which faces the ocean. The terrace clearly extends farther than what I had traipsed over. It's like the house has been spun around so its residents can take full advantage of their coastal view. Angela barely raises her voice, as she calls up the curving marble staircase. She forces a wry smile at me as footsteps above intensify. Doors overhead swing open, and two screeching girls come bolting down the hall.

"No, Josie! That's mine, give it back. Maintenant," the older one says in an accent entirely different from her mother.

"You have two already, Manon!" the younger one says in an identical accent. They're English. Guess this is a popular holiday spot for the Brits.

"Because I asked for them for my birthday. It's not my fault you wanted a Nintendo."

"Girls!" Angela's voice doesn't dare enter shouting territory.

Her daughters turn their heads over the railing, halting their argument over a pair of wireless Beats headphones.

Angela gestures toward me. "This is Kat. Votre au pair for the summer."

Manon, by my guess the eleven-year-old, tilts her head, and her strawberry-blond bun droops to one side. "Maman, we don't need a babysitter," she insists, rolling her eyes.

"Yeah," Josie says, crossing her arms and sticking her tongue at me. By that move alone, I match her with the eight-year-old listed in the information packet.

Angela's lips tense, accentuating her mile-high cheekbones. "Joséphine Lavergne Chessley!"

Chessley? Why was that name so familiar?

"Maman, Maman!" Footsteps scuffing the stone hallway come into earshot.

A boy runs to Angela's waist. Is this her eldest son? He looks younger than Josie even though he's supposed to be the same age. His index finger, purple and throbbing, has a piece of wood poking out of it.

"Oh, Milo." Angela holds up his hand. "Que s'est-il passé?"

"I-I-was in the olive grove and," Milo pauses to catch his sobs. "And I wanted to hang . . . from the trees like George. And my hand . . . slipped, and now I have . . ." he blubbers before wailing into his mother's waist.

Enough summers spent climbing trees in my backyard taught me a thing or two about splinters.

Angela tries to mar her impatience while she pats his back and smooths the mop of hair out of his eyes. "His favorite show. C'est Américain."

"*Curious George?*" I ask.

Angela's caught between a nod and an eye roll.

"I can help," I say. My tone is half asking and half declaring.

Milo's face is blotchy from the tears. Angela peels his hands off her pants and spins him to me. I kneel down to his eye level.

"Hi, Milo. I'm Kat. You watch *Curious George?*"

He nods, but his frown remains.

"You know, I like to climb trees at home, and I've gotten my fair share of those too." I point to his affected finger. "Lucky for you, I know how to get them out. Want me to show you?"

"Will it hurt?" he asks.

"Not for more than a second. C'mon." I hold my hand out to his, and to Angela's surprise—and mine—he takes it.

I whisper to Angela for a pair of tweezers as I walk Milo to the kitchen where I grab a pot off the wall, using Angela's nod as my permission. The faucet knobs labeled with a C and F throw me for a loop. I start with the F, thinking it'll dispense warm water but Angela clears her throat and shakes her head.

"You want chaud."

I nervously smile, completely aware that she and her kids are watching me as if I'm about to perform surgery. After filling the pot with warm water from the sink, I sit Milo on a stool. His sisters have followed and now watch with intense focus. Maybe they're waiting for me to mess up, but I won't give them the luxury.

"Milo, do you remember that episode when George went to Australia with the man with the yellow hat?" I spent every morning from ages five to ten watching the show before the school bus came. When Milo nods, I continue. "Do you remember what they were looking for?"

"The Perseids," Milo mumbles, and I stick his hand in the pot of warm water.

"So when George goes out at night hunting for the creature, he might've been a bit scared, but it was all worth it for the adventure." Milo doesn't see me grab the tweezers that Angela had placed behind him. "George was brave, wasn't he?"

Milo sniffles and nods. His sobs have slowed.

"Okay, Milo. I'm going to pull out the splinter."

His face crinkles, and he pulls away. More footsteps echo down the hall and toward the kitchen, but Angela pays no mind, and the girls are too enraptured in my procedure to notice.

"Do you think you can be brave too, like George?" I say to Milo. "I know you can. Your sisters think you can too, right?" I smile at the girls, and they quickly agree. Milo doesn't say a word. He just nods and looks away.

"I think you might just be the bravest boy I've ever—"

"Owie!"

"—met. That's it, it's all out."

Milo heaves a relieved sigh and brushes his dusty blond hair out of his eyes with his dry hand. Angela pulls out a box of bandages from the cabinet underneath the wine shelf.

"Well, now that that's all settled," Angela says, lifting her son off the counter before diverting her attention to me. "Are you ready for your picnic?"

"Picnic?" My first thought is wow, these people are hosting a party for me. But that daydream quickly crumbles as I set my eyes on the unpacked hamper I'd noticed earlier.

"When you get back, we will go over the remaining détails for your summer with us. Sylvie prepared your lunch. And Kat, please make sure Joséphine actually eats her food and doesn't spend the whole time picking daisies."

"And who is Sylvie?"

"Our cook," a familiar voice rumbles behind me.

I turn toward the voice and come face-to-face with the six-foot-tall pastry chef I'd been speaking to not forty-five minutes earlier at La Cave.

Jamie.

This is Jamie's family! Of freaking course it is. Over two million people live in the French Riviera and the family I get placed into belongs to the man that makes my tongue dry up and palms go clammy when his soft, rounded eyes land on me. A burning warmth invades my cheeks, already tomato red. He's washed his hands of any cherry juice stains. My focus lingers around his forearms. Toned and tanned.

Realizing I'm staring, I quickly retreat my gaze to the marble countertops. But my eyes can't stay away for long. I smile at the somewhat familiar face, but he doesn't reciprocate. There's not a hint of recognition of me in his eyes.

"So. Wait. You? Wh-what are you doing here?" I ask, tilting my head and putting down the tweezers I haven't yet released from my constricting grip.

"Suppose Mum didn't put me on the advert." Jamie ignores my curious gaze, walking right past me and fishing over the cheese and bread selection waiting to be packed.

"But—" I scrunch my brow. The air conditioning is icy against my sweaty forehead.

"Jamie Chessley," he says, tapping two fingers to his chest. His tactless tone reeks of arrogance. A complete 180 from the guy I met in the wine shop. "And no, you won't be in charge of me."

"Maybe if she was, we'd actually be able to get a hold of you, hmm," Angela says, intently avoiding eye contact with her son.

Jamie's eye roll isn't as indiscreet as he tries making it.

"Maybe I like to be left alone," he grumbles.

Angela lowers her voice, but the kids are too busy arguing how to pack the picnic hamper to notice.

"Why? So you can drink until the wee hours of the morning and shag every girl who walks by you?"

My eyes widen.

"Better than anything going on here," Jamie responds coolly. I stand awkwardly between mother and son duking it out, unsure of which side I'm to take, if any. Angela is by no means offering a warm welcome, but Jamie's standoffishness, toward me and his mother, has bad attitude written all over it.

The Jamie I'd met today doesn't match the one a few feet from me. The one I met was gentle and approachable. This one has a snarling look in his eyes.

"Well, Kat." Angela turns to me. "You won't have to worry about this one," she says, barely nodding in Jamie's direction. His nostrils flare, and his knuckles whiten as he clenches them into fists. "Probably won't see each other unless you're up at four in the morning to see him sneak in, back from wherever he was . . . *whatever* he was doing."

I scrunch my brow in confusion. Was the Jamie I'd met in the wine shop an illusion?

"Jamie." Angela's accent thickens as the recollecting ire fuses into her tone. "How is your father to trust you with Chessley Enterprises when you still act like you're seventeen? Et qu'il est temps de grandir."

Jamie digs his hands into the countertop behind him. He drops his voice. "Maman, don't tell me I need to grow—"

"Milo, stop!" Josie whines.

Josie and her twin nearly knock over the vase of carnations on the little round table, tugging on a bottle of sparkling lemonade.

Angela raises her eyebrows at me, and I scramble to subdue the bickering, packing up the hamper and sweet-talking them with promises of a wonderful get-to-know-each-other picnic. Milo is game, but the girls won't have it.

Apparently, I'm intruding on their lunch. Manon, the oldest and only a few years away from adolescence, is not too keen on being watched over for the whole summer. And Josie quickly forfeits her own opinion to assume Manon's attitude.

"I don't want to go with *you*," Manon huffs. "Do you even speak French?"

"Well, I'm learning."

"Kat will teach you Spanish," Jamie says unexpectedly, but still with a curt chill to his voice. Angela scrunches her brow, but her ringing phone impedes her from pressing on his comment as she addresses the incoming message. Manon crosses her arms. "I *don't* need a nanny."

Jamie kneels down to Manon's height. "Bien, parce qu'elle est journaliste incognito," he says, casting a playful grin my way. For a mere second, the Jamie I met in downtown Èze shimmers in his emerald eyes.

Angela looks up from her phone, catching me studying Jamie. Her brows narrow, and her lips purse as her eyes cloud with suspicion. I give her my most professional smile, trying to communicate that in no way will I be pursuing her town-flirt jerk of a son. In his best cinematic voice, Jamie announces, "Here to document the rare Chessley wildebeests in the wild." Jamie gives his giggling sibling's hair a quick tousle. Angela's tensed brow softens as her attention returns to the kids.

Josie grabs her older brother's hand. "Jamie, will you come with us? Please."

"Josie," Angela says, resuming her email scrolling. "Jamie has other things he's spending his day doing."

Jamie scoffs. We catch each other's gaze.

"I'll go," he says.

"You will?" Manon asks, pausing from chewing on her thumbnail.

Manon's and Josie's enthusiasm picks up. Milo seemed like he couldn't care less, as long as there are profiteroles packed next to the gouda rinds. Jamie takes his sisters' hands. I take Milo's, and we follow Jamie's lead out the kitchen.

As Angela waves us off, she calls out, "Oh, and Kat?"

I let the others go on ahead as I circle back to Angela.

"Don't forget about the rules." She raises one eyebrow before abruptly strutting off. "You are here to work, remember. Ce ne sont pas des vacances."

I stand gaping in the kitchen for a second longer. The whirlwind of meeting the family and Jamie's plot twist of an appearance is enough to send my mind spinning, but I'm determined to get some answers. For one, why he's pretending not to have met me.

CHAPTER FIVE

*I*s it unfair of me to have had a few expectations? I mean given the fact that the website's description of this family was "modest couple with three mild-tempered children in need of basic assistance." Something must've gotten lost in translation.

The quaint cottage I'd been duped into believing would be my home for the summer turned out to come with a major upgrade. I shouldn't be so angsty about staying in one of the most pristine villas along the French Riviera. But as it turns out, the peacefulness of the house doesn't match the juvenile creatures I'm now tasked to watch over. My preconceived notions of the *type* that would live here were teased out in my shock at their style of dress. When I first stepped foot on the property, heard their English accents, I'd pictured them dolled up in polos and sundresses. Rather, I found Josie boasting what looked like something picked up at France's version of an Old Navy, Manon in a Twice K-pop band tee, and Milo in basketball shorts and a grass-stained cotton T-shirt.

At least a few of the mysteries could be solved now that Jamie was with me, forced against his will by Josie's puppy-dog eyes. We find our way through the olive groves adjacent to the mansion and eventually come to a dirt road lined by chestnut trees. To my right and over a few verdant hills, a conical stone tower pokes out, but I can't see the entire structure it's connected to.

"C'mon," Jamie says, nudging my elbow. "This way." He forges ahead to the end of the lane. I refuse to let any other heat splotches invade my body. It can't happen, not with Angela's strict *no-frisky-business-with-the-eldest* rule. I won't give into temptation. It's not worth getting fired and forfeiting my destined spot in the Young Soarers program.

The road spills into an open field dotted with wild daisies and buttercups. The ocean shimmers in the distance, its current lines clear and fierce. We set a gingham blanket out before arranging the food buffet-style. If this isn't an aesthetic, I don't know what is.

The kids scarf down a few pieces of bread with figs and brie. Jamie makes them each have at least ten green beans before they start playing games in the field.

"You'll thank me later," he says. His siblings don't catch a whiff of what he means, though I can't help but chuckle. We've all been there.

Then, it's just me and him. In forty-five minutes, I've met two Jamie Chessleys. One gentle and kind. The other a callous and supposed flirt. But which one is real?

I'm hoping he's the first to make the small talk, but lo and behold, he just drinks in the sun, leaning forearms behind him. At this point, I'm over it and starving for information.

"What was that all about, back at the house?"

Jamie shrugs, sips on some lemonade, and says indifferently, "Can't imagine what you're talking about."

"Why'd you pretend not to know me?"

Jamie squints his eyes at me. "*Do* I know you?"

"Oh come on, cut the crap."

A smile tugs at the corner of his mouth before settling back to neutral.

"You didn't know your family hired a complete stranger to watch your siblings for two months?"

"Not sure if you can tell, but my parents and I aren't exactly close." Jamie looks off toward his siblings who are currently chasing each other around the daisies swaying in the sea breeze. "I wouldn't have told you about what I do if I had known you'd be——"

"Why does that matter?"

Jamie shakes his head. "You wouldn't understand."

God, I really hate that line. How assuming. How pretentious. How degrading to my emotional intelligence. I leer back at him.

"Try me."

"Well for starters, you'd probably be on your way back to the States if it seemed like we'd already bumped into each other. I didn't mean to come off like an asshole, but I had to keep Mum off my scent and yours."

Huh, that's a relief. Jerk-wad Jamie is just an act. But he seems to lean into it sometimes even when Angela isn't around, like he's trying to temper the buoyant side of him.

"So you know about the no-frisky-business rule too?" I tilt my head and chew my inner cheek, my gaze sheepishly straying away toward the field.

Jamie paws through the picnic basket for some grapes. "Practically ingrained in my brain for the last decade. And every year, I get the same lecture on it. Mum's a bit of a control freak about it, if you can't tell."

"Well, have you ever . . ."

He shakes his head, a few loose strands of hair framing his sharp cheekbones. "No, no, I've never been interested before."

Before? As in, something's changed this time around? My sternum and neck are set on fire. Any moisture on my tongue evaporates after I muster a miniature gulp. I catch Jamie's still gaze for a few milliseconds, his face solemn, like he'd just said something he shouldn't have. He quickly peels his eyes away and continues assembling a plate of fruit and cheese.

"Besides that," Jamie says assertively, as if erasing the moment that just transpired. "If Mum knew we met, she'd go down every rabbit hole to figure out when and where. She doesn't need to know about my spare time and that's the end of it." His jaw tightens, but before I can respond, he adds, "No one knows about my job at the Vigne besides Emi, Marie, and Antoine . . . I don't know why I told you. It just came out." He scrunches his brow.

"You don't think *I'm* gonna tell your parents?"

"I don't know. Are you?"

"Why would I?" I don't give him the chance to answer before I blurt out, "Why the big secret anyway?"

He wraps his arms over his shins. "Because I'm not looking to change who they think I am."

"They think you're a tequila-obsessed womanizer." The bite of bread and soft brie I take loosens my scrunched brow. Creamy, pillowy, wholesome. It takes the utmost concentration to bring me back to the conversation.

"Exactly." Jamie stretches out his legs, kicking off his brown suede sneakers. "What I do between four and twelve has nothing to do with them."

I shake my head. His jigsaw answers confirm his intention not to get any clearer than he already has. But it leaves more to be desired.

After a few prolonged moments, the breeze intercedes our silence, sending my piece of baguette flailing down the hill, and we both laugh. He proceeds to fill me in on *some* useful details about his family.

They are the Chessleys. His father, Nicholas, just so happens to be the tenth Earl of Harrowby. But what that means, Jamie tells me, is a spot on the guest list at the Queen's Jubilee and other exclusive London parties. Having grown up in farm-country England, Nicholas leveled up to become one of the top commercial real estate brokers in all of Europe. He'd met Angela on a business trip to Paris, where she was studying fashion at the time. They were inseparable. She agreed to marry him on the condition that she would finish out her remaining school years first and that no matter where they settled, that they'd vacation here in the French Riviera every summer.

Now he is Nicholas Chessley, European real estate magnate on the verge of settling one of the largest deals in retail properties across the Netherlands. It's a pinnacle career moment, thirty years in the making, worth well over fifty million euros. And then of course, there's Angela Lavergne, CEO of France's leading sustainable luxury fashion brand. It baffles me why the au pair company wouldn't advertise their accolades.

Jamie shrugs. "Mum's a pretty guarded person."

I huff through my nostrils. Fair enough. Truthfully, I can't confidently say I would've clicked submit on the application had the villa's photos been posted on the site. My level of luxury usually stops around a Best Western with breakfast included.

"What about Emi and her parents?" I ask. "They know about you and the Vigne. And they've never let it slip?"

"We have an arrangement," Jamie says. "I've convinced our head chef to source local. Local ingredients. Local businesses. The Vigne gets all its wine from Aunt Marie and Uncle Antoine. So their business always has a client even when tourist season slims down."

"And in exchange, they keep your secret?"

"They'd keep it anyway. They know the chaos on the other side of Mum and Dad finding out that I'm shattering the career plans they've manufactured for me. What I'm doing at the Vigne is pure mutiny, but I'm not throwing my life away to appease them. It'll be the big family blowout of the century, and I've been avoiding it ever since I started shaving."

"If you feel so strongly about it, why not come out with it?" I press, kindly but firmly.

Jamie, taken aback, broadens his shoulders. "Dad's spent half his life dedicated to this deal he's finalizing now. He's sacrificed more than he's willing to tell us. And he's told me a million and one times that there can't be a shred of bad press about the family if this deal is going to go through. So his clients can't find out that the heir to Chessley Enterprises is clearly not fully invested in the company."

"Not the most credulous," I tack on.

"Exactement," he replies, twirling a buttercup stem he'd picked from the grass. "I'm playing along until the contracts are signed and the deal is done. Then, I'm out. I'll help Dad find a new heir to the company, even if they aren't blood." He pauses to take a breath. "I don't hate them, you know. My parents. Sure we don't get along most times, but I won't get involved with things—at least not publicly—that might put a dent in their image and hurt their businesses and everything they've worked for."

I nod. "So you allow yourself the moonlighting job at the Vigne. What have you said no to then? What aren't you getting involved with?"

Jamie looks me up and down, flares his nostrils, and gulps quickly. My heart flutters for a split second. My palms go a bit sweaty as I wait for him to expand, but he looks off to the ocean. The wind has picked up, twirling our hair in a frenzy.

Manon, out of breath, comes running up to Jamie and me on the blanket for their promised desserts. Jamie only concedes after he redirects the request for my approval. My brow lifts ever so slightly. A tingly feeling dances along the crown of my head and back neck, but I dispel it, giving my nod to Jamie and his sister.

He hands her the pastries sitting in scalloped paper shells. She thanks him and me at Jamie's demand. By the way she tears her side-eye glance from me, I can tell I'm not included in her idea of a perfect holiday in France.

Jamie hands me a golden-brown cream puff filled with fresh-picked strawberries and the lushest, fluffiest whipped cream I've ever tasted. I'm about halfway through when it occurs to me that Jamie had been watching me pound it the entire time. My abdomen tenses. I wipe the cream off the corner of my mouth and put the half-eaten pastry on my napkin.

"Too heavy on the vanilla, isn't it?"

Feedback. He wants feedback. I relax.

"Did you make this?"

He offers a bashful shrug in response.

"It's amazing," I say, taking another bite. "Seriously. I judged the bake-off at my mom's parish fundraiser, so I think I know what I'm talking about." A grin pushes through my cheeks.

"And how do I compare?"

"Slightly better than Marjorie's mega-goopy lemon squares, but not as enticing as Roxy's burnt brandy snaps with curdled cream."

Jamie clears his throat, forcing away a brimming laugh. "Well, I'll have to up my game then."

"Oh, if you want a chance at beating Karl's raw apple strudel, big time." I bow my head, suppressing the giggle bubbling in my throat.

Sighing, Jamie straightens his spine, a coolness bristling over him.

With Angela at least a mile away, I didn't expect him to resume the can't-be-bothered act so soon. Was it something I said?

"So," he says firmly, paring an apple into slices. "What's your story?"

That question. It irks me. Always has. It's like asking someone how they're doing. Like, do you want the quick, conventional response, or do you want the gritty truth with more nuanced layers than a croissant made from rough puff?

"What do you want to know?"

He tilts his head. "You're in on one of my secrets. Don't you think I'm owed a bit more detail on Kat McLauren."

"I don't *owe* you anything." My tone chills.

Jamie plays with a loose string on the blanket.

"Can I then *request* some more detail?"

Broadening my shoulders, I fix my gaze on the ocean while dishing out full name, age, place of origin, education, and career plans a la Continental Air.

"Any hobbies? You know, what do you *like* to do, rather than what you *have* to do?"

I swallow hard. Though his face remains solemn and tense, he leans back on his forearms. The sun gleams over the wavy sun-bleached curls caressing his neck, his hickory roots are almost imperceptible in the sunlight. From what little I know about Jamie Chessley, he's used to putting on airs for others while harboring truths unbeknownst to anyone else. He values his passion. My gut feeling is that his curiosity in my own is genuine.

Am I really going to tell him? My pleather backpack is glued to my hip. I tug at the strap, and my hand moves to the zipper pocket where my journal sits inside. My cheeks warm with a blush, but the moment is cut short when Jamie's cell phone rings.

When he sees the caller, he answers hastily in French. The only words I pick up are, "no, no, no, no, no." He scrambles to get his shoes on before he bolts off the blanket. "I need to go," he says to me.

"What, but . . ." I gesture to the kids.

"You can handle it." Jamie waves to his siblings. "Au revoir!"

They don't seem to notice, too busy climbing some olive trees outside the groves.

In a matter of moments, Jamie's disappeared and the kids, exhausted and covered in dirt, are sitting at my feet asking what's next. Like I have any clue? I don't have an agenda. I haven't brushed my teeth since I left Massachusetts, and my knowledge of this area is beholden to the car ride I just had and what I remember of the movie *To Catch a Thief*.

Manon rolls her eyes when my silence crosses the four-second mark. Her expectations are going to be the hardest to please. Fortunately, Milo and I seem to be buds. At least, that's what I'm assuming based on the way he requires that I hold his hand on our way back to the house. The sisters lead, snickering as they occasionally look back over their shoulders.

"This way!" Manon takes a sharp left turn, clearly opposite the direction of the villa and straight through the olive groves.

"Manon!" I duck underneath the low-hanging branches. The kids make it through without a problem. The trees form a canopy above them. Milo releases my hand, and they're at least thirty feet ahead of me. The brambles and trees seem to thin out in front, and when I've finally made it to the clearing, my feet sink into a shallow ditch filled with sun-baked mud. The fertilized stench reeks of manure.

The kids erupt in roaring belly laughs. Even Milo did me dirty, literally. And I thought we were friends. At least that hopeful truth is confirmed when he comes over and assures me that he'll show me where they keep the towels.

I thank him gratefully, though I hold back that my concern isn't about my being dirty. It's about Angela's reaction should she still be at the house. I don't want to make it a habit of not living up to their mother's standards.

CHAPTER SIX

*M*y unzipped suitcase looms in my peripheral vision. The en suite bathroom, though a marble masterpiece, unfortunately can't block reality from sticking out like a sore thumb.

I haven't committed to putting my clothes away yet. I did the same when I spent a semester in Sevilla. Kept piling clean, folded laundry over the unworn items in my bag. Pretty soon I just started wearing the same five pieces that scattered the top of the pile. Somehow, it made the temporality of it all that much more prevalent. It was soothing, and at the time, an antidote for homesickness. That's not the reason I'm avoiding it now though.

There's just no good reason for me to stay here. I mean the kids, besides maybe Milo, think I'm Satan in disguise. Angela clearly isn't too impressed with my Americanness. And Jamie . . . I can't get a firm read on him. Sure, he's devastatingly gorgeous and makes my whole body blush just by glancing my way. But he goes from warm and charming to robotic and indifferent faster than the speed of light. Besides, Angela's rules prohibit me from getting involved with him anyway; not that I'm convinced that he's even interested, with his freight train of mixed signals. But there's one good reason for me to stay here: the Young Soarers program. How great would it look on my application if I au paired for eight hours before booking a one-way flight home? I'd be cast as a flake before my would-be cubicle had a name tag.

I flop onto the bed. Of course it's the most comfortable mattress I've ever laid on. I rest my head on the pillowcases made of satin-like cotton and stare at the wood beams crossing the ceiling. A small copper chandelier dangles overhead. I figured Angela would put me in the shabbiest room in the house. Assuming she did, this is still Ritz-Carlton level. The tapestry rug, wooden dresser, and boutique blush love seat give it a homely charm. Out the window, warm twinkle lights on the terrace glisten against one of the large chestnut trees. I poke my head around the drapes, and through the glass is a view of the water assuming the color of the night sky. City lights speckle across the juts of land and on board the sailboats in the bay.

The thump of a shutting car door twists a knot in my stomach. Gentle lantern light graces a stocky man with an indistinguishable face but a head as shiny as if it's been squeegeed all afternoon. From the driveway, he scuffs under the trellis and toward the main foyer.

How many people are at this family dinner?

I curl my toes as the muffled voices get louder below.

Get your shit together, Kat.

My pep talk draws me toward my suitcase, languidly at first. But the more affirmations I chant, the more semi-temporarily energized I feel.

"You're not some whiny loosey-gooser." I climb into my forest-green jumpsuit, pop in some pearls, and spritz the perfume that managed not to spill during its overseas jumble. I eye my reflection in the mirror, snarl, and flex my biceps inward. "I eat kids for breakfast . . . Okay, too far. Too far . . ." I broaden my shoulders and tilt my head, my chestnut curls tumbling over my shoulders. "At least I look fucking fire."

Leaving the cringe behind, I head down the hall with the bottle of wine in hand. The housewarming gift had completely escaped me in the flurry of my arrival.

Conversation bubbles beneath the grand spiral staircase. Leaning over the banister, I spot a few men chatting with Angela. The stocky, bald man I saw outside my window wears a red and white striped ascot. The other, tall with slicked back salt-and-pepper hair, gives Angela a peck on the lips. He must be Nicholas.

The rubber ends of my half-inch Target booties thump over the hardwoods. The men don't notice, but Angela snaps her head upward. I smack my back against a wall drenched in shadow. Angela, as it turns out, is a nightmare of mine come true. Getting on her good side is like a code even an FBI agent couldn't crack.

Earlier when I was self-touring the house, I'd found a secret staircase in the easternmost wing tucked behind a pastel-painted door that leads to the kitchen. I'm guessing it'll look better if I drop the wine off in there first before addressing this yet-to-be-determined group.

The descent down the wooden staircase transports me back in time. Sweet and musky hickory meld with the coolness of the unlit plaster walls. I crack open the door and see platters of food spread over the countertops.

Someone grabs the handle on the other side and swings the door open, a fluster of wind attacking my face. It's a woman about six inches shorter than me and forty years older, resting hands over the apron tied around her hips.

"Bonjour," I say, my voice wavering.

The woman tilts her head, her silvery strands of hair glistening in the warm kitchen light. She firms her grip on a rolling pin. Her biceps alone could qualify her as an MMA fight.

"Qui es-tu?"

While I could berate myself for eternity on why I didn't bother to practice a bit more basic French on the plane, I have to somehow convince this woman that I'm not a party crasher or a jewelry thief. But someone else takes care of that for me.

"Sylvie," the raspy voice says.

Jamie. He walks into the kitchen and rests his hand on the cook's shoulder before gesturing to me. The woman's eyes light up when she sees him. I can't help but stare a bit. He's cleaned up nicely. *Real* nice. Navy pants and blazer. Chocolate leather shoes. His hair, wound in a low bun, is still warm from the sun.

"C'est Kat. Notre au pair. She's from the States."

"États Unis?" Sylvie returns her gaze to me. "Est-ce que tu parles français?"

I know that phrase, so I shake my head without Jamie's translation. Sylvie makes what sounds like a disappointed "hmm" and crosses her arms.

"Sylvie is from Marseille. About a few hours' drive down the coast. She understands basic English, but she doesn't speak it."

"Ah. Um . . ." I quickly sort through the cobwebs in my mental arsenal of French lingo, but for the life of me, I can't remember what's informal and what's formal and which this situation would be considered. I don't have time to consult Google or my language learning apps, so I just have to swing for the fences on this one.

"Comment ça va?" I ask Sylvie. Wrong choice. Sylvie lets out a sigh through her nostrils. But I recover with, "I mean, I mean, comment allez-vous?"

Jamie forces away a grin. He couldn't be any more transparent. Fortunately, Sylvie seems to appreciate my efforts.

"Bien, merci," she says. The wrinkles on her face soften as a warm smile pushes through her freckled cheeks.

Sylvie understands when I lift the wine bottle, grabbing it from my hands and thanking me.

"Well I'm glad you're amused," I whisper to Jamie, though my voice doesn't stray from annoyed territory.

"I like that color," Jamie says, pointing to my jumpsuit. I look down and tug at the pant leg to distract from all the wrinkles that amassed from being shoved in a suitcase last minute.

"Oh, thanks," I say. "I like your . . . hair."

I like your hair? Really, Kat? Why don't you follow up with, "that heavenly cologne of yours is making me swoon."

"Well, I'll be sure to thank my mum and dad for the genetics." He smiles.

Okay, seriously. If Jamie Chessley's main priority is to keep his distance from me physically and emotionally this summer, this flirty side of him isn't helping us one bit. I wonder if this is how it'll be. One moment, he's the easygoing baker Jamie, and the next, it's the well-rehearsed stuck-up rich-boy act, complete with a bad attitude and no time for anyone, let alone the au pair. I'd rather he just pick a single persona, preferably the option that wouldn't get me fired, nor get my feelings involved.

A loud clacking sound steals our attention as Angela bustles into the kitchen, flicking her black dress out like a flamenco dancer.

"There you are," she says to Jamie. "Viens." She claps at him before readjusting her satin shawl. "You too." A nod in my direction lassos me with an invisible rope.

Jamie and I follow her out with a wave to Sylvie, who hums along as she finishes up the meal's preparation. Turns out the pots and pans aren't just decoration. And by the looks of the plethora of vegetables, meats, fish, and bread spilling over the countertops, I'm starting to think this dinner feeds a bit more than the family of six.

We're not two steps onto the terrace when I hear someone shout my name. Sitting at a long dining table underneath the trellis's canopy of wood beams, vines, and twinkle lights is Emi, Antoine, and Marie. Emi hugs me, and I stiffly comply as she kisses both my cheeks. Amid the day's events, the fact that Emi and Jamie are cousins had escaped my mind.

"Ça va?" She looks like she spent the afternoon by the beach. Her skin is golden. She's glowing. Either from the refreshment of a shower after wading in salty sea water or the fact that she's wearing a stunning coral-colored maxi dress with gilded stitching.

"Kat, how are you liking the place?" Antoine scratches his fluffy mustache.

"Just fine."

"And the kids?" Marie asks, sipping her sparkling water. She does a poor job at hiding her amusement.

"Um, well, they're fine too." I inadvertently catch Angela's gaze. "Great, I mean. They're great. It's great. It's all great."

"Great," Jamie says. He smirks at me.

Angela waves her finger between me and Antoine. "Tell me, how do you all know each other?" Antoine opens his mouth, but Angela cuts him off to ask me. "Did my brother drive you?"

I hardly nod, not sure if that's the correct response here. Angela pops one of her hips.

"Antoine, if it's money, you know Nico and I will help."

"Not everything is about money, Angie."

"Then pourquoi?"

Marie pipes in. "Conversation."

"Ah," Angela says, nodding though unimpressed. "Je comprends."

Even I *comprends*. Who doesn't need a bit of space.

I've been fidgeting with a loose string in my pocket long enough as I deliberate where my duties begin and end in the day. Angela and I hadn't gotten that far.

Does she expect me to get the kids? Is that overstepping? Does my role pause when she's present?

I twist my head around me, examining the rectangular table set for twelve—what is this? A state dinner for the French Parliament?—and start taking a few steps backward.

"Where are you going?" Angela daggers a stare my way.

"Um, the kids." I point behind my shoulder but lower my thumb as Angela shakes her head.

"Nico doesn't need help bringing his own children to dîner."

I suppress an eye roll, trying not to let the sting shine through. Jamie walks beside me and pulls out a cushioned wicker chair at the table. He gestures for me to sit and then takes the seat adjacent.

"She's tough on all the au pairs," Jamie whispers in my ear. "Just wants to test you early. Make sure you'll last."

The Jamie I'd met in Antoine and Marie's shop is returning in waves.

Moonlight sneaks through tree branches and casts itself over the ocean miles in the distance. My stomach howls. It's nearly nine o'clock. Dinnertime was late like this in Spain, too, so I thought I'd be used to it. Guess I'm rustier than I thought. Angela takes her seat at the head of the table while voices crescendo down the hallway leading to the terrace. Manon and Milo come bolting out the open door followed by the men I saw in the foyer. I get a clearer view of Nicholas Chessley this time around. He's about Jamie's six-foot stature, though a touch lankier, and they share the same emerald-green eyes, as clear as sea glass. He takes Angela's hand, and they share a moment's gaze with each other. Years of love, probably a few turmoils, and the treasures of a family created together all wrapped up in those few seconds.

The second man, a guest I presume, holds Josie's hand all the way to the table. He's beefy, but not as rotund as Antoine. His accent is a bit more Cockney than Nicholas's and Jamie's posh London vibe. The ascot wrapped around his neck leaves room for a jade pendant and gold chain to shine through. His dark skin and pudgy cheeks look entirely familiar, but I can't figure out why.

Angela orders her kids to stop playing with the rose bushes and to take their seats at the table. She glares at me as if to imply I should have been the one to summon them before she gestures her arm out in my direction.

"Nico," Angela says. "C'est Kat." Her lips tense as she examines me once more.

"Ah, the au pair!" Nicholas walks over with a smile and the same lackadaisical stride as Jamie. "How was your trip across the pond? Bloody turbulent I bet. Always is whenever I fly back east too. What airline did you take?"

"Um, United?"

"United?" The second man bellows, raising his bushy gray eyebrows.

"Ah, allow me to introduce my dear pal, Howie. Godfather to every one of these little rascals." Nicholas tickles below Manon's armpit. "Jamie included."

"Oh, I'm not automatically assumed a rascal, too?" Jamie spins a wide silver ring on his pinky finger.

"Jamie, don't be fresh." Nicholas points at his son, who sends an eye roll right back.

"Ah, he's twenty-six, Nick. Let him be a little fresh," Howie says, patting Jamie on the back. He extends his hand to me for a shake. "Howard Gupta."

I don't do much to lessen my dropped jaw. My future boss.

Good one, Universe.

"You-You own Continental Air." My voice is on shaky ground.

Angela finishes sipping from her water glass. "My, Kat. You already know everyone here, don't you?" I can't tell if that sarcasm is playful or vexed.

Howie tilts his head and smiles proudly. "You must've read the write-up the *London Times* just did for me." He broadens his shoulders, tugging at his blazer.

In person, his features are more aged and sharpened than anything in the media.

"You're my boss. I-I mean. You will be." I pause, scoffing nervously for fear of coming off obsessive or threatening. Jamie's knuckle nudges a glass of water next to my plate, but I ignore him. "I'm interested in the Young Soarers, sir."

"And look at you, here for the summer." He leans one arm against the back of a chair and gestures to the villa with the other. "A real traveler's spirit indeed. Kat, we'd be lucky to have you aboard."

He winks, and I swallow harshly.

Angela clears her throat, and, as if by hypnosis, it summons the kids and the men to take their seats. My eyes remain locked on Howie as he takes the chair two spaces away from me.

My soon-to-be boss. Here. Godfather to the Chessley kids. Wait a second.

The clanging of silverware as we unroll our napkins masks my hoarse whisper to Jamie on my left. "Why didn't you tell me he . . ." I pause and nod to Howie, ". . . would be here."

"Figured it'd stir the pot a little," he says with a wink.

All the seats are taken except for the one to my direct right, leaving a clear view of my future boss. It takes everything in my power not to devour the bread basket in front of me. But Jamie rips off a piece of baguette and places it on my plate. My blush evaporates as soon as he dispenses more bread to Manon and Emi.

"Sylvie." Angela raises her voice. "Qu'est-ce que c'est?" Among the six or seven on the table, she lifts the wine bottle nearest her. When Nicholas inquires what the problem is, Angela insists that Sylvie must not have seen the chardonnay she had picked out to go with the bouillabaisse. Sylvie only points in my direction. I grip the tablecloth hovering over my knees.

"You brought this?" Angela's voice is as rich as the butter tabs beside the bread, but stern as a dictator's.

"That's thoughtful," Nicholas says, ripping a piece of bread between his teeth. "Your favorite, Angie. Bourgogne."

Angela hardly lifts her mouth to a smile. "Hmm, lucky guess . . ." She stretches her gaze to my left.

It's Jamie's turn to grip something. He opts for crinkling his pants. But Angela continues trailing her sight to her own brother.

Antoine lifts his hands and says, "Wasn't me. The girl knows her wines."

Angela politely grunts as Sylvie continues on with the dinner courses. All seven of them. Fortunately, Jamie explains the order, starting first with an apéritif to stimulate digestion. Like a liquid appetizer. Following the others' leads, I take small sips of the dandelion-gold liqueur. Either it's supposed to taste like this or the bottle has gone rancid, because as soon as the sweetness dissipates, I'm left with a grassy aroma permeating my mouth. I reach for my water glass to get the dry taste out of my mouth, but Manon, who was watching my entire reaction, snickers at me. To spite her, I push my water back to its place and slug the rest of the aperitif only to regret it two seconds later as I cough against the fireball scorching my throat.

Manon: One. Kat: Zero.

The starter is a chilled veggie ceviche featuring green peas, cucumber, herbs, and local goat's cheese. After we gobble up the introductory plate, Sylvie serves small portions of the bouillabaisse soup. Saffron, fennel, white wine, and a hint of orange zest infuse the chunky pieces of poached rockfish floating in the bowl. The conversation pitters as we dunk our baguette pieces in the luxurious broth.

Howie asks Angela how her fashion line is doing. To her credit, it's been deemed the most sustainable luxury French brand, and they've just exceeded their fiscal year's goals. The feat turns heads, but her modesty squelches any praise that might follow. Rather, Angela dons the glory to Sylvie who's delivering our main course: braised lamb shank over a bed of truffle risotto and grilled garden vegetables. As a finishing touch, she drizzles the aromatic red wine sauce that tenderized the cooked meat.

"Délicieux, Sylvie!" Antoine lifts his glass of wine in her direction. She only bows bashfully before returning to the kitchen.

"How do you like your food, Kat?" Emi asks, popping a piece of eggplant into her mouth.

"Délicieux," I say without much confidence in my accent. Angela's eyes burn into the right side of my cheek. Her spot at the head of the table is fitting, where she can see everything and insert herself into conversations that she deems fit to intervene.

"There's more where that came from," Emi says.

Angela clears her throat. "Mmm, the French know food." She continues massacring her lamb shank with delicate silverware cuts.

Howie wipes his mouth. "Ah, you mean you don't like a good old Olive Garden meal when you visit the States?"

"A what?" Angela raises her brow.

"I fancy their breadsticks," Nicholas says.

Angela rolls her eyes.

We polish off a few more bottles, but I don't feel the regular topsy-turvy tipsy I do when I have more than a glass at home. Perhaps the food's just soaking it up. And amazingly, I'm not even full by the time Sylvie brings out the fourth dish.

"You're gonna like this," Jamie says to me with a sly eye.

"What is it? Snails? I've tried escargot before you know. Doesn't bother me as long as I chew quickly . . . and don't look at the plate."

He chuckles. His attention feels like sunshine.

"Le trio de fromage," Sylvie announces, placing a platter before us with three cheeses.

A long cylinder of goat cheese sits between a wedge of Roquefort, speckled blue cheese, and a circle of Camembert.

Cheese? *After* dinner?

My scrunched brow widens Jamie's smile.

Howie leans across the empty chair and says, "Don't worry, I thought it strange myself the first time I tried it."

"It is not strange," Angela sighs. "It is a delicacy, and if we had it earlier, it would've spoiled our meal."

"That's why you don't like mozzarella sticks, right, Maman?" Manon says, proudly looking quickly at Jamie to reciprocate her giggle.

Angela grunts in disgust.

"If only Maccy D's had those, Manny," Nicholas said, high-fiving his daughter.

The few bites of cheese actually do settle the meal quite nicely. And for the finale, we have Tarte tropézienne. After the piercing glare Angela sent Howie for calling it cake, I hesitate to call it anything but a sweet bun filled with a layer of cream. And either the wine is catching up to me or it's the fact that it's almost eleven, but this tarte transcends me to a whole other world. The light-as-air brioche melts in my mouth, leaving the luscious orange cream to be savored.

The feast has intoxicated me so entirely that I hardly catch on to Nicholas pouring the pièce de résistance, a twenty-year-old cognac. The knots in my shoulders and upper back have unwound themselves throughout the meal, and I slump back in my woven chair, swirling around the dark amber brandy. The licorice and vanilla notes perfume my lips.

"Enjoying yourself?" Jamie asks. His eyes have relaxed too, his shoulders dropped. Even the once-tight low bun has loosened, pulling out his wavy side bangs.

Before I can expand on my smile, Nicholas hijacks Jamie's attention.

"Jamie, are you ready for Amsterdam on Thursday? Did you read those contracts?"

I can tell by the way his knuckles whiten as he crumples his napkin that it'd be days before I see his presence at calm again. "Yeah, Dad," Jamie grumbles, avoiding eye contact with his father.

"Can't you sound a bit more enthusiastic? You of all people know how long it took to make this deal. We don't always host sales celebrations."

Jamie cocks his head. "So why the need for one now?"

"James." Nicholas's voice cools. "We are a family business. So we're going to act like one. I think you can take two days off from the clubs and the girls for a trip with your colleagues from Chessley Enterprises."

Jamie mockingly smiles and raises his glass. "Always business or bust, isn't it, Dad?"

Nicholas mumbles his stern response. "Yes. Now more than ever." He adjusts his collar. Jamie, now engaged in a game of sugar cube table hockey with Josie, doesn't seem to be paying much attention.

Angela twists her head to her husband. "Nico, quel est le problème?"

"Nothing, mon trésor." He pats her hand and takes a swig of cognac, but Angela's pursed lips tell me she isn't convinced. Howie takes the opportunity to shift the subject, though Angela and Nicholas remain disposed in their own side conversation. I keep my ear open to it, so that if it's about me, I can quickly prove their disappointments wrong.

"Speaking of properties," Howie says. "Sure are a lot for sale 'round here."

His declaration only allows me to catch the tail end of Angela and Nicholas's semi-private chat. "It could ruin everything. Maybe this'll set the record straight."

What does he mean?

No one else seems to notice. Antoine, Emi, and Marie are dozing off. Sylvie is close by, but her focus remains on clearing plates.

Nicholas addresses Howie, hammering on about the area's real estate market. How tourists flood the streets of Nice, Cannes, and Monte Carlo and can't seem to break the spell that the French Riviera has over them, so they resort to purchasing any and all property they can.

All this talk of buying and selling has reeled Jamie's attention back in.

"Whoever snagged that shabby little chateau a few miles down the hill"—Howie points in the direction of where Jamie, the kids, and I took our picnic—"has their work cut out for 'em."

"Pardon," Angela says, reengaging with her guests. "But what idiot would buy that dump?"

Howie rubs his shiny head. "Beats me. They're gonna have to pave the whole road to even get to it. To each their own, I suppose." He sips his cognac. "If it were me, I'd spend that kind of quid on enough pottery to fill my four houses."

Humblebrag. But a fan of the arts. Interesting.

"Ah," Antoine says, batting his eyes open. "But it has potential, no?"

"Only you would think so," Angela responds, clasping her fingers together.

Antoine smooths out his peppery mustache, leans back in his chair, and smiles wryly at his sister. "You and your standards, Angie."

Angela scoffs. "Well, where would we be without them, hmm? Certainly wouldn't have had the meal we just enjoyed or the view we see now," she says, sweeping an arm toward the harbor in the distance. "Il ne faut rien laisser au hasard. Pourquoi prendre le risqué."

Jamie's cheeks hollow out at the word *risqué*.

"Leave nothing to chance," Nicholas translates.

Marie pipes in with, "Comme avec la nouvelle assistante." She winks at Angela, who swats her hand playfully and toys with the pearls adorning her neck.

"Ce n'est pas vrai. C'est juste une rumeur," Angela defends.

Emi sees my befuddled expression and explains.

"Tante Angie allegedly set a private detective on her new assistant last year to make sure she wasn't selling trade secrets."

"Oui," Angela affirms. "Allegedly."

"And she was let go soon after. For undisclosed reasons," Marie adds. With a sly grin, she pokes fun at her sister-in-law. "What was it for, Angie? Not punctual enough?"

"Maybe because she wore a leopard blouse with striped pants," Emi jokes.

The chuckles sprinkling around the table aren't enough to convince me whether or not Angela is telling the truth. Regardless, the idea has ingrained itself in my brain. Angela spies on her employees, looking for a reason to fire them. Lovely.

The conversation returns to the crusty old chateau across the field.

Antoine crosses his arms. "I suppose you think these buyers then are hoping any leftover ghosts will tile the salle de bains and install a toilette."

Nicholas stretches his arm over his head. "Whatever their intentions, they better hope those ghosts charge a fair fee for the new furnace and flooring," he says.

Laughter sputters throughout the table as Angela and Emi tack onto this place's list of dire refurbishments. Marie doesn't add but chuckles along. Jamie straightens his spine and takes a final swig. "Windows could use some glass, too," he says.

I blurt out, "Mmm, to block the manure downwind."

Howie bellows deep-belly chortles and reaches out to shake my hand. "If you can roll with the punches of this lot, well, you're going to do just fine at Continental, Ms. McLauren."

A twang in my abdomen sobers me.

I *have* to stay in Èze. I can't quit. I can't get fired. My future depends on how well I do with the Chessleys this summer. It could make me. I could be best friends with the Continental Air CEO before I even get accepted into the Young Soarers program, or if I completely fail, I'd be doomed from the start. There is no going back. My vision board isn't going to manifest itself without a little elbow grease.

This is fate. This is serendipity. Like hell will I let it pass me by.

And according to the ten-year plan, I'm well on my way to attending the Young Soarers alumni brunch in eight Septembers, reminiscing on my brief but brilliant tenure before transitioning to world-renowned filmmaker—route to get there, TBD, but I'll narrow it down eventually.

As the conversation peters out and yawns catch like wildfire across the table, Milo walks up to me, his eyelids heavy under the mop of dusty blond hair. It's my cue to get the kids in bed, and soon, the others follow with hazy goodbyes.

I melt onto the mattress, my body nourished. Though what occupies my mind is a resolve to get on with the show. But without warning or reason, another thought lingers in my head. *His* room resides in the opposite wing of the house, yet its distance does little to squelch my instinctive interest in his presence. When I see him next, will he be the warm, inviting Jamie I met in the village or the cool, debonair Chessley he affronts to his family?

I scoff and turn off the lamp. Doesn't matter to me.

CHAPTER SEVEN

*T*he morning after, I'd expected to wake with a pounding hangover. But instead of feeling like my forehead is packed with boulders, I feel cleansed, like the evening and rest washed off a coarse layer of rigidity I didn't even know encased me. Trouble is, I sense its rebuilding as soon as I step foot on the terrace.

On the far right side of the balconied patio, two women enjoy their breakfast inside a glass birdcage that resembles a gazebo. It's Angela, dressed to the nines in her finest 8 a.m. satin summer dress. The woman beside her looks to be an alter ego, boasting a pixie cut, chunky dangling earrings, and a multicolored tunic. Angela drops in "Jamie" a few times. My weak comprehension for French can barely decipher the essence of their conversation.

"Je ne sais pas ce qu'il fait. Il doit être plus sérieux. Il est temps de grandir," Angela asserts herself, ripping through a croissant. She must be talking about Jamie. She said something similar to him yesterday when I had just finished tending to Milo's splinter.

The bohemian woman at the table rests her chin in her palms and shrugs. "Il trouve son chemin."

"Il appartient à Chessley Enterprises," Angela says, swatting her jam knife in the air.

"Dit qui?" the other woman challenges. Maybe she's not so keen on Jamie following in his father's footsteps.

"Estelle," Angela says, resting her wrists on the table and searching her friend's eyes for a more concurring comment.

"Je voulais juste remuer les choses," the woman replies with a grin. Her coral lipstick doesn't even smear onto one tooth.

I watch them long enough to see Angela's genuine laughter and intimacy with a close friend. But, as if she smells me, her eyes immediately shift to my figure decked out in "Shake Your Coconuts" pajama bottoms. Sighing back into her chair, Angela waves me over and points to a seat beside her friend.

"Estelle, this is Kat."

"Ah," Estelle says. "Wonderful to meet you. Angela's told me all about you."

All about me? She hardly knows me. I shudder thinking of what Angela must've spouted to this woman.

"Here," Estelle says, grabbing the basket of croissants. "Have some breakfast. Oh, and try that raspberry preserve. From the farmer's market. Do you like coffee? Tea?" Estelle holds up pots of both before setting them down and taking a bowl of chopped fruit and spooning the contents onto my plate. "Have some pears, too. Amazing."

"Before you dig in," Angela interrupts. "Some instructions for the kids."

She slides me a folder with neatly typed-up pamphlets of each kid's obligations and a master calendar to keep it all straight. Tennis practices, equestrian lessons, and pharmacy orders, among others. Though the family is on "holiday," Angela occasionally has to handle something for the fashion line, and Nicholas really only pauses work between Christmas and New Year's.

"You should take them to the Matisse museum. I got caught up there last night. Docent duties," Estelle says, sipping her espresso. "Why I missed your welcome dinner."

"*My* welcome dinner?"

Angela creases a volume of *Vogue* rather aggressively and sets it on the table. "Well, Estelle," she says, standing up. "I think we'd better get a move on to the vineyard, hmm? And remember, Kat, I take my rules very seriously. All of them."

Estelle nods my way and wishes me well. Angela strides across the patio without so much as an "au revoir," but her unblinking eyes don't separate from my own until she's inside the mansion again.

Could she be any more suspicious? I'm not out to steal her diamond earrings . . . or her eldest son.

For a few moments, the only sound is of the crashing waves miles below. I crunch through the flaky, buttery croissant and surrender to a few calm seconds of bliss before Manon, Milo, and Josie come storming through the breakfast area.

Guess this is my life now.

———*—*—*———

PERHAPS IT WAS a bit bold of me to assume I'd be just fine in acclimating to the family atmosphere, to the culture, to the language. I figured my relatively well-stamped passport would have prepared me well enough. This week, however, I found out I'm not immune to touristy fumbles, which Manon devoured as if more entertaining than any song from a Twice album.

In France, there are quite a few *erreurs* to make. Like not saying *bonjour* or *bonsoir* to shop owners upon entering. None of that bow your head while you browse and hope the cashier doesn't make eye contact. Here, chin up, greet the human running the show, and chug along. And another note, if you ever miss breakfast, do not squish a banana into your bag and devour it in the middle of the street unless you're prepared to get nasty scoffs tossed your way. Meals here are sacred and shouldn't be a second thought.

Regardless of my touristy fumbles, I'm rather proud of getting somewhat into a morning routine with the kids with only minimal help from Sylvie. It's like clockwork. A seven-minute temper tantrum from Milo and Josie about wanting to sleep in before they rise like zombies and reluctantly brush their teeth. Manon is usually good about getting herself dressed in time. She's more mature than I initially gave her credit for.

Breakfast is another ordeal, but I'm getting the hang of it. Milo only likes eggs with orange slices in the morning. Josie, nearly burnt toast with orange marmalade. Manon pretty much eats anything without dairy, given her severe intolerance to it. Sylvie helps with breakfast so long as I take the grocery shopping, which I don't find disagreeable at all. Supermarkets abroad always give me a strange high from perusing local produce to out-of-the-ordinary potato chip flavors.

I rely on Antoine to be our main driver, and once the kids are dropped at their lessons and classes, I can do as I please. Angela suggests I use that time to conjure up methods for handling the kids better, given that whenever she happens to be around, the kids are on their worst behavior. It's usually after we return from their scheduled activities. Hungry, tired, and irritated doesn't set the groundwork for the siblings to get along.

I've never been fired in my life. But I feel like I'm skirting that line now more than ever with Angela breathing down my neck and Manon determined to kick me to the curb.

After that snarky little "joke" about Angela spying on an old assistant, I can't help but look over my shoulder every five minutes. One wrong move and out I go.

It's only been a week, but I feel like I've been here an eternity already. I'd only seen Nick, as he asked me to call him, a handful of times. His client calls often require him to make short trips across the country and Europe. He and Jamie just got back from the Netherlands yesterday. And if I thought Jamie had a wall up around him before, it's gotten five feet thicker. On the night of their return, as I was closing out my reading session on the moonlit terrace, I overheard the tail end of a disgruntled conversation in the villa's library.

"Don't even think about it. Leave her alone," Nick had said. "Your actions have consequences, Jamie."

"What do my choices really have to do with you?" Jamie's voice was a screeching whisper.

"James. You know." Nick walked out on Jamie then and there.

Without a moment to dissect my eavesdropped morsels, I shuffled up the secret kitchen staircase and into my room ever so quietly as to not be seen or heard.

But what was the warning about? Leave who alone? Me?

The Jamie at the picnic denied his women, wine, and song act. But I haven't known him long enough to validate if there's complete truth to that. Clearly, Nick isn't convinced either. Even *if* Jamie ever feels some type of way about me, would I be just another girl whose name he'll forget the second someone else comes along?

I don't know why I entertain such delusions. It's clear whatever vibe I had felt between us in the Cave on that first day has entirely evaporated.

Before Jamie and Nick left for Amsterdam, I hadn't seen much of Jamie, except that time at breakfast when he gave Manon a head tousle before heading out the door without even a glance in my direction, erasing any semblance of our budding repertoire. Now that he's back in town, is it wrong to assume he's actually avoiding me? I get he doesn't want to be too talkative when Angela's around, but what happened to those British manners?

This is why I don't let myself get attached. Okay, too attached. To be honest, I feel rejected by a guy I never even made a play at.

He's twenty-six and has most definitely been around the block. I'm almost twenty-three and still waiting to cross the street.

But it doesn't matter, really. I didn't come here to have a fling.

I know what brought me here. Wine. Damn red wine. And if my hopefully soon-to-be boss wasn't the kids' godfather, I'd be on the next flight back to Boston, playing the "leaving for personal reasons" card.

In the meantime, it's like mission impossible. Don't quit, and don't get fired.

But so long as I have to wait out the summer, I can't deny that I'm in a breathtaking place, and I promise myself not to wallow my free time away in self-pity. I'm gonna see the riviera for *all* that it has to offer, starting with enjoying lunch under an awning at a café in Nice. With the kids at painting class in their "aunt" Estelle's apartment up the street, it's my turn to see what makes this neighboring city so alluring.

During the twenty-minute car ride from the green slopes of Èze, I had made mental notes of the crêperies and soap shops lining the turquoise waters. Its naturally high tourist levels make me feel a little less alone when I'm not the only one questioning why there's no ice in the glass of water I asked for. Fortunately, Manon, in a rare moment of kindness, implied to specifically request water from the tap if I don't want a bottle of sparkling to be brought out when I ask for *de l'eau.*

From my umbrella-shaded table, I purvey the scenery and orchestral summer frenzy. The city has few green spaces. It's mostly apartment buildings and shops towering over one another, but it's not suffocating. It's bright and airy with a whiff of salt water and coffee.

The streets bustle with tourists and locals making their way to the beach down the street. There's a mixture of local frustration with some ignorant visitors who don't care to learn an ounce of French and a reluctant acceptance that they live in a vacationland.

Clothing, makeup, and grocery stores embed a few English translations below their French signage. It's the evolution from resisting the encroaching language to a general succumbing. Still, I think the locals have a right to be firm in their hesitation. Language ties to the soul of the culture. And French, it's always been one that's transfixed me.

In the past week, while I've tackled a few more phrases and words to help me get by in town and with the kids, I'm eager to learn more. I *could* practice with the millions of French natives buzzing around me, but I resolve to the privacy of my language-learning apps. Duo, the Duolingo owl, doesn't laugh when I mix up *cucumbers* with *constipation*.

I'm halfway into my daze when someone taps my shoulder. Chills race up my spine. I could've sworn I just heard the whirring flutter of a camera lens shuttering.

When I turn around I see Emi. I peek over her shoulders. No camera or spy in sight. Maybe the summer heat is getting to me.

Her head held high and face lit up, Emi adjusts the brim of her straw sun hat and shines a smile. In her sundress and wedges, she looks fit to be on the cover of *Vogue*. She greets me with la bise, the double cheek kiss.

"Minou," she says in a soft voice, matching the murmuring tones of diners chattering around us. Minou means kitty. It's her nickname for me.

"Niçoise salade, s'il vous plaît," she says to the waiter as she pulls out a chair, taking a seat and turning to me. "I've missed you. We really should find the time to see each other more. How are the kids?"

"Oh, well, you know." I raise my eyebrows, and Emi can only chuckle.

"They're good ones, really." Emi smiles as she butters her bread. "How's Jamie?"

What does she mean by that? How should I know? Did Angela ask her to say that?

My turbulent tirade of thoughts muddle my answer. "I, um. I don't . . . I'm not sure. Do . . . Do you know how he is?"

"Uh, no," Emi says. "Why I asked you." The smile lifting in her cheeks tells me she detects the red in mine.

"Haven't seen him much." I grab a piece of bread and start cutting it with my knife. Emi's hand stops my back-and-forth motion.

"Like this," she says, picking up a piece and tearing it in two with her hands. She lifts her silverware. "For the meal."

"Can you follow me around and tell me all my faux pas?"

"You're doing better than most of the au pairs they've had. Here, trying to adapt is appreciated more than you think."

We chat more about the almost-always-sunny weather, top attractions in the area, and some of the foods I apparently *need* to try. I tear a piece of paper out of my notebook for her to use.

"What's that?" She points to the journal I'm hastily stuffing in my bag.

"Nothing." The pang in my stomach hits differently this time.

"I have a diary too," she says.

"It's not a diary. I-I like to take notes of my surroundings." Gosh that sounds creepy.

Emi's inviting eyes make me feel safe enough to divulge a bit more. How the sensory details bring me to the moment itself. Like a recorded book of inspirations.

As Emi nods encouragingly, she takes a slow sip of her café au lait. A gentle sea breeze sweeps through the streets and ever so slightly rattles my coffee cup and saucer. The madeleine beside it nearly blows away, but I rescue it before it goes flying. Yet, I can't save my napkin, which goes soaring to my right. When I bend over to pick it up, a strong, tanned hand decorated in fine fashion rings meets the napkin on the stone patio. A tall, gray-eyed man at least a few years older who looks like he's just walked out of a Louis Vuitton factory, shines a half smile. He's coated in the finest cologne France has to offer.

"Bonjour, Mademoiselle," he says, standing up and folding my napkin. "On devrait t'arrêter pour excès de beauté sur la voie publique." The way the canvas awning blocks the sunlight above us and his cream and beige outfit billows in the breeze, he's glowing. But of course, and most especially when an angelic man stands before me, my tongue decides not to touch base with my brain.

"Je ne . . ."

Crap! What's the rest?

"Je ne parle pas . . . beaucoup le français," I say with a butchered accent and an awkward smile, hoping to goodness there's no tuna or egg wedged in my teeth.

Emi leans toward the man and introduces us both. Fortunately, he knows English and switches for my comfort. Lucky me. He pulls out a chair that Emi invites him to take.

"He was saying that you should be arrested for showing so much beauty in public," she whispers not so subtly to me.

Out of the corner of my eye, his debonair, bright grin gives me chills.

"What a pickup line," I say, taking a sip of coffee.

Is that a flirtatious edge I feel coming on?

"What, it didn't work?" he says. His teeth seem even whiter against his tan skin.

"Damien," the mystery man introduces himself—pronounced dah-mi-uh(n). Ah yes, the silent "n" that's more like a suggestion.

When Emi excuses herself to go to the restroom, even though she had just gone five minutes before, my abdomen quivers, and I rub the ends of my napkin to send the energy somewhere else.

"So, um, do you come to Nice a lot? I mean, well of course you do, you probably live here. Or, wait, do you live here? Where are you from?" I bite my lip to stop the rambling, but Damien appears amused.

He leans his elbow back on the seat rest, hardly creasing his beige blazer. "I'm from Antibes. Just a few kilometers away. Close to Cannes."

"Have you ever been to the film festival?"

"Mhm, I walked the red carpet too."

My voice drops its shaky nerves. "Really?"

He nods. "An actress had asked me to be her date."

"Oh." Because I guess that's regular around here?

"But we waited for hours for the screenings to start. By the end, we just got drunk at the bar and left early."

"It wasn't worth it to stay?"

Damien shakes his head and takes a sip of water before changing the subject to my reasoning for sitting in a café along the French Riviera. I give him the cliff notes version of how and why I happened here.

"I'm au pairing for a family in Èze."

He inhales deeply through his nostrils. "Don't tell me. The Chessleys?"

"You know them."

Tracing the rim of a glass, Damien nods. "I've had the unfortunate pleasure of crossing paths with Jamie a time or two. But that's in the past."

Emi returns to her seat, fluttering her napkin over her lap and interrupting with, "Damien, before you got here, Kat was just saying how she'd love for someone to show her the area."

A grin spreads over his face. "That so? Well, Kat, would you like to join me in Monte Carlo next Saturday for a charity gala? I've got an extra ticket. And you really shouldn't miss it."

"I-I, um . . . I don't . . ." I catch a glimpse of Emi's encouraging smile. "I guess so. Oui."

"Merveilleux," Damien says, rubbing his palms together. I bite my lip.

"Bien. Pick her up at six," Emi orders.

"Oui. La villa Chessley," he adds. His phone blitzes awake, and he shuffles out of his chair. "Ah. Désolé. Sorry, I've got to get going."

Damien takes my hand, pecks it, and places it back in an ensuing pool of sweat on the white tablecloth. "Enchantée, Kat." He says goodbye to Emi, but with less fanfare. Apparently, I've lost my tact for words, if I ever had any, and can only manage to nod helplessly.

"Looking forward to seeing more of you," he says with a final wave as he strides back into the street.

For a good half hour, Emi pokes at my giddiness, and I so gladly let her. We decide to take a long walk from Nice's city center back to residential Èze before we surrender to the cobblestone streets of its old town. The smell of flower bushels wrapped in brown paper tempt my already heightened spirits as we make our way to the wine shop for a quick hello to Emi's parents.

Stone arches adorned with climbing flower vines form tunnels over the narrow, inclined streets. Someone strides down the stony walkway, catching my eye. I can tell by his gait and the toned arms that it's him. Jamie.

Emi sees him too and is about to wave when I press on her elbow. To my right, another presence catches my attention. Only *she* would still wear the clickety-clackety heels in this completely stiletto-averse terrain. Her commanding voice doesn't cascade beyond a muffle as she says goodbye to Antoine and Marie at the wine store.

I nudge my head and Emi catches on. Two seconds later, she's hustling to stall Angela at the store a bit longer, and I set off toward the steps to get Jamie out of sight.

When he sees me, his emerald eyes flicker with a burst of curiosity that hardens to unnecessary coolness.

"What are you doing here? Where are the kids?"

"They're fine. Come on." I press my hand against his forearm and move back up the cobblestone hill.

"Hey, I gotta go to the Cave." He's dressed in his chef whites.

"No, you don't. Your mom's there."

"What?"

Angela's voice gets louder as she insists on heading out of the Cave. Jamie can hear her now. His dropped jaw tells me so.

Without much thought, we quickly shuffle into the closest shop. The unlocked seafoam-green door leads us into a quiet, vacant bookstore. My knees squeeze against my jeans as we kneel to the floor below the windowsill to peek outside.

Angela struts down the cobblestones and faces the shop where Jamie and I are hiding. She tilts her head, not one hair-sprayed auburn curl falling out of place. Instead of investigating, she shakes her head and strides toward the car park at the bottom of the village.

"What the bloody hell," Jamie mumbles to himself, untying his apron. "She hasn't been down here since she and dad bought the house."

"When was that?"

"Thirty years ago." Jamie stands and holds out a hand. But I'm already halfway off the ground. Still, it doesn't stop me from awkwardly taking it even when there's no need for balance. Thankfully, my chuckle sparks his own, and the tension brushes off.

In a few milliseconds of silence, my eyes meet his, and the coolness from the past few weeks evaporates. Only about a foot separates us, and I can feel his body heat unintentionally encroaching on mine. He's just naturally really hot. I tear my gaze away and bumble around the shop, creaking the floorboards.

Jamie does the same, though I'm not sure why he hasn't just bolted back to work at this point. He's made it clear that he's not looking to get involved. And neither am I.

A few rays of sunlight pour in through the smudged windows, illuminating the clouds of dust swirling in the air and caking on the empty bookshelves. Cardboard boxes filled with books from poetry volumes to mystery novels are scattered around the wooden tables. Toward the back, a rickety staircase leads to a horseshoe balcony and loft stocked with more reads. In its glory days, this place must've been a treasure trove.

I feel a pair of eyes on me as I admire the architecture and the atmosphere of a store that once was. I sharply turn around, catching Jamie, with an open cookbook in hand.

"Amazing, isn't it?" His tone is genuine, and I immediately feel guilty for mentally accusing him of otherwise.

"Mmm," I say, nodding. "If this place were functioning, I'd spend hours here." I mention a sampling of my favorite genres. A blend of classic literature, contemporary, and anything on space or world travel. "I practically lived at the library. Used to read these back to front," I say, picking up a guidebook on the Mediterranean coast collecting a thick layer of dust mites. I flip through wafer-thin pages peppered with hotels, attractions, and language tips.

"We're kindred spirits, then. Because I was a few aisles down checking out these," Jamie says, lifting the French pastry volume splayed in his hands. "And anything Greek philosophy. They knew their shit."

A smile creeps along my face as I picture it. A lanky 4'8" nine-year-old with comic books tucked under one arm, an encyclopedia of chocolate-based recipes, and a Socrates biography in the other. Now, mid-twenties, roughly six foot, and he's still intoxicated. My stomach sinks for him, wondering what his fate will be once he starts working at Chessley Enterprises full time.

"But as for fiction," he says, slicking his fingers back through his hair. "I'm more of a movie buff."

A smile paints my face. We geek out over some favorite films. Him: *Castaway*, *8 Mile*, *My Cousin Vinny*. Me: *Star Wars*, *Mamma Mia*, *Forrest Gump*.

"I'm guessing *Apollo 13* is in there too?" he says coyly.

"You guessed right."

"A superfan, then. Sure you didn't go to school for this?"

Before I can catch myself doing it, a laughing scoff tumbles out, as if convincing myself that I'm completely happy with the decision of going the business school route. "I wish," I mumble so softly that Jamie's head doesn't turn.

My phone chirps incessantly inside my bag. In my haphazard attempt to retrieve it, I ever so elegantly manage to spill out half of my belongings. My journal included.

Jamie rushes to help me recover everything.

He picks up the notebook, which I had labeled with a "Write Like You Mean It" sticker.

He lifts the leather journal.

"So, you're a writer?"

I reach underneath a table for my lost strawberry ChapStick. "Um, no, well, not exactly."

"But you write," Jamie underscores.

"Well . . . yeah," I strain as I plunge my arm farther underneath the wood siding. "Sort of."

"Then, you're a writer."

I sigh. Well, I'm not exactly penning the next great American novel. More like a few documentary treatments and an attempt at crafting novellas out of select study abroad escapades.

My fingers locate the ChapStick's cool plastic tube. I press back onto my knees. "It doesn't work like that."

"Doesn't it?"

"Does heating up oatmeal make me a chef?" I retort coolly. I'm not in the mood to go into it with him anymore, so I politely, but forcefully, request my journal back. He concedes and places it in my outstretched hands, while I swallow my embarrassment through a clenched throat.

A voice outside the window steals our attention. Leaving Jamie on the ground, I quickly stand and brush the stone floor's residue off my pant knees.

"Damien," I say with a perky lift in my voice. My, with his sky-blue button-up and linen slacks, he's looking fit for a Dolce & Gabbana photo shoot. I'm about to gather my bag and head out the door to "bump" into him, but he disappears into the shady cobblestone alley that leads to the car park.

"How do you know . . ." Jamie trails off. "So that's your type?"

I scoff, and my eyelids go to thin slits.

Before I can retort, Jamie shakes his head and flips through another cookbook, mumbling. "I didn't peg you as a girl who'd like guys like him."

"And what's that supposed to mean?" I face Jamie.

He shuts the cookbook and turns away. "I shouldn't get involved."

But now he's opened a can of worms that I'd like to know more about.

"Hold on. So you know Damien?"

"Yeah," he says and can't help but add, "the less you know him, the better."

"Oh really?" I cross my arms over my chest. "I'm old enough to decide who to hang out with, thank you very much."

"Hey, I'm just looking out for you."

"Oh, like you really care?" I want to add, "when you don't even pay *me* any mind . . . or your family for that matter?" but I hold my tongue.

Jamie's nostrils flare, and he steps closer to me. "Of course I . . ." There's a fire in his eyes. "Kat." His voice softens. "I . . . I can't show you . . ."

"Why not?" I challenge him, taking a step closer. I feel the heat of his body inches away.

"You know why not . . ."

Angela. A deep breath swells in my lungs. Jamie looks away. I have to peel my searing focus from him.

I peek at my phone and realize how late I'm going to be picking up the kids from Estelle's. As we leave the bookshop, bashing shoulders through the entry door, we steal one more glance. His eyes are warm and green. But the momentary warmth freezes over in seconds.

"I shouldn't be here," he says, swallowing and tearing his eyes away. He promptly starts storming up the street toward the Chateau Vigne d'Argent, but pauses his strides. Without turning around, he says, "Kat. Don't see Damien, okay?"

I cross my arms. "Why's that?"

"Just don't, okay?"

"I think you should get back to work," I say, spinning around and thumping down the street toward the car park for Antoine's ride, resisting the urge to look back at Jamie. I don't hear his scuffing footsteps, so I assume he's standing firm in place where I left him.

Once in the car, the entire way back to Nice, Jamie's words linger in my mind.

Does he find it amusing to challenge me? How can he sit on his high horse and question me like that when he's the biggest sneak in his family? And what's with him and Damien?

And the second that frozen exterior of his begins to thaw, he sticks it right back into the blast chiller. I get that he's trying to keep our interactions on the down low so Angela doesn't suspect anything. If nothing else, his maturity and care in making sure I don't get fired is part of why I feel so magnetized to him. Still, if he's gonna be cold out of obligation, I'd prefer he stay consistent in it, rather than inadvertently toying with my feelings.

CHAPTER EIGHT

"Just wait till I tell my mum," Manon grumbles as she climbs into the back seat of Antoine's Porsche.

I'm really late. Not a casual French fifteen minutes late. But a whole hour late to pick the kids up from art lessons with Estelle. My interlude with Emi, Damien, and Jamie had usurped much of my free time.

And if I hadn't stayed in that bookshop with *him*, maybe Manon wouldn't be as upset as she is now. But she's not the temper tantrum type. No, for this eleven-year-old, she's dishing a disappointed scolding. Like mother, like daughter.

Milo and Josie don't seem as bothered. More time with Estelle means the more mango ice pops she'll give them. But for Manon, today is not the day to be late. She had strictly instructed that she *absolutely 100% needed* to be back home by 3 p.m. Twice, her favorite band, was releasing concert tickets, and Angela had given her the go-ahead to purchase them with my assistance. Because Estelle chose to do without Wi-Fi in the summers to "enjoy the simple pleasures of *la vie*," and given her apartment's already spotty connection, the transaction would really only work at the villa. Knowing how well off the Chessleys are, I'm shocked Manon couldn't just order someone to do it. But it's not like they have a waitstaff besides Sylvie, and she's off Tuesdays and Wednesdays.

Antoine chats up the younger ones as we drive along the verdant cliffs. From the passenger seat, I take a look at the three of them smushed together in the back. Josie and Milo hold up their watercolors proudly. Manon's stone face shifts to a warm, artificial smile as she plucks a piece of paper out of her art portfolio and hands it to me.

The clarity in her pastel work is actually quite commendable, but I take issue with the subject. It's a brunette in a green jumpsuit—cough, cough—seated on a plane's wing that's headed back to a mountain with an American flag. I'm surprised she didn't draw smoke and flames too. I swallow my discomfort, complimenting her use of color. Manon only purses her lips.

From the driver's seat, Antoine takes a quick look at the picture and muffles a chuckle. His wink to me makes me feel like maybe this is normal. So what if it is? They've had au pairs before who didn't fare well. Emi had told me that almost all of them either quit or got fired within six weeks of being here. That can't be me. By the disgruntled look plastered on Manon's face, if I'm going to make it through twelve weeks of this without being tossed on the street and risk my name being tarnished at Continental, I'm going to need to put pedal to the metal on learning the language, cultural nuances, and the family's necessities. My incompetencies are piercing through. I'm going to change that.

—*—*—*—

TURNS OUT, WHETHER or not Manon actually filed a complaint with her mom about me, I didn't get fired last night. When I was cleaning up from dinner—caving in and making the kids boxed mac 'n' cheese at their begging request—Angela was returning from a photo shoot for her winter line. And she only managed to get through half an eye roll when she passed me in the kitchen and saw the empty pasta box. In my book, it's a major improvement compared to the exaggerated sighs of disappointment I received my first week.

What gave me a bit of comfort was that Angela was taking the kids on a road trip over the Italian border to Sanremo, where they'd be visiting cousins of hers. Which meant forty-eight hours of Kat time.

The thought did cross my mind that I was intentionally being left behind. I mean, Angela's shelling out a few hundred euro my way every week for au pairing. Wouldn't she want to make use of the help she's paying so much for?

Unless she's hoping to nab me with that spy of hers. It's the perfect trap. Both parents, a.k.a. bosses, out of the house. No kids to watch over. Just a horny girl drowning in hormones, or so Angela presumes. I swear it's like she's waiting for me to mess up and snog Jamie—Ha! Like that'll happen—just to justify her suspicions.

Before I open my eyes to a new, unimpeded day, I can feel the yellow morning light pouring in through the window. I left the balcony door open last night to carry in the sounds and scents of the ocean. The French sun must be as rejuvenating as it's hyped to be, because I haven't slept this well in I don't know how long. I reach for the pillow next to me, but my hand rests on the cotton sheet. Something warm is beneath it. For a moment, I wonder what the hell I did last night.

Did I break into the wine cabinet and drink myself silly? Am I even in my bed? Who the hell is in here with me? It can't be him. I wish. *No.* No way. But the sounds that follow confirm that it's no human in bed with me.

Baa!

Pushing myself up, I lift up the sheet.

A lamb!

Baa!

What the hell is a lamb doing in the house! In my room! In my bed!

The animal is covered in mud from hoof to sternum, and now, so are the eggshell sheets. My mouth gapes wide, and I try to shuffle the bichon-sized creature off the mattress.

Baa! Baa!

"Oh, no, no, no, no, no! Don't get on the rug!" If that tapestry gets stained, I'll be spending my two days of freedom with a sponge and carpet cleaner. Lifting the animal up, it squirms in my hands, kicking dirt on the oversized T-shirt I wore to bed.

That's when I see her. The bedroom door is cracked open, and half of Manon's face watches me with a maniacal sort of pleasure.

Manon: Two. Kat: Still zero.

Payback. I knew she was going to get me, I just wasn't expecting this!

A car honks outside.

Angela's voice echoes up the main staircase. "Manon, allons-y!"

Manon whips a cunning smile in my direction before bolting down the hall. In a matter of seconds, car doors shut, tires crunch down the gravel driveway, and I still have a baaing lamb in my arms.

I run down the hall, down my special secret staircase, and through the kitchen, forgoing pants in favor of finding the quickest solution to the lamb problem. "A lamb, a frickin' lamb. Where the hell did she get a frickin' lamb?"

The villa, thankfully, is secluded enough that no neighbors will see me if I put the little sheep in the enclosed tea garden until I figure out where it came from and what to do with it. "Emi, call Emi, she'll know what to do with this." I calm the squirming creature and scuffle around a hall corner. "Then I— Ah!"

My right shoulder bashes into someone.

"Whoa!" Jamie exclaims.

Of course it's him.

Baa!

I resecure my grip on the lamb.

He examines my slumping ponytail and the fidgeting lamb smooshed against my chest. Heat races up my spine and around my neck as Jamie's eyes land on my bare legs.

"I-um, I-I found this in my bed," I say, nodding like this is all completely normal.

Jamie leans his shoulder against the wall, crossing his arms and holding back a grin. "I mean, I like some company too."

"Gross, ew, no. No, I didn't put it there."

A breathy chuckle passes through his nose as he scratches the back of his head. "Manon?"

My shoulders loosen. Seems like he just got up too, still in his boxers and a red Manchester United T-shirt. His wavy side bangs are tumbling out of his low bun.

"Mum leave with the little ones?" Jamie asks looking over my shoulder.

I nod, nearly smacking my jaw against the lamb's head.

"C'mon," he says, turning around. "Knowing Manon, she probably got it from the Duponts on the other side of the olive groves." By the way he's loosened his shoulders, I can tell the warm, charming Jamie Chessley has returned. Part of me wonders how long it'll last before we're caught in another quarrel. I make a mental note not to mention Damien again.

I fumble with the agitated animal. Jamie takes the lamb from my arms, an amused grin forming as our arms tangle awkwardly.

"We'll put it in the garden for now, and I'll bring it back on my way to work."

He sends the animal outside, and it immediately begins gnawing the hydrangeas. Jamie, acting as if this is just a regular Wednesday, heads down the hall, and I follow him until we land in the kitchen.

"For now? Why the delay?"

"Because," he says, stretching his arms out wide. "I have this place to myself . . . ish, and I'm gonna make us breakfast."

"Us?"

Mr. Nice Guy returns. Guess he's putting our bookshop argument behind him. He shrugs. "If you want."

I do want. But only because this is strictly platonic, and there will be no funny business under the surface. I'm sure he intends the same.

"I'm just going to put on some pants first."

Jamie glances down as if he's just now noticing I am missing a key article of clothing. I blush as I realize he can see my butt poking out under my shirt. Don't get me wrong, I'm quite proud of my fondness for squats. But it makes me nervous for Jamie to see the results, even if deep down, I kind of want him to. He presses his lips to a smile and winks before I bolt back upstairs.

Parsing through my still unpacked suitcase for a clean pair of pants turns out to be a nightmare. That little lamb not only muddied the sheets, but my clothes too. Manon must have let it snuggle all around in my bag before plopping it under the covers.

When I come back downstairs, Jamie's in the midst of conducting a gastronomic symphony. He's entrenched in a rhythm between the crack of an eggshell, the fibrous chop of fresh fruit, and the crinkling of a bag full of baguettes and croissants.

I take a seat at the island, and he pours me a cup of pressed coffee. He may be half-French, but his English side doesn't let it steal the spotlight as he pops a dollop of milk into his mug of tea.

"When did you start cooking?" I ask, sipping the coffee with a splash of whole milk.

Jamie looks at the clock on the wall. "'Bout ten minutes ago," he says with an expected smirk. I roll my eyes at the joke. "Ever since I was about this high." He holds a hand up to his waistline. "When did you start writing?" He grabs some jam jars from the fridge, and I squirm back on my stool.

"Few years ago."

Jamie takes out two plates from the cabinet. "What made you start?"

Before I can stop myself, I speak the thoughts swimming around in my brain. "It needed to come out."

"Hmm. Your head was 'bout ready to proper burst."

I nod and slug another long sip of coffee. It's true. I've always been thinking up a story or seeing them unfold in real life. Being the last stop on the school bus came with its daydreaming perks.

"So what is it you write, exactly?"

I shrug. "Scripts. For film. Documentaries mostly. Some fiction pieces too. Short stories."

"What are your plans for it?"

Jeez, what's with the game of twenty questions?

Sighing through my nose, I tilt my head to the side. "It'll be my job. Eventually."

It's still early days. I've got years to go of polishing up my prose to become an artistic beast before I even debut. The collection of half-written outlines stored on my computer only prove my progress. Trouble is, I just have to finish them before hopping onto the next logline like a lion to its prey.

"Ever thought of film school?" he asks. "There are some great ones in Europe."

"Here and there. But I don't have time. Not right now."

Jamie prepares a plate, adding scrambled eggs speckled with fresh herbs next to strawberries, kiwi, and a piece of bread ripped from a baguette loaf. He must detect the dejection in my tone, much as I try to perk it up.

"I'll figure it out though," I say, nodding. ". . . In a few years."

"Why the wait?" Jamie slides the plate toward me.

"Well we can't all follow our dreams right out of college." I lay a napkin over my lap as Jamie leans his palms on the edge of the island's countertop.

"I take it you mean me? Well for your understanding," he says, grabbing his cup of tea, his tone not at all accosting, "I'm not sittin' on buckets of cash. Sure, I'm blessed to have been born into this." He gestures to the kitchen. "But I don't get to take it with me when I move out."

I scrunch my brow as I take a bite, mentally ordering myself to focus on the conversation instead of the freshest, fluffiest eggs I've ever had.

Kat, whatever you do, do NOT moan.

I swallow my pleasure. "You mean, you don't have anything set aside?"

"Only what I've made myself. Mum and Dad never believed in trust funds. They help us with university, and that's about it."

"They want you to work."

"Bingo."

"Wouldn't they be happy, then? That you're . . . you know, going at it on your own?" I lower my voice. "At the Vigne?"

We're most definitely alone in the house, but even Jamie looks over his shoulder.

"I know their expectations," Jamie says, toying with the lid on the raspberry preserves. "It's like they can't picture success outside of the boxes they're accustomed to."

I lean forward, the loose ends of my bun mingling with the food on my plate.

"Have you tried telling them about pursuing culinary arts? Aren't you a bit curious to give them the benefit of the doubt?"

"Look, it's not to their standards. They'd say I'd be throwing my life away." It's his turn to take on a cynical attitude. "We're doing just fine as it is. They have their ideas about me, and it gives me all the liberty to do as I really please."

"But it's not true," I press. "You're not this womanizing party jerk." As I say the latter half, I wonder if I'm wrong about it.

"What we have is enough to get through the week, have a laugh here and there, and make Christmas just barely tolerable. If they knew the truth about me, their perfect *family portrait* would be shattered."

And they'd be left with a slap-in-the-face reminder that their re-lationship isn't what any of them wished it really was. Angela pegs him as a delinquent. But it's his secretism—for fear his parents won't accept him—that birthed the shady behavior. So he'd rather maintain the lie and hang on by a fraying thread than completely cut himself off from his family forever.

Jamie tears through the crust on his bread. "It sucks when the peo-ple biologically programmed to love you think you're a fuckup."

Lowering my shoulders, I swallow one more bite. My mind flick-ers to my own family—cousins and aunts and uncles who don't care to make an effort with me all year except for obligatory small talk at the holidays while we share shrimp cocktail. "I know what you mean. It's always an act."

His eyes flash as they trail to my face. "Exactly."

We eat in silence for a few moments. Jamie wipes the corner of his mouth where the jam he'd smothered over his bread had landed. His gaze searches his plate.

"You know, I didn't even think twice when I signed the contract to acquire the company when Dad hits seventy." He sighs. "Like a voice in my head was shouting at my hand to stop, but I just kept watching every letter of my signature come onto that page . . . Can't back out now, not yet anyway."

"What about all this?" I wave my hand to the array of food he's prepared.

"It'll have to wait."

Why do *his* dreams get a delayed start, but he's so adamant that I don't put mine on hold?

"Wait for what?" I lift my brow at him, and he blends a scoff with a chuckle.

"When the time is right. Can't rush the rise." Bread. He's talking about bread. Thank you, *Great British Baking Show*. "If I back out of the deal before I can find someone to replace me, Dad's reputation would be worthless. He's put all his trust in me, and I can't walk out on him like that, embarrass him like that, especially after he's touted me to the company's clients and partners. So, as much as I fervently disagree with him on multiple points, I couldn't do that to him. I won't."

Damn, he's posh. I open my mouth to say something, but Jamie's caught in a fluster.

He takes a big sigh and bows his head. "Sorry."

Without thinking, I reach across the counter and rest my hand on his.

"Hey, no, it's okay. I get it. I do." Jamie looks at my palm, and I'm immediately mortified. Swiping it back, I feel everything in my stomach halting its digestion and swelling to nausea. "Oh my gosh, look at the time. I told Emi I'd meet her for the market." Every bone in my body feels as if it's been dunked in a bath of awkwardness, and I nearly stumble off my stool.

"Kat, wait."

I stop him before he has the chance to tell me it's okay and that he either a) has a girlfriend or b) isn't interested in me like that. But I wasn't trying to even come on to him! After repeatedly thanking him for breakfast and for helping with the lamb and mentioning at least five times that I am going to get ready for the day, I finally make it back to my room. Shutting the door, I slide my back down until my butt reaches the hardwood. My fingers tug at the fringes of the rug.

Why in the world did I just do that?

There's no explanation for why I took his hand, only that something intrinsic in me cannonballed it there.

Is it a full moon tonight? Did I have too much caffeine?

In reality, I don't have much time to ponder the error of my ways, because I truly do need to meet Emi for the farmer's market before hitting the beach, and it'll take me a good fifteen minutes to walk to Èze village where we'll catch the bus down the hill. Perfect. Plenty of time to reprimand and remind myself why I'm here and why getting emotionally involved with a guy who my boss strictly prohibited me from dating is not in the game plan.

Besides, I'm not here to fall in love. Like that would happen. I'm here to be the best damn au pair this family has ever seen and to catapult myself on to the corporate ladder at Continental Air.

CHAPTER NINE

*T*he Marché aux Fleurs turns out to be just what I need to distract from mulling over this morning's sequence of annoyingly chaotic events. Down in the heart of Old Nice, parallel to the sparkling sea, Emi, Marie, and I traipse through café-studded streets, where the dandelion stucco shines bright in the sun. For the first time, I don't feel *so* touristy. It might have something to do with my outfit or the fact that I now feel confident navigating the city without relying on my iPhone Maps.

Even Emi had commented on the former when I met her earlier at the wine shop.

"Ça va, Minou?" she asked. "Comme c'est chic." Emi eyed my outfit from top to bottom while I bashfully tucked my hair behind my ear.

A few days earlier, upon discovering the lack of functionality in my crop top with less wiggle room than a straitjacket, I'd decided to go shopping. Fortunately, the lamb's muddy tracks hadn't made it to this new outfit, still in its bag. I wasn't sure if I'd actually wear it, so I'm glad today's events forced me to. Now as we stroll through Nice Historique, sporting a floral-dotted sundress and sandals, I feel as comfortable as the locals always look when they stride past.

Turning onto the street Cours Saleya, we come to an open-air market. It's bustling, but not overwhelming. Lines of coral and white-striped awning tents stretch for blocks. They shelter a buffet of flower bouquets nearly spilling out of each stall. Peonies, orchids, baby's breath, and carnations. Lots and lots of carnations. Vendors wrap up fresh bushels in brown paper and string, replacing the just-sold items in a matter of seconds.

Emi grabs my elbow and then her mother's, and we walk with arms interlocked through the entirety of the floral booths. Marie picks out a bushel of violet tulips along the way, and I drink in the sweet earthiness swirling around me. Groups take leisurely strolls, admiring the day's offerings. Many walk like we do, elbow in elbow.

"Well, Minou, what do you think?" Emi asks, readjusting her creaseless wheat straw hat over tightly-coiled auburn locks.

"Magnifique," I respond, my eyes still trailing the umpteen blocks left.

Emi's eyes go to thin crescents. "Come, see ahead."

In a matter of moments, the flower stalls transition to tables stocked with vibrant fruits and vegetables of all kinds. Squashes, leeks, melons, lemons, and oranges. Locals pick up loaves of bread, cartons of raspberries, and dried meats while tourists mull about, peeping in at every stall like it's a wonder of the world. I fall into the latter bucket, in awe of the assortments of cheeses, spices, and spreads.

At one stall, what looks like gallons of olives from the narrow purple to plump light green varieties have been spread out in shallow dishes. Marie points to the smaller black ones and instructs the man to fill up a plastic baggy. Following Marie's lead, we each try one out of the scoop he's offered to us.

"Delicious, no?" Emi says to me, though it's an understatement to the briny, buttery flavor coating my mouth.

The next stall isn't as welcoming to visitors. The "Ne touchez pas s'il vous plaît" sign matches the temperament of its vendor. Hands on her hips, she glares at each person perusing her selection, ready to pounce on anyone who dares hover a finger over her cured sausages.

Once Marie finishes gathering her groceries, we finally get to what Emi cares most about here. Confection and bath products.

Just as we reach the booth hailing tubes of bath salt and rows of color-coded fragrant bar soaps, someone taps my shoulder under the striped tent.

Every muscle from my shoulders to my knees locks in place. My mind immediately goes to the worst case scenario: Did Angela somehow find out about me getting all *touchy-touchy* with Jamie? Has she sent someone to spy on me, just like she did with her former assistant? And now based on the alleged spy's evidence, *la police* are here to collect and deport me?

"Âllo. Ça va?" The voice is cheery and breathy.

When I turn around, Estelle tilts her head at me, the ends of her silky headband poking her collarbone. My shoulder blades loosen, yet my insides still feel like mud. Like when I used to stay home alone while Mom traveled for work and every creak in the floorboard instantly meant a samurai assassin was creeping behind the shower curtain.

Get a grip, Kat.

"Comment allez-vous?" Estelle asks us all, readjusting the strap on her crocheted grocery bag.

I repeat the "bien, merci," that Marie and Emi reply.

"Kat," she says, grabbing the sides of my arms before the double cheek kiss. I've become so accustomed to it at this point that my body takes it on without having to think.

Over her shoulder, my eyes widen at the sight of a camera and a long, wide-brimmed lens being yanked behind a grand oak tree at the end of the cobblestone street.

Oh my God! I *knew* it!

I make to chase the cameraperson down, but Emi rests her hand on my elbow, startling me. My eyes dart around the nearby tent stalls and between the hundreds of shoppers admiring their goodies, but I lose sight of the onlooker.

"Looking for something?" Estelle asks.

With one more glimpse at the oak tree, there's no sign of the spy I *swear* I just saw.

But I shake my head, even though my mind swarms with possibilities.

Estelle gives a coy grin.

"So, you've met my *marraine*. Godmother. Well, mine and Jamie's," Emi says.

Estelle nods with me. "Glad to see you're still with us, Kat."

Same, Estelle. Same.

"Lovely day for a market walk, hmm?" Estelle lets her eyes wander around the bustling venue.

"It's good to know the vendors too," Marie says in her thick accent. "When la fromagère and le boulanger do well, so do we."

"Are you thinking of selling in the market?" Estelle asks her. Not even the breeze coasting through the streets is strong enough to move one strand of Marie's shoulder-length brown bob.

"If we have enough hands to help."

Emi resumes sifting through sachets filled with dried rose petals, herbs, and lavender. The bright expression on her face has subsided. When she looks at the stall a few steps down, she immediately perks up, grabs my elbow, and takes me to the confection stand.

Marie and Estelle follow, mumbling in French.

"Bonjour," the vendor says to us as we peek over the glass barrier between us at an assortment of fine chocolates, crystallized fruit, and jars of citrus preserves. They must've set the display over ice packs, because in this eighty-degree weather—twenty-six Celsius—the candy would normally be sweltering.

"Un coffret de calissons s'il vous plaît," Emi says, pointing to a box of almond-shaped confections topped with pastel glazes. She and the vendor exchange smiles and informal niceties while I glance a few times over my shoulder, scrunching the periwinkle fabric over my thighs. The swells of visitors wandering in and out of each stall are now all suspected stalkers.

Holding out the box in front of me, Emi nods. "Calissons d'Aix. Spécialité provençale."

What I thought was a cookie turns out, as Estelle explains, to be a mixture of ground almonds and candied fruit, like melons and oranges.

"Like marzipan?" I ask. I shudder, remembering the glob of overly sweet almost-paste.

"Better," Emi insists, handing the box around to Marie and Estelle.

She's right. The sweet, nutty bite practically melts on my tongue, leaving a lingering echo of cantaloupe.

Estelle shakes her head with pleasure. "More people need to try this. Now they take their phone pictures and move on. They don't stop to enjoy the *joie de vivre*."

Marie shakes her head. "C'est dommage."

Emi whisper translates. Pity.

"Which is why we need to be in front of the tourists," Marie continues. "They won't know about us otherwise."

"You could try social media, Maman," Emi mumbles, popping another calisson into her mouth.

Marie can only grunt her distaste. "We *cannot* turn out like Solange."

"Solange?" I ask, and I am promptly filled in that the empty bookshop where I happened to find myself alone with Jamie belonged to Solange Martin. When her grandfather passed, she assumed the reins of running the bookstore in Èze until fledgling revenue levels forced her to close its doors.

"I hear she is trying to start a new business," Estelle says, gripping her wrist below her back.

Marie scrunches her brow. "Comment?"

"Oui. A magazine of sorts."

"About what?" Emi asks.

Estelle shrugs. "I've seen her walking in and out of the hotels by the Matisse museum. Something for the tourists, I imagine."

Travel magazines. We have those back home. I used to work for one as an intern. Eighty percent of my job was devoted to marketing materials, but the remaining time, I scribed write-ups on local happenings, hidden gems, shops, and restaurants. Though small compared to a Condé Nast, it proved relevant and prosperous in its own right.

"But . . ." Marie lowers her voice below its already low-hum level. "Ces touristes only read what is online."

"Maybe she wants to do the same as you, Marie. Be in front of the people. Physiquement. But with papier."

"I for one," Estelle begins as she walks to a stall emitting a nutty smokiness, "give her full support."

Emi, Marie, and I follow her, departing the tent sheltering assorted honey—*miel*—jars for the stall with a painted sign reading "Socca." A man pours thin batter onto a circular cast-iron skillet at least a foot in diameter. He sticks it into the pizza oven behind him, a crackling, glowing orange fire alive inside. The heat caresses my face and makes the sun shining down feel somewhat cooler. The dough bubbles as it cooks, and using a long paddle, the man retrieves the skillet, revealing the dough's char-speckled texture. Off the heat, he slices it into triangular pieces and sticks it into a paper cone before handing it to Estelle.

She gestures for us to try a piece. I'm beginning to think that this sharing nature isn't a temporary mood for these women, and that it's rather culturally customary.

I tilt my head as I grab a warm piece, still steaming. "Crêpe?"

Marie shakes her head and points to the bucket of yellowish flour next to bowls of olive oil. Apparently, the *pois chiches* label on the container means garbanzo beans. And astonishingly, the minimal ingredients in this relatively brittle chickpea pancake understate its savory, salty, earthy flavor.

Estelle harps on about Solange. "She already has one reader. I prefer paper."

"Is that why you don't use your portable?" Emi lifts her own cell in the air.

"Ah, Emi. Tu es si drôle. Hahaha." Estelle gives Emi a smirk and a nudge. "There is a lost magic in how we used to talk. Waiting for the post to come every week, hoping for a letter from your closest friend . . . or lover," she says. "It's so . . ."

"Transfixiant," Emi finishes the sentence with a slight smirk.

"Oui." Estelle returns the grin and snatches the cone of socca back. She leads us through the pastel-striped tent colony to meander and bask in the sun. As we walk, I keep an eye out for the wayward camera lens.

When Estelle pulls me under one stall selling vintage stationary, I pause my momentary sleuthing to consider the options. Slightly discolored stamps boast sketches of the palm tree-lined riviera. Thick cardstock paper smooth on the surface and gruff on the sides. Red and blue stripes bordering postage envelopes. I exchange ten euros for a package of each, hugging my purchase tight to my chest, not sure who I'll write to just yet.

Not two seconds later, I hear Howie Gupta's voice bellowing a hundred feet away.

Jesus. Did *all* of Èze decide to show up today?

He's guzzling down a satchel of dried fruits and nuts as he saunters over.

"I thought that was you," he says to the group. After exchanging cordialities, he strokes his chin and says, "So, did you hear the talk of the town? I was up at the Cave earlier to refill my merlot stash. And I ran into a woman starting her own travel agency."

"Solange," Emi interjects.

"Righto. That was her name. Might not be a bad gig for Continental to sponsor," Howie ponders aloud.

"Did she mention her promotional magazine?" Estelle asks.

"Briefly. Something about needing an English editor."

Marie turns to me. "You have a creative eye, Kat. Emi tells me so."

"Are you considering the position, Miss Kat?" Howie asks.

My palms start to go sweaty. The sun's rays feel more abrasive against my shoulders than they did five minutes ago.

"I um . . . well, I haven't heard much about it. I'd . . . I'd have to check with Angela, of course."

And meet this Solange woman *and* read the fine print of whatever the hell I'm signing up for. I won't lie, penning a travel magazine would be a glorious creative outlet and great practice for when I eventually work my way up to international content editor for Continental Air—after I get inducted to the Young Soarers and spend three years in the rotational program.

"Miss Kat, your ambition hasn't failed to impress," Howie compliments.

My mouth is gaping, and I struggle to come up with a response.

"She hasn't said yes yet," Estelle says.

I shrug and exhale. "I guess I'll have to look into it."

Howie's grin lengthens a mile wide. A rock sinks in my stomach.

Oh God. What did I just do? I know exactly what I've done.

My hopefully future boss now expects me to edit a travel magazine, and I haven't even met the woman running the show nor have I addressed the feasibility of the role in addition to au pairing and perfecting my Young Soarers application.

But the smiles painted across the group's faces sear into me.

This is why spontaneity is overrated.

CHAPTER TEN

O
can't believe Angela would do something like that. Correction,
I can't believe I believed she *wouldn't* do something like that.
Really though, what kind of host mother sics a private investigator on their guest? Is this her version of a background check?

Unfortunately, for all I know it might not have been *her* doing at
all. Maybe it's Nick's way of vetting the au pair service. Or perhaps
Howie's trying to weed out any rotten eggs from joining Continental.
Hell, at this point maybe Jamie's plotting against me. The further I go
down this rabbit hole, the less logic I find in my arguments.

To keep myself seemingly sane and refrain from voicing such ac-
cusations to Angela's direct kin, I don't mention a peep to Emi on our
way from the market to the beach.

By the time we hit the coastline, most of the sun chairs and umbrellas have been snatched, so we unroll a large blanket in front of the
water. Where I'm used to sand back at home, here sits an assortment
of faded gray and charcoal-colored rocks, no larger than the palm of
my hand.

But the sound of the tide is ever much the same. Hypnotic. And
the brilliance in the way the Mediterranean's shoreline transitions
from misty white to cobalt blue captures nearly all its onlookers'

attention. Something I love about the ocean; it brings people together. Different opinions, backgrounds, income levels, uniting us as humans who just want to cool off and fall under the spell of its white caps.

After parting ways with Marie and Estelle at the end of the market, Emi and I had swapped our day clothes for our suits. Her, a scanty polka-dot bikini, me, a maroon one-piece, a.k.a. the only swimsuit I packed. Lying down on her back, Emi soaks up the sun.

I peel a piece of paper out of my backpack. It's my typed-up short answers to the first round in the Young Soarers applications. Biting off the cap of a red pen, I scan my sentences for syntax errors.

The first section passes with flying colors, and I silently dote on my academic achievements in every area from Economics to Spanish. The next needs some work.

Question: How does your international work experience prepare you for life at Continental Air?

I can't exactly say my host mom is a Type-A disciplinarian with a never-ending list of rules and demands, making me well-equipped to meet the requirements of any future boss or team leader. Rather, I toss in a few phrases like "strengthening intercultural competences" and "enriching my active listening capacity." That'll sure keep the admissions folks happy.

Emi opens one squinted eye. "Minou. Can't that wait? You won't be in la Côte forever." She gestures to the beach swarming with sunbathers and swimmers ages four to eighty-four.

Slumping my shoulders, I respond, "Hmm, I know."

I tuck the lightly marked-up page back in my bag and decide to follow Emi's lead of actually relaxing. Leaning back, the sun coats my skin. Emi fishes around for a tube of sunscreen in her bag and points at the clunkiness of mine.

"Minou, what do you have in there? Briques?"

With anyone else, I'd say it's just summer reading. But I don't want to lie to Emi, so I show her my bag's jumbled contents. Language learning books. Everything from French 101, Intro to French Grammar, and French Vocab Speed Course. If I'm going to meet Manon's and Angela's standards, conquering a bit more of the language will at least keep me from crashing and burning when needing to function in public spaces.

Without much thought, the idea percolating in my head comes straight out.

"Will you help teach me? I promise to be a great student. I can show you my transcript to prove it." I clasp both hands at my chest and offer an Oliver Twist pout.

And it's like Emi had been waiting for me to ask her since the day I met her. She claps and sways side to side. "Oh, oui, oui. Une étudiante! They say once you can teach une Américaine, you can teach anyone anything. But," Emi says, holding up an index finger. "You have to do one thing first."

"What?"

Emi rests her tongue between her teeth as a grin nudges itself through her cheeks.

"Suis-moi," she says, rising to her feet and stripping off the sarong at her waist. "Follow me!"

I press off the blanket and follow Emi's lead, dunking into the sea. It doesn't take much effort, so joke's on her. We float in the gentle current, joining other sea bathers. The water isn't like the Atlantic where it takes a good few minutes for my body to get acclimated to the temperature. Here, the radiant sun almost seems to warm up the sea like a big bath. It's refreshing and balmy all at once.

I lie back, letting the ocean tickle my scalp and play with my hair as I float, drinking in the sun shining through the puffy clouds. To my right, Emi's broadened her strokes farther from the coast and the groups of people around us. When I catch up to her, she lifts her brow.

"Ready?"

I shake some water out of my ear. "For wh— Emi!"

With a gleeful holler, Emi strips off her bikini top and lets it dangle around her wrist. I tear my eyes away from her and look down at my blurry feet sinking into the sea floor.

"Your turn!" Emi shouts, and I turn my neck sharply to her, shaking my head ferociously.

"No, no. Emi, I can't. I can't." My toes struggle to grasp the mushy sand.

"Oui, you can. When in France!"

Not when there's a fat chance my host mom sent a spy to watch me!

I grip my elbows with opposite hands. "The expression is when in Rome," I grumble. "I should get back to editing those application questions."

Emi chuckles. "Just do a quick flash. Face toward the horizon at least. It'll make you feel better," she says. "What's life without a little carpe diem!" Emi exclaims.

You know, if someone asked me in April how I thought my summer would look, I wouldn't have said "Oh I expect to be flashing the Côte d'Azur to win French lessons." No, definitely wouldn't have guessed that.

My knuckles go white, gripping the inch-wide, red straps on my suit. A deep breath fills my lungs. The sun has gone from energizing respite to intense spotlight in mere moments. Emi splashes around, still naked from the waist up.

"Merde."

I pull the straps down, feel the water cool the skin of my torso, and whip the suit back up, snapping my head in all directions to detect any potential witnesses.

"Ah," I gasp. Adrenaline pumps from the crown of my head to my toes.

Emi whoops, cheering me on as she hops up and down.

"Oh my gosh. Did I just do that?"

"Feels good, no?"

Emi was right. Uncontrollable laughter sputters through my diaphragm. She joins in, and I splash a bit of water her way.

"See what a bit of spontanéité can do," Emi teases.

"You're not gonna make me cliff jump as compensation for teaching me future tense, are you?" I jab.

"Of course not," Emi says, swatting her hand. "Juste un peu de parachutisme."

"Parachute what?"

Emi smiles mischievously instead of answering. She looks to the shore, her head tilting as something catches her eye. I follow her gaze to someone standing across the street from the beach. My spiked energy turns to dread. Jamie.

A million thoughts rush through my head with the overarching being did he just see me half naked! He's already gotten a glimpse down below from this morning's lamb debacle. So unfair. And I've only seen him fully clothed. Not that I want to see anything otherwise!

I swallow hard, feeling my heart pound in my chest.

Wait a second, is *he* the spy Angela sent?

The warmth has drained from my face. I must look like a ghost. Now this is *merde*. A big, big *merde* show.

I sink my entire body except my head into the sea.

"Hé!" Emi tosses her outstretched arm side to side, but Jamie, leaning against the exterior of a gelato shop, doesn't notice her or us. The swarms of beachgoers, city walkers, and trams populating the road make it a bit difficult to identify a far-off wave from someone lapsing in the water.

Thank goodness.

The breath I'd been holding tumbles out, and my shoulders loosen.

"Ah, he's busy." Emi winks at me and returns to floating on her back.

Back on shore, a young woman around Jamie's six-foot stature approaches him from behind and affectionately grazes his shoulder before whopping a major smooch on his cheek. I inhale sharply and sink deeper so my chin touches the ocean's surface. My eyes are magnetized to his hand placements. Her biceps for the double cheek kiss, then back as she squeezes her arms around his neck for a long-time-no-see kind of hug.

So that's his type.

Given his concentrated interest on her—that and the fact that there's no camera on his body—I can only surmise that he's not my street stalker.

"Emi, who is that?" I nod in Jamie and the woman's direction. "She looks . . . familiar." I tilt my head sideways. "What's her name?"

"Vivian. I don't know her well, but I know she owns like four motos. And that she was once an assistant in Angela's office. Now she's some sort of higher up at a major fashion company. Hermès, I think it was."

Impressive. And she's most likely not even thirty yet. I wonder if Vivian has a ten-year plan. Well, she probably doesn't need one. She's obviously crushing it professionally.

Given her high-rise white satin pants and jet-black button-up, she either had style before working at Lavergne Designs or she got it there. But knowing what little I do of Angela, I assume it to be the former.

Vivian. Tall, brown skin, luscious black locks, who's badass and rides a motorcycle. That's it. She's in a photo with Angela in the villa library.

"She and Jamie have been friends for years."

We watch Vivian get cuddly close to Jamie as they walk into the gelato shop. Just friends? The jealous, jumping-to-conclusions side of me lingers on Jamie's most likely type: a career-oriented woman who's made her dreams a reality. And here I am, just holding onto my visions for the future by a lone thread.

I figure switching the subject will say to Emi *like I care what Jamie does in his free time or with whom.* Because I don't.

"So that'd be cool if the Cave starts selling at the market, huh?"

I tread gently, swishing water in a semicircle with my arms. Emi reattaches her bikini top.

"Yeah, do you wanna take my shifts?" she jokes. "I cannot stand it when she does that."

I feed off her earlier sarcasm. "What, volunteer you for something you never agreed to?"

Her palm taps the surface of the water. "Exactement. She doesn't want to see me actually use my degree."

"I'm sure she does."

"Well, bien. She does. But she only wants me to use it within ten kilometers of Èze so that I can always pick up a shift at the Cave." Emi shakes her head and leans her face to the sun, though a cloud quickly blocks its rays. "I want to go to Paris. To be a teacher in the city."

"Does she know that?"

"She should. I talk about it all the time, but she pretends like I won't take a job if I get it or that I'll change my mind. But I don't care what she says. I'm moving up there in a few months whether she likes it or believes it."

"She'll warm up to it, I'm sure."

"Well if she doesn't, ce n'est pas mon problème."

I thought the same when I first shared some of my writing projects and short films with Mom back in high school. Let's just say "nice hobby" isn't exactly what wide-eyed young artists want to hear. After that, it kind of just became a habit not to share anymore. Sure, I can pretend that the trust and support roots in our relationship aren't ruptured, but the act can only last so long.

Emi and I wade in the water a few more minutes until she claims she's feeling a lemonade. When we get back to our towels, I struggle to find my button-down. And this bathing suit's lack of padding doesn't offer much coverage when wet. A narrow shadow appears on our blanket and gets more defined as its owner gets closer.

I clench my jaw, waiting for the clinking of handcuffs, but the distress melts when I hear his voice.

"Did you lose something?" The French accent is heavy, like merlot.

I spin around. Damien. He lifts up my button-down with an index finger.

"It blew down to my chair." He points to a cluster of white pool chairs under blue pin-striped umbrellas.

Rising to my feet, I scrunch my eyes in the sunlight and cover my chest.

"Did . . . did you see us . . . in the water?"

A smile tugs at his cheek, and he shrugs. "Peut être."

Emi giggles but doesn't offer my begging eyes a translation. "You could have joined us," she says with a polite smirk. "Kat would have liked that."

"Emi." My eyes widen at her.

"I would too." Damien directs his attention to me. "But I had to deal with something." He waves his hand with minimal effort.

"Oh, that's . . . that's okay." His soft gray eyes mesmerize me.

A gust of wind sweeps through the beach, spraying sand over our blanket and fluttering open the flap of my backpack where I had stuffed my market purchases. The stationary goes flying in every direction.

"No, no, no, no!"

Without much grace, I lunge for the flying papers, jerking every which way to retrieve what I can like a puma on the hunt. Engorged in laughter, Emi and Damien help me scuttle around, collecting most of the flyaway sheets. We forfeit some to the wind, where they'll eventually be blown onto someone's seaside apartment balcony.

"That's a lot of postage," Damien says, catching his breath and placing the stack of envelopes in my hand.

I bashfully shrug. "I was thinking of writing home this way. Old-fashioned, I know."

"Oui. I've read my grandparents' old letters before. C'est roman-tique. I think," Damien says, curling up one corner of his lips and tossing in a wink.

I scramble for the sunglasses tucked in my hair, but I push them off the back of my head completely. As I bend down to grab them, another hand meets mine.

Not Emi's. Not Damien's. The wide silver ring on the pinky tells me who it is. I lift my eyes to confirm. Jamie smiles and hands my glasses back.

"What are you . . . where's . . ." I don't know how to finish that statement without sounding like I've been prying into his personal life. I look over his shoulder, but there's no six-foot, gorgeous, proba-bly-has-her-career-sorted woman behind him.

"So," Jamie says, shoving his hands into his pockets. "Beach day, huh?"

Damien's cheerfulness has completely evaporated from his face.

"For some," Damien replies, examining Jamie's less than beach ready jeans.

"Well," Jamie begins. "Some of us have real responsibilities."

I bow my head. Jamie's tense jaw line softens.

"Kat, I didn't mean—"

"Ah," Damien lifts both his palms. "I forgot, you have to be very dedicated to your silver spoon. Very dedicated. Je suis désolé, Jamie."

Jamie squints back. "Piss off."

"Well then, if you're finished, please excuse me," Damien says to him. "I have something to ask Kat."

Me? What? The next thing I know, Damien steps in between Ja-mie and I and gently rests his hand on the back of my elbow. We take a few steps away from the others, but not out of their earshot.

"Kat, are we still on for this Saturday? The Monte Carlo gala?"

I feel Jamie's head snap toward us. When I glance his way, his brow is scrunched.

Turning back to Damien, I shine a toothy smile. "Yes. Of course. I—"

"I can't tell you how excited I am. Did you ever see *To Catch*—"

"*A Thief?* Of course. With Cary Grant and Grace Kelly."

"Mm, she actually became—"

"Princess of Monaco." I finish the fact.

"The auction is bringing in some big items. I hear some cars from the movie are going to be there as well."

Jamie's eye roll is hard to miss.

Ugh, why do you care, Mr. Hot and Cold?

"Pick me up at six," I remind Damien, returning my gaze to the bronze-skinned Hercules standing in front of me.

Emi sports a proud grin.

"Merveilleux," Damien says, slicking his hands through his jet-black hair.

And after a few bumbling moments of forgetting my own phone number, Damien pops it in and gives me a double bise on my cheeks.

"Who's going to watch the kids, then?" Jamie says, his arms crossed.

Emi steps forward. "I will. A little bonding time with the cousins can't hurt."

I smile gratefully toward her before sneering ever so slightly in Jamie's direction.

"Merveilleux," Damien says again and bids us bonsoir.

A daze stirs in my body. As Emi and I head up the scorching cement stairs from the beach to the street, I overhear Jamie confront Damien back at his chair. Their bickering is hard to ignore.

"Laisse-la tranquille." Jamie points in our direction.

Damien scoffs. "Occupe-toi de tes oignons."

"*Ce sont* mes affaires."

Emi doesn't hear any of this as she's on the phone with Antoine who's agreed to give us a lift to Èze. And I don't have the wherewithal to memorize Jamie and Damien's conversation. The day's events are catching up to me. The market, the potential spy, flashing in the sea, and the upcoming date. My second date ever—if I'm also counting a group of ninth graders seeing a Liam Neeson movie and getting frozen yogurt before our parents picked us up.

But this. This is a real date.

Whatever Jamie's problem is with me—and Damien—will have to be dealt with later. I'm over his flip-floppy attitude. It's not worth sacrificing my peace of mind. *He* can deal.

CHAPTER ELEVEN

"P'tit déj!" I call up the villa's grand staircase in a not half bad accent. It's been almost a week since Emi and I began the French 101 instruction, and I slipped right back into the language-learning groove I had when poring over flashcards in eighth-grade Spanish.

In the kitchen, I scoop three bowls of thick porridge and arrange them beside jam preserves, honey, fresh fruit, and glasses of orange juice on the table. I detail the morning's breakfast menu in my journal to record the scents and flavors that hallmark the morning and ring in the new day. When only Milo and Josie come running down the hall, I inhale slowly and tense my shoulders, preparing for whatever Manon has in store this time. More stolen farm animals running rampant in the house? Maybe she smuggled in Monaco's royal jewels and planted them in my room. After I finish tying Josie's hair into two red braids, Manon saunters in, seats herself at the table, and shines a close-mouthed grin in my direction.

"Alors, qu'est-ce qu'on fait aujourd'hui?" she asks me as I scarf down some breakfast.

My spoonful of milky oats plops back into the bowl. "Um. Pardon?"

I should have seen the eye roll coming.

"C'est *par*-don," Manon repeats with an emphatically rough "r."

Really, she's gonna harp on my pronunciation? I thought I'd come a long way in just twelve days.

"Quoi qu'il en soit, quel est le plan, huh?" Manon tilts her side ponytail.

Josie nor Milo offer any translation help as they're quite occupied flicking orange peels at one another.

"Josie, Milo, s'il vous plaît arrêtez," I beg, rushing to the table. But I'm a second too late. Josie sends a piece of rind flying in my direction. The second I duck to the side, I regret it immediately. I should've let it hit me.

"Joséphine!" Angela's voice boomerangs around the room. All of us at the breakfast table go quiet. She's standing in the entryway with arms crossed as tight as her pursed lips. Her thick bracelets clang against the stone tile as she bends over to grab the orange rind.

When she rises, she brushes away the minimal wrinkles on her leopard-print blouse. Angela transfers her gaze from her youngest daughter to me. Her eyelids coated in olive shadow send chills up my spine.

"You call this taking care of things?"

"We were fine before, really." I gesture to the remaining breakfast set up.

Manon stands up from her chair and throws her napkin down.

"C'est une imbécile. Elle ne sait rien." She throws her hand in my direction. "Nous n'avons pas besoin d'elle ici."

A sneer lingers on Manon's face, her body language marinating in the bitterness soaking her words.

Angela nods, acknowledging Manon's comments, but doesn't indulge them further. She only beckons me with her index finger.

"If you cannot do the job, it is better I know now." Her gaze invades my own.

So you can stop sending randos to watch me from behind bushes?

While I'm starving to offer her a little unsolicited opinion that maybe the estrangement-inducing parasite in their family *isn't* me, I fear that cluing her in would only shatter her sovereign pride. But like hell am I gonna let this woman paint me to be a conniving man-eater, effectively ruining my reputation and crushing my shot at the Young Soarers. Enter Kat McLauren, smooth-talker saleswoman.

"I-I can do this. I promise. Please, I want to stay."

"J'ai besoin de plus de preuves." My blank stare generates her follow-up. "I need more proof than this." She gestures to the three kids kicking each other's legs. Milo, dangling chewed orange rinds over his blond eyebrows, tempts the idea of launching them into Josie's bowl.

"I'll take care of it." With a confident nod, I quickly whip out the first phrase I asked Emi to teach me. "Je suis là pour aider."

I'm here to help.

Angela leans her head back and lifts a perfectly waxed eyebrow. "Est-ce vrai?" She snaps and gestures to me to follow her. "My office. *Maintenant.*"

Josie and Milo have resumed their breakfast, bickering while Manon snickers as I trudge down the hall behind Angela.

In her office space drenched in the perfume emanating from the numerous vases packed full of lilacs, she takes a seat at her desk and points to one of the upholstered velveteen sofa chairs.

"Sit," she orders.

My tongue goes dry, and my breathing deepens.

"This summer will not go well if there are secrets being kept," Angela says, readjusting her rose-gold Rolex.

Crapcakes. Every brief moment Jamie and I have shared flashes through my mind as I try to think of whatever incriminating evidence has been relayed to her via her spy.

I open my mouth to interject, but Angela quickly says, "Howie tells me you're considering signing up to be Solange's editor."

I let out a small sigh of relief.

"Well. I-I don't know much about the job, but of course I wouldn't take it on if it would affect my responsibilities here with the kids."

"Nonsense." Angela waves her hand. "I've already sent her a recommendation letter for you."

I dig my canines into the inside of my cheeks.

She what? She's trying to squeeze me out. Of the house. Of the family circle. Keep Kat and Jamie separate as much as possible.

And since when did I let my fate start being smacked around like an inflatable beach ball.

"But," I pause to laugh lightly and subdue my burning irritation. "Why would—"

"You clearly have a lot of energy to expend. And I see you with that notebook of yours, always writing . . ." Her gaze trails to the leather journal glued to my side.

I brought it with me from the kitchen. There was no way I'd leave it behind, risking the chance that Manon would tear the pages out for origami practice.

"But." Angela lifts her index finger. "When I spoke to Solange about your recommendation letter, she told me she saw you and Jamie . . . mingling . . . in her shop. We have an agreement, Kat. Jamie is off-limits, eh?"

Nervously scoffing, I push the hair out of my eyes, hoping she doesn't catch the blush invading my cheeks and neck. "Of course. I was just . . ." I have to come up with an alibi for Jamie that won't out his gig as the pastry chef at the Vigne. "We were just—"

"I thought I made my rules very clear," Angela interrupts. "I'm not blind. And I have eyes everywhere."

My jaw clenches. So she *has* been watching me!

"He was just showing me around," I say, shrugging.

Angela's eyes go to thin crescents. "Hmm. Ask Emi next time. Jamie doesn't need any more distractions. It's time he steps up at Chessley Enterprises."

I nod fervently, and she clears her throat.

"We wouldn't want to give Howie the wrong impression of the type of employee you are, now would we?"

I sharply inhale through my nostrils so fast it burns.

Oh, so she's playing that game. Noted.

Both of us catch the echoes of Milo and Josie fighting over the last glass of orange juice.

Angela nods toward the door and says, "Well then, as my husband would say, tout suite." She offers me a polite smile as I head out the door, my hands shaking.

—*—*—*—

WITH ANGELA KEEPING one eye on the situation until she has to leave for work, gathering the kids and washing up the breakfast dishes brings on stress levels I can only imagine Olympic athletes have to endure. Though I haven't been able to confirm if there are secret cameras hidden in flower vases or bookshelves, erring on the side of caution seems to be the best option, so I make sure to wear an extra wide smile in every communal space.

After a long morning of sibling bickering and temper tantrums, I figure I'll take the kids into the village to say hello to their aunt and uncle. Really though, it'd give me a chance to find respite with Emi. Walking over the villa's gravel driveway, I can't help but notice the lack of Jamie's convertible. He hasn't been home in days. Probably with Vivian after work at the Vigne's restaurant. Not that I care. Just observing.

Narrowly avoiding a verbal badgering from the sandwich shop owner after Milo scarfed down every tomato mozzarella baguette sample slice, I find out the disappointing news from Antoine and Marie at the Cave. Emi is out of town for a graduation party and won't be back until tomorrow. Antoine promises to entertain the kids while I run down to the corner market for some cans of San Pellegrino. I hand over a few euro bills at the checkout and pay for a bag of chocolate cream cookies, knowing that the kids will want a snack in an hour.

Look at me, already anticipating their hunger pains. I tuck the treats into my newly purchased wicker purse.

Taking the long way back around the corner to the wine shop, I rustle around my bag for my notebook and pen. Some of these details are too immaculate not to document. The echo of the ocean washing over shoreline pebbles. Cobblestones still wet from last night's rain. Yeasty leavened bread. I duck into a stony tunnel that brings me to another windy street. The pastel green window frames adorning the former bookstore catch my attention as much today as they did the first day I saw them. I now know the shop belongs to Solange and is currently under renovations to become a travel agency. Overgrown vines dangle above the main entrance. Most of the boxes I had perused with Jamie seem to be gone, but with the sun glare against the window glass, it's difficult to make out the rest of the interior's state.

I practically press my eyes up against the window. Where there were once tables now sits a large desk and two loveseats facing it. A singular bookshelf has a few rows stocked. There's also an espresso machine hooked up in the far corner. I'm curious if the prior contents had been moved to the loft upstairs. When I glance to check, I find another set of eyes peering back at me.

I inhale sharply.

The eyes belong to a petite woman with frizzy brown hair half clipped back. Rectangular glasses sit at the very tip of her nose in the middle of her elongated face. It must be Solange.

I lean my head back quickly and "accidentally" drop my pen. My acting needs improvement, that's for sure. Not two seconds later, the woman yanks open the door in front of me.

"Qu'est-ce que tu veux, huh?" Her nasally voice nearly batters me down.

"Je suis Kat." I press my sweaty palm to my torso. "Je suis la au pair de la famille Chessley."

That information doesn't change her sour expression, like the corners of her mouth are stuck in an ever so slight frown.

"Je sais," she says. Expectedly, the woman introduces herself as Solange and leans her shoulder against the door.

"J'apprends encore le français," I say before she lets out another word.

"Bien. Then I can practice my anglais." Solange's fuschia-lacquered scowl thaws to neutral. Nodding to the journal in my hand, which I quickly stuff back into my bag, Solange tilts her head. "What do you write in there?"

"Oh, nothing," I say, though a pang in my stomach twists. I would've peeled off the "Write Like You Mean It" sticker if I knew it'd be such a conversation starter.

"Do you like to . . ." She makes scribbling motions with a closed fist.

I shrug. "I guess." The pang gets tighter.

"Are you good?"

Scuffing my sandal against the cobbles, I avoid eye contact.

"I mean, I don't know. Maybe?"

"Would you like another job this summer?" She tucks her chin down, looking over her glasses and piercing me with her sapphire eyes.

"I, um . . . I don't know if . . ."

"I've heard good things about you. Angela provided a glowing reference."

Glowing? She must really want me out of the house if she's going to embellish her remarks about me to another potential employer.

"I'm starting a travel magazine about Côte d'Azur to accompany my new travel agency. But I need someone to write les articles en anglais et take les photos," Solange explains.

I furrow my sweaty brow.

Who'd be this trusting of a complete stranger's credibility without even a glance at a portfolio?

"But you haven't seen my writing," I press.

"You speak English. You write English. You évidemment like travel and the Côte enough to stay with those Chessley children."

"Well I'm still not—"

Solange takes out a rectangular business card from her pocket. "Here, my email is there. I'll need your answer by next week so I can stay on schedule. Hmm?"

I thumb the ivory cardstock bordered with lavender sprigs. Before I have the opportunity to accept or reject the opportunity, Solange retreats inside and shuts the door.

A few thoughts stir in my mind. The overarching one is how I will juggle being a first-time editor with my au pair duties. But will I regret giving up the chance to write for a magazine?

CHAPTER TWELVE

*T*onight's the night. My second date ever. I can't help but wonder if Damien saw me how Jamie has—jet-lagged fresh off an airplane, half naked in my pajamas, sweating from head to toe as I chase his siblings around—would he have still asked me out? Or maybe Damien really is a stand-up guy.

Maybe this *is* my time. After legit *years* of waiting for someone, a gorgeous Frenchman has taken an interest in me. And I am going to enjoy it.

These thoughts linger in my head for the rest of the afternoon after picking the kids up from Estelle's, on the train ride back to Èze, and along the walk back to the villa, where Emi greets us.

While Milo has been my fan since day one, Josie took some warming up. But I'm skating on thin ice with Manon. It could be one more snide comment to Angela about me and out I go. Hopefully, a bit of space between us tonight will be enough to soften the tension and maybe mend the fences enough to hold it together.

Still, another two months of this won't work if things stay the same. I'll be sent packing if I can't figure something out. My French is getting better, sure, and my cultural competence has sharpened, absolutely. I know each of the kids' favorite dinners, shampoo brands, and board games. I can even get through half a day now without a prolonged temper tantrum from the younger ones.

But Manon's quick wit and hyper-independent spirit are getting the better of me. Just the other day, she left equestrian practice on her own. The stable attendants hadn't seen her leave, and after half an hour of panic and clambering for the French 911, I found her a few blocks down the road, eating a pear by the bus stop.

If Angela or Nick thinks I'm going to lose their kids in the French Riviera, there's no shot at me keeping this gig, not to mention a spot in the Young Soarers program. Fortunately, Angela's yet-to-be-verified personal detective hasn't caught me in the act. But I won't always be so lucky.

I can't let that shake me. Not tonight, anyway.

Now sitting in my bedroom, the coral sunset over the peninsula fades into twilight, and the room's scattered lamps send a warming glow over every surface. The boudoir seat seems like it belongs to a movie star.

"Eyes closed," Emi says. She puts down one makeup brush coated in mauve blush and picks up another caked in a shimmering taupe. Emi has been the MVP of the night, from taking over childcare duty to helping me get ready for this gala. It feels nice. The way the brush tickles my skin and how the creamy lipstick glides on. Athleisure and moisturizer had become my go-to for the past few years out of sheer functionality.

But if my time in France has taught me one thing about myself so far, it's that I like a good dress-up too.

"Ready for the gown?" Emi asks as she finishes tying my hair into an intricately braided low bun.

I pull a long yellow sundress off its hanger in the closet. It's the closest thing I've got to a ball gown. Emi and I face the mirror with me holding the cotton dress over my lounge clothes.

"No," a thick, heavy voice mutters.

Spinning around, I make eye contact with Angela. She invites herself in through the crack in the door, holding a white box close to her hip. She's wearing a satin bathrobe and wide rollers in her hair. I assume she's going out with Nick tonight.

"Here," she says, placing the bow-tied box on the edge of the bed. "A proper dress for a proper gala."

I raise my eyebrows and quickly close my dropped jaw.

"An extra from last year's collection. I saw it in the office storage and thought you could wear it. You are always representing the Chessleys, you know."

No words come out of my mouth, but if she could only see the invisible gratitude pouring out of me.

Or wait. Is this a test? Am I supposed to politely deny?

Angela toys with her dangling gold earring, examining her Versace slippers. "And. You have been doing much better with les enfants," she admits reluctantly, clutching opposite elbows.

A genuine gift. So she *does* have a heart. A grin pushes through my cheeks. "Merci, Angela. Merci beaucoup."

Half a smile stays on her lips for no more than a millisecond.

"Bien. Amuse-toi, and be careful with that dress, eh? I'll see you there."

I scrunch my brow until her explanation unwinds it. She and Nick had been invited months prior. Initially, conflicting work schedules had prevented them from confirming their attendance.

"And is Jamie going too?" I ask, brushing a stray piece of hair behind my ear.

Angela shrugs. "Qui sait?"

Good point. Who really knows except him.

I straighten my spine and thank Angela once more. We exchange nods, and she retreats to the hallway.

Emi eagerly bounces over to the box and asks to untie the bow. I give her the go-ahead while I bite my lower lip. Below flaps of tissue paper, scarlet-red sequins shine back at us. With one quick swoop, Emi lifts the dress out of the box, swishing it in all its glory. A form-fitting V-neck masterpiece aglow with a million ruby sequins. It even has flowy sleeves. The design is flawless, timeless, and quite aerodynamic.

I tug on the fabric a few times to make sure all the threads are intact. Can't walk into this party only for the potentially faulty ballgown to slip right off my body. Now *that* would be enough of a scandal for Angela to send me packing.

Adorning a pair of comfy wedges, an effervescence reverberates through me as I take a peek in the mirror. Whoever she is. She's glowing.

Emi sits back in the boudoir seat while I twirl like a young girl playing dress-up in her mother's clothes.

"Oh mon Dieu," Emi says.

"What?" I gaze down at the dress hugging my thighs and brushing the rug. "Is there a rip?"

Emi shakes her head, grinning. "C'est absolument magnifique."

A smile brims at my scarlet lips.

Damien announces his arrival—a few minutes early, peculiar for a Frenchman—with a few horn beeps out on the gravel drive. I figure he's avoiding a meet and greet at the front door out of precaution for a chance encounter with Jamie. Emi takes both my hands and gives them a squeeze.

"Go, have fun." She hands me my gilded rhinestone clutch. "I put an extra lipstick and some peppermints in there."

I sigh. "Emi, thank you. Merci, merci, merci." My eyes trail to the clutch, and my stomach drops. My face must tell the same story.

"Minou, quel est le problème?"

"I-I haven't . . ." I drop my voice. ". . . kissed a guy in . . . well longer than I want to admit." Jitters flutter through me, and I can't control my tongue's speed. "And I'm not saying that he wants to. I'm just preparing, you know?"

Emi rests her hand on my shoulder. "Minou, that doesn't matter. Guys can hardly tell the difference, so long as you've got la *confiance*." Her smile encourages mine. We hug, and a few minutes later, I'm locking eyes with Damien who's leaning against a pastel-yellow vintage convertible. My gosh. Where does he work?

The moonlight's reflection on his slicked-back, jet-black hair is as bright as his white tux. His gray eyes, luscious eyelashes, and strong jawline send heat racing up my spine.

"I have to ask you to do the spin, eh?" he asks, twirling his fingers.

Confidence. Confidence, Kat.

A giggle accompanies my compliance, and the sparkling dress floats in the air as I take a few turns on the gravel. He opens the passenger door for me, holding my hand while I take my seat.

We cruise along the streets tucked into the mountain ridges, and I watch lights on the yachts and sailboats glitter across the harbor down and to my right. Wiggling my toes in my shoes, I take inaudible deep breaths, trying to make sense of where I'm going tonight, who I'm going with, and what I'm going to *maybe* do with him.

"Have you been yet? To Monaco? Monte Carlo?" Damien asks.

"No. I know it's silly. We're only, what, twenty minutes from there?"

Damien shakes his head, running his fingers through his perfectly quaffed hair. "No, no, it isn't silly. In fact, it was wrong of me to ask. You must not get a lot of free time having to take care of Jamie's brother and sisters."

"Oh, well . . ." It's strange to hear Damien utter Jamie's name. Part of me wants to join in on the griping, but another part instinctively wants to defend. "I get enough . . . free time."

"Hmm, enough is never enough. Especially when you are in La Côte," he says.

Damien listens more than talks, nods intentionally, and makes sure to glance my way with some eye contact and a smile every so often. He lets me ramble, encourages me, almost understanding how nice it is to just vent sometimes. I go on about my time with the Chessleys so far, my routines with the kids, my own fumbles along the way. I start to veer off into what I think of the village, the shops I've frequented, and I'm almost comfortable enough to divulge Solange's proposal, but Damien—apologizing for cutting me off—points ahead.

"Here we are. Monte Carlo."

Rounding a wall of cypress hedges, a horseshoe-shaped harbor aglow with hundreds of neatly lined-up yachts comes into view. Overlooking the water and graced with soft lamplight are the cleanest plaster and stucco buildings that date back a few hundred years.

Next to more modern mid-rises sit churches, hotels, and shopping centers fit for royalty. The entire country of Monaco is less than one square mile, but the winding pedestrian streets that must glow with their pastel color in the daytime would render one to get lost rather quickly.

We pull onto a perfectly paved street with trimmed palm trees occupying neat patches of soil along the clean sidewalks and smudgeless lamplights. Vintage cars sporting teal, white, and cherry red paint park adjacent to the street.

At the end of the road comes a rotary with a fountain as large as a house in the center. Damien parks the car next to a line of other retro convertibles.

Swaths of guests decked out in their finest suits, gowns, and jewels make their way to the two-story building dominating the street. Awash with golden lamplight, the beige exterior glows to life. Decorated with intricate molding around its lines of rectangular windows, moonlight cascades over its two pointed domes that sandwich an operating clock face directly north of the main entrance.

"The Monte Carlo Casino." Damien nods in the building's direction, where guests twinkling in their attire make their way to the party, like bees to honey. It's so different to the few casinos I've ever been in, usually to catch a concert or to fuss with the penny slots with some college friends. Those places only offered the facade of luxury, and we got what we paid for: mediocre steak dinners and ash-caked carpets.

This is the opposite. Damien places his hand on my lower back, guiding us toward the red carpet rolled out before the entrance. I wouldn't call them paparazzi, but a pack of eager photographers shout in French, English, and Italian to the guests strutting their stuff along the backdrop peppered with the auto show's gala logo.

"Come, we walk it too."

My eyes widen at Damien. "But I'm not, we're not celebrities."

"They aren't either." He points to a few women decked in pant suits and ball gowns. "It's what we do at galas."

Oh, right. Come on, Kat. You've only been immersed in this world for two seconds of your life. Shouldn't you know this stuff already?

When it's our turn, a bashful smile crosses under my nose, and I clench my stomach. The incessant clicking from the cameras draws my attention in every which way. Some of the cameramen and women sit on the ground. That can't be a good angle. The photos are relentless, like a row of a thousand semitrucks flashing their high beams into my pupils.

Damien places his hand around my waist and tugs me closer to him. I rest my hand on his mid-back, and for a moment, I feel pretty secure. He leans to my ear, turning his head away from the cameras.

"Lift your chin, smile like you just got a whole week of vacation, and turn your neck to the right. It's your best angle."

So he *has* been looking! Heat travels around my sternum and straight to my armpits this time.

Following Damien's tips, every vertebrae in my spine rises and straightens. Like I just took an espresso shot of confidence. He hugs my waist closer to his side before we make our way off the carpet and to the main floor.

But the second we step through the glass entry doors to the casino, all else escapes my mind. Attendants hand out glasses of champagne, guiding us and the other guests through a wide hall lined with marble columns. Along the ceiling, a stained glass window illuminates with the help of adjacent lighting.

Seconds later, we enter the main reception. The sound of clicking heels disappears on the soft carpet and is replaced with the chatter of hundreds of people enthralled in their own conversations. It seems I'm the only one gazing at the complex sculpted wall panels, the ceiling's murals and molding, and the dramatic pure-crystal chandelier. There must be nearly a thousand glittering diamonds magnifying light over the room.

Card and roulette tables have been moved to the room's perimeter and are replaced with dinner tables. At the far end of the room, next to the jazz band blitzing their instruments, sit three prized cars up for auction. Each had been used in renowned Hollywood films from the 1950s.

"Kat." I spin around and see Angela in a silky copper slip making her way toward me. She nods her auburn updo to Damien but addresses me solely. "Come. Let's see Estelle."

"Estelle is here?"

"Oui," she says, like I should have known.

Damien affirms that he'll be over in just a second after he gets a new drink at the bar. The champagne is just "customary" as he says.

Angela locks her arm around my elbow and smiles brightly toward Nick and Estelle sipping bubbly by one of the windows.

"How are you?" Angela asks. For the first time ever, her voice sounds maternal.

"Um, fine."

Should I not be? I hastily glance around the room at the people practically oozing money. Conversations on the second-best yacht clubs and debates on Ritz Carlton versus Four Seasons float around the room. If they tried to ask me a question, I'd have no material for them. Discomfort sprouts in my abdomen until we make it to Estelle, donning a multicolored chiffon muumuu. She's dyed the ends of her blond pixie haircut silver.

"Ça va, Kat?" Estelle smiles wide, giving me a grand hug.

"Uh, bien." I shrug.

Nick is a bit less perky than his usual self. There's a stiffness about him tonight and it's not the hair gel in his thick salt-and-pepper quaff. He nods my way and aggressively checks his watch.

"Where in the blazes is he?" Nick says, darting his eyes to the entry hall.

Angela pats her husband's shoulder. "He never promised, Nico."

"No, but he should know better. He's got to start coming to these functions. Chessley Enterprises was built off of goodwill and network-ing. Jamie needs to learn that."

Angela nods along to her husband's mumbling rant.

Estelle taps my elbow. "Seen any celebrities you recognize yet, hmm?"

"No." I shift my gaze around the room, wondering what's holding up Damien at the bar. "I wasn't looking."

"See there." Estelle points to the marble hallway where guests continue to pour in. A man wearing a plum suit strides in. A bright, captivating smile plastered on his face. "That man is one of the biggest football stars in France."

It's a shame I watch nearly every other sport. Basketball, Ameri-can football, hockey, Formula 1.

Behind the famed soccer player, someone I do recognize walks in solo. His hands stuffed in the pockets of his deep green suit, his hair neatly tied back. Still, the hints of summer sun are detectable in a few lightened strands. I don't know how long I've been looking, but it's long enough for him to take a glance around the room and meet my eyes. He stops in his tracks. The crowd muffles for a nanosecond. Instinctively, a grin begins to play at the corner of my lips. I feel my hand, as if I lost all control of it, rising to wave.

I regret it immediately. He's not alone. Vivian appears at his side. She's absolutely stunning. A satin silver dress with a slit up the side and all the confidence of an astronaut launching into space completes her look. I see my hand, still frozen in the air mid-wave, and tear it back down. Instead of acting like a normal adult and saying hello to Jamie and his date, I rush to the bar to find Damien.

He's chatting with the bartender. When he sees me, he pushes an empty glass away from his knuckles and clasps a freshly poured old-fashioned. A suave smile tugs at his mouth and he proceeds to ask if I'd like anything. Before I respond, Jamie's voice grows louder behind me.

"Nice party, isn't it?"

Damien's happy-go-lucky countenance goes cold. "Jamie."

Vivian shines a smile, taking me by the shoulders for la bise. She's careful not to smudge either of our makeup. Gosh, her perfume is freaking amazing. She and Damien hardly exchange glances.

"So nice to meet you, Kat. Je suis Vivian," she says, placing a hand over her cleavage-bearing sweetheart neckline. "Jamie has told me so much about you."

"Oh, really?" Nothing embarrassing I hope.

Jamie turns his head, putting his attention on the party's grandeur.

Damien leans forward. "Qu'est-ce que c'est, Jamie? Not to your standards?"

"Not tonight, Damien, eh? And don't talk to me about standards. Your moral ones could use some work."

Vivian looks away, the glow in her eyes fading.

"Don't change the subject." Damien points to Jamie, stepping closer so they're only a foot apart.

Jamie instinctively tightens his fist.

"What's the deal?" Damien prods. "Looking out for your father again?"

Jamie sneers. "Va te faire foutre."

"Okay," Vivian says abruptly, grabbing Jamie's arm in one hand and lifting her dress with the other. "Let's find our seats."

Damien and I do the same, though we unfortunately find ourselves only a few chairs down and across from Jamie and Vivian at the long rectangular table.

Dinner is a spectacle filled with Michelin-rated specialties delivered on individual silver platters. Still, even the overflowing candle and greenery centerpieces aren't enough to block the terse glances between Damien and Jamie.

A few times, Jamie and I lock eyes, but he quickly looks elsewhere. Angela and Nick mingle with people I assume to be acquaintances and neighbors, though to keep such a high-profile name in these parts, they also need to treat strangers like their new best friends. Estelle takes to chatting with the waitstaff about the materials used to craft the murals overhead.

When dessert finishes and the cognac has been rolled out, the silent auction commences. My focus draws to Howie Gupta at a baccarat table. Except for the card dealer he's currently engaged with, he's completely alone. This could be my chance to squeeze in some one-on-one flattery/networking. A perky laugh a few seats down pulls my gaze to Vivian, draped over Jamie's right shoulder.

Damien leans to my side. "Want to see something cool?"

Surely Howie will be down here when we return.

I nod and Damien leads me out of the room. I glance back at my seat to make sure I didn't leave anything, but as I do, I catch Jamie's eyes on me. This time, he doesn't remove them. His jaw tightens, his stare unwavering.

On any other day, that fact would consume me with questions. But right now, as Damien whispers to a security guard near a grand staircase, my focus is on him. He pats the guard's shoulder, and they exchange cordial laughter. Taking my hand, Damien leads me up the carpeted steps, out of view of the party. Conversations and music muddle as we find ourselves alone on the second floor. We start up another staircase tucked behind a door perfectly hidden within wall panel moldings. He gestures to me to follow him, but I hastily glance around.

"It's all right. You're going to want to see this," Damien assures me.

I take his hand the rest of the way. At the top of the fluorescent-lit stairwell, we step onto the casino's roof. A swoosh of the chilled night air tickles my ankles and races up my legs. I hadn't realized how hot my cheeks had gotten—from the alcohol most likely. Sighing and drinking in the fresh air, Damien follows behind me as I totter around the roof lit by lights carved into the stone floor.

"Étonnant . . . beautiful. Isn't it?" Damien leans his elbows on the wide stone railing. In front of us lies nearly all of Monaco. Moonlight caresses the roofs of the elongated U-shaped sliver of land. The harbor buzzes with life and light. "Like you," he says leaning toward my shoulder. A singular hair lock falls from its gel binding, curling at the tip of his forehead. The cognac lingers on his tongue.

I bite my lower lip and muster a playful scoff.

"It's a pity you don't have more time to yourself. Always running after those kids."

"I don't mind it too much. I still have plenty of time for other things . . ." I say, toying with the stone gargoyle to my left. I leave a silence for Damien to inquire more, but he changes the subject.

"Pardon for asking, but how can you even make it through the summer? They don't pay you much, huh?"

"Um, well. I mean . . . it's enough."

"What do you do it for? The experience?"

It may have started as an inebriated application and evolved into the future of my career resting on my current performance. But he doesn't need to know that, so I nod and shrug.

"Oui. It's not really about the money for me."

"Impressive." Damien turns around, leaning his back against the railing. "I won't take a job if it doesn't hit my minimum." He lifts his hand flat to his chin level.

There's a whisper of defiant arrogance in his tone. But I'm intrigued to dig up his rationale.

"You don't care if you hate what you're doing?"

Damien shrugs.

"If it pays well enough, I can spend my time off doing things that distract from how much I hate my job." He laughs, then continues the thought. "My family . . . we didn't have much when I was growing up. There were some weeks where we only ate lentils and bread. Eventually, my father had his first success in business. And it, how you say, snowballed from there."

"What kind of business?"

"Oh, all kinds really. He invested in construction at first. Then he purchased an architecture company and a perfumery. And now he and my mother own a public relations firm. Essentially, we're venture capitalists."

"They really cover everything, don't they?"

"Not everything." Damien's voice goes solemn, but he quickly perks up. "Kat." He takes my hand and gently rubs my fingers. "I'm going away for a few weeks. A family cruise around Italy. I hate to leave when I only just started to get to know you."

"Distance makes the heart grow fonder?"

Oh my God. Is that me talking or the champagne?

Damien steps closer. My heart rate picks up. "I won't have much service on the boat."

"We can write each other letters," I say jokingly, though part of me really means it.

"Like my grandparents did," he says, and I remember his comment from the beach the other day.

"Could be fun," I say, offering a little shrug.

He grins. "It could be. Oui. Je l'aime bien."

He likes it!

"But," Damien continues. "Kat. First . . . I'll regret it if I don't try now."

Oh my gosh.

He takes two steps closer, his hand traveling up my arm and toward my face until my cheek lies in his palm. I fall under the spell of his soft gray eyes. Intoxicated by his cologne and mesmerized by the moment, I tilt my chin upward.

Our lips are only centimeters away when the staircase door whacks open. My stomach sinks. Snapping my head to the right, I see Jamie. A cold expression plays across his face, and he flexes his fists.

Damien drops back from me.

"Kat, we need to go," Jamie says.

I cross my arms, infuriated that he just ruined the first moment in my European love story.

"What, why?" I scrunch my brow so tight, it might get stuck like that.

"My mother wants you back with the kids by midnight."

Mother-flipping Angela cock-blocking my European love story.

"Wh— They're already sleeping. Plus Emi is with them. Why do I need to . . ."

I sigh, succumbing to Jamie's long stare. Whatever the reasons, logical or not, I need to follow Angela's demands. Especially with Howie downstairs.

Friggin' craptastic. I gather my dress and apologize to Damien for cutting our evening short. His face hardens when he makes eye contact with Jamie.

"Piss off, Damien. Laisse-la tranquille," Jamie orders him while gesturing in my direction.

Damien insists on taking me home, but Jamie retorts saying his parents don't want any non-family, non-approved guests at the house later than the current hour. I give Damien a hug and a *merci* for a wonderful evening.

"We'll stay in touch, Kat?" Damien says, motioning a pen in his hand. A hopeful glint flashes in his eyes.

I nod without commenting further. So, he *does* want to be cutesy and old-fashioned.

Thanks for the idea, Estelle.

Damien kisses my cheek, and I keep my focus on him until Jamie and I are alone, descending the staircase, where my annoyance brims over.

"Why would you do that? Right then? Couldn't wait two minutes?"

Jamie rushes down the stairs avoiding an answer.

"Jamie."

That turns him around. The stress lines along his forehead soften only for a moment. Our gazes lock. My heart swells to my throat. From a few steps down, his eyes trail from the bottom of my red sequin dress to the top.

A blushing fire scorches over my sternum.

He barely shakes his head, like he's reprimanding himself, before he continues down the steps. As we make our swift exit out the casino and past the now-empty red carpet, a hoard of photographers sit on the sidewalks. They're too busy enjoying their smuggled glasses of champagne to take more pictures of the party guests.

Jamie unlocks a cherry-red convertible. He swings open the passenger door for me but hastily makes his way to the driver's seat.

"What about Vivian? How's she getting home?"

Jamie rips off his jacket, unbuttons his collar, and takes what seems like his first deep breath of the evening. The cloth of his shirt curves attractively over the muscles in his shoulders and forearms.

"Mum sent a company car."

I grumpily take my seat, cross my arms, and we're off. It's infuriating how good the wind feels going through my hair as we zip down through Monte Carlo and make our way along the moonlit roads following the mountain ridges back to Èze. I exhale and slump my shoulders, drawing Jamie's attention.

"We . . . She has her reasons, okay?" He steals a glance my way.

"We?"

Jamie grips the wheel tightly. "I didn't mean that."

"Oh, well. Please, enlighten me." The sarcasm in my tone pushes his buttons. Jamie's brow furrows, his emerald eyes flash in my direction, but I quickly tear my gaze from his.

"I'm not . . ." Jamie lets out a sigh through his nose.

The wind heartily pushes against us on the road. It's sending my hair straight back.

"Why can't you let other people be happy? Just because your secret is eating you alive doesn't mean we all have to share in your misery."

Jamie turns his head and ruffles his brow. "Are you fucking kidding me?"

"Why else ruin my night?" I scoff. "Damien probably thinks I'm just a flake."

Jamie raises his voice over the whipping wind. "That guy is bad news, Kat."

My nostrils flare. "Oh yeah? Let me be the judge of that. Oh, but how could I?" I shrug aggressively. "When every time I'm with him, you manage to A, show up right in the middle and B, piss him off. What did you do to make him hate you so much?"

Jamie slams on the brakes at the stop sign.

"Me? What did *I* do?" He shakes his head. The grin is one of disbelief. "What's he told you?"

"About what?"

He releases the brake. "So he hasn't. Figures."

"What are you talking about?" The wind smacks a loose piece of hair into my eye, and I grab hold of the once-perfectly curled braided bun and twist it into a firm top knot using the hair clip Emi tucked into my clutch.

Jamie leans back against the cream leather seat, loosening his shoulders.

"So, what's the deal?" I press.

Jamie inhales slowly, barely shaking his head.

His refusal irks me. "Really?"

"It's not my place. You wouldn't believe me anyway."

I roll my eyes and thank the universe for the confirmation.

Damien de Dandonneau. Charming. A bit haughty at times, sure. But at least he's upfront.

Jamie Chessley. Kind one minute. An absolute ass the next. He's refused to be upfront with me ever since we found out I'd be au pairing for his family. The boisterous breeze has calmed as we cruise along the line of cypresses bordering the road.

"I'm sorry," Jamie says, bringing his focus back on me. "For ruining your night."

My shoulders drop from my ears. "I'm sure you are."

Past the automatic gate, we pull onto the gravel driveway. A few lights glow in the bottom row of the villa's windows. Jamie walks me inside and to the staircase, where he nods up the marble steps.

"I'll make sure the kitchen's all cleaned."

"No, you don't have to—"

"It's all right. You deserve it after tonight."

Our eyelids hover halfway open, both exhausted. I pick up the red-sequin fabric and make my way up a few steps, taking my heels off in the process.

"And Kat."

I twist around.

"I truly do apologize. For tonight. Really. And for getting in your way. Maybe . . ." He kicks his shoe against the floor. "Maybe he has changed. Maybe you bring out the good in him."

I stare at Jamie, waiting for the other shoe to drop, but he seems to be sincere. I nod in acknowledgment, then turn away. I can feel his eyes on me as I ascend the stairs. It's getting harder and harder for my hormones to disengage when he's actually nice like this. I am only human after all.

After rinsing off and pulling on my cozy pajamas, I lean back on the bed. Shutting my eyes is only plausible for a few seconds before I bust them open again to firmly assess each conversation from tonight. My throat, hoarse and sore, aches for something to soothe it. By now it's past midnight, and I tiptoe down my secret staircase to the kitchen where Jamie has indeed cleaned up.

I pop the kettle on and fix myself a cup of tea. I'm a few sips in when my phone lights up. *Great, what is it now?*

But my smile and airiness from earlier this evening return when I see Damien's name.

Will you meet me tonight? By the club in the old town? Here is the address.

Directions pop up to a hole-in-the-wall kind of discothèque, as Angela would say with nausea on her tongue.

I lean on the quartz island and stick my tongue against my cheek. Clubs aren't really my thing. Sweaty bodies and strobe lights, no thanks.

I'm more of a wine on the beach at sunset kind of girl. It's past 2 a.m. at this point, and I'm not in any mood to try to fake my enjoyment, especially when it'll take me a good forty minutes to get down to Nice at this hour.

Instead, I offer an alternative.

When do you leave for your cruise? How about coffee tomorrow morning?

I chew on my lip and bury my chin in my palm. No new messages. I wonder if my connection has gone out or if my international phone plan has hit its limit, any excuse for why he hasn't responded.

Making my way back upstairs, eyes glued to the phone, I can only keep my eyelids from shutting for so much longer. Within twenty minutes, I'll be passed out asleep. Reasoning that Damien had a busy—and no doubt disappointing—night as well, he's probably caught up finishing goodbyes at the gala. He'll get back to me in the morning.

CHAPTER THIRTEEN

*T*he past week has been surprisingly rhythmic between the now-familiar routine with the kids, French lessons with Emi, and quick passes with Jamie in the house. I try my best to not be awkward around him so his parents don't think there's something fishy between us and have me on the next Delta flight back to Boston.

Damien did get back to me before he disembarked on the cruise. A few apologies for missing my message and how he'd like to see me when he gets back. I like it. A man who can actually say "yes, I'd like to spend some time with you," rather than giving silly pickup lines or crude requests. Plus, after about an hour of sleuthing on the cruise ship's website, I figured out how to send him mail. It was an absolute treat to put my farmers market stationery goodies to use.

A few days ago, I wrote the first letter and with Emi's help, got the correct postage and plopped it in the villa's yellow mailbox. I figured that I'd have something back by now. But maybe it got lost in the mail room on board. So I resolve to write a follow-up just in case.

With Milo and Josie chasing each other around the living room, I plop myself on the canvas couch and lift my knees toward my chest. Resting a notebook against my thighs. I tap my pen against my forehead. How do I *not* make this sound pushy or naggy or obsessive. I've only written *Dear Damien* when someone asks, "Brainstorming your Oscar-winning documentary?"

I jolt forward, clutching the paper to my chest.

Jamie walks into the room and takes a seat on the sofa chair. He props his feet up on the wooden coffee table, catching his neck in the web of his fingers. A soft smile spreads over his mouth. It's genuine Jamie today.

We haven't addressed the gala night's proceedings, and neither of us seems eager to do so anytime soon. His beef with Damien is still a mystery to me. But I won't deny that the *vibe* I felt with Jamie my first day in Èze, at the Cave, reemerged that night on our way back to the villa. It's like my body and soul are drawn to him whenever I find his emerald eyes. That is until he shuts it down, flash-freezing his exterior and cooling the simmering heat. And it's not just because of Angela's rules. I'm sure of it, because his attitude is so back-and-forth even when she's not around. There's got to be something more causing him to pull away from me. What, I don't yet know. But I can't let myself fall into that smitten pit, not when I could actually make something really magical with Damien.

I rub the cardstock between my fingers. Loosening my shoulders, I say, "It's personal."

"Ah." He nods. "Understood." Though he continues eyeing the empty piece of paper resting on my leather notebook, overstuffed with travel memorabilia from taped-in ticket stubs to polaroids to journal entries. "Can I ask what you put in there?"

"Ideas. Details."

"On?"

I sigh, resting the paper aside. "So when you . . ." I have to remind myself that Nick and Angela are somewhere in the house, and I lower my voice. "When you cook, you don't just see a leek or a tomato or an egg. You see the bigger picture. Right?"

"I fancy calling it an ensemble of sorts."

"Exactly. They don't exist in a vacuum."

This is my bread and butter. He leans elbows near his knees and tilts his head, his loose hair falling to the left.

"It's the stuff around me that might get passed over if I look too quickly. Pieces of conversations, people's clothes, their mannerisms, architecture. And then I tie it all together with words or film. Or at least, I try to."

From my sternum to my stomach, buzzing butterflies flutter through. I rarely speak about this stuff to Tiff, let alone the guy I just met a month ago.

Jamie smiles. "So you're a professional eavesdropper?"

I toss a pillow at his torso and lean back into the couch.

"It's called inspiration," I snap back.

"Well, I hope you use it."

My eyebrows turn down. "What's that supposed to mean?"

I meet his green eyes, already latched on mine. My focus doesn't waver until Milo jumps on my lap. "Kit Kat! Kit Kat!"

Angela marches into the living room, her heels attacking the terra-cotta tile. She strains her brow and rubs her temple.

"Milo. Baisse la voix s'il te plaît." I make a mental note of that phrase for the next time the kids are getting too loud. Angela whips her head in my direction, placing her hands over her wrinkle-free Chanel skirt. "Kat. Où est Manon?"

My stomach clenches.

"Where is she? Um . . ." I know this, but Angela's unrelenting stare halts my capacity to access memory and quick thinking. "She's, um. She's with her friends. Elle est avec ses amis." And even amid Angela's foreboding aura, I manage to sputter out, "Elle sera à la maison pour le dîner."

"Et toi?" Angela forcibly pokes Jamie's shoulder. "Will you be joining us?"

Jamie closes his eyes as if he forgot something. "It's Monday, isn't it?"

"Oui."

"I'll have to get back to you on that, Mum." He doesn't even turn around as he speaks to her.

Angela crosses her arms, an infamous eye roll following suit. "Incroyable."

Nick walks down an adjacent hallway, hanging up his cell phone. He'd been speaking in Dutch, presumably with his infamous Amsterdam clients. Angela beckons him over.

"Nico, tell our son how much you want him at dîner tonight, eh?"

Nick leans against a bookshelf, complying though his tone seems to know the answer he'll get.

"Jamie," Nick starts, but Jamie stands abruptly.

"I've got plans. Sorry."

Josie bolts into the room, rocketing into her father's leg for a hug. Milo tugs on my arm.

"Kat, Kat, Kat, Kat. Let's go to the olive groves. Josie and I wanna play monsters and race cars."

"Monsters and race cars?" Nick says, tickling Josie's side.

Jamie nods in my direction. My cheeks flush with heat.

"Kat made it up. The kids love it. Even Manny."

Angela raises her brow.

Milo swats my arm with my pen, repeating his request. But my head shake resolves him to finish with a "pretty please." He's giving me Benjamin Button vibes, and even Angela's impressed with Milo's improved manners.

"Okay, okay," I say, stuffing my notebook in the bag at my shins. I had shoved my phone in there earlier and set it to silent while I drafted my letter to Damien. A message gleams on the screen, snatching my attention and draining all the color from my face. It's from Noémie's mother—Manon's friend. Fortunately, the Frenglish she uses translates clearly. Unfortunately, the message relays that Manon bolted out of the ice cream shop and hasn't been seen since. That text came two hours ago.

Jamie must notice the panic in my eyes, though I do my best to shield it from Nick and Angela.

"Everything okay?" he whispers, directing his attention out the window to not seem too obvious.

I nod with a closed-mouth smile and wrangle my hands around Milo's and Josie's shoulders.

"C'mon, let's go for our walk," I suggest.

Nick sips on his afternoon coffee. "Have a jolly time!" He raises his espresso cup with eyes glued to his cellphone. Angela picks up the latest volume of Lavergne designs but keeps one eye on me.

"Jamie, stay here a moment," she orders. Licking her index finger and flicking a page, she reminds me, "Revenez avant cinq heures."

Back before 5 p.m.? Sure, I'll be back before 5 p.m. so you can handcuff me yourself and send me off to be deported for losing your daughter for real this time.

I stop in the kitchen to grab our going-out bag—a tote filled with water and the kids' favorite snacks—before the mad dash across the lawn begins. I swallow gulps of air, calming my climbing heartbeat. I need to get to town. Screw the olive groves. I should've freakin' suggested that we go get ice cream ourselves. Now Milo and Josie are a quarter of a mile through the villa's grounds and making their way straight to the rows of trees ahead. I run after them, for the first time ever failing to enjoy the gentle sun or the soft breeze wafting off the ocean. Coursing my fingers through my hair and scraping my scalp, I curse as loud as an aggressive whisper allows.

"Kat." Jamie's voice centers me. He jogs up and hovers a hand behind my elbow. "Hey, is everything okay?"

Tears don't brim in my eyes, but I get that tugging feeling in the back of my throat.

"Manon," I huff. "She's . . . she's gone."

"Gone?"

"She ran away in the village."

Jamie rests a hand above my bicep. "We'll find her. I think I know where she might be. Well, a few places."

"A few?"

Jamie and I start walking quickly toward Milo and Josie.

"She's run away from me before too."

"Oh, so I'm not the only one she despises for no reason?" The kids' bag nearly falls off my shoulder, so I tug on the canvas straps with a reinforced grip.

"She's just busting your balls. She's a real Chessley."

"She's a little Angela Lavergne." I shut my eyes as if that'd erase what I just said. "Sorry, I didn't mean that."

Jamie surprises me by letting out a laugh. "Don't be."

"Where are we going?" I ask as he leads us through an opening in the stone wall separating the Chessley-Lavergne villa from the neighbors' farm.

"Milo! Josie!" Jamie waves his siblings over. "I think she could be here," he says, nodding his head toward a stone hut only about eight feet tall and right by the pen holding the infamous lamb and its brethren. Given the satchels of potatoes propped outside, it seems to be an old medieval dwelling turned modern pantry.

There are small muddy footprints on the granite slab step by the entrance. A smile grows on my lips.

"Manny?" Jamie kneels down and taps on the wood door. "Manon, are you in there? C'est Jamie."

No response. He taps a bit harder until the door creaks open a few inches. A sliver of sunshine illuminates the interior stone bench. Jamie charges in, but no one is inside, just burlap sacks filled with root vegetables.

My stomach sinks. No, no, no.

"What are we doing here?" Milo asks, plowing his way onto the stone bench. "We want to see the olive groves and the castle."

"The castle?" Jamie tilts his head.

"Yeah. The really big house way, way down," Josie says, swatting her arm. "It's got a little tower too."

"But it's on the top floor," Milo adds. "So the queen can see everything."

That sounds like the decrepit old chateau I caught a glimpse of on my very first day. I've been eyeing it at a distance on our grove walks.

Jamie nods slowly. "Ah. We don't need to go there. Manon's playing hide and seek, and it's our turn to go seek her."

"Wait, maybe . . ." I scan my memory. The kids always pretend to be royalty when we take picnics in the field. And Manon always insists that . . . "She's the queen," I blurt out.

"What?" Jamie rises off his knees and grabs Josie's hand.

"What if Manon is hiding in the castle?"

Jamie looks away. "I don't know . . ." He shakes his head.

"We have to try." Milo and Josie don't pick up on the urgency in my voice, but Jamie concedes with a reluctant sigh.

The trek across the field is reminiscent of my first day and our picnic in the tall meadow grass.

Today, however, an infantry of ominous gray clouds hovers in the distance. The "castle" comes into view through the tall, skinny cypress trees, and the kids bolt off again.

A silence brews between Jamie and I. Our shoes scraping on rocks nestled in the soil serves as the only sound. Out of the corner of my eye, I see him hesitantly turn his head.

"Here," he says, placing his palm on the canvas tote currently weighing down my left shoulder. "Let me take this."

"No, it's all right, it's fine. I got it. I got this." I pull the bag's strap tight, the strain of both it and my personal backpack slung around my other shoulder twist my muscles. I have to be able to fix this, otherwise, I'm most definitely and completely a hot mess express that can't handle this job.

"Please, let me help," he insists, his green eyes full of concern. The strap digs further into my shoulder. It's my turn to concede, and I hand him the bag.

"I hope you know," he starts, glancing away. "I really feel awful about the gala. I wasn't trying to—"

"What, ruin it?" I snap my head in his direction. "No, I'm sure you weren't trying to ruin *my* night, but you had no problem trying to ruin *his*."

Jamie exhales through his nose.

"So congratulations, mission accomplished." I cross my arms, hindering my balance as we traipse over some lumpy molehills.

I don't realize Jamie's stopped until I'm five steps ahead.

"That wasn't my motive," he urges.

"Don't tell me it was because your mother wanted me with the kids. Because I asked her the next day."

Jamie swallows fiercely, but I go on, stepping a few feet closer to him.

"She never sent you up to the roof. So explain that one."

His cheeks redden, and he looks away sheepishly. I step closer to him with my index finger raised, prepared to point out more flaws in his logic. His crystalline green irises search mine. My chest grows warm, and I falter. Less than twelve inches separate Jamie's nose from mine. I tear myself away. A short sigh tumbles out of my mouth. "Doesn't matter now anyway. Like he'll ever talk to *me* again. Or write back. It's been five freaking days since I sent the first one," I mumble to myself. Shaking my head, I mount the peak of the hill. The chateau is less than a hundred feet from us, though a colony of chestnut trees camouflage its lower exterior. Milo and Josie trot ahead.

"The letters? Those are for him?" Jamie guesses, probably remembering the packet of envelopes I had splayed out in the living room.

"There a problem with that?"

He clenches his jaw as I roll my eyes. Annoyed, I step forcefully to the uppermost point of the hill, but trip. My face lunges toward the grass until Jamie grasps my forearm. He pulls me back. My heartbeat races as I grip his bicep for balance. Our chests are closer than they have ever been.

The wind rustles branches from the nearby tree line. A shadowy figure sways in my peripheral vision, and I swipe my head toward the forest. My stomach clenches. Someone's there. Watching us. I can feel it. I return my gaze to Jamie and quickly step back, regaining balance and clearing my throat. Jamie does the same.

"Jamie. We need to stop this. Whatever this is." I look at the short distance between our bodies. Much as we've tried, we keep ending up inches apart and seconds away from spilling our feelings—at least I have.

"I know." He lowers his head.

"It won't bode well for either of us."

Jamie pours his gaze back into mine, making my knees tremble and my heart leap.

"I know."

"Look." I point to the shabby building. "The castle."

Jamie scratches below his neck. "Oui," he affirms, taking a colorless, almost disappointed tone.

We follow the younger ones down the grass. A medieval moat surrounds the three-story chateau. Columns of limestone bricks, faded from the sun, wrap around the building's exterior. Most of the wooden window shutters remain, though they are quite frail from years of storm battery.

The charcoal-shingled roof is still intact, even with its few little towers poking alongside the chimneys. The place really only needs a little tender loving care to bring it back to what I'm sure it was in its eighteenth-century heyday.

Jamie and I take Milo's and Josie's hands to walk over the make-shift drawbridge. Beside the gravel walkway, a real estate sign hitched in the grass has a big "Vendu" sticker plastered across.

"Whoever bought this place . . ." I begin as we ascend the front porch balcony. ". . . is a genius."

Jamie draws back. "A genius?" He examines a dangling shutter. "I don't know about that."

"You don't buy something like this without a vision."

Jamie shrugs. "Or a fondness for bankruptcy."

Milo reaches for the brass lion knockers on the front door. After giving them a few thuds, no one answers.

"It's locked," Jamie says. I turn toward him, and he quickly adds, "It has to be. She can't be inside. Maybe we should try the garden 'round back."

"How do you know there's a garden?"

"It's France. There's always a garden." Jamie bounds down the front steps just as Josie twists the front door's knob straight open. The creak makes Jamie's head turn back toward us.

"Josie, how did you . . .?"

"It wasn't locked." Josie shrugs, and she and Milo bolt inside.

"Wait up, you guys," I shout after them.

Jamie looks wearily through the open door and succumbs to follow me in.

"What?" I poke his arm. "Scared there might be ghosts?"

His demeanor quickly shifts, those jade eyes brightening in an instant. "Well if there are, they're sure to fire out of here once those two start fighting." He nods toward his younger siblings scuffing their feet on the hardwoods in need of polishing.

"They're like our own personal sage sticks," I kid.

Jamie chuckles, coursing a hand through his wavy hair.

Sunlight pours through the crystal windows above the entryway, piercing through the thick layers of dust bouncing around us. A grand wooden staircase marks the center, and two wide hallways spill out on either side of the railing's banisters. The explorer in me wants to venture around with the kids, but the Continental Air hopeful wants to find Manon so I've got a shot left at saving my career prospects. One could call it selfish. I'll call it coincidental multitasking.

Up the rickety stairs, a few rooms have locked doors. We knock on each but get no response. Josie pushes one open, revealing a room where someone's started cleaning up. Floorboards have been stripped, and sitting at the ready are fresh wood pallets, paint buckets, and brushes. Whoever purchased this place has already gotten started on renovations.

Jamie rests his hands behind Josie's shoulders. "Let's keep going. Best not to touch anything that isn't ours."

It may be an old mansion, but I can't help but revel in its sweet hickory wood and chilled limestone.

A dilapidated spiral staircase toward the end of the hall leads to the roof's level where the towers sit. Josie runs up and pounds on the little wood door at the top. Sunlight outlines the crevices in the doorframe. A gasp from inside gives us all pause. Milo joins Josie in banging on the door.

"Manny, Manny, Manny!" they shout.

I rest my hands on their shoulders. "Hey, hey. Maybe a bit lighter, guys."

They continue shouting until the voice on the other side of the door pelts us back.

"Go away!" Confirmed. Manon.

Jamie taps on my shoulder. Our bodies are mere centimeters away as he brushes past me, ascending a few steps to the door. Disinterested, Milo and Josie run back down and around the hallway.

"Soyez prudents!" I shout.

Be careful. Another one of Emi's necessary-for-the-Chessley-family phrases.

Jamie knocks on the U-framed door with his knuckle.

"Manny. C'est Jamie. Will you open up? Please?"

I can see the shadows of Manon's shoes in the crack between the door and the floor as she scuffs closer to it. Her voice doesn't waver in aggression.

"Leave me alone."

A sigh sinks Jamie's shoulders.

"Let me try," I say to him. We stand side by side on the final, narrow step. He's disheartened but still offers me a kind half smile, and I lean my head against the door.

"Manon. It's Kat. Can I come in?"

Her response is even more muffled this time, as if she's talking with her elbows crossed over her face. "Why?"

"Well, we don't get to talk much. Now's as good a time as any, huh? Maybe you could show me the view from in there." No response. Jamie bows his head. But I press on. "We can speak French. Show you all I've learned. Maybe you can help me with my R's."

"I don't want to speak French ever again. I don't want to come here anymore. I just want to go home. My real home."

"Her real home?" I whisper to Jamie.

He rings a hand through his hair. "She wasn't born here. Mum and Dad had her in England, but the rest of us here. Just worked out that way."

It clicks with me then. She had gone to get ice cream with her friends, but with her lactose intolerance, she can only get the nondairy options, sparsely available in this neck of the woods. That shop in Èze for sure doesn't have any, which is why I've only taken the kids to Nice for gelato.

Manon boasts the culture but can't claim citizenship by birth or consume a foundational food group in the region's cuisine. For someone so proud of her heritage, I wonder if she just doesn't feel French enough.

I lightly tap on the door with one hand and fish around my backpack for my journal.

"Manon. Can I show you something?"

"What?" She sounds depleted.

"You'll like it. I know it."

Her feet approach the door, and the knob twists to the right. Jamie and I raise our brows to each other. She cracks open the door an inch wide. Enough to see her puffy red eyes and cheeks.

"Only you," Manon says, pointing to me. Jamie gestures me in, and I join Manon in the tower. It's only about six feet wide. A stone bench horseshoes the perimeter, giving way to the trifold windows latticed with copper rods. It's like Brothers Grimm came here before crafting Rapunzel. The view of the ocean and mountain ridges is immaculate, but I can't see below the treetops. No wonder she hadn't seen us approaching. And the headphones she wears explains why she hadn't heard us come inside.

"Twice?" I point to her phone. She doesn't respond. Still holding on to that grudge for making her miss the ticket window, I see.

Manon takes a seat on the bench and stuffs her knees to her chest. I smile awkwardly at her, trying to make eye contact.

"I know how you feel."

She looks out the window. "No you don't."

I brush the dust off my palms from the cool stone seat. "Well, I can imagine how you feel."

Manon huffs and shakes her head.

"You know," I say, leaning my elbows on my thighs and playing with a hair tie. "Sometimes—well, more like six times outta ten—I feel like a stranger wherever I go. Fish out of water, you know?"

Like I just keep getting into situations that I *think* will feel right, but never do. My memory trails all the way back to college applications that seemed right at the time. To internships I had no interest in. To walking across the graduation stage, collecting a degree that doesn't really light me up. Manon keeps her head toward the window, but her eyes trail to me.

"All that to say. I know what it feels like to be a bit lost. Out of place."

"It's not fair," Manon says, kicking her heel against the stone bench. Her strawberry-blond bangs falling out of her ponytail and shield her eyes.

"Can I read you something?"

"Whatever."

Exhaling through my nose, I open my journal to June 7 and clear my throat.

"'Today, Milo, Josie, Manon, and I went to the grocery store. Manon took care of nearly all the shopping. She knew where to get everything on the list. She even ordered for us at lunch because I had yet to comprehend the fact that entrée means starter, not the main.'"

I sprinkle in a few of my major fails, garnering a laugh from both Manon and myself. A light smile lingers on her mouth until I close the journal and her moodiness sets in again.

"Did you know you have a type of citizenship your brothers and sisters don't?"

"Yeah, rub it in."

"No, no." I scoot closer. From the international law class—thank you, business school—I had taken last semester, one of the principles had stuck. "You have *jus sanguinis*."

Manon scrunches her brow. "Ew."

I chuckle. "It means you are French by blood." I hold out the underside of my forearms. "It runs in your veins," I say, trailing my finger along the blue lines visible through my pale skin.

Uncrossing her arms from her chest, she examines her own with curious eyes.

"Plus, I know someone who doesn't do anything dairy either."

"Who?"

I nod to her graphic tee with song lyrics printed across the front. "Billie Eilish."

Manon widens her eyes. "Really?"

A spark of hope is there that I latch on to. "Mm-hmm. And Lizzo."

"No way."

"Yes way."

She does a quick Google search on her phone to fact-check me, her jaw dropping when she gets her answers.

I lean closer. "You're not any less French for not eating yogurt. Besides, coconut milk ice cream is super underrated."

The smallest smile of satisfaction crosses Manon's face. It's maybe one of the four times I've seen her *not* looking like a sourpuss. And then, she does the unexpected. She wraps her arms tight around my waist, nestling her head against my side.

"Merci, Kat."

I return the hug.

The door creaks open. Jamie leans against the doorframe, his face alight with relief. As Manon and I unravel from our little embrace, my hip lowers back onto the stone, and something in my back pocket pokes at my tailbone.

Solange's business card. I must've left it there from last week. Recovering my contact info from Estelle, Solange had sent me an email last Friday outlining her need for an editor in chief to help run her French Riviera magazine while she focused her efforts on her up-and-coming travel business.

Manon gets off the bench and runs over to Jamie, who tousles her hair.

"There she is," Jamie says. Mid-hug with Manon, Jamie sends a grateful smile in my direction.

We may have mended this fence between us, Manon and I, but holding it together will be another thing. At this point, the key to me keeping this job is keeping her happy. And what does Manon enjoy more than berating my pronunciation? Autonomy. Before I know it, I agree to Solange's offer.

"Manon." She turns back around, her smile slowly evaporating. "How would you like to help me with something?"

The rest of the way back to the Chessley villa involves Josie and Milo climbing up nearly every tree with branches low enough to grab, Manon changing the name on her social profiles to Assistant Editor in Chief, and Jamie and I sharing amused glances.

Just before we step onto the terrace, Jamie leans into my shoulder. "Thank you," he whispers in my ear.

When we step inside the villa, it's like we cross an imaginary border, and he dissolves from my side. Hopefully, the potential stalker didn't see the smitten gaze I just shared with Angela's eldest son. Otherwise, she will surely send me packing for US customs.

Down the hall, Angela and Nick have gotten to chatting with Sylvie over the dinner menu. The little ones are back to racing around the house, and Jamie has disappeared.

Manon struts past me, clapping for my attention. "C'mon. We have work to do."

CHAPTER FOURTEEN

Summer's scorching heat hasn't mitigated the hordes of tourists flocking to the south of France for the country's beloved Bastille Day tomorrow. They pack the streets of Nice like sardines, but Èze remains relatively quiet.

Manon and I have joined Solange for our first staff meeting. Her shop is in its next stage of evolution with a freshly painted sign waiting to be hung outside, a few new pieces of furniture still wrapped in cellophane, and stacks of posters outlining her services. The next level up will be air conditioning, I hope. The little white fan can only do so much to dispel the sweat glistening on my forehead. Besides, she's only got enough in her budget for electricity between the hours of three and four, so we haven't got time to waste.

Solange's vision for the magazine is clear. Unique, attention-grabbing, *incroyable*.

Sure, sounds attainable.

Waving her pen in my direction, she instructs that we'll need at least six articles for every publication. When I inquire about the categories we should cover, Solange shrugs and tilts her head down, eyeing me over the glasses glued to the tip of her nose. "That's for *tu* to decide."

"Noted," Manon says with a confident nod, sipping her glass of lemonade.

Solange tosses a smile in her direction.

"How much is it? The magazine?" Manon asks.

"It's free," I say, scribbling in my notebook and hoping it passes off as me brainstorming article ideas.

Manon halts her leg-kicking against the flimsy fold-up chair. "*Gratuit?*"

"Oui." Solange rests her crossed forearms on the table. "Because we offer space for *publicité*."

We've already decided that I'll do the article writing in English and Solange will translate to French. It'll be a bilingual mirror.

"Just as long as there's a clear . . . euh . . . how do you Americans call it. Call-to-action? To contact the travel agency at the end. C'est ce qui est important."

I gulp, though my nod doesn't impart any facade of confidence.

"You know what I was thinking?" Solange leans back in her desk chair. "How do you feel about video, Kat?"

I nearly spray my sip of sparkling water all over the tchotchkes littering her desk. "I um—"

"What if we started one of those," Solange snaps. "YouTube channels."

My abdomen squeezes inward. "Well, I mean—"

"You can be our spokesperson, trying out the popular sites in the area, hmm? Our very own *porte-parole*. It will go well with the paper volumes." Solange's agility in the business realm is respectable. She most definitely has a keen eye on her prospects. But, I'm no spokeswoman. Put me in front of a camera, and I'll forget every word in the English language, let alone French.

"I don't know if I can commit the time," I lie without giving it real consideration. Manon's eyes burn into the side of my face. "With the younger ones and all."

Solange doesn't even try to mask her disappointment. "Bien," she says, sighing. "Still. Think about it. And we'll need something to keep the locals interested, something to spice up the content. I was thinking, 'Èze-clusives.' Town buzz. Juicy stories. That sort of thing. Comprendre?"

I offer up a soft "oui," though gossip pieces aren't really my forte.

Solange spreads out a map of Èze on her desk and uses a black marker to circle a spot not too far away from the Chessley villa address. "Check on that chateau that just sold."

Leaning forward to look at the map, Manon gasps. "The castle."

Solange chuckles. "Find out who the new owners are," she says to me. "It's the big question in town."

Four o'clock rolls around, and Solange is forced to turn off the computer and the rotating fan. Manon and I thank her for her time and make our way back onto Èze's narrow cobblestone streets. I clutch my notebook against my chest, wondering how I'm going to produce six full-fleshed quality articles every two weeks. Solange insists that the publication schedule needs to be frequent in the summer to capture tourists' attention.

I bury my nose in two blank pages staring back at me. Making bullet points for article titles one through six is easy, but filling them in proves to be much harder than I anticipated.

My writer's block only magnifies as we pass a local band practicing in an upstairs apartment who thought closing the shutters would mute their practice. Trombones wail, their vibrations fluttering flower petals in window boxes. Shop owners run up and down the street, plastering blue, white, and red streamers from door frame to door frame.

Manon had resumed listening to her music, but the second she looks up from her phone, she bolts a block ahead of us, striding to Howie as he kneels and opens his arms. He was just leaving a table under a red café awning, patting his adequately rotund belly and exuding practiced kindness to the waitstaff, even though he doesn't speak a word of French.

"Manana Banana!" Howie bellows, embracing his goddaughter in a bear hug. When I'm within conversational distance, he nods to me. "Kat, how are you going?"

"How am I . . ."

Manon turns around. "Translation. What's up." She spins back to Howie and says, "Kat's still learning *our* English too."

I shrug, stuffing my lips together in a forced smile.

Manon's gaze bounces between me and Howie.

"Howie, guess what?" she says.

He kneels again, his eyes alight and wholly interested. "What?"

Manon lays out the magazine spiel, the assistant to the editor bits, and the busy publication schedule.

"My, I'm glad you went through with it." He looks up at me and nods. "Can't wait to see what you do with the gig. You know, Kat. You have just the initiative we look for in our Young Soarers."

The blood drains from my face.

"Now I don't have any part in recruitment or admissions, but I can tell you, this magazine would be wonderful for your portfolio."

I try to slow my aggressive nodding. "Definitely, yes. Of course."

Now I just need to make sure these next few magazine issues blow their freaking socks off.

Howie rises, smoothing out the wrinkles in his pant creases.

"Well, I've got to be off. Heading to see your father, Manana Banana." He bows his head toward me. "Miss Kat, always a pleasure."

This time, my nod is appropriately even-tempered. But I have to remind myself to say the words floating in my head.

"Yes, likewise," I manage to get out with a grin.

As Manon and I depart from her godfather, she plugs in her headphones and resumes her album, but my head is in a daze as I chew my inner cheek. Not even the blank notebook pages can steal my attention now. The Young Soarers application is due in just over a month. So I better get this magazine thing right.

We only make it a few more doors down until we round the corner to the flower shop, displaying loads of vibrant sunflowers and violet iris bushels on the sidewalk. I hope to see Emi next door in the Cave, but someone else has just exited the store.

Vivian steps out onto the winding sidewalk, hoisting her couture bag over her shoulder. Before she starts off toward the car park, she squints at me and Manon. Lifting her hand over her eyes, she starts to walk closer.

Immediately, I pretend to be picking out a bouquet.

"Bonjour!" Vivian prances over to me and Manon. "Kat, right?"

I push a smile through my makeup-lacking cheeks. "Oui."

Don't be cold to her, Kat.

"Lovely seeing you again." Vivian leans in for the double bise on the cheek.

My gaze travels to Vivian's sparkly sandals and pearly toenail polish. I quickly clasp my hands behind my back, hiding the chipped burgundy on my fingernails.

"Funny running into you," she says. "I just finished a conference call at the Hermès office with some buyers in Asia, so forgive me if I look a mess. I'm actually on my way to the crêperie for a birthday party."

Damn. She's really got her stuff together. Corporate fashion house mogul with an afternoon rendezvous with friends.

"You look great," I insist. "I love those shoes."

"Oh," she says, waving her hand. "Just some goodies Angela sent me. But you probably get so much yourself, huh?" She clears her throat as she reads my blank face. "You know, I'm actually looking for Jamie. Do you know where he is? He's not answering his phone," she says, wagging her cell.

I grip the straps on my backpack.

Does *she* know about the Vigne? I can't risk telling her if she doesn't know. It'd be unfair to him. Besides, I'm not entirely sure he's there. Not having seen him or the tire marks in the gravel driveway since we rescued Manon from the chateau last week.

"I, um . . . I'm not sure actually."

Vivian crosses her arms. "Hmm. Seems like no one does. I can't believe he would just ditch me like that."

"Oh, did you have plans?" I twirl my ponytail.

"No, but he just runs off every time before I get the chance to ask."

So maybe they *aren't* a thing. Butterflies tingle in my stomach.

Stop that.

"He could just be busy with the business. With his father and everything," I suggest.

She rolls her eyes, but not at anyone directly. "All of a sudden, *now* he cares about that. But maybe you're right. Where else would he be?" she says rhetorically. She must not know about him moonlighting as a pastry chef.

I politely smile and notice a bored Manon leaning against the exterior of one of the stone buildings. Vivian and I bise on the cheek again. She emphasizes how great it was to run into each other, and I conventionally nod in agreement. We wave each other off, leaving Manon and me to head for the house.

The entire walk back, I try to compartmentalize all that just happened in the last forty minutes from the publication's first due date, to bumping into Howie and getting the inside scoop on the program I've been clamoring for, to coming across Vivian in her pursuit to find Jamie.

Annoyingly, that last part is rather stickier than I'd care to admit. It's not like she's done anything wrong to me, so it's unfair for me to dislike her. I shouldn't even care anyway. I know what this feeling is— jealousy. But I don't need to feel jealous. I'm not going for Jamie. He wouldn't go for me. Or else he already would have, I'm sure. Besides,

I'm not gonna crap on Vivian for existing when she's actually kind and career-driven. An inspiring acquaintance. In any other circumstance, we'd probably be the best of friends.

When Manon and I reach the villa's front gate and traipse over the crinkly drive, I check the yellow rectangular box adjoined to the house's exterior. Its painted letters read "La Poste". It's where I drop off my letters to Damien and the postcards to Mom every morning at 8 a.m.

Normally, the only mail is for Nick or Angela. But at the bottom of today's stack is one addressed to me. And it's from Damien! From aboard the Ocean Cloud IV somewhere in the Mediterranean Sea.

I bite my lower lip. Finally, someone who shows up for me.

CHAPTER FIFTEEN

"Smell this one," Emi says, thrusting a bottle of peony-colored fragrance at my nose. Earlier this afternoon, she'd insisted that we visit the perfumery on the mountainside overlooking Nice, and much to my apprehension, she swayed me.

It's not that I don't want to admire the stacks of freshly made bar soaps or try my hand at concocting an eau de toilette. Rather, I don't want to run into Damien, whose parents own the perfumery. Even if all logic points to the fact that he won't be popping in when he's on a family vacation, I maintain a steady gaze over my shoulder.

"Why are you so nervous to see him, eh?" Emi pokes my forearm, and I push the wicker basket holding our bath goodies hard against my waist.

"I'm *not* nervous." Ha! Tell that to your churning stomach! "It's just . . . I'm not ready."

Emi takes a whiff of a lemongrass lotion. "For what?"

"It's so easy for me to write to him. He picks up on the littlest of nuances or what I might be feeling even if I don't put it into words."

"And this is a bad thing?"

"No. That's the problem."

Emi furrows her brow, leaving me space to explain.

"On paper, it's like we're in symbiosis. But whenever I've spoken to him in person, I go on like a babbling idiot without a stop button."

"Trust me. The heart knows what it's doing. Your mouth will follow."

"My mouth?" The thought of our lips touching—like they almost did on the casino roof before *someone* interrupted—sends chills up my spine. But it's a mix of tantalizing excitement and pure dread.

"You know, your words," Emi says.

My shoulders loosen. "Oh."

As we exit the shop, Emi begs me to read some of Damien's latest letter, which I accidentally let slip that I tote around in my backpack.

"Mademoiselle Kat," Emi reads, but Damien's velvety voice overlays in my mind.

Apologies for my delay in getting back to you. Désolé. While the Amalfi Coast may tempt me greatly, it hasn't taken my mind off you. So it seems your summer hasn't been without its share of adventure. As for the magazine, I admire you for it. Not every person would be brave enough to take an opportunity like that. But it might just be your blessing in disguise. Your spirit is undeniable. And what transfixes me all the same.

I toy with the straps of my backpack, eyes glued to the verdant cliffside view of the dazzling Côte d'Azur.

Emi continues on to the part where he recommends steering clear of touring the nineteenth-century prison or else Manon might try to lock me inside.

A small chuckle tumbles out of my nose as my eyes melt into the view, a warmth caressing my shoulders from the gleaming sunshine and a tingling at the crown of my head from his words.

Somehow, the universe was looking out for me when I bumped into Damien that day in Nice.

It was fate. *La destinée.*

———*—*—*———

OF COURSE OF all the times to catch a case of writer's block, now it decides to show up in full force. Manon had drawn up a list of three bistros, two boutiques, and a smoothie place for us to visit and review. Sure, treating ourselves to loads of coffee (me) and pain au chocolat (Manon) wasn't difficult. No, the horrendous part was the collection of words that needed to pour out of me piping hot and into a pristine, cookie-cutter format. But every sentence I form, I eventually cross out for being too flowery or too abrupt. It'd be easy—well, easy*ish*—to stick to the facts. Year founded, owners, what it offers. The basics. Plain, simple, informative, with no room for my rebellious creativity to nudge its way through.

Resolving to take this approach, I hunker down in the villa's library after making dinner and putting Milo and Josie to bed. Manon says she doesn't need to be part of the actual writing process. For that, I'm quite thankful. The excess judgment would only inhibit me further, not that I should care what an eleven-year-old thinks of me or my craft.

At this point, though, she wouldn't have much to judge. A blank laptop screen stares back at me. My cursor blinks persistently, awaiting the first sentence, the first word, a single letter. Another open tab taunts me. My half-completed Young Soarers application. With the clock ticking at T-minus thirty days until I need to hit submit, I've lost my momentum in getting around to the second portion. But it's becoming increasingly difficult to teleport myself into corporate American lingo when I'm basking daily in the awe and beauty of the Côte d'Azur.

I turn my attention back to the magazine contents due by midnight. If I'm going to wow the Young Soarers admissions team, the publication has to do well. I've already notified Solange that I'd be omitting the gossip piece on the crummy chateau's new owners without enough time to get a real lead. Her response email had reluctantly expressed her temporary leniency. The computer churns heated air onto my open-faced notebook, the pages only containing a few scratches of in-the-moment descriptors on each business. I lean my forearms over the cool wooden desk. The few lamps sprinkled around the room cast a soothing glow over the plush sofa chairs.

Oh, how I'd much rather pluck a book off of the well-stocked hickory shelves and cozy up under one of those faux-fur blankets draped over the cushioned seats.

A knock on the double glass doors stirs me from my procrastinated haze. Jamie enters the room with two large mugs of tea. He smiles and hands me a cup. My tensed shoulders drop.

"Chamomile," he says. "No milk, no sugar."

"You didn't have t—"

"I wanted to."

We exchange soft glances before a playful smirk spreads across his face.

"Even if it's sacrilegious to drink it plain," he says, glancing toward the translucent liquid in my cup. "But hey, I'm not judging."

Because I've already spent thirty minutes "looking" for a dictionary only to confirm that there aren't any bugged microphones or security cameras, I play back.

"Oh, I forgot to tell you. I'm not actually here to au pair for your siblings. I'm here to teach you all the correct ways to drink tea."

We snicker into our chests. My hands wrap around the ceramic mug, allowing the herbal steam to kiss my face. I don't know if I'm supposed to be angry with him or if we've remediated our toils. It's been a roller coaster ever since I met him last month. There's something about the villa's confines that makes him a bit more relaxed, and it seems to be where we get on the best.

"So." Jamie takes a seat in one of the chairs. "How's it going with the first issue?"

I chuckle without a drop of humor attached. "Getting there." I twirl my loose ponytail and fall into a deeper self-denying chuckle. "Jamie, I have no fucking clue what to do with this."

My honesty spurs his own amusement, and we share a few hearty chortles.

"No one said you had to come in and be the next Condé Nast."

I lift my eyebrows.

"What?" Jamie asks.

"Just kind of surprised you know what Condé Nast is."

"Hey, a well-rounded businessman has his toe dipped in the waters of all enterprises."

"You sound like your dad."

"Good. I'm practicing."

My eyes return to the aggressively blank screen. "I don't know what these people want to read. And Solange wants to take this to YouTube . . . I just. I can't." I lose the words to the rest of my ramble.

"It doesn't have to be perfect on the first go 'round," Jamie offers. "Take what comes naturally. Change from there if you need to."

"I wish it were that easy."

Jamie scrunches his brow and leans his elbows on his quads. "Why can't it be?"

"Because, this has to go right. I can't afford the trial and error."

Boss man—that's what I'm unofficially officially calling Howie Gupta now—said it himself when Manon and I ran into him in the village. These earliest publications would be the pinnacle of my Young Soarers application.

Jamie sits back, keeping his focus on me. "You've wanted this for a while, the Soarers program, haven't you?"

"I call it my healthy obsession." Even if I'm properly avoiding the very application right now. The neat, clean, monotonous paragraphs I'd have to pen for the written questions aren't the sexiest way to spend my night.

"Well," Jamie says, nodding to my laptop. "I vote that you write that magazine from your gut. It knows the way."

I smile.

"And if you decide to go the video route, I'd gladly volunteer as cameraman."

I tilt my head, and he hurriedly swallows a sip of creamy beige tea. "You sure Angela would be okay with that?"

"Probably not. But you're always representing the family. The better you do, the better we all do."

"Why though? Who's she trying to impress?"

Jamie shrugs, glances to the left, and says, "It's the way it goes." He sips and quickly reroutes the conversation, but I can tell there's something more. "Besides, Chef says I gotta work on my food shoots. Figure a little practice with the camera can't hurt." He shines a dimpled half grin.

"Noted. Thank you." I take a sip of my correctly prepared tea. "How's everything going down there?"

"Where?"

I thought it was obvious. "The Vigne?"

"Oh, right," he says, casting his gaze toward the window. "It's going. Really going now."

"Care to share?" I push the laptop to the side and devote my full attention to him, sipping my warmed tea.

Jamie scratches the back of his neck. "Rumor has it a Michelin inspector's comin' to the hotel this month. The place already has two stars, but it lost its chance at a third a few years back."

"Really? What didn't they like?"

"The dessert." Jamie's eyes go stoic as he opens up to me. "If I can help secure the Vigne's third Michelin star, it'd be my break out of the Chessley Enterprise shackles."

He falls silent at the admission. So this is it. The accolade would be his trophy, proof of finding success outside of the business world.

"Jamie. Hey." I try to stir him from his self-purgatory. "It's going to work out the way it should." He doesn't move. "From what I know about you, you don't half-ass anything you really care about."

He lifts his head. A soft smile tugs at the corner of his mouth.

I fiddle with my mug's handle, breaking eye contact once I feel the rush of butterflies swarm around my stomach.

"And if it doesn't work out," a grin spreads across my face, "I'll hire you as the kids' personal chef."

A laugh tumbles out of his mouth, and he rests his hand on his reverberating abdomen.

"See, Kat. You know exactly what to do with your words."

Our eyes lock for a few seconds before my phone nearly vibrates off the desk. At first I think it's Damien, but then I remember from our letters that he wants to keep it strictly old-fashioned to magnify our in-person reunion. Such a romantic, I know. But he is French after all. Then I remember it's ten o'clock on Wednesday, which means Mom's calling for her weekly check-in.

"Do you mind if I . . ." I lift up my phone, and Jamie waves his palm.

"Of course, of course."

I send him a smile before answering. I get up and walk toward the window, gazing out at the lantern-lit sea beyond the cliffs. Jamie removes himself from the sofa chair in the process, making his way to the library's double glass doors.

Mom and I cover the niceties of how the week went. She gives me the low down of who went to church, what the choir sang, and what she got at the farmers market. I give her the CliffsNotes version of how I'm doing, circling around the same descriptors. Good challenge. Never a dull day.

And maybe it's the conversation I've just had with Jamie that's spruced me up about the magazine, but I finally share the news with Mom about my editorial position. I bite my lower lip and play with a houseplant's leaves on the windowsill, acknowledging the fortuity in getting to run a travel magazine on the French Riviera.

But that lightened feeling comes to a screeching halt. "Are you sure you're going to have time for that?" She belts through the phone as usual because she doesn't realize I can hear her regular speaking volume just fine.

And now I'm dealing with the exact reason I didn't want to tell her in the first place.

I exhale through my nose. "Seriously. Why do you always do that?"

"What?" Mom says. "Look, Kat, I just want to make sure you're not spreading yourself too thin."

"Will you let me be the judge of that?" I try not to raise my voice too much. "I don't know why I even bother telling you."

"Kat—"

"No, it's fine. It's fine. Mom, it's late here, and I'm gonna go to bed."

I hang up the phone and turn back around to the desk. Footsteps shuffle down the hall. Did he hear all that? Great, not only do I get to go to bed with refreshed embarrassment, but as I shut the blank laptop screen, my impending deadlines—one for the magazine issue and the other for the Young Soarers application—rear their little heads once more.

CHAPTER SIXTEEN

*M*y body anticipates the day's events before my eyelids open. I sense the encroaching morning light pouring into the room as my hands grip the bedsheets tighter. A swirling breeze sends in notes of sea salt and earthy cypress.

It's debut day for *Conseils Sur la Côte*—literally translating to tips about the coast.

I squirm all over the mattress, scrunching my toes and curling into the fetal position with the duvet consuming me completely.

I was elated to finally send my write-ups to Solange earlier this week. She didn't have any complaints as she translated the mirror-image to French. My guess is because we're on a strict schedule to get the forty-pager to the printer in order for the copies to hit shelves on Thursday morning. So she couldn't have had the time to consider what could be improved for the next go around. This debut issue would be a bit hodgepodge given that we're using stock photography, pictures from my Canon, and local businesses' advertisements to feed the visual attention. Sure the pixels might be dodgy, but I doubt she'd let it go to print if things were *too* blurry.

I finally crawl out of bed, only to find out it's only a few minutes past six, meaning the kids won't be up and ready for breakfast for at least a good hour and a half. So rather than sit with my impatience, I figure I'll take a walk to the boulangerie to quell my toe-tapping nerves. Not a sound emanates throughout the entire villa, save the magpies chirping outside and the distant snores coming from Nick and Angela's bedroom. I tiptoe down the winding marble staircase. I still feel like a stranger even though I've called it my place of residence for well over a month.

Once I'm outside, the cheery morning brightness greets me, and I strut with newfound confidence down the driveway. Jamie's car is gone, shocker. But my mind doesn't linger too long on where he was all night or who he was with. Because it doesn't matter to me.

Along the sidewalk, a few cars whiz past me, nearly sending my sundress flying north. But I pay no mind, biting my lip, wondering what those first few readers will think when they see *my* words. I can't wait to tell Damien how it goes. He's requested that I send him every copy.

Ascending the cobblestone paths, everything is just as I suspected: locals mull about the shops with their crochet produce bags. They huddle arm in arm, walking leisurely but with intent. Cafés welcome their regulars for morning coffees and pastries.

I've placed imaginary thumbtacks on the shops that had agreed to display the free magazines. Swallowing hard when I come to the first place, I plant my feet firmly on the stone walk and stare at the boulangerie. Under a yellow and white-striped awning, a window display shows off baguettes and a stack of *Conseils*. The front cover shows a ground-level view of one uncommonly straight street in Èze. An electric blue sky serves as the backdrop for a polished chestnut door in the foreground enshrouded in leafy vines. Adjacent, a stony walkway with a strip of terra-cotta tile running straight through lets the eye follow it just until the narrow road starts to wind again. My knees still have scrapes from where the tiny stone debris scuffed at my skin. But it was worth it for a shot like that.

Solange took inspiration from other travel magazines with a bold cursive title and a few headline snippets sprinkled along the left and right. I wrap my arms across my torso and take wide steps to the bakery, beckoning me with the warm, yeasty scent of fresh croissants and baguettes.

Inside, the thin-framed boulangère greets me with a short-lived smile. At this time of day, she's used to the neighbors who know what they want and how much. She leans her left hip into her palm and raises a brow while I peruse the glass display, stocked with everything from sourdough boules to cream horns. To my far right, a few women chat at two white tables, pecking at their breakfast pastries. A stack of the magazines sit on the table behind them. I watch one grab a copy and flip through the pages.

My heart nearly skips a beat.

"Mademoiselle?" the boulangère says to me. I glance back at her quickly. Given that no others have stopped in the shop yet, her impatience baffles me.

To stall, I point to three different bread loaves. While she wraps them in paper and twine, I slyly watch the woman reading. She flicks through rather quickly and, unless she can read five hundred words a minute, she isn't actually taking it in.

The boulangère hands me the bread and holds out her hand for my euros.

"Um," I mumble. "Six croissants aux amandes." Thank goodness Milo loves the almond ones, otherwise I wouldn't be able to nail that pronunciation. "Et six croissants r . . ." I stumble through "réguliers." Noted for my next lesson with Emi.

The baker woman smiles at me. A real genuine smile, not a polite "thank you for your money, now get out of my store" smile.

"Merci d'avoir essayé," she says and packages up the pastry while I return my attention to the women in the corner. The one who had picked up the copy passes it to her friends.

"Se lit comme un livre," one of them says, tossing it back on the stack.

It reads like a book? Not exactly the five-star review I was looking for.

Queasiness stirs in my stomach. I need to get out of here. With a nod to the owner and my baked goods piled in my canvas tote, I make my exit.

Just steps out of the boulangerie, I come to the next pin-pointed display: a popular breakfast and lunch café. At the outdoor tables, a trio of men light cigarettes after finishing their juice and coffee. At first, I think they are actually enjoying the magazine, given that it's splayed out across their table.

But then one man exhales smoke and smears his cigarette butt all over the write-up I'd done on that very restaurant.

I inhale deeply, shuddering at the thought of anyone else reading this. I'm tempted to go around town and hoard every copy so no one else has the chance to lay eyes on it.

My stomach drops as I remember what Sylvie had told me a few days ago. That she'd bring plenty of copies from the fish market before arriving at the villa this morning.

No, no, no. Angela can't read this. Nick can't read this. They'll think, *What is this girl getting herself into? Writing garbage and taking time away from the job we hired her for.*

What I'd intended to be a nerve-relieving stroll to town turns into a hightail back to the villa. Doesn't matter that the fully risen sun now accosts my bare skin, making me break out in a sweat. What matters is that I get to the villa before anyone's finger touches the front cover of the magazine.

I must not have seen his car as I nearly trip across the gravel driveway in my sprint to the kitchen, because not a few steps inside as my vision adjusts to the interior, I bash right into Jamie. Our elbows smack each other right in the funny bones.

"Oof. Kat, you all right?" His eyes search the frenzy in mine.

"Yeah, great, great." I push past his arm, not failing to realize the inches between our bodies yet again. But I plow through the feelings and straight to the kitchen, where Sylvie has just finished scrambling a dozen eggs.

"Sylvie," I say, nearly out of breath. "Les magasines. Where are th— I mean. Où sont-ils?"

Sylvie readjusts her gray ponytail and nods her head toward the direction of the ocean.

"A l'extérieur," she says, wiping her hands on her linen apron. "La terrasse."

My wrists hit the chilly marble island, where platters of fruit sit adjacent to the cheese tray. I drop the bag of bread and pastries on the counter and stagger past Sylvie. Jamie has made his way to the kitchen entry with a curious gaze. I nearly run into him again on my way outside.

"Kat, wait." His voice reverberates through my bones, but I lock my focus on the sea directly beyond the terrace's overlook.

"I-I can't."

"Wah!" Milo jumps out in the hall, pelting me with his new water cannon. "Got you!"

A line of lukewarm water strikes across the lower half of my dress. But I haven't the time to consider how embarrassing this looks. Behind me, I hear Jamie's muffled reprimand to his brother as I stumble onto the patio, where Angela and Nick are already midway through their copies of *Conseils*.

My shoulders drop as Angela sips an espresso. Neither acknowledge my presence for a few seconds until Angela lowers the magazine below her gaze and eyes me up and down, wrapping a fluttering scarf around her neck. "Bien joué, Kat."

She *likes* it?

I stand frozen, waiting for Nick's reaction.

"Oui, oui," Nick says in his overtly Britainized French. "Bravo."

Something compels me to take the third seat at the breakfast table. The shade of the chestnut tree and the wafting sea breeze soothe my already sun-scorched shoulders.

"Well written," Angela says.

Elation permeates every cell in my body. I take a croissant from the pastry basket next to the vase of carnations.

"Café, Kat?" Nick says, pouring me a cup. "You know," he says to all of us, "the town needed something like this. Something to slow everyone down—the tourists really. Get them to appreciate where they are, eh?"

I nod fervently. My emotional jitters are now combining with those brought on by the coffee.

As I reach for a glass of juice, I realize the half-drunk one in front of me belongs to someone else. The round table had been set for three. That's when I hear the extra voice plummeting down the far side of the terrace.

By now, I recognize that booming, deep-belly tone.

"Ah, Nick," Howie says, walking across the patio with his copy of the magazine in one hand and a coffee in the other. "Oui, oui. But to slow the traveler down, you must first grab their attention, eh?"

The few bites of croissant churn in my stomach, souring my appetite completely.

Jamie walks outside, his hands on Milo's shoulders, restraining his brother from making a beeline for the pastry assortment.

Howie continues his spiel, though I so wish he wouldn't.

"Miss Kat," he says to me, leaning against the limestone balcony. He holds up *Conseils*. "You write beautifully, you do, and it's a great effort. But may I suggest, next time, you think more like the tourist, huh? Meet them where their minds are. Greet them in the clouds before anchoring them on the ground."

The blood drains from my face, but Jamie's interjection saves me from having to form an immediate response.

"Spoken like a true airline CEO," Jamie says, swatting his godfather's arm, not a crease forming on Howie's polka-dotted Continental-branded polo shirt.

I thank Howie for the advice before gathering myself, still partly drenched from Milo's water attack. "I think I'll go check on the girls."

"I do hope you continue with it," Angela says, lifting her copy but not making a single effort to glance in my direction.

While I could spend an hour dissecting whether she meant that as encouragement to isolate myself from her son or true creative support, I'd rather dunk myself in an ice bath to repel the soul-sucking idea that I might've just blown my entire Young Soarers portfolio with this debut issue.

Jamie takes a step toward me as I make my way off the terrace, but I swear I catch him and Nick sharing a terse glance, and Jamie retreats. Agony stirs in my chest as I make my way back upstairs to flop on my bed. I obviously had no right to expect an immediate success.

A little chuckle bubbles through my diaphragm as a voice in my head starts getting louder. It's an imaginary Emi saying, "Mon Dieu, Kat! Give yourself a break. At least you know what doesn't work for the next *Conseils* issue. Now, pick yourself up and let's go swimming topless again!"

Imaginary Emi has a point. I *did* just co-launch a travel magazine while au pairing for one of Europe's most suffocating families and letter-writing a romantic French heartthrob.

Kat McLauren is making waves in the world. I take a moment to pat myself on the shoulder before returning to the drawing board to drum up new ways of catching and keeping readers' attention.

CHAPTER SEVENTEEN

OCEAN CLOUD IV
ATTN: DAMIEN DE DANDENEAU
CABINA #148
00053 CIVITAVECCHIA, RM
ITALIA

 Well, I'm glad you found the debut Conseils *"informative" and that the extra five euro I spent on shipping your copy was worth it for your kind words. Still, you're being too nice. Almost everyone else thought it was a bore. To be honest, it was crap. Not my finest work, I'll admit. I nearly fell asleep writing the damn thing. But get ready for the next issue. Kat McLauren is about to rock these readers' socks off with what's coming next. I just need to figure out what that is first. Anyway, hope you're well. Enjoy all that lovely pasta! Can't wait to hear about your time at the Colosseum.*

Cordialement,

Kat :)

———*—*—*———

KAT MCLAUREN
22 RUE DES FLEURS
06360 ÈZE
FRANCE

Je me réjouis! Je suis ravi de le lire. Trust your instincts, Kat. They know the way.

Try not to think too much about it. Let it flow. As for anyone's opinions, pick out the useful feedback, then picture throwing the rest into the Mediterranean. You don't need that.

And thank you for asking about Italia. The country is incredible. The food, the wine, the architecture, the landscape. I could live here. I'd love to explore it with you one day.

Bisous,
Damien

———*—*—*———

"It was awful, Emi."

Four days had passed since the first *Conseils* launch, and though I'm mortified beyond belief that large stacks still remain in nearly every display, Emi insisted on grabbing lunch after my meeting with Solange. *That* was another embarrassment in itself.

At a café by the wine store, Emi paws through the magazine while I press a palm over my strained forehead. Waiting in agony as she reads, I momentarily surrender to the humdrum cacophony of ceramic cups hitting saucers and feet scuffing over tile.

"Kat," Emi says, twisting her hair into a high bun. "It's not awful. There's just no passion."

She always has such tact in her French bluntness.

"Funny, that's what Solange was getting at too."

"How did that meeting go?" Emi sips her lemonade.

"Actually awful. And I'm not exaggerating." I lean my forearms on the table and sink my shoulders lower. "Five hundred copies were distributed, and not even thirty were taken. Fifteen of those had to have been between your family and the Chessleys."

"What's the plan then for the next one? What'll change?"

"Everything," I say, locking focus on the notebook next to my water glass. "It has to. Some of the sponsors already threatened to take out their advertisements. And no ads means no funding, which means no *Conseils*."

"I think you need to use your creative instincts. Write some more from here," she adds, patting her heart before pointing to her forehead. "Rather than here."

I chuckle. "Damien said something like that."

Emi gasps. "Mm, dis-moi tous les détails."

"What details?" I laugh nervously, playing with the ends of the tablecloth.

"Minou," Emi says with the utmost endearment. "As your French best friend, I am required to know how it's going between you and your *très sexy* man."

My shoulders vibrate with giddiness as I think about the letters.

"He's not my très sexy man."

What makes him a dreamboat isn't even his looks, though those go a long way. It's how open we can get when we write, like we've entered another dimension, another degree of closeness I worried I'd never find with another person. I relay his suggestion to mentally gather up every single person's potential opinion of every present and future *Conseils* magazine issue and chuck it into the sea. And when Emi is satisfied with the gossip and a fair dose of kissy noises, we part ways for the day so I can resume my kid-caring duties.

My way back to the villa lets me digest the conversation with Solange. This magazine doesn't just belong to her. I'm responsible for it too. And when I agreed to be editor, I agreed to making each iteration the best it can be. The rest of the walk, I draft ideas to try out for the next issue. Put myself in the tourist point of view. Meet them where they are. In the driveway, I see Jamie's refurbished red Porsche. I know what to do.

CHAPTER EIGHTEEN

*W*hen I get back from Èze village, I head straight to Jamie's bedroom and knock on his door. It is the first time I'm exploring this side of the villa in all my weeks here. He greets me with a bit of shock before welcoming me in.

Jamie's room is nothing like I pictured it. There are no stacks of cookbooks on the shelves. No dirty sneakers lying about from his afternoon runs. In its place are neatly pressed bedsheets, framed copies of his university degree, and a barren work desk. Even on holiday, the Chessleys keep up with the Joneses. The balcony's double glass doors overlooking the terrace had been swung wide open, allowing every one of Nick's muffled belly laughs to echo through the room.

"Something the matter?" Jamie asks.

I shake my head and follow up with my quick business proposal, removing all emotion from my voice, as plain as if I were ordering a bag of rubber bands online.

"Solange and I have agreed to start a YouTube channel to go with the new *Conseils* issue. All revamped. Can you help us?" I hold my head high to maintain the formal tone.

I'm a bit embarrassed to admit, but I assume Jamie will poke fun at me for taking him up on his cameraman offer.

Jamie steps closer to me, smiling gently. He smells of fresh laundry and cloves.

"Of course."

My shoulders fall from my ears. This can't be what I think it is. I can't *like like* him.

Sure, he's objectively attractive, but no way in hell am I throwing out what I have with Damien.

Seconds later, footsteps thump down the hallway.

"Yay!" Manon storms the room and wraps her arms around Jamie's waist. "Does this mean you're coming with us?"

"We're getting coverage on a few places around town today," I explain.

Jamie kneels to his sister's height. "Well of course. You're looking at your brand-new cameraman."

"Kat," Manon says. "I'll be in the library coming up with our list of places for the week. Don't let me do *all* the work." When I don't follow behind her within three seconds, she puts a little more oomph in her attitude. "Okay?"

I send one more grateful smile Jamie's way before turning around. "Right behind you, Manon."

While Manon races down the hall, Jamie follows me out of his room.

"Figure I can help too. I know a few hidden gems."

Before joining Manon in the library, I check that Milo and Josie are perfectly occupied with their new chapter books. We'd picked them up at the most adorable bookshop in Nice. Jamie taps my arm as we descend the staircase.

"Hey, are you okay about everything?"

I scrunch my brow.

He expounds, "I know Howie's comments can be a little . . ."

I shake my head and broaden my shoulders. "It was just the advice I needed."

"For what it's worth, I'm glad you're still going with it. You've got spunk."

The back of my neck tickles with delight. It's the kind of comment I only dream of hearing but never expect to receive.

"Merci, Jamie."

Manon's "Allo?" bounces around the marble tile in the foyer, dissolving our widened grins.

— ✻ — ✻ — ✻

IF IT WEREN'T for Howie Gupta's comments on the first issue—that, and the overwhelmingly dull reaction from townspeople and tourists alike—I would never have thought to completely unroot the format I'd been using. Goodbye, densely packed, elongated articles. Hello, traveler's quick guide to navigating the French Riviera.

I scan Solange's feedback.

Too many words. Not enough pictures. Make me feel like I'm in France. Transport me.

The opportunity to revamp and revise drums up an exciting challenge. I combine ideas from other magazines I already love and toss in a few of my own. A monthly calendar of can't-miss events. A one-page featurette of a hidden gem that flies under the radar. Plus, lists. Everyone loves a good list. "Five Places to Gather Ingredients for a DIY Charcuterie Board." "Seven Locations to Enjoy Your Personally Assorted Meats and Cheeses."

Manon had a thoughtful idea of letting businesses and organizations post their event fliers too. This got Solange and me thinking. We can reduce the regular advertisement section and pepper in posters. The more relevant to each page, the better.

The last section of each publication would be dedicated to Le Journal de Kat. Kind of like my own column. I'd document what I interacted with in town that week, taking advice from locals on what to try next. I negotiated with her to put off the gossip article if I were to do my own column. I'm a creative, not a reporter.

As for the YouTube channel, we'd ironed out that we'll have a segment that coincides with a write-up in each publication. It'll be called "Only a Day Trip Away," cataloging what to do and how to get to a renowned location within a two-hour drive of Nice's city center.

To say I'm eager to get started on next week's *Conseils* publication would be an understatement. Unblocking my creative spigot, I'm ecstatic to channel some of that visionary spark into a tangible outlet. Even the kids are stoked that they get to join me on our little escapades. And they're even more excited that Jamie's coming with us. Apparently, time with their big bro is scarce with his schedule.

Frankly, the more time I spend with Jamie, the more he seems to warm up to me. And I to him. I promise I don't like him as more than friends, but he's a good punching bag to practice my flirty energy on once in a while.

After a romantically stale high school and college career, I've come to realize one very important truth about myself: flirting is fun, and I will employ it when the mood strikes. Maybe it's the European water, but since I've stepped foot on foreign soil, I'm liberated more and more every day to actually take charge of my love life.

I won't deny the electricity that sparks inside me when I'm around Jamie. But I attribute it to nerves.

On the other hand, with Damien's letters, there's a calmness that feels like a safe, warm hug. Plus, he actually verbalizes his feelings. He is transparent. He starts and ends almost every letter with a nod to how beautiful he sees me inside and out, even the parts I used to despise. Like how one iris is a slightly darker shade of brown than the other, and my tendency to word vomit over people I'm comfortable around. His words make me feel seen, heard, and encouraged, even when I feel so out of place. He recognizes my fierce go-getter spirit but wonders if I can see it myself.

These thoughts linger as we pack Jamie's car up for the start of our weekly adventures. We're popping around the village for "Six Must-See Spots—One Weekend in Èze." I tell myself not to compare the two guys as Jamie loads the car with water and the kids' daypacks. Damien may be suave and sultry. But man, can Jamie really rock the suntanned, works-with-his-hands aesthetic.

I wish Emi were coming with us. She'd be the ice cube between me and Jamie to keep away temptation. But when I asked her to join, she said she'd taken a shift at the Cave. That came as a shock to me, since she'd mentioned last week that she was close to securing a teaching gig in Antibes.

"It's a minor detail," Emi had told me. "Besides, they need my help."

When the convertible trunk is all packed and I've wrangled the kids into the back seat, Jamie holds the passenger door open for me, but I remember I've left the snack bag in the kitchen.

As I scuffle through the main entry to grab the canvas tote on the island countertop, a few muffled sobs ripple through the hall. It sounds like they're coming from the library. I tiptoe toward the open door.

"When is this going to be over?" Angela cries.

I lean into the hallway to catch Nick's voice comforting her. "Soon enough, mon amour."

When is what *going to be over?*

"I can't even walk in my own house without feeling like I'm being watched."

What is she talking about?

"Let them pry. We have nothing to hide."

Who?

"We have a right to our privacy, Nico."

"I know, amour. It'll be over soon. I promise."

The conversation swerves as Angela's emotions sweep her further down a rabbit hole. She blows her nose vigorously.

"And I want him back, Nico."

"He's still here."

"But for how long?" Angela's voice croaks. Silence falls over the couple, and before they think to enter the kitchen, I tiptoe out of the house.

In the driveway, Jamie's entertaining his siblings from the driver's seat. He gives me a smile and a friendly double horn honk to commence the adventure.

Just when I thought I had this family sort of figured out, I'm thrown a curveball. Angela thinks the Chessleys are being watched? Why? Who? Is it the photographer I've seen around town the past month? Or worse, does she think it's me? Regardless, someone's a spy. No doubt about it.

And another thing is perfectly clear: the Chessley's familial ties are loosely held together like worn pieces of string, frayed to the last few threads.

Question now is, how long will the facade last?

If that woman thinks *I'm* the fault line in her family, she's got another thing coming. She can send her private detectives. Even the damn CIA if she likes. But I'm not going anywhere. Not until I've aced my Young Soarers portfolio, chummed up Continental Air's CEO, and had a real and proper snog—with Damien of course. And I won't let Angela be the one to muddle it up.

CHAPTER NINETEEN

*I*t wasn't my intent to get Jamie all hot and bothered. With a hectic week, it just so happened that our drive to Èze's Jardin Exotique made for a few quiet moments to write Damien. The cliffside ocean views occupied the kids' attention, and while the road should have been doing the same for Jamie, he started squirming in his seat when I pulled out my pen and paper. I caught him glancing but didn't say anything.

What's his deal? Does he really despise Damien that much?

Whatever the beef between them, of course I want to know, but I also don't want to be the one to wedge myself into their quarrel.

One thing I've noticed about Damien, through his letters at least, is the passion with which he defends himself and his family. He refuses to have a bad word spoken about them. Regardless of the snobby ignorance their venture capital successes have afforded them, they are good people, he insists.

Funny. I'm sure Jamie would say the same about the Chessleys. If only he and Damien could just air their grievances, I'm sure they'd realize they're less rivals and more similar than they'd care to admit.

We've crossed the neat and tidy paved avenues that wind through upper-class Èze to the more rustic, gravelly side streets along the cliffs, and I resolve to finish the letter later when the bumps from the road aren't as harsh, no thanks to Jamie's poor pothole avoidance. It's like he aims for them.

The wind stirs with ocean air, flinging my hair in all directions. I turn back and see Manon's and Josie's doing the same, while Milo shakes his new buzz cut like he's wearing an invisible wig. The back seat drowns in infectious laughter, and the contagion spreads to Jamie and me in the front.

After a few more minutes up a rather steep road, we arrive at the botanical gardens. They expand over the peak of a small mountain, overlooking all of Èze village, with Nice and the Saint-Jean-Cap-Ferrat peninsula off in the distance. The kids dash out of the car for a game of tag, but Jamie and I holler at them to come back.

"Revenez, tous," we shout.

"Careful on the railings," I add in, noting the steep descent down the adjacent cliffs.

Part of me wants to drink in this moment, how the view offers the illusion that one could simply step right onto the cobalt-blue expanse stretching from one side of the globe to the other. There is more wispy-cloud sky than land and sea, like we're just little figurines in a gigantic snow globe.

Then the other part of me—the au pair responsible for three human lives in addition to my own—wants to hold each of their hands. But Manon, being the mature teen-like tween that she is, assumes that task.

"I've got it," she says rather proudly, gathering her siblings while Jamie follows me around the garden's base with the Canon camera.

Stone and brick staircases wrap around the mountaintop, a plethora of plant species consuming either side of the walkways. Squat cacti plants share cliff space with fuchsia blossoms and five-foot-tall palm trees.

"It's like the desert had a baby with the Mediterranean."

Jamie points at me. "Hey, that's a good line. Have you ever considered the writing profession?"

"Haha. Your humor is unparalleled."

"There's more where that came from." He winks at me, and I resolve to make my way up the steps, shoving away any encroaching feelings he's inadvertently awakened.

I reach my hand out for the camera, and Jamie hands it over. One of many sun-washed Earth goddess statues that populate the Jardin stands tall amid bushels of botanicals.

It's as if she herself admires the all-encompassing view: the sunburnt terra-cotta roofs against a backdrop of jagged cliffs kissing the sea.

Snap. My camera clicks, capturing the scenery.

So few visitors wander around us. Easy to guess that most tourists are probably soaking in rays at the beach. It's quiet enough to hear a soft breeze bristle palm leaves together.

Jamie sighs and leans his arms against a railing. "I love it here."

"Taken the au pairs here before, have you?"

He scrunches his brow. "What?"

I shake my head and continue up the steps. "Nothing, nothing. Just figured you've probably shown people around." I tap my fingers along the metal railing. "No?"

"You really think I'm some sleazy geezer?"

That London accent gets me.

I shrug, but my sleeve tumbles nearly halfway down my arm. Damn these adorably cute shoulderless rompers. I sweep it back up to physically communicate "no, that was not me being flirtatious."

"I did at first, but then I figured your night shift spiel had to be true." I snap another picture of striped lilies.

"How's that?"

"My third week here. I saw you come in around midnight covered in duck fat from the waist down."

"Ah, pretty cheeky looking down there, now aren't we?"

I dagger a glare at him. He chuckles and lifts his palms.

"Kidding. Hey, maybe I really *was* trying to swoon a lady."

"Mm. Hot grease. Never been more turned on myself." I lift my brow and give a smile.

The staircase ascent leads us to a planked deck enshrouded by raw mountain rock and a human-made waterfall. Wooden lounge chairs invite us to take a seat and feast on the oceanic view. It's tempting, but my attention darts to getting a visual on the kids. Jamie notices my hasty glances as I try to detect their voices, and he points to our right. A few staircases below us, his siblings are battling over who gets to use the binocular stand.

I follow Jamie as he sinks into one of the wooden deck chairs. The waterfall's misty droplets and the sweet, earthy poppies take hold of my senses. The tension below my neck I hadn't even known was there slowly releases.

"So," I begin, cracking open one eyelid. "Any intel on the Michelin inspector?"

Jamie shakes his head and runs both hands through his sun-soaked hair. "Rien." He slices the air with a horizontal hand gesture. "Nada. Niente."

"Well, no matter *who* they are, I'm willing to put my money on the Vigne."

Curiosity melts his tone. "Have you been yet?"

"It's on the list," I affirm.

"Let me know what day works for you. I'll reserve a table. Bring Emi, if you'd like."

I notice he doesn't mention a certain someone.

Well, maybe because he knows a certain someone's away on vacation, but still. The more I think about it, the idea sounds like a win-win.

"You know, I can do a write-up on it for *Conseils*."

He looks over at me. "You don't have to do that."

"No, I'd love to. I'll keep your name out of it. Don't worry. But I will be brutally honest, so make sure you bring your A game." A warm spaciousness swells in my throat, culminating in a little side grin.

"Well, I hope it's good enough for your standards." He returns the grin, but it dissolves into distracted stoicism. "I'm gonna need all the good press I can get. If we blow it with this Michelin star, I might as well hand Chef my apron on the way out. Dessert has been our Achilles heel for the last few years."

"Until you came around and gave the pastry team the boost it needed," I encourage him.

A small smile graces his lips. "Thanks. I hope you're right. I can't drop the ball now, not when I'm so close." He scoffs to himself.

So close to what? My eyes search his face.

I assume I know what he's thinking, at least in part. "Well, say the inspector is missing their taste buds . . . and the Vigne doesn't get that third star, Nick and Angela won't find out, right? You've done so well at hiding it."

Jamie pushes his tongue against his inner cheek. "That's because there hasn't been a spotlight on it. Once that review comes out, all eyes are gonna be on us. If it's good, all the posh neighbors are gonna brag about it. And if it's bad, they'll damn it for being the reason they all flock to friggin' Monaco for dinner."

He pauses, calming his voice. "And the pastry team will either be the MVPs or the culinary equivalents to washed-up gutter rats. Either way, secret's coming out."

"We can't predict the future, Jamie." But I know what it's like to want to live in it.

"Can't we though? Don't we have some influence?" he challenges.

My cheeks hollow out as I suck them in. "Well . . . maybe a little bit, but who are any of us to say how it'll happen exactly."

"I still think it's up to us to give fate a little nudge."

We share a silence, allowing for the pittering waterfall to soften the air. Though my own camera sits in my lap, I swear I hear the shuttering of a lens nearby. I toss my head over my shoulder, but no one's around. My throat clenches, and goose bumps spread along my skin.

Jamie doesn't seem to catch on. He stretches his arms out. "So I really gotta put these bad boys to best use," Jamie says, wiggling his fingers. Heat races up and down my neck.

I clear my throat and stand up, flicking my palazzo pants backward. "Well I guess you really better get your shit together, then."

We chuckle together, then depart the little sanctuary and make our way to the kids, who've run to the other side of the mountainous garden. Selfishly, I can't help but think that he was right.

If he loses his Vigne shift, he's not guaranteed the same hours elsewhere. Without a cameraman, I'll have to resort to vlog-style videos. It's not the end of the world. But without his help, would I be able to deliver the same quality of content? What would Mr. Gupta say if my work for *Conseils* wasn't up to snuff? And would that affect my admission to the Young Soarers?

—*—*—*—

YOUR MOST MAGICAL TRIP TO THE LAVENDER FIELDS OF PROVENCE

There's so much more to these rolling hills of blue-violet flowers than their intense aroma.

How to make your trip even more spécial:
- *Have a photo shoot on the grounds*
- *Stroll through the adjacent sunflower fields*
- *Visit nearby towns to sample lavender-infused gastronomic specialties like eclairs and truffles. Delicieux!*

- *Pop the question! Gorgeous setting and a bonus, the calming scents may help to quell those nerves too! Win-win.*

When to visit:
- *Capture the blooms starting in late July through early August!*

Lavender fields to give a try on your French vacay:
- *Valensole Plateau*
- *Sault Plateau*
- *Luberon Valley*

Book your next trip with Solange Martin!

—⁂—⁂—⁂—

THE ESSENCE OF EASY LIVING IN MONACO

Show off your chic at the Café de Paris Monte-Carlo.
    Where? À la Salle Empire de l'Hôtel de Paris Monte-Carlo.
    Oui oui! Add some dazzle to your day & embrace the moment.
- *Wear a sunhat, don some fine linens, pop on some red lipstick*
- *Let your inner royalty shine as you indulge in the fancier side of life*

Editor Kat's favorite bites:
- *Braised Beef*
- *Salmon Tartare*
- *Fruit & Custard Tart*
- *Chocolate Glacier*

Book your next trip with Solange Martin!

—✳—✳—✳

THE KIDS ARE fast asleep in the back of the convertible, leaving me to pen the rest of the week's write-ups with them fresh in my mind. It's been a half-month-long whirlwind since the *Conseils* revamping and our trip to the Jardin, and I've gotten my writing rhythm down pat. I try my best—ish—not to take too many glances at Jamie in the driver's seat. But damn. I can't resist admiring his sun-washed locks dancing in the wind and the golden hair on his tanned forearm glistening under the cloudless sky. We've actually kept les hormones under control. Not too many flirtatious gazes or incidental grazing of our hands. The icy exteriors melted to a neutral playing field.

Over the cliff, the cobalt sea exudes a vibrancy that never gets old. I rest my eyelids for a moment, and my mind slips into a daydream, replaying the afternoon we just spent gorging on ice cream and fine French cuisine in Monte Carlo.

We had just wrapped up filming the café's exterior: a palm tree-lined patio in front of the foaming fountain across the street from the casino. We strolled and recorded plenty of clips capturing my in-the-moment food reviews.

Jamie may have signed up to be cameraman, but I gladly took on the role of director, coordinating all the shots that we'd eventually tie together. As per Solange's orders, I also had to be the star of the travel guide series for *Conseils*'s YouTube channel, much to my hesitation at first. I suppose my comfortability on camera has been increasing day by day, as I'm not so quick to cringe when I hear my recorded voice anymore.

At the table, Jamie laughed as I made a big show of deleting a clip of me running from a swarm of bees in the lavender fields a few days prior.

Then, Milo successfully smeared the entire perimeter of his mouth and the rim of his shirt collar in chocolate ice cream while Josie neatly spooned raspberry sorbet like royalty in training. Manon was busy downing the rest of her sparkling lemonade.

As I dabbed a wet napkin over Milo's shirt, Jamie said, "Kat Mc-Lauren, world-class au pair by day, media mogul by night."

I tossed him a sarcastic chuckle.

"Damn, wish I had someone to clean me up when I make a mess like that," he added.

I hadn't detected any following cameras around us, so I conceded to flow with the flirt. Angela wouldn't know.

"Didn't realize you were so dirty." I winked.

He grinned coyly. "You don't know the half of it."

The kids didn't notice our exchange. Before my cheeks could get too scarlet red and my palms too sweaty, Jamie abruptly pulled back in his seat, the humor and lightness disappearing from his eyes. I couldn't understand.

He had started it.

Either this is how people flirt in Europe or he's surely keeping me in the dark. If anything, he's consistent in his inconsistency. Just when I think we're verging on friends, we get kicked right back to square one.

I'm pulled out of my reminiscing when a sleepy Manon tugs on my sundress from the back seat.

"Kat. Can we go to the chateau? Maybe the new owners are home."

"Maybe later, Manon," I say.

Jamie snaps a glance my way. "What's the deal with that, anyway? Solange still wants the gossip article?"

"Mmm. Oui. But she's not getting it anytime soon. I'm not TMZ," I affirm.

"That's good," he agrees. "Glad to see you putting your foot down."

"Well, merci. Hopefully I can keep it there. I can't risk upsetting Solange and losing the gig that's pretty much the golden ticket to my Young Soarers application."

"Well, let's hope things'll stay as they are," Jamie says, keeping his focus on the road. Though, his tightened grip on the leather steering wheel makes me curious what's gotten him so invested. When we arrive back at the Chessley villa, it only takes Jamie three seconds to bolt inside without so much as a wave or glance in our direction.

"What's the rush?" I shout after him.

"Nothing, nothing," Jamie says. "I just. I've got to meet . . ." He looks off toward the harbor, stopping himself from revealing this supposedly precious information.

My tongue goes dry. Just say it. It's Vivian.

I get that he's trying to stave off Angela from picking up anything between us, but does that mean he has to forfeit all sense of cordiality? He does every time we return from a *Conseils* excursion. Frankly, it's peeving me off.

CHAPTER TWENTY

OCEAN CLOUD IV
ATTN: DAMIEN DE DANDENEAU
CABINA #148
84121 SALERNO, SA
ITALIA

    So, what do you think of the new and improved Conseils*?? Have you been watching the YouTube videos?? We can't pump them out fast enough. (By the way, do you have WhatsApp? Maybe we can use it to text when you're in range of a Wi-Fi signal).*

    Every day gets better and better. I mean, I'm getting paid to film beautiful places, write about them, and share it all with the world. I think I'm living my dream. I just never imagined my summer taking a turn like this. Emi's a good influence. She's got me sporting the carpe diem lifestyle. Your country seems to have better practice at that.

    Also, there is something you should know. Jamie's been helping me with the filming for Conseils*. I know you guys aren't on the best of terms—you can confide in me when you're ready. But, truthfully, we're becoming good friends, he and I. And I don't say that about just anyone. I hope you two can reconcile one day.*

How's the Amalfi coast?

Bisous, Kat

* * *

KAT MCLAUREN
22 RUE DES FLEURS
06360 ÈZE
FRANCE

Kat! I just finished reading the latest Conseils. *It is perfect. Tu es vraiment incroyable. I watched your travel guide through Valensole. You really know which shots will capture the essence of a place. Très impressionnant. And you look so natural on camera. Tu es d'une beauté ravissante. Je n'ai jamais vu un visage aussi beau de toute ma vie. :)*

And don't worry about Jamie and me. That's in the past. Sometimes the truth needs time to breathe, and I wouldn't want things to get messy. Not now. But do me a favor and ask him what's got him so shaky when he's holding the camera. He's not nervous, is he? Hahahaha. Je plaisante.

Honestly, Kat. Je n'ai jamais rencontré quelqu'un d'aussi originale que toi. You enchant me. I can't stop thinking about you. My whole world shifted when we met. The way you stand up for your dreams and won't take no for an answer. I've never encountered such conviction in another person. Have you always been this way? Or is it something in the water?

I'll be back within the month. I'd like to take you out when you've finished your au pairing, of course. I'm sure Jamie's mother wouldn't want you to get too distracted. It's been a few months of unfortunate circumstances, eh? Quand même, whatever happens at the end of summer, I want to tell you how special you've become to me. Keep being you, Kat. The world needs more of it.

Bisous, Damien

—✳—✳—✳—

"ILS SONT PARTIS!" Emi shakes her fists excitedly, nearly whacking her feather earrings out of their clasps.

"Every copy?"

She nods. "Every single one. I checked la boulangerie, la crêperie, et le café with the salade niçoise that you like."

My jaw drops, and my hand loses all feeling. I nearly spill my steaming cup of tea all over my notebook and maxi skirt. But I'd rather burn my thigh than get a drop on these plush sofa chairs in the Chessley sitting garden.

"Quoi!" A smile radiates over my face as I lean back into the cushion. I web my fingers behind my neck and lean back, welcoming the shade of the azalea bushes. The garden's limestone fountain trickles its gentle lullaby. "Is this what bliss feels like?"

Emi plops down next to me, swiping a madeleine biscuit from the tray on the weather-resistant coffee table. "Whatever you are doing," she starts, wiping off the crumbs from her linen tank top, "it's working."

My exuberance subsides as I realize the harsh reality that comes with such success: maintaining it. Not just for Solange's sake, but for mine as well. The half-filled copy of my Young Soarers application peeks out of the backpack by my legs, taunting me.

But another paper on my lap regains my attention. Emi makes kissing noises when she sees it. Damien's latest letter. He doesn't seem bothered that I'd spent nearly four hours a day with Jamie for the past week and would be doing so for the rest of the summer. But that's just the kind of guy he is. It's refreshing.

Emi slyly peels the letter off my lap and grips either side of the handwritten note, scouring every line. She gasps and points to the middle of the page. "Que c'est beau," she comments, pressing her hand to her heart.

A blush invades my cheeks, and I return to the flowery shade, sinking back in the couch cushion. My smile dissolves as I nod in Emi's direction. "Read the rest."

The last paragraph had turned the best letter I'd received all summer into the worst one.

Emi traces her finger toward the end of the paper. "Quel est le problème?" she asks.

"'Whatever happens at the end of summer,' just means he doesn't see us working out. Doesn't it?" I hug a square pillow to my stomach and rest my gaze on the villa's stucco.

Emi tosses the letter in between us on the couch. "Not necessarily."

I shrug, but my loosened muscles freeze in place the second I hear those clacking heels against the terra-cotta tile inside. Angela struts out the double glass doors and into the garden. She bats an accordion fan by her neck without pause as she prepares for her miniature speech.

"We are going for a family outing. Nico, myself, and all the children."

I lean forward, packing my backpack. "I'll make sure dinner is ready when you get back."

Angela inhales as if her next words were already implied. "You are coming with us. We are going to Nico's favorite . . . pub. Emi, your father said that you are working at the Cave tonight. Otherwise, you would be welcome."

I shift my attention to Emi, who after thanking her aunt looks down, her dark orange curls shielding her eyes.

The situation rattles me. In my nearly two months at the Chessley villa, not once has there been a group outing of any kind.

"Are we celebrating something?" I ask.

Wrong question, Kat. Angela's nostrils flare.

"We do not need to celebrate to be with each other, eh?" She swerves around and shuts her fan, jolting it above her head as she walks back inside. "Dix minutes."

I crane my neck to Emi. "What's this about?"

Emi's reply is only a one-shoulder shrug. She insists that she needs to be off, preemptively avoiding my eventual question on why she keeps picking up shifts at the Cave.

So rattled by the letter I'd received, I hadn't known how to reply to Damien, and it had delayed my scheduled 8 a.m. drop-off in the post box. Now with this Chessley escapade stealing the rest of my afternoon, I have to condense my letter writing time from sixty minutes of thought-through cursive to ten minutes of rushed scribbles two notches above chicken scratch.

And with the local post taking a week off for their holiday, this letter can't wait. After all, I couldn't have Damien thinking I'm ghosting him, not after he poured a few precious words straight from his heart. No, if I left him high and dry, he'd probably figure "might as well make some moves on these gorgeous Italian women." Well, maybe not. Knowing what I do about him, from how he carries himself—from how he writes, really—he's probably among the men with the highest integrity traipsing across the Amalfi Coast.

I condense my own feelings down on the sheet of paper and add a final line without filtering it through my "too flirty, too forward" scale. Nearly slicing my tongue as I lick and seal the envelope, I plop on the stamps and check my phone. Just a minute past noon.

The slap of a metal box's thin lid rattles.

No. Crap! The postman came early.

Abandoning my things in the garden, I charge barefoot through the house, scrunching up the skirt that had seemed like the perfect decision four hours earlier. I barely catch garbled Chessley conversations in the living room as I bolt out the front door and off the marble steps. I quickly regret not putting shoes on as each gravel stone pricks the bottoms of my feet. But that doesn't matter now.

The postman is about to take a hard left out of the driveway on his yellow moped.

"Wait!" I wave my hands.

He turns around and flips up his helmet's visor, allowing me to meet him at the villa's gate.

"J'ai une lettre." I hold up the note for Damien.

"Kat!" A voice shouts behind me. It's Jamie, running down the driveway, his mouth set in a firm line.

I return my focus to the postman, lifting up the letter. "C'est très important," I say. "Comme les autres." Really though, it's more important than the others, but I don't have a moment to finagle that sentence out.

The man tilts his head. "Quoi?"

Was my French messed up? Did I say it wrong?

"Here," I say, holding out the letter. Just as he opens the box fastened to the seat behind his, Jamie's footsteps reach a crescendo. He stops next to me, taking a moment to catch his breath.

"Kat, wait. No."

I scoff and cross my arms. "Seriously, are you that bothered by me writing to him?"

He sighs and shakes his head. "N-no, it's not that." His eyes avoid me and search the mail hamper on the moped. Jamie gives a slight nod to the postman before returning his focus to me. "That won't get to him for another week. They may be collecting the post today, but it won't be dispatched until the week after. One of the chefs at the Vigne lives over the border in Ventimiglia."

"Italy?" I say.

Jamie nods, a few of his wavy hairs falling out of the low bun. Now noticing his fresh-pressed button-down, I surmise he's also joining the Chessley excursion. Odd for him.

"I can have him drop it in the Italian post after his shift is over tonight." My wary eyes cause his to soften to that gentle emerald I know well. "He won't read it, promise."

Day-one Jamie is back, at least for a moment.

Despite the friction between us this summer, I can't deny that he's been there for me. With the lamb in the bed, with *Conseils*. I don't have any incriminating evidence to prove his intentions to be malicious. So I nod my agreement, and we walk back to the villa after we say our "au revoir" and "mercis" to the postman.

"Bonnes vacances, Monsieur," Jamie says with a final wave.

A warmth localizes near my lower back, but it dissipates as soon as it arrives. It was Jamie's hand. I catch him swiping it back and scratching the back of his neck. He clears his throat, clearly embarrassed, like he hadn't even realized he was doing it.

CHAPTER TWENTY-ONE

"Bloody hell," Jamie grunts, peering out the car window. His unabating leg shake hasn't stopped since the second we got into our Uber.

To say it's yet another eventful week would be an understatement. Accompanying the Chessleys for their rather orchestrated "family" outing at the only English pub in the south of France had its fair share of roller coaster ups and downs. Starting with me rubbing thighs with Jamie in the third row of Nick's Audi because Josie and Milo *had* to occupy the second row or else the sky would fall. And of course my feelings for Damien burn bright, but I am a mere mortal and not completely immune to Jamie's enchanting cologne. Orange. Ginger. Cloves. I can still smell it!

Then, even in a wood-paneled bar exuding oak and ale that looked to have been plucked straight from a quaint English village, Nick couldn't rip the plastered, crooked-tooth grin off his face. Kept asking if we were all très bien every three minutes. The awkward silence brewing among us only interrupted when we sipped our hoppy drinks or shifted an inch in the red vinyl booths.

Next, the barkeep beckoned Nick and Angela to face off in a game of darts against Jamie and me. While I would've politely declined, I couldn't say no to Angela's demand that we comply, even if she was trying to show me up. Unfortunately for her, I've retained an impeccable aim ever since high school basketball. The challenge rallied each of us to up our game while the kids noshed on pretzel and peanut mixes. If I didn't know any better, I would've called it the Chessley's version of family game night, but why it needed to be so orchestrated was another question.

I wasn't lucky enough to evade Angela's eye when Jamie and I secluded ourselves for another drink at the bar. She most definitely saw my rosy cheeks as he gave me a horrendously cheesy pep talk before the match point. And that's when Jamie got the text from his coworker Mathéo. I only had to read the first sentence.

L'inspecteur Michelin est à la Vigne! Viens vite!

With Emi's help, despite the spotty service from the pub's bathroom, we figured out a plan: Antoine and Marie needed Jamie and me to cover at the Cave due to a family "emergency" with Marie. We told Nick or Angela that the red alert is car trouble. They automatically assumed it was something to do with the twenty-year-old Fiat that Marie's sister drives, supposing she'd broken down on the side of the road in Antibes. Fortunately, there was no real crisis, and our little white lie held up.

Nick was all for it. "Anything for family!" He'd shouted across the bar, blitzed up on ale. But Angela had traces of skepticism in her eyes. Still, we made it out and into the nearest rideshare option.

"Bloody effin' bollocks," Jamie grumbles next to me.

The driver, an older gentleman with few teeth and a relaxed posture, occasionally smiles back at us. "Ça va?" he repeats over and over.

I tell him we're fine, even though I could do without the sweat and mildew baked into the carpet flooring. But the man clearly takes pride that his little tuna can on wheels is pushing 300,000 kilometers.

Jamie checks his phone about ten times a minute. His knuckles go white as he grips his thighs.

"It's all right." I lean to him, though the seat belt yanks me back into place.

His eyes dart to mine. He abruptly leans forward and asks the driver, "Pardon. Comprenez-vous l'anglais, monsieur?"

The man twists his head. "Pas un mot."

Jamie sits back.

"Kat, if this doesn't go well," he starts, but I have to interrupt him. "It will."

"I'll be an absolute joke. They'll *never* respect me for it."

He twirls the silver ring on his pinky. I notice the engraved word now. *Chessley.*

"Hey, you've got so much going for you. Don't assume the worst. Try to give yourself more credit." I rest my hand on top of his fidgeting fingers. My gaze drifts out the window. "It's not the easiest thing. I know. When all you want is to prove yourself, but somehow, you can't stop and appreciate how far you've already come."

"I take it you've been down this road before," he says. Of course he means it figuratively, but I decide a little mood-lightening joke might alleviate his anxiety.

"Too many times to count. All you can do is your best in this moment. Leave nothing on the table."

A smile of gratitude tries to push through his stiff cheeks. He and I both look down at my palm spooning his. I yank it back. Why do I keep doing that?

Jamie raises his head again. A field of sunflowers passes behind him out the window.

"Would it help if I gave *you* a pep talk?" I say, a lift in my voice.

"Go on then." He smirks.

"Jamie, get your head out of your ass and get on with the show. Second star to the right and straight on till morning."

I stole that last part from his buzzed pep talk at the dartboard. Airiness returns to my stomach as a full grin emerges on his lips.

It distracts from the stunning coast coming back into view.

"All right, fair play," he says. "Now, my turn. If ever you start to doubt yourself or your work, I want you to think of me."

Heat flashes through my cheeks.

"Picture me saying, 'Kat, tell the haters to sod off and c'est la effin' vie.'"

"C'est la vie!" the driver exclaims, raising one palm toward the roof, surprising us both.

"C'est la vie," I repeat.

The atmosphere in the back seat, now loosened, lets Jamie and I admire the view outside. To the left are the dramatic, scraggly cliffs hugging the Mediterranean. We wind past secluded beaches, where visitors mount rock landings about twenty feet above the sea.

"Ever thought about taking a dive?" Jamie asks me.

"Well, I don't, I don't know. I, um . . ." I trail off, distracted by the beachgoers doing backflips off their makeshift diving board. "Maybe I will, you know, when I've finished up the au pair stuff."

"You mean when Damien's back in town," he teases.

Annoyed, I cross my arms. "You're actually much more similar than you think."

"Really?" Jamie crosses his arms too.

I twist my torso to be square with his. "You both have ambition, you both are great older brothers."

"You think I'm a great older brother."

"Manon does."

"Well," Jamie sighs. "At least I've got that going for me."

"I'm just saying."

The tension creeps back in, and Jamie's voice goes stern. "That guy is nothing like me. He hasn't told you about what really happened, I'm guessing."

"Not exactly."

Jamie scoffs. "Exactly."

I furrow my brow, searching his gaze for an explanation.

After glancing at the driver once more, Jamie leans toward my shoulder.

"He's a snake. And when he tried poaching every business in Èze, trying to convert it to some shopping outlet, I went to every shop owner to let them know who they'd be dealing with if they sold to Damien. But they didn't need me to help make up their minds. His money isn't worth shit. And selling out would mean going against everything they stand for, seeing their town turn into that."

I slowly nod, as I take in the information. Though a lump is swelling in my throat for fear I've been lied to this whole time.

"You're not the first girl to fall under his little spell," Jamie adds.

I suck in a breath.

"He's only out to please himself no matter who it'll affect, and I don't give a flying fu . . ." He calms himself with a quick glance at the jovial driver, who can barely see over the steering wheel.

"That's it? That's all you're gonna say?"

He flares his nostrils. "It's not my place," he says almost inaudibly.

I actually laugh. "You're so typical. If you have a problem with someone, why not fix it rather than moping about it?"

The vigor in my voice stirs his gaze toward me.

I lift an eyebrow back at him, but my thoughts course through every memorized letter line, scraping for any argument Damien provided in their feud, but I come up short. The way Jamie paints it certainly makes him look like a rose and Damien the thorn. But Jamie's human after all. There are multiple sides to every story.

Jamie and I seem to notice the mere centimeters between our faces at the same time. He pulls back. Twirling his fingers, he seems to be trying to suppress the trembling as we near Èze. "I hope you find the answers you're looking for," he says.

"Not that I'll get them from you," I mumble, staring out the window and feeling his bright green eyes scorching the left side of my face.

The stirred-up tension now searing between us, I tell myself that what matters in the next hour is getting to the Vigne as quickly as possible. Sure, Jamie's attitudes—kind and compassionate one minute, cold and callous the next—may drive me up the wall, but I'd promised to help him. After all, *Conseils* wouldn't be doing as well as it is now without his help.

The driver drops us at the car park in Èze. We clamber up the cobblestone streets, stopping at the Cave to meet Emi quickly and scour for Jamie's extra set of chef clothes. Marie and Antoine keep an additional set there in the event of emergencies or wardrobe malfunctions.

While Jamie changes into his chef whites in the stockroom, his phone dings, and he curses. Reflexively, I look at the curtain separating us, his shirtless back visible through the slit in the fabric. I quickly glance away, and he reemerges, fully dressed.

"What is it?" I lift my back off the cool stone wall.

He sighs, tucking in the high-collar button-down. "Our hostess has the flu."

Apparently, the inspector will knock them for anything out of place. Incorrect silverware orderings, overly minted ceviche, missing staff.

"I can do it," I burst out the words before the thought fully forms.

Jamie lifts his brow.

"I used to be a hostess back in high school. Well, I did it for a summer at an Applebee's, but I know the basics."

Jamie inhales deeply through his nose, and he squeezes my forearm. "Thank you."

The sound of clinking wine bottles being packaged for customers disappears as our gazes lock. "C'mon, let's get going," I say, tearing myself from the situation.

Jamie has been my camera guy for the past few weeks—milking the opportunity for me to teach him something about exposure and aperture—keeping him away from the Chessley villa at most daytime hours. Reducing his father's chance to snatch him for a business chat had been strong motivation, I presume. Nonetheless, his help hasn't gone unnoticed, and I don't think twice when it comes to helping him knock the socks off this Michelin inspector. The Damien fiasco will be dealt with later.

We pass the kids' favorite little crêperie and Solange's office on the way to the Vigne. Every editorial meeting that goes by, the more the space transforms. This time, a few framed posters decorate freshly painted peony pink walls. Now that it's well after four and the lights have gone out, she's probably off enjoying dinner with her family, celebrating the past week's success with *Conseils* and the uptick in agency clientele.

Coming to the end of the narrow lane, it's my first time actually approaching the Chateau Vigne d'Argent. Up close, I can now see its scuffed yet endearing layered stone exterior. A fresh coat of paint could do on the periwinkle shutters, but the vibrant flower boxes distract from the more rustic elements. Guests staying in its rooms make their way to the cottage-style lobby, but Jamie leads me to the right of the building and through a small alley where there is a forest-green door with a digital padlock.

Jamie enters the code and guides us down narrow halls lined with piles of dishware and tablecloths. Clanging metal pots, the hot sizzle of oil, and dissonant shouts bounce over the walls as we enter the raucous kitchen. Five men and three women halt their racket along the stainless steel counters when they see Jamie and me standing in the doorway.

Jamie nods to the group. "Faisons-le," he says, tying his apron straps around his waist and rolling up his sleeves. He *bonjours* the head waiter, who's busy memorizing tonight's menu before he points his thumb toward me. After their short discussion, the waiter beckons me to follow him out of the kitchen. On my way out, I give a quick thumbs-up to Jamie, who's about to commence the dessert prep at his station. When our eyes meet, his heavy breathing slows, and he returns the grin.

The head chef saunters in, snapping their fingers, and the six line cooks stand tall, awaiting direction. I sneak one more you've-got-this smile at Jamie before the waiter nearly yanks my arm out of my socket.

I wander behind him down the hall. He examines me from head to toe and parses through a closet full of black trumpet-sleeve dresses. Decoding my size with only a look, he hands me a dress and obsidian wedges that fit to a tee.

"You have done this before, no?" he asks when I emerge from the bathroom after changing.

I'm guessing Jamie didn't include the Applebee's detail. I nod fervently as he takes my clothes and tosses them into the closet.

"Bit rusty," I admit.

The waiter rolls his eyes and keeps walking down the dim hall and up a wooden staircase. He rather quickly details my duties. The place is reservation only, so the tables have been preassigned to the waitstaff. All I have to do is greet the diners with, "Bonjour. Bienvenue au Château Vigne d'Argent. Suivez-moi, s'il vous plaît." And if they don't speak French, "Hello. Welcome to the Chateau Vigne d'Argent. Follow me please." At the top of the stairs, the waiter presses on the door, but he hesitates and cranes his neck to me. "Make sense? Do you need anything else?"

"Glass of wine might help." Shrugging, I crack a smile.

Wrong moment, Kat.

Clearing my throat, I shake my head.

"Bien," the waiter says. He reminds me of Stanley Tucci's can't-be-bothered yet affectionate character in *The Devil Wears Prada.*

He swiftly opens the door and glides through. Swarming around us in elegant strides are the rest of the waitstaff, attending to every patron's need on the stone terrace. A wire fence separates the twenty candlelit tables from the steep cliff. The view is immaculate. The Côte d'Azur is on full display, and with the sun now set, an electric indigo hue provides a stunning backdrop to the moon hovering close to the sea's horizon.

At the hostess podium, I squint to examine the guest list. The twinkling lights dangling around the terrace's perimeter add lovely ambience but horrendous reading light.

New arrivals interrupt my curious scanning, and I escort them to their table without messing up my lines.

Way to go, Kat!

A few more parties arrive to be seated, and I manage to peep out a little conversation with one elder gentleman and his dinner partner. But when I resume my post at the podium, the Stanley Tucci maître d'—whose actual name is Charles—grumbles.

Stick to the script, Kat.

Now that my eyes have adjusted to the light, and my stomach has calmed its hungry howling, I wonder who on the guest list could be the infamous inspector. If the waitstaff is on edge, they certainly don't show it in their nimble feet as they dance between tables.

Whoever the inspector is, I doubt they'd be dining solo—too obvious—and they're most certainly using an alias. I examine the list of names, both those that have already arrived and the ones yet to come.

Louis Martin. Sounds too normal to be suspicious.

Eliza Bernard. Hmm, maybe.

The next name makes my gut drop.

No.

But I can't do anything about it. The second I read it, I hear his voice. He approaches the terrace, his salt-and-pepper goatee trimmed and combed to perfection.

"Miss Kat," Howie says, his arms lifted. "What are you doing here?" He leans his elbow on the host stand. "They're not underpaying you over at Casa de Chessley, are they? Otherwise, I'll be having a chat with old Nicky."

I hastily assure him quite the opposite, but I have to think of something to explain why I'm here without blowing Jamie's cover.

"I, um . . . I'm doing research. Got to meet the traveler where their mind is."

Howie taps his forehead. "Look at that. If it were up to me, you'd certainly belong with us at Continental."

I try not to let him pick up on my jittery hands. Instead, I bow my head and gather a few menus for him and his business partners. After showing them to their table right along the center of the balcony, I consult a nearby waiter who I had heard speaking English earlier.

"Do the chefs ever come out here?" I whisper to her.

"Not usually."

Hopefully it stays that way.

The rest of the night goes off without a hitch. All of the guests on the list have now been seated, but I can't tell who is the Michelin inspector and who is just a yacht owner with a craving for thirty-euro hummus.

But the one guest I do know, Mr. Howie Gupta, has thoroughly enjoyed his seven courses and presently polishes off his table's third bottle of wine. His comment has been ringing in my ear for the past hour. It's not long before my mind wanders to Jamie again. I've seen various dessert plates come through the kitchen door, catching glimpses of molded mousses, elegant petit cakes, and immaculate pastry. Part of me wants to slip downstairs and give him a wave, but the other part of me says "Kat, stick to your post."

Maître d' Charles scurries over to the podium, alerting that some kitchen staff is coming upstairs to greet a woman dressed in gold. Louisa Roy. I sat her near a potted plant over an hour ago. They think she's the inspector. I bite my lip, hoping that Jamie gets selected but also hoping he's forced to stay down there.

A minute later, three individuals donned in their chef whites step through the staircase doorway. The first is the head chef, followed by the sous chef, and then Jamie. Without hesitation, I grab Jamie's arm. Relief swells in his eyes when he sees me, but he insists on following the group ahead.

"No, Jamie," I whisper, making sure his face stays out of view of any diner. "Your godfather's here." I lean my head to the side, so he can see for himself.

His face goes white. "What?"

Howie rolls his neck back, consumed in laughter. He hasn't detected Jamie. Yet. But the terrace is small enough to pick up on the slightest shift in energy.

"You deserve to be up here with them." I nod toward his coworkers coalescing around the woman in gold. "But . . ."

"But I can't," he finishes, bowing his head. "Bollocks." Strain smears across his brow, but he dissolves it, coursing his hands through his tied-back hair. Before he ducks behind the door he came in from, he gives my hand a squeeze. My heart leaps in every direction. The twinkling light shines over his toned, tanned jaw and the gleam returns to his eyes.

"Merci, Kat."

I whisper, "Je t'en prie."

Before we know it, the night is coming to a close, and the last table has just taken their final bite of profiteroles. Howie and his party stumbled away earlier. Their arms wrapped around each other's shoulders, they'll have the scent of Syrah on their breath for the rest of the week.

I help clear tables alongside the waiters, who've now dropped the stiff upper lip and assumed a more casual repertoire of playing makeshift hacky sack with lemon rinds. They abandon playtime, however, when maître d' Charles storms back through the door to check on them.

"Thank you for your help, Mademoiselle Kat. Where shall we send your pay for the evening?" Charles asks me.

"Oh, no. Please, don't worry about it. I was just helping a friend."

For the first time this evening, a grin grows at the corner of Charles's mouth.

"Je comprends," he says and gently pats my shoulder, leaving me to admire the cascading view, equally captivating at night as it is in the day. Navy-blue sky and darkened cobalt ocean meld together, lit by boat lanterns and house lights strung along the peninsula. I still can't get over how the salty air makes its way miles above the cliffs. Nonetheless, I drink it in.

"You're still here," Jamie says. A hint of surprise lingers in his voice.

I spin around and give a grin. It hits me that I haven't taken him up on the coffee and dessert invitation he made when we first met. "Just cashing in what I was promised," I say, making obvious glances to the espresso cups and pastry crumbs left at someone's table.

Jamie crosses his arms and bows his head, concealing the grin spreading under his nose. "I'll do you one better," he says and curls his pointer finger for me to follow him.

Back in the kitchen, now cleaned and scrubbed to perfection after the night of soup making and duck braising, Jamie uncorks a local Cabernet Sauvignon from Provence and pours me a glass while he prepares two dinner plates. From one convection oven, he pulls out a sheet pan of leftover chicken breast, roasted potatoes, and steamed green beans.

"Chef lets us take the leftovers for our dinner. I figured you'd be hungry."

My cheeks go rosy.

"And I saved us some chocolate mousse," he adds, plating our meal.

We take the long-awaited dinner up to the terrace and sit in satisfying quiet for a few moments, enjoying the lemon, rosemary, and tarragon infused in every morsel.

Jamie clears his throat and lifts his glass. "Cheers, by the way, to pulling all this off," he says, glancing around the now-empty terrace.

We clink glasses, but I notice his bliss is fleeting.

"Jamie."

"They didn't come. Whoever they are," he sighs. "We had a faulty tip."

"The woman in the gold dress, it wasn't . . ." My brimming question trails off when he shakes his head.

"You know, I'm glad, really. I'd rather not be in the know when they do come," he says.

I sweep my gaze to the view at our side.

"Takes the pressure off."

"I'm quite jealous of you," Jamie says, taking a long sip of wine.

Jolting my head back to him, confusion paints my expression.

"You handle it all so well. My sisters and brother, for one. And my mum. And the magazine. It's impressive. Now that's pressure."

"Well," I start, "I'm not alone in it. I have Emi and . . . you." A tingle ripples in my throat, and I don't know how to stop it. More water and wine don't help as it travels down my neck and back.

Jamie finishes chewing and nods. "But you didn't think twice about it, you just went for it."

I shrug. "Hmm, some call it impulsive . . ."

"You don't think it was your gut taking the reins?"

"I think wine helped push some of those decisions along," I say, tipping back my crystal glass. "Hard to tell if my gut knows left from right anymore. I never do stuff like this."

Jamie leans back in his chair. "Maybe you've always wanted to."

I look over my shoulder at the French landscape before us.

"Never gets old," he says. When I meet his eyes, he nods to the moonlit sea.

"It's a great setting," I say, resting my chin in my palm.

"Hmm . . . for a great McLauren film."

"Yeah." I exhale through my nose, recalling the goals on my vision board that perpetually seem out of reach. "Right."

"What? It'll happen. You've already proved your dream is possible. Some would say you're living it already." He fiddles with his thumbs. "If anything, *Conseils* is at least a preview."

I think of all the footage we've taken for the magazine's YouTube channel.

Peering at the view once more, I rest my napkin on the table. "Maybe someday. When I've got some credits to my name. You know?"

"Kat," Jamie says, leaning back in his chair. "If you keep pushing it off, aren't you worried you'll never get to it?"

I squint at Jamie. "Look, no offense but you don't know what it's like. Your food is Michelin-rated. Everyone here loves it. I don't have that luxury yet. And it'd be a disservice to rush it."

"It didn't happen overnight," he says, swirling the last drops of wine in his glass. I trace my upper teeth with my tongue while he continues on. "Kat. Your work might not mean something to everybody. It's not supposed to. But I'm sure it'll mean the world to someone. And it sure as hell should mean something to you."

"Well, true as that *may* be, I've got Young Soarers to focus on for now."

Jamie shakes his head. "I don't get that whole thing. Why settle for some stuffy corporate gig just to have your soul sucked out of you?"

I straighten my spine. "Who says it would?"

"Won't it? If you sacrifice your calling just to be there?" Jamie sighs. "All I'm saying is, you can't fake peace of mind."

We hold each other's gaze for a few prolonged moments. When he speaks to me like this, it's like he's talking to the person I hardly show to the world, the one who looks back at me from the mirror. The one who wants to be utterly free from the suffocating grip of years of expectations. Expectations that have lost their origin but have glued themselves to my identity—that if I act out of accordance with them, part of me will rupture. How can I break the mold I've outfitted for myself?

The twinkling fairy lights land gently on his wavy, low bun. My eyes go to his lips, but I blink ferociously and sit up straight, crossing my silverware over the empty plate.

While I digest his last comment, he clears his throat and takes my plate, promising to return with some dessert and coffee.

When it's just me on the terrace, thoughts badger my skull one after another as I fidget with my rings.

Don't think about it. You have Damien . . . sort of . . . almost.

You've got a good thing going with him. Something that'll really stick.

Don't throw it away.

Still, I hadn't visualized what it'd be like to kiss Jamie until tonight. Sure, I've had flutterings, I'm not too vain to deny it. But tonight, something has shifted. Before, the idea would have only floated around my brain for a few seconds until I quickly dissolved it with a laugh. Tonight, I can see it with such clarity, grabbing his face and pressing his lips against mine.

But I won't do that. It'd violate rule number one I've set for myself when it comes to romance: *Do not make the first move.* That way, I avoid making a complete fool of myself. If they act first, then I know for sure I hadn't been imagining things and that the vibe is *actually* reciprocated. Whenever I'd been the first move-maker in the past, it had failed. Catastrophically.

Like trying to force a fantasized relationship onto my childhood crush only for him to say he's got someone special already. Or the time I thought my chance elbow brushes with the football player in my accounting group meant he had the hots for me. Or, my favorite of all, when I saw my university's star basketball player in the dining hall and I forced my roommates to drop him my phone number while I suggestively licked an ice cream cone at our table.

But all I've learned from my romantic strikeouts is that just because I'm looking does *not* mean they are. Anyway. Jamie's off limits.

"Let it go," I mumble coarsely.

"Let what go?" Jamie stands at the door with two bowls of chocolate mousse.

I stand abruptly, almost knocking over the wine glasses. "Nothing, nothing." I make my way toward Jamie with a quick stride and jitters in my voice. "I'm feeling tired," I lie. "It's been a long day, and I really should be getting back."

Jamie nods and offers to accompany me on the walk back to the house after he swaps his chef clothes for jeans. I don't bother changing, except trading the heels for my tennis shoes wedged in the waitstaff closet. Jamie lends me his jacket to brace against the evening wind. After I thank him, silence mulls, and I keep a three-foot distance between us the whole way back. He doesn't seem to mind though, his head bowed to the ground and hands stuffed in his pockets.

When we make it to the villa's front door and tiptoe up the stairs, we pause at the banister. My room to the left, his to the right. Only a few hallway nightlights provide any illumination, but as I turn away, Jamie places two fingers on my elbow.

"Kat," he says. His whisper is rich and tender. "Thank you."

He takes my hand, sending electrifying chills up my arm. He places a single kiss on the back of it, never dropping his gaze from mine. A warmth burgeoning in my heart spreads across my entire chest, cascading to butterflies in my stomach. In a second, my entire body is tingling. Jamie curls his lip to a half grin.

The hot and cold frenzy he's been boomeranging between all summer evaporates with that kiss. Has he felt this all along? Has his icy exterior and keeping me at arm's length been his way of avoiding any suspicions from his parents? Maybe he's like me; once the feelings start to roll, it snowballs quickly, and there's no stopping the avalanche. Yet neither of us can go through with it, not when there's too much at stake. My job here for one, and therefore, my spot at the Young Soarers. And if he does feel the same as me, then if we fall, we'll fall hard. At least, I will.

"I want you to know how sorry I am, truly. For sometimes being a right arsehole to you. Guess it's my defense mechanism. You don't deserve that," he says with a melancholy air. "I thought that if I came off rude, it'd stop me from . . ."

Muffled voices echo from down the hall. I pull my hand back and look over my shoulder, knowing Angela is just twenty feet away in her bedroom.

"Kat, I—"

"Bonsoir," I whisper to him.

His shoulders drop. He knows as well as I do that this is a road we can't go down.

And just like that, we go our separate ways. He to his room, and me to mine. Pressure builds behind my eyes, a knot tightens in my throat, and my hand still tingles from the press of his lips. And just like that, an uncontrollable heat scorches my neck until I step into the shower, rinsing off the mayhem of such a tumultuous day.

CHAPTER TWENTY-TWO

*W*e're at the entrance to what looks like a stone cottage, but anything beyond the wooden door is lost on me. A balmy air wraps around my arms and legs and through my knee-length dress as the sun slips below the coral horizon. My eyelids melt together, blurring the swaying grass and buttercups around us.

He grabs my waist and gently pushes me against the door. Everything below my belly button tingles and cheers. He presses his lips against mine, firm but tender, before moving to my neck and shoulder, pulling my smocked sleeve down my upper arm. I layer my wrists behind his neck, pulling him in tighter and running my fingers through his hair. He moans.

I run my fingers through the strands. His hands squeeze my hips.

The *he* has no face. But he's warm and smells of musky vanilla and red wine. I taste it on him too as our tongues swirl together.

It's the most intimate I've ever gotten, yet my body knows exactly what to do.

"Oh," I gasp. He kneads everything south of my back like bread dough, with more and more grip on each squeeze.

His groans grow louder. I grind against him, and he reciprocates. The heat between us could burn a hole right through our clothes. He bites my shoulder. I nearly break the skin along his shoulder blades with my nails.

"Ah," he lets out. "Oh God. Kat."

"Oh, Jamie."

Chilly night air sweeps through my lungs.

I lurch up in bed, my eyes flying open to reveal my actual reality. The bedroom is still dark. Moonlight filters in through the window. A layer of sweat coats me from head to toe. I lie down, face to the ceiling, out of breath. I try my best to forget what just happened, but no matter how hard I press my eyelids together, there's no unseeing what I just saw . . . what I felt.

CHAPTER TWENTY-THREE

*I*n the morning, all I want to do is remain in my bed, but I resort to freshening up with another shower and getting back to the regularly scheduled programming: au pairing and *Conseils* work. When I open the en suite door, a cream-coated face stares back at me with frenzied eyes.

I jump back, stifling a scream.

"A-Angela. Is everything ok—"

"Pas du tout," she whisper yells. Underneath the cream, her face is pinched in anger.

I grip the towel wrapped around my torso, the condensated shower steam on my shoulders still fresh.

Angela points her index finger at me. "Reste loin de lui."

"Stay away from who?" Of course I know who, but I want to hear her say it. I cross my arms, not letting her win this one.

"I saw you on the stairs last night."

I should've known those beady eyes had been watching us, even in pitch black. And I hope to goodness one of her spying cronies hadn't followed Jamie and me to the Vigne. If I were responsible for outing his secret, I'm certain he'd never look my way again.

"Don't lie to me."

Her pursing lip begins to tremble. She may be Angela Lavergne Chessley, European fashion guru, but she's also a mother.

My voice reciprocates her hoarseness. "Look. I'm not here to get in the way—"

"Bien. Then you're not to speak another word to him this summer."

"Not even a bonjour?"

"Not even a bonsoir."

I bite my inner cheek and cross my arms. Normally, I'd just swallow the instruction, but Kat McLauren is not a doormat. "Or what?"

"If this is your true character, I'm sure Howie would like to know before he makes any mistakes."

My tensed shoulders surrender, and a satisfied grin makes cracks in Angela's hardened face mask. I agree to her demands with a bowed head and a "bien." She swipes her satin robe off the floor and disappears down the hall while I clench the ends of my towel. The ten plus years I've spent pining after Young Soarers cannot and will not be tossed aside because I can't keep my emotions in check, as much as it aches me to bear it.

—*—*—*—

IT COULD'VE BEEN easy to forget my responsibilities with the kids after the emotional tornado battering inside me. If anything, though, resuming au pair duties is the perfect antidote for dismantling whatever last night was.

Also needing a topic for this week's *Le Journal de Kat*, I draw on Estelle's recommendation to visit her at the Matisse Gallery. After a small chat with Sylvie about how delicious the croissants were this morning and hurrying the kids through breakfast—because I didn't care to take my chances with running into Jamie—the kids and I take the little train from the top of Èze village across the mountains and into Nice. In the few moments where Milo isn't attached to my hip on board, asking me to name every US state capital, I dive straight into editing the next batch of *Conseils* videos. Solange and I decided to pair them with articles and must-see lists from the magazine issues, meaning most turned into short travel guides with music overlays and a documentarist flair.

The electric train lightly sways my body side to side as I watch the footage on my laptop, chopping out any moment where the kids' faces appear. We've been nearly everywhere from here to Cannes in the past few weeks.

The B-roll whisks me back to the gelato shop downtown with its freshly mopped floors and plentiful tubs of swirled dessert. One clip of Jamie mimicking an abstract bird statue makes me snort so hard that I smash my palm over my mouth.

Manon furrows her brow at me but continues listening to her music.

I readjust my own earbud and immerse myself in our day trip through the vibrantly clean streets of Monaco. It's as pristine as a movie set. At the roundabout in front of the sun-washed casino, I relive when we had taken lunch outside at the Café de Paris.

Besides a few clips of our French onion soups, Jamie had managed to catch me looking rather posh like Audrey Hepburn with my top bun, cat-eye sunglasses, and cherry lipstick. He'd swayed me to give a few elegant kisses to the camera and bashful side glances. The camera stayed on me a few seconds longer than I thought, even after playtime was over.

Editing together pieces of footage was an elixir I hadn't yet tasted, though it was quickly growing on me. There's an intriguing wonder in everyday travels and a soothing cadence in the Riviera's lackadaisical rhythm. There's the foreign aspects—the snail appetizers and nude beachgoers. Then there's the universal bits—babies giggling and palm leaves bristling. The way the day welcomes an electric coral sunrise and bids farewell with a cotton-candy sunset. While its visitors and residents flock to the shores in the morning, evening is where the true magic happens, revelry bursting from the lamplit stone cottages and stuccoed villas tucked in the mountainside.

Before I finish the clip from an olive oil shop's tasting event, the train halts at our stop, giving us just a few minutes to deboard. It serves me right for thinking I'd get much done on a route that gets us to the museum in less than twenty minutes. Now I understand Estelle's impatience for us to visit.

Sitting flat on a platform a few hundred feet above sea level, a blood-orange building is surrounded by stately manicured hedges and rose bushes. It's three stories tall, though the top floor is decidedly four window lengths shorter than the two wider floors below it. In its entirety, the museum is a symmetrical melody, and the attention to detail on its exterior can only hint of the immaculate artwork inside.

The kids and I are greeted at the front desk, where Estelle holds out her arms for hugs and kisses. In her multicolored shawl, she nearly blends in with the painting hanging behind her. It takes a moment for my eyes to adjust to the ecru-white walls fixated with miniature spotlights over an array of paintings. The air conditioning adds a nice touch though.

As we set off through the gallery's many halls, Estelle wags her finger at the kids. "Remember. Ne touchez pas."

Estelle links arms with me as we walk into a room dominated by vibrant paper cutouts in all shapes and sizes.

I'm surprised the kids have gone this long without needing to take a seat or have a snack, and one particular painting catches their attention. It's a floor-to-ceiling and wall-to-wall piece made up of blue, pink, green, and yellow cut-out flowers, almost like mosaic tiling. Manon challenges her brother and sister to see who can count them the fastest. Her siblings accept, leaving Estelle and I to take a seat on one of the leather ottomans in the room's center.

I suck in my lips and pretend to admire the collection while Estelle not so subtly examines my face.

"You look different," she says abruptly, her comment skirting the line between compliment and observation.

"Thank you?"

"France has been good to you." Estelle leans an elbow on her thigh and maintains her googly gaze through those thick-rimmed square glasses.

Has it? Right now I'm one glance away from being strangled in my sleep by a delirious host mother who's ready to chuck my career plans down the toilette if I even think about saying bonjour to her eldest.

"Must be the sun," I joke. "All that vitamin D."

"Peut-être. That's part of it. But you look . . . je ne sais pas."

"I'm sure it's the sun," I reaffirm. It has nothing to do with *Conseils* or Damien . . . or Jamie.

Estelle shakes her head, her chunky dragonfly earrings bouncing side to side. "I knew," she says, toggling her finger from her chest to me, "you were going to be a difficult case."

Ah, the French bluntness again. It never gets old.

Estelle chuckles, bobbing her pixie cut up and down. "It was written in your face, of course. In your shoulders," she says, scrunching up her own to ear level. "And now look at you, totally relaxed, and the kids aren't running away on you."

She's right on that front. Some things certainly have improved. Now that I'm on Manon's better side, I just might make it through the rest of this summer with flying colors—at least with the kids. Angela is a different story.

"You know," Estelle continues. "Everywhere I go, people are talking about *Conseils.*"

"Good or bad?" I sense my shoulder blades squeezing upward.

Estelle rests her hand on my forearm. "Excellente. Even my neighbors read it every week, and they've lived here for fifty years. You look surprised. Pourquoi?" Estelle nods to the blush swelling in my cheeks.

"It still feels so strange," I confess. That people are reading my work. Caring.

"Well of course." Estelle turns toward me. "Anything new takes a bit of . . . comment tu dis . . . breaking in."

The shuffled footsteps and murmurings around us fade as my ears hear only Estelle.

"When I met you, I couldn't see the glow in your eyes as I do now. And I hope you don't ever lose it."

Many factors could be at play, and I internally analyze them. Conquering my initial au pair screwups, impressing my future boss, growing feelings for someone, and reveling in creative pursuits.

I sigh. Estelle tilts her head.

"It's just . . . I didn't come here to go soul-searching."

"Well, too bad. Because your soul found you." Estelle nods assuredly. "The journey is yours to take. Maybe *Conseils* is your first step, hmm?"

She doesn't get it. The world doesn't work like that. As much as I'd like to claim myself a full-time *artiste*, I can't just dive into it without an income yet.

"Henri." Estelle gestures to Matisse's works and sculptures peppered around the room. "He was set to be a lawyer until his mother gifted him painting supplies. He fell in love with the craft."

"Lucky him," I mumble a bit bitterly.

Estelle laughs. "You think it was easy? Look around. This is only a sample of his many expressions. *He* followed the spark." Estelle gestures around the room. "Why else would thousands come to see this place every year?"

By this point, the kids have ceased their counting competition, with Milo beating out his sisters much to Manon's annoyance. Estelle and I decide to end the tour here while they're mildly even-tempered.

On our way toward the exit, one painting I had brushed past initially now catches my eye. "Joy of Life (Le Bonheur de Vivre)" is engraved on a gilded placard. More than ten minimally outlined human figures dance and sprawl themselves out in the nude, surrounded by washes of orange, coral, and jade oil on canvas. An uncontrollable smile appears on my face as a blissful sensation runs from the crown of my head to my toes.

Manon, Josie, and Milo burst outside through the glass entrance doors, chasing each other into the garden hedges.

Estelle waves me off and says, "Ne peigne pas la girafe, Kat."

Don't comb the giraffe?

Before I can question her further, she walks off to guide a new set of tourists through the gallery. She discreetly points to one of the women in the group who has a rolled-up copy of *Conseils* wedged into a pocket in her backpack.

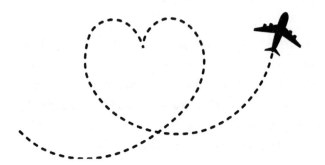

CHAPTER TWENTY-FOUR

*T*hanks to Emi's text explaining the full origin and meaning of the expression, as it turns out, "ne peigne pas la girafe" is slang for "don't do something unnecessary."

What the hell does Estelle mean by that? For a culture that has no problem being blunt, her selective indirectness comes at the worst times. She obviously knows how much I've enjoyed writing *Conseils*. It's part of what's given me the glow she talked about. She lauded it herself.

And if she's referencing Young Soarers, well . . . well, how dare she. A decade's worth of meticulously written A-plus papers, dream boards plastered with the Continental Air logo, and a killer interview record would have another thing to say.

Fortunately, I have all day to ruminate on it, given that I'm dropping the kids off with Angela at Le Negresco, Nice's finest waterfront hotel. Considering its castle-like exterior waving French flags from the green tin rooftops, I'd expect nothing less from a place on Angela's go-to brunch list. Angela sees us before we see her. We share a quick, cordial greeting and goodbye. The briskness of our exchange amuses me. I'm rather proud that I've come this far, not going to jelly-legs in her presence, especially after our little confrontation the other morning.

As I turn to go, Angela calls my name. "Enjoy some alone time, hmm?"

Can't imagine what she's insinuating. I suppress an eye roll. Now with the rest of the day wide open, Emi and I agree to rendezvous downtown. The sunshine coats my neck as I navigate through Nice, around sunscreen-covered tourists making beelines for the salt water and the leisurely-walking locals on their way to pick up loaves of bread or wedges of cheese at the Cours Saleya market.

My unencumbered strides are only temporary. Satiated café-goers swing open a bistro's door, and an herbal aroma occupies my entire sense of smell and stops me in my tracks. Almost instinctively, some commotion simmers through my body, making me feel ravenous. And it isn't just hunger for food. The calendar taunts me. Aunt Flo's monthly visit is coming up. It explains the dream from the other night and why my hormones are blitzed up to eleven.

Seriously, imagine that. I've never kissed a guy beyond a few pecks, but I can fantasize like I know exactly what I'm doing.

I cast off the persistent feelings ensuing *down there*.

But doing my best to force those feelings away has minimal power against the romanticism baked into these French streets. On my way to meet Emi at the bistro with the best café au laits in town, an adjacent window display debuting a new lingerie line seizes my attention.

The mannequins, of various heights and sizes, boast lacy bra and underwear sets. The cherry blossom pink and jet black colors are enticing, but my eyes settle on the scarlet red. I inhale deeply, realizing I haven't taken a full breath in a minute. I bite my lower lip, pulling my shades down my face.

"Looking for something in particular?"

I want to run, but not a muscle moves as panic glues every cell in my body together.

It's Emi. She examines the display with me. My shoulders at my ears, I shake my head.

"Pretty," she says. "Wanna go in?"

"Oh, n-n-no. I was just looking. Come on, let's get some coffee." I take a few steps down the sidewalk before checking over my shoulder. Emi doesn't try to hide her smirk.

"So," she says. "You guys making plans?" She wiggles her brows lewdly.

"What. No. What do you mean? No."

"Okay," Emi says, lifting her palms. "Just asking."

"Why would we, why would you think we would—"

"Kat, you've spent weeks writing this guy letters. I just figured you were gearing up for a bit of physical touch."

An internal sigh cascades through me. Damien. She's talking about Damien. My pent-up nerves manifest in a relieving chuckle. "No, no. Not yet anyway."

"Oh?" Emi's grin returns.

As much as I want to share, I don't think it'd be right for me to air what Jamie had told me in confidence—how Damien was looking to poach all the shops in Èze for commercial investment properties. But it happens to be the reason that's detained me from responding to his latest letter. I want there to be another side that I'm missing that'd remedy his character. It's gut-wrenching to question whether he's the guy I thought he was. Especially now that I've already pictured what names we'd pick for our imaginary kids. I have a knee-jerk habit of doing that with every guy that tosses me a pickup line.

I crack a sheepish smile. "He's coming back from the last leg of the cruise in a few weeks. We'll see then."

"Didn't he ask you out?"

I shrug. "I haven't responded."

Emi does a poor job at hiding her confusion. It doesn't help the thoughts pouring through my mind either. The spark I get in those letters, it's indescribable. I can tell he's really reading my words. He's listening to me, assuaging my initial doubts about *Conseils*, championing me in every pursuit. But the picture Jamie illustrates of Damien, in the business and personal arenas, leaves a sour taste in my mouth. Jamie said it himself. That I'm not the first girl to fall under Damien's spell. A pang in my stomach forms as I consider that there may be someone else in the picture.

Ugh, but what does Jamie know, really? Sure, maybe Damien has had flings in the past. I mean who could resist that Mediterranean masterpiece of a man? Besides, all Jamie can assess is the exterior Damien presents to the world. But through our letters, I know his inner world. Jamie's judgments can bite me.

The business-poaching, however, is a point I'll have to investigate. There's got to be another angle to that story.

Emi and I take our seats at an outdoor table under the shade of an umbrella and order our coffees.

I tilt my head, sipping the foam off my drink. From the impromptu Chessley outing to the Michelin inspector fiasco, I've been a bit delayed in penning Damien. If Emi hadn't mentioned the letters, I probably would have pushed it off further, but that wouldn't be fair to him. I make a mental note to write it tonight.

The waiter brings a few napoleons to the table. They're almost too pretty to eat, with sandwiched layers of pastry and cream and immaculate feathering of pink and white chocolate icing on top. Emi leans forward and whispers.

"These are Jamie's. The Vigne is selling his stuff all over town. The cafés and restaurants. They can't get enough. Must be that write-up you put in the last *Conseils* publication."

My mind flashes to the past few weeks. His hand on my lower back, the meal we enjoyed on the terrace, his help with the magazine. Combined with the hormonal symphony taking place in my body, the memories are aphrodisiacs.

Emi's fork crunches through the flaky, buttery pastry, sending the layers of cream oozing to the sides. A warmth below my waist amplifies.

To keep myself from sighing, I grab the water glass coated in condensation and guzzle down the cool drink.

I am *not* throwing away what I have with Damien because I'm starting to get the hots for someone else. And I am *not* throwing away my au pair job or my chance at becoming a Young Soarer because I couldn't keep my hands off the family's oldest.

When we finish our coffees, Emi tosses down a few euros and stands proudly.

"Kat, allons-y," she announces.

"Where are we going?"

Emi tosses both palms up toward her shoulders. "It's *journée des filles!*"

Girls' day.

"Come on." Emi waves her arm. "When's the last time we've had a full day where neither of us needs to work? Do you have any writing left for this week's *Conseils?*"

I shake my head.

"And you are off duty with the kids for the rest of the day, so . . ."

"Girls' day it is," I say with a smile. Emi claps and bounces down the sidewalk, tossing ideas around. Spa? Kayaking? Horseback riding tour in the lush mountain trails?

"Ah, I've got it," Emi says, halting on the sidewalk. A group of passersby nearly stumble right into Emi in her enlightened moment. She doesn't seem to mind, though, taking me by the elbow and exclaiming "Saint-Tropez!"

A smile spreads across my face, and a sense of urgency jolts through my voice. Maybe it's the caffeine. It's one of those places I've had in mind ever since I heard it in that Taylor Swift song. "How do we get there? Train? Ferry?"

Emi winks and pulls out a set of keys from her purse, dangling them in front of my face. Then I remember, it's Monday, also known as Antoine's day off from Ubering, which means Emi has free rein of the family's Porsche. I couldn't think of a better way to navigate our girls' day in style.

Emi clicks the key fob, directing my attention twenty feet down the street. The soft *beep-beep* of the unlocking car and a flash of its headlights bring me back to the moment I stepped out of the Nice airport that early June day. While the car is pretty much the same, I feel completely different. Think of all the emotions, embarrassments, and wins I've endured in eight weeks. At first glance, someone might say Europe was changing me, that France was changing me, but I say France is finding me. It's putting opportunity on a silver platter and saying do what you will.

And I've seized every opportunity flung my way in order to be a better Young Soarers applicant. Now I feel like my dream is finally within reach, a reality not too far off. And it'll be out of my hands once I send in the application next week.

The doors thump shut, and Emi scrolls through her playlist on the dashboard screen.

"Harry Styles?"

"Of course," I say.

We roll the windows down and fall into our own real-life music video, floating our palms in the breezy sea air, our hair flying in all directions as we laugh.

And an entire album of songs later with a pit stop at a fancy gas station for some quick-fix bathing suits and towels, we round a mountainside road. Ahead sits Saint-Tropez at the end of a small peninsula jutting into the coast.

This part of the Riviera boasts a softer pastel color palette than the vibrancy of its neighboring towns. Striped awnings outstretched over cafés and pop-up markets characterize the historic heart of Saint-Tropez. Its coral and dandelion plaster exteriors exude the same toned-down brightness found in Nice. These buildings have braced oceanside conditions for decades, yet share a modernized charm, evolving with the times. The streets are abuzz with locals selling fresh produce and with tourists flocking to the harbor dotted with sleek sailboats and yachts carrying rowdy partiers. A number of people stroll through soap shops or savor a treat at crêperies. In the distance, I can just make out the towering villas on the outskirts of town, where the infamous glitzy and glamorous residents live.

We take a detour through the peninsula, ascending rolling green hills that give way to verdant fields peppered with lush vegetation and tall, fluffy trees two shades darker than the grass beneath them. At times, there's only a two-foot-tall brown stone wall separating our car from the steep descents on the left. Feeling slightly squeamish about the drop beyond the wall, I glance in the wing mirror, taking notice of an obsidian-black car with shaded windows. I keep my eyes on it as our car continues to follow the curves of the road. Emi glances in the rearview mirror every so often, but only to check that her mascara hasn't smeared over her eyelid.

"What beach are we going to exactly?" I ask Emi, wondering if she maybe got lost with her directions from memory.

Emi snickers through her nose. "So impatient, Minou. Sometimes I forget you're Américaine."

I retort with a smirk, and she points to a stack of signs standing in the shade of full oak trees. Four white rectangles, short and wide and outlined in blue, point in different directions. Emi reads the top one. "Pampelonne."

The car trailing ours turns down a side road, releasing the tension knotting through my upper back. But after my last conversation with Angela, I wouldn't put it past her to send a tracker two hours down the coast to make sure I'm not secretly meeting up with Jamie. She must really think I could do some damage to that family dynamic. More than that, she must really miss her son.

Within ten minutes, Emi parks the car, and we find ourselves sitting oceanside at one of the most precious open-air cafés I've ever been in. On the nearly white sand beach, some guests drape themselves over cushioned lounge chairs. Others, like Emi and me, take a rest by the bar, where neatly set tables with pin-striped padded wicker chairs host hungry beachgoers. Wooden columns support a rustic pallet ceiling that still allows a few sunrays to peek through the slits.

The hypnotic turquoise waters beckon our attention. The sea on this side of the peninsula looks like a blue topaz crystal.

When a waiter approaches our table, Emi surveys the wine list.

"Une bouteille de Champagne Rosé," she says to him.

"Moët et Chandon?" he asks to confirm. With Emi's nod of approval, he smiles generously, fills our glasses with sparkling water, and trots back to the bar.

I lean forward. "A bottle?"

Emi sips her water and swats a hand. "Don't worry, we'll order another."

Something between a laugh and a scoff forms in my throat. "It's not even noon, Em."

"It's girls' day!" Emi reminds me.

As we gorge on truffle fries, burrata with fresh tomatoes, tuna tartare, and dressed salad greens, Emi eyes me curiously.

"So, Minou," she says. "You will be coming back next summer, yes?"

I swirl the rosé and trace the glass's condensation with my finger. "I, um, I don't know. I'll have to see what my schedule looks like."

"Do you not get to travel as a Young Soarer? That seems contreintuitif."

I don't answer and pile in another mouthful of peppery arugula.

"Minou, what will you do when the program is over?"

"That's if I get in, Em."

"Okay, *if* you get in. What do you do when it ends?"

My lacy sun cover-up starts to itch my shoulders. A bit more at ease to answer with the bubbly flowing in my bloodstream, I reveal my plans to level up to travel writer for Continental before experimenting in bringing my own creative projects to life. Like that study abroad memoir.

Or a documentary on the Riviera.

"Why wait?" she says, twirling her fishtail braid.

I pause my chewing. A few breathy sighs come out before any meaningful words form on my tongue. "Why does everyone think it's so simple?"

"Isn't it?"

"How so?" I press. "I can't just walk into Continental and say here I am, pay me millions to traipse around the world."

"I mean," she starts, watching me take a long sip of wine. "What's stopping you from your own projects?"

I cast my gaze to the sea. "Because it's not as black and white as you think. I don't know the *how* part yet, so that's what I'm using the next few years to figure out."

"Isn't that part of the fun though? Trying?"

"Fun isn't always stable."

Emi pushes back, leaning her forearms on the tablecloth. "Life isn't meant to be stable, Minou. It's an evolution."

"Since you're so passionate about my career, I have to ask, have you told your mom about teaching in Paris?"

Emi swats her hand. "C'est sans importance. I'm working on it."

I breathe out, not realizing I'd been holding the air in my lungs. I meet Emi's eyes. They're gentle, reassuring me of her kind intentions and her instinctive ability to read me with ease despite our rather young friendship. I take another breath and smile weakly at her, though tingles still rush from my fingertips to my toes.

Then, I see *him*. Or at least, I think it's him.

I sit forward abruptly, nearly spilling my glass of rosé on to my plate of fish and fries.

Damien. What the hell is he doing here?

Walking down the wooden boardwalk connecting a strip of beach bars to each other, a group of twenty-somethings mosey from one joint to another. In the middle of the pack, I could've sworn I saw Damien's clean-cut dark hair and deep olive skin. But the group moved so quickly down the path that they were out of sight as soon as they came into view.

Emi couldn't make him out either.

"Probably some Italian," she says to assure me, but it's too late. The arches of my feet have already soaked my flip-flops in sweat.

This is silly. Damien's sailing around the Amalfi Coast, not meandering about the French Riviera. Come on, Kat. Get it together.

Emi begs to hit the shops in the beachy village and to grab something sweet. The rosé's buzz makes me compliant. We intertwine our elbows as we head into the town of Ramatuelle. There's something about the salty air kissing my bare neck, the simplicity of the pale stone buildings drenched in sunlight and vines, and the increasing silence as we head deeper into the winding streets, that eases my thoughts. Or maybe it's the three glasses of rosé champagne.

I don't have the patience to filter myself, and I wouldn't have it any other way right now.

Emi pokes at me about my increasing flirtation with my beau. I wave her off saying it's nothing and insist that we grab whatever the heck smells so good out of the bakery up ahead. Through the glass, I spot shelves well stocked with baguettes, a rainbow of macarons, lemon tarts, layered rectangular cakes, and delicate palmiers.

"Deux feuilletés à la pomme," I say, pointing out two circles of flaky pastries topped with caramelized apples.

The baker, with his paper bag at the ready, asks if we want anything else. He even suggests trying it with a café au lait.

I respond enthusiastically with, "Eh bien, si vous le recommandez, bien sûr!"

Emi raises her brow at me and gives me a little clap.

Normally, if I completely botch my French and the person knows English, they'll switch without asking—to practice themselves. But this boulanger nods and pours two coffees followed by hefty splashes of fresh dairy milk.

Part of me wishes I had my camera with me to capture these precious moments, but I resolve to blink hard and make a mental note to remember all the sensations going through me this afternoon. We take our culinary treasures down the streets, and Emi compliments me on my linguistic progress.

"I've never seen you so sur de soi," Emi says, taking a bite of apple tart. "C'est très sexy."

I shrug and toss in a chuckle. "I don't know. There's something about France that makes me feel so much more like a woman."

"Minou, you're almost twenty-three. I think you've been a woman for a few years now," Emi says, nudging my elbow.

"Yet somehow, I *still* haven't slept with anyone." I know she wasn't even going there, but I couldn't help myself. Drunk words, sober thoughts.

"And what does that have to do with anything, hmm?" she asks. Emi tosses her paper wrapper and empty cup into a trash bin. "À mon avis, having sex doesn't make you a woman. What makes you a woman is your confidence, your spirit, and your compassion." She offers me a comforting smile. "Besides, sleeping with someone doesn't give you sexual prowess. You already have it. Just rock it."

Emi casts me a gentle smile, and an internal heat churns through almost every cell in my body, like something's awakening.

We continue our stroll through town, and a storefront's plum-purple window frames catch both our eyes. Emi's drawn immediately to the outdoor display of children's books neatly arranged on a table. Some stories I recognize like *Ferdinand* and *Madeline*.

"Don't you love this smell?" she says, lifting one binding below her nose. Her eyelids press together, and I can imagine what she's picturing. A bookshelf full of stories like these nestled around desks and tiny chairs and a humongous rug where she can read to all the students.

My gaze wanders to the next table over. The stacks of books on sale are categorized by topic. *Jardinage. Cuisine. La navigation à voile.* Gardening. Cooking. Sailing.

I brush over to the index card labeled Philosophy, and that's when I see it. Tucked beneath a stack of Greek volumes, a hardbound leather book with gilded engravings sits unassumingly. I tilt my head, reading the title from the philosopher Epictetus. Also known as Jamie's free-thinking ancient hero. He couldn't stop gushing about him after we visited an ancient ruins site a few towns away from Èze, close to the Italian border.

And now *The Art of Living* sits before me in a rare trilingual edition. I grab it as if it were the last discounted television at a Black Friday sale and pull it close to my chest. I'm glad I did, because now that it's past the afternoon snooze session, the streets have become a bit more populated.

Examining the copy, a few inches of its binding are scraggly looking, but the rest is in good shape. I flick through the pages, scanning the tightly printed font and whiffing the tobacco baked into the pages after years of sitting on the shelves of a pipe smoker. The bookshop owner sits inside, dutifully reorganizing haphazard piles of old newspapers, maps, and vintage magazines. Given his hunched back and thin frame, my guess is that he's been doing it for years.

Emi points at the Epictetus book snug in my elbow's grasp. "Light reading?"

"It's not for me."

"Ah, for your beau then," Emi says, resuming her perusing.

I roll my eyes playfully. "Jamie is not my beau."

Emi's dropped jaw swaps places with her grin. "Jamie?"

Oh God. I feel the color drain from my face. Damn rosé!

Emi steps closer. "You and Jamie?" She raises her brow.

I shake my head and wave my hands out aggressively. "No, no, nothing's happened. Nothing will happen. I just saw this and thought he'd like it." I drop the Epictetus copy on the table.

Emi's playful grin returns as she pulls her sunglasses down. "Okay, if you say so."

"There's no way he likes me," I resolve, poking at a few gardening pamphlets.

"Uh-huh. Oui," Emi says unconvincingly. My cheeks are beet red I'm sure.

"Who doesn't like who?" a voice behind us rings out. I turn and see the uber-fashionable Vivian nearing us in the street. The sun dances over her silky black braids as she struts across the bricks in a sunshine-yellow bikini peeking out from her lacy cover-up.

She points our way. "Kat. Emi. Bonjour! Ça va?"

My body casually leans in for the obligatory hug and cheek kisses, but my mind is in full-on panic mode, deliberating how much she might have overheard.

"Kat," she says, clasping my elbow.

Oh God, she's probably going to yank my arm out of my socket.

"Un petit amour d'été?" she presses with a grin.

Summer romance. Yeah, something like that. While a love as passionate as Danny and Sandy's has been on my bucket list since I first watched *Grease* in seventh grade, I didn't exactly plan for Jamie and my stop-and-go relationship this summer. It sort of just happened. And I most certainly can't let Vivian know that there's any relationship at all. In fact, there isn't. Feelings, emotions, impulses. That's not a relationship. Still, she doesn't need to know any of it. So I shake my head bashfully until Emi pipes in.

"What do you mean, Minou?" she says, tilting her head at me.

I try to use my eyes to beg her not to spill what little she's heard me talk about it. But she doesn't even bring him up.

"Damien," she says as if I lost my brain.

"Oh, right, yes. Oui." I hope the breathiness in my voice doesn't give the impression that I forgot.

Vivian turns away from us and focuses on the spread of magazines. "Ah, Damien. Right. And, um, how is he?"

"Still drop-dead gorgeous," Emi adds in, alleviating my silence.

Vivian quickly exhales through her nose and offers me a tight, closed-mouth grin. "I bet . . . Well, I'm glad at least someone's got a bit of romance going on."

She sighs, leaning into her right hip and flipping through an issue of *Vogue* from the '70s.

"Guy troubles?" Emi asks Vivian. I gulp, awaiting her response.

"And girls," Vivian says. "Maybe it's the universe telling me to take a break." Vivian slaps the cover on her magazine shut. "There was this one guy from last summer. I was head over heels for him. We had an amazing night together by the beach where he said he loved me." She briefly shuts her eyes and bites her lower lip, soaking in the memory. "But the *connard* ghosted me two days later, and I haven't heard a word from him since. Guess he moved on."

Surely she would've name-dropped Jamie if it was him. Right?

"Ugh, men," Emi says, shaking her head.

"Not all of them are like that," Vivian says. "I know a few good ones."

My voice cracks as I mutter, "Like Jamie."

"Exactement," Vivian agrees, therefore verifying the mystery man who dumped her isn't my British-French side crush.

Emi bites her tongue from saying something.

"He's the best brother I've never had," Vivian says, sighing and slumping her hip.

Brother! She thinks of him as a brother.

Emi catches my bugged eyes and prods Vivian for me. "Oh, so you and Jamie never . . ."

"Jamie et moi?" Vivian nearly tears up chuckling. "No. Never. Jamais."

It's moments like these that I realize the stories in my mind, when unchecked, can run wild and rampant. And thankfully, Vivian corrects my extrapolation that just because she and Jamie are undeniably attractive people, they're not exactly into each other as I had assumed.

I watch her check her phone. She answers with impressive speed, not needing to reread her message or manicure her words.

"Désolée," she says, putting her phone away.

"Work?" I ask.

She shakes her head. "I never answer when I'm off the clock. Unless it's an emergency."

"Wow. That takes discipline." I think of my own lack of boundaries when it comes to work and play, a.k.a. the Young Soarers application that's been by my side all summer.

"Don't get me wrong, though, it's tempting to answer after hours, but why waste your twenties burning yourself out for a title that you might not even want in five years. I learned that from experience."

I examine Vivian's sweat-glistened forehead. There are the faintest of crease-lines decorating her temples.

I'd painted her as this untouchable idol, and now the veneer is wearing off.

"I need a speed course in work-life balance, the French way," I confess with a grin.

"Happy to grab some café with you anytime if you want some tips," Vivian offers.

A smile burgeons across my lips, and a warmth burrows in my stomach. "I'd love that."

A car beeps behind us. Four people squashed into a compact shout for Vivian to join them. She gives them a wave and yells back, "J'arrive!"

Emi and I salute her with la bise, and in thirty seconds, she's packed into the little car and speeding off down the bumpy road with her friends.

My shoulders loosen, and I heave out a deep sigh, but the relief only lasts a few seconds. When the group's car is about to turn the corner, the taxi behind them snatches my attention. Someone props a camera lens in the taxi's rear windshield and aims it straight at me.

Oh no. No, no, no!

I knew it. I knew Angela sent one of her spies to tail me even on my day off! And I'm so flippin' sick of it! What makes her think this is at all okay? It's an invasion of privacy. And I'm over it!

My jaw and fists clench simultaneously as I fume with ire. Snatching our paper bag from the bakery, I bolt down the uneven cobblestones toward the taxi slowing at a stop sign.

I dig my hands in the crumpled bag and scoop up a handful of sandwiched macarons, chucking them right at the car. Emi's shouts echo behind me as I get closer to the vehicle. I can't make out the photographer. They've snugged a baseball cap over their head and hidden their face behind the camera.

"Take all the damn pictures you want!"

Angela will love these shots. A sweat-drenched, lobster-red American with too much vino in her system to have any aim.

"Enjoy!"

I pitch a chocolate macaron right at the taxi's side view mirror, the ganache staining the glass. A plummeting feeling makes my stomach feel about twenty pounds heavier. The car slows down for a moment, and I hope to goodness I didn't just piss off the driver. Then again, I'd like to confront the photographer and give them a piece of my mind.

The taxi with the spy speeds off down a side street. Emi runs up to me. Catching my breath, I sheepishly hold up the empty paper bag sticking to my wet palm before divulging my suspicions about being watched all summer.

"It's just driving me nuts! Why does she care so much?" I vent.

"You've run wild with the idea. Literally! My aunt *wouldn't* do something like that," Emi insists.

As the wine wears off and the sun wanes across the sky, Emi and I pack the Porsche with our bookstore goodies and the second bag of macarons from the boulangerie before taking the sober drive back to Èze. Word of advice: chasing a detective while slightly buzzed and on the verge of dehydration, not a good look.

We pass through highway tunnels carved through the mountain arches. Eventually, the terra-cotta tops of Nice peek out from the rugged terrain to the right of the road. The speed limit ticks down as we approach town. Blue road signs for Èze pop up on our route, but I make a special request to take the exit ramp down toward the Matisse museum.

Emi complies, but kindly asks for a reason.

"I want to show you something," I say.

A few miles down from the neatly trimmed hedges and topiaries surrounding the stately reddish-orange museum, a sparsely populated street looks almost abandoned. Not one car is parked alongside the stretch of stone buildings, despite the small but vibrant green field at the top of the street. It's perfect for a picnic or an outdoor reading session.

I point out a building toward the end of the lane and request Emi to park in front. She eyes me curiously as she follows me out of the car toward the window plastered with renovation papers. The flier taped to the front door catches Emi's attention, as I had hoped.

"Estelle told me that one of the gallery docents is starting a primary school. And she'll be needing teachers. Like you." I nudge Emi, whose face is awash in surprise, angst, and fear.

She examines the flier intently, crossing her arms and biting the inside of her cheek. But her eyes turn cold and any flutter of excitement dissolves from her body as her nostrils flare and her lips purse.

"Ce n'est pas ton problème. Occupe-toi de tes oignons."

"But Emi . . ."

Emi storms back to the car and shuts the door. Fortunately, yet unfortunately, I know the expression take care of your onions. It's the nice way of saying, "Kat, keep your nose out of my damn business."

"I have to get back to the Cave," she says out the window, pulling her sunglasses over her eyes. I scurry toward the car, but she puts it in drive and tosses my bag at me. "Angela's probably waiting for you in town. And Kat. Don't try to fix my life when you have plenty of work to do on your own."

In an instant, our day of intoxicated bliss morphs to shaky, crumbling ground. Emi revs the engine and flies down the street, the wind sweeping up my hair in all directions. No one is around for blocks, but I keep the tangled curls in front of my face, masking the tears threatening my dry eyes.

CHAPTER TWENTY-FIVE

OCEAN CLOUD IV
ATTN: DAMIEN DE DANDENEAU
CABINA #148
90133 PALERMO, PA
ITALIA

Damien, my apologies for such a late reply. I must say, you certainly have a way with your words. And truly, I feel the same as you, like my perspective has completely shifted ever since we've been writing. I've never felt so seen before, so safe to share. Speaking of, I need to get this out . . . well a few things.

First, I'd be lying if I said I didn't know some details about Jamie's and your past, and it's not the prettiest of pictures. Something to do with buying out businesses in Èze for a commercial shopping center and him undermining your efforts? It's only fair to hear your side of the story. I'm sure you both had your reasons and both probably felt they were valid.

The other thing I'd like to get your thoughts on—why'd you get involved in your line of work? When you started with venture capital, was it for your family? Did you find interest in it? I've been thinking about this lately. How do we know when our goals are really ours, or if they're just what we thought people wanted of us? So we spend years clamoring for it, fusing them to our identity. And going back now would completely disintegrate the archetype we've structured our life around. I'm not sure how, but every passing day in France, I lose a few degrees of interest in the Young Soarers program. It's strange and so unlike me, yet I've never felt more myself. Or maybe my nerves are playing with me.

Eager to read your thoughts. Hope you enjoy the last few days of the trip in Sicily.

Bisous, Kat

———✳—✳—✳———

THE LAST THING I needed today was to wake up with sun-scorched shoulders where my spaghetti strap cover-up hadn't done its job. I wanted to put yesterday out of mind, but the fire dancing along my red and raw skin had another plan.

This, of course, is no concern to Solange, who, after handing Manon her lemonade and me an espresso at our weekly editorial meeting, sinks into her large leather desk chair, humming with glee.

"You see this?" Solange points around the room. We've come a long way since our folding chairs and paper cups to a well-furnished travel consultant's office. A coffee cart with fresh pastries sits beside plush sofas and a bookcase stocked with copies of *Conseils* and travel guides categorized by region.

She nods toward the lamps alight behind her desk and taps on her watch. It's nearly five in the evening.

"L'électricité!" Manon exclaims.

Solange interlaces her fingers. "We are, how you Américains say, back in business."

To think that we've done all this just with words on paper and videos online—and Solange's clientele management. The moment pulls me out of my low spirits, sharing in the delicious triumph. But my pride shrivels up in a matter of seconds when she rips a piece of paper from a notebook and hands it to me.

"What's this?"

Solange raises her brow. "Your next assignment. Don't think I forgot."

Chicken scratch questions lie underneath a taped-on picture of the crumbling chateau near the Chessley villa. It's the gossip piece she's wanted since the beginning. Except now, she's reframed the angle to be a little less tabloid-like and a bit more new and noteworthy town buzz.

Manon leans over, peering at the paper with excited eyes.

Under another pretense, something more along the lines of writing up the building's history, its features, or its landscape would have been a pleasant task.

But Solange's notes take a starkly different tone.

"Your articles and video guides are impressive, oui," Solange says. "But I want something juicy. I want to do a 'Bienvenue à Eze' spread on these mysterious new owners. Do some digging. Find out who they are, where they've come from, and why they're keeping secrets."

"Who says they're keeping secrets?" Manon asks.

Solange folds her arms over her desk. "They've owned that property for two months and haven't introduced themselves. They *must* be hiding something."

"Privacy maybe," I mumble.

Solange pulls her head back. "Is there a problem?"

I cross my legs and straighten my spine. "We're not a tabloid."

A gentle smile crosses Solange's mouth, layered on thick with a neon-orange lacquer.

"People love a little friendly gossip no matter where they go. *Conseils* needs something fresh. And it's not a tabloid piece. We're welcoming them to the neighborhood," she says.

Hmm, by putting their names and backstory on display. Whoever they are, they picked the wrong place for anonymity. And as much as I detest those publications with outlandish headlines and weakly strung, conjectured story threads, succumbing to pride at the present really wouldn't do any of us good. Solange knows that my time with *Conseils* is temporary, and though her average weekly clientele has picked up at the agency, she'll rely on advertisement revenue in *Conseils* until that amount has doubled. Fact is, she'll have to hire another writer or put a spin on her service. The more readers means the higher the price she can charge to companies seeking advertisement slots. So she'll do anything to boost the number of eyes on *Conseils*.

Besides, I don't want to leave the magazine. Not yet anyway. There's still so much more to write, to film. Plus, if I leave her high and dry now, I'd only be tainting my Young Soarers application with a flaky work ethic.

I raise my head, seeing where Solange had hung a poster that Howie had gifted her: an illustrated world map with Continental's logo prominently stretching across the bottom banner.

"Très bien. Je suis d'accord," I say without an ounce of hesitation. Solange and I reciprocate smiles. One invasive little article can't hurt all that *Conseils* has become, I hope.

———✳—✳—✳———

"YOU LOOK SAD," Josie says, picking up some blush from my makeup collection strewn out on the living room floor tile. "Let's fix that." She swirls a brush over my cheeks, dabbing many, many layers of rosy powder. What I get for agreeing to play salon with her and Milo.

Milo toys with a few scrunchies, wrapping them around his earlobes.

"Now what'll we do with this," he says, flinging my hair from side to side.

Normally, I'd be hesitant to do anything with them that may cause Angela to raise a brow. But with her and Howie in the home office, fully invested in concocting a collaboration between Continental and Lavergne Designs, I'm out of the direct line of fire at least for a little while and out of sight, unless she's fixed cameras in the Renaissance tapestry hanging on the wall, maybe in the lute player's eyes. In that case, there's no escape route from the caricature the little ones are making me out to be.

I'd figured Angela's spy had immediately divulged to her what a nutcase I appeared to be after they witnessed the macaron chase. But nothing yet. No French police escorting me to border control. It might have something to do with the fact that I haven't spoken to Jamie in a few days, not after Angela threatened my job and future reputation if she sees us alone together again.

Milo tugs my hair, stretching my scalp, but I stay quiet, marinating in the transpiring events August has brought so far. It's been half a week since I talked to Emi, when she left me in Nice at the primary school. Technically, it's only been a day since I've seen her. She was mulling about the Cave when Manon and I were on our way back from Solange's editorial meeting yesterday. The shop door was propped open, and I could see her stocking bottles of merlot along the shelves. Her face cooled at the sight of me, and she promptly marched to the entrance and kicked the door stopper out of its place, letting it slam shut.

As angry as she may be, I'm entirely grateful to her. So far, there hasn't been any inkling that my little crush on Jamie has left her lips. And with Jamie and Nick away at negotiations for real estate acreage in Belgium, he hasn't been around at all. Still, I can't help but wonder if he'll prolong the trip because he somehow knows that I've come down with a silly little case of feelings.

My phone buzzes from inside my backpack. I ask Josie to grab the bag from the couch. She dramatizes her tug on the strap.

"Do you carry rocks in here?"

Just tri-lingual Greek philosophy books I drunkenly buy for a twenty-six-year-old dreamboat I've been harboring feelings for because love triangles aren't just for the movies.

"Yes," I say.

I haven't decided if I'll give it to him or if it'll be a random souvenir I lug back to America.

The text is from Mom. She says good luck on my Young Soarers application, knowing that I'll be submitting within the week.

I type back, *Thanks. I hope it turns out well. Maybe this time next year, I'll be moving on to my second rotation.* My insides churn seconds after I send the text because there's not an ounce of excitement funneling through me as I think of the program. But I rationalize it as getting too attached to Èze. Who wouldn't be sad to leave a city so easy to fall in love with?

I don't have expectations for when I'm talking with Mom, but there are certain things that I'm not looking for. And her reply is one of them. *And making a real income!* She adds a winking emoticon. My stomach tenses. Apparently, if I'm not working in corporate America, then I must be doing something wrong.

She's one to talk. She works for the government!

Jamie said it best. People only know the versions of success they've seen in their life.

I respond with a bland and simple *Yeah* to Mom, even though it twists the wrench further into my abdomen.

Josie peppers my eyelids with the darkest shade of purple on the shadow palette. I'm either gonna come out mimicking Liza Minelli or Dracula. My money's on the latter.

"You are looking so good," Josie reassures me.

Milo fervently agrees, tightening the two ponytails sticking out of the top of my head.

"Like a queen!" he says.

An airy chortle diffuses behind me, the haughty note to it telling me it's one person. But I didn't hear her clacking heels attacking the hallway tile. I turn my head ever so slightly to see Angela, covering her mouth, trying to contain herself. She swipes her Hermès neck scarf and waves it in the air as she catches her breath from the intensifying cackles.

"Mon Dieu," she says breathlessly.

A rock sinks in my stomach, realizing Howie must only be a few steps behind. Playing salon in the living room had seemed like a fool-proof idea when Angela firmly requested that there be no interruptions during their lengthy business meeting.

I stand quickly, abandoning my "salon chair" pillow on the ground. The bathroom door is in sight, but Howie rolls up behind Angela. At least he keeps it contained, avoiding eye contact and sucking in his lips.

Merde.

I stuff my arms across my chest and smile nervously. "Kids," I say, shrugging my shoulders.

"Oh, Howard," Angela says, through the last of her chortles. "What was it I came in here for again?" She composes herself as Howie tugs on the flaps of his blazer.

"Le party," he exclaims, lifting his arms around his puffy belly.

"Ah oui. La fête," Angela says. "Kat, we will have a launch party for the Lavergne-Continental collection. And I need you to assist our party planner."

"Me?" Thank goodness for the thirty layers of blush.

Angela sighs, placing her hands on her hips. "Oui, Kat. Tu. Do you think we have time to run our businesses and plan a party by Saturday?"

"Saturday?" Lovely. Less than seventy-two hours.

"It'll be marvelous," Howie reassures me, resting his hand on my arm. "If you can help pull off a Chessley—"

Angela clears her throat.

"And Lavergne party, you're going to be the cream of the crop with the Young Soarers admissions. I just know it." He gives a wink. "Not that you aren't already."

A deep breath sweeps through my lungs. Milo tugs at my leg and holds up sparkly butterfly clips, and I sit down to let him finish decorating my hair.

"Okay then. Bien," I assure them.

Howie claps, and Angela—apparently no longer amused with my ridiculous hair and makeup—gives a terse nod and makes her way back to the office, beckoning her new colleague to follow with a finger snap over her head.

The dread of them seeing me in embarrassing states has become more and more palatable as the occurrences seem to only increase. However, I now have to top off my portfolio with "assistant to luxury event planner," and the closest I've ever been to that was organizing a group trip to a Celtic's game for fifty half-drunk college kids in student programming.

I got this.

I think.

CHAPTER TWENTY-SIX

$\mathcal{G}$ 've decided that there's no better time than the present to drown my thoughts into a pot of coq a vin, only stopping my incessant stirring when the kids start impatiently banging their silverware on the kitchen table. The red wine braising the chicken and vegetables will have cooked off by now, so I let them feast before getting them ready to wind down for the night.

After putting the kids to bed, I return to the symphony of thoughts racking my brain. I volley between the last unfilled portion of my Young Soarers application, the pesky little gossip article that Solange demands be ready in three days, and the fact that Damien hasn't gotten back to me yet. I hope I didn't offend him with the business poaching accusation. I refuse to believe that Damien's some conniving evil mastermind who cares more about his bank account than the baker that's fed him his entire life. I tell myself that his backstory will amend things and put my mind at ease.

I hunker down in the villa's home office while Angela departs for her dinner out with Howie and Estelle. My face slumped in my palm, I bounce my gaze from the almost-complete application on my laptop to a notebook page spread out on the desk. The latter is empty except for the picture of the chateau paper clipped to the left-hand corner and the title I'd quickly scribbled, "Bienvenue à Eze, nouveaux pro-priétaires!"

Slapping a cutesy title at the top doesn't erase the fact that the contents are more than a touch nosy.

I take in a deep breath and return to the Young Soarers applica-tion. I've been avoiding it for too long, and I need to send it no later than 7 a.m. tomorrow. Examining the final essay question, my stom-ach sinks.

It reads, "Why is the Young Soarers program your dream?"

I sigh, my entire posture collapsing. Fuck. I don't know.

Past the office's double glass doors, the other end of the darkened hallway illuminates as the foyer's light comes on. Muffled voices ac-company the unexpected arrival.

Nick's and Jamie's voices get louder, their conversation becoming more crisp as they walk through the house. The negotiations must have ended early. And by Nick's tone of voice, they might not have gone as planned.

Jamie peeks his head down the hall, noticing me at the desk. He smiles and Nick hoarsely calls after him.

"Watch it, Jamie," Nick warns.

"What's the damage, Dad?"

"I'm sure neither of us wants to find out."

Jamie's exact response is inaudible but undoubtedly coarse. A few moments later, he taps at the glass doors and gives a smile. There are bags under his eyes from only a few days of Chessley Enterprise meet-ings, though his hair is as lusciously hickory golden as ever.

My toes curl while butterflies tickle my stomach.

Until the image of Angela's cream-masked frown pops up in my mind.

Screw it. She's out tonight anyway.

I wave him in, and he melts in the sofa chair beside me, loosening the collar of his button-up.

"Well you look great," I joke.

"I know, right, never felt better." He leans forward, groaning and rubbing his forehead.

"Tired?"

"The opposite actually."

"I know what you mean," I say, slouching my shoulders back in the leather swivel chair.

The week has left me in a whirlwind. From emotional analysis to au pairing to gossip writing, I'm aching to expend some energy.

Jamie stares at a bookcase and clicks his tongue.

"I know a place. If you want to come, grab your bathing suit and meet me down here in ten minutes."

Anticipation courses through me, and I gladly slap my laptop shut. I'll plug in some cookie-cutter responses later. Besides, given Howie's encouragement, I'm fairly certain my resume will outshine anything I scribble onto the essay portions.

—*—*—*—

DID I THINK twice about sneaking out past ten with Jamie? Yes. In fact, I thought about it thirty times over. And all the ways Angela would publicly defame me. But my hormones got the better of me. Still, I hadn't mentally prepared for the onslaught of nerves that'd be electrifying my body while sitting in the passenger seat of Jamie's convertible.

The silence between us isn't awkward or draining, however. We've simply learned to enjoy each other's presence. Still, I try to distract myself by the impressive mountains, jet black against the deep navy night sky.

"Where is it we're going exactly?"

"A place I used to go to get drunk with my summer friends."

"Oh?" I look out the window but feel Jamie's eyes searching me. He takes a moment to respond.

"Some mates I knew down here when I was in high school."

We take a turn onto a grassy dirt drive, following two lines of pine trees toward a gorgeous two-story limestone manor. Warm floodlights caress the neatly trimmed hedges and cypress along the exterior.

"Are you sure we can be here?"

"Positive," Jamie says. He raises a finger. "Pinky promise."

An impenetrable contract.

He leads me around the rectangular building to a side door. He taps a sequence on the electronic keypad, and we head down a dim, humid stone hall that smells of chlorine. It leads straight to a giant indoor swimming pool. Moonlight shines through the glass ceiling, making the water's surface appear smooth as glass. Potted ferns and plush lounge chairs surround the perimeter.

"Care to join me?" Jamie asks.

He removes his shirt. The moonlight dances over the curves of his muscles, accentuating his form.

I catch Jamie sneaking a few glances as I take off my clothes and sport my ruby-red one-piece.

"Hey. Eyes up here, buddy," I teasingly scold him.

Jamie's dimpled grin sends chills up my arm.

"As you wish." He winks before raising his arms to the side and looking around. "So whattaya think of this place?"

"Not bad," I say, placing my hands on my hips, examining the slanted glass roof.

As if I'm lured, my feet make my way to him.

We stand millimeters apart, his heels on the edge of the deep end. I'm so tempted to close the distance and press my lips to his. But again, Angela's face flashes in my mind, so instead, I push my palm against his chest and send him flying into the water.

I gasp. Oh my gosh, did I just do that? He flicks his head back, curving a line of water with his hair, and wipes his eyes. A wide grin plastered on his face. He points at me. "Oh, you're gonna get it now."

My tongue peeks out between a bashful smile as he wades toward me, but I dive in right past him. The water is as chilly as the ocean, and it liberates my entire being. When I emerge to the surface, Jamie's there waiting for me with the most genuine smile I've ever seen on him. We paddle back and forth on our backs, examining the starlit sky. In addition to the ceiling, the walls are glass as well, giving way to a view that I can only imagine is just as breathtaking during the day.

I kick my way to the edge of the pool, resting my elbows on the tile edge. The view of Monaco lit up and glittering in the distance catches my eye. Jamie joins me, resting his chin on crossed arms.

"Nice, isn't it?" he asks.

"It'll do." I bite my lip. "So I'm guessing this is the grand Lavergne Vineyard?"

"X marks the spot."

"Just when I thought you were the bad boy sneaking me onto private property."

"C'mon, you're saying you don't get the same thrill from legally entering?"

"Hits different." I shrug, catching his grin.

Apparently, the neighboring lavender farm hosts their spa and bath shop on the bottom floor of the manor while the second story houses the winery's tasting room. The entire property is completely booked when it's not being used for a wedding or private event. It'll be perfect for the big bash that Angela's volunteered me to help arrange.

"I don't know how you do it," Jamie says, searching my face.

My top bun slumps a bit. "What do you mean?"

"It's like you have this well of ambition that never goes dry."

The compliment tenses my shoulders, and I swallow hard as he goes on.

"I mean you come in and take, let's be honest, not the most relaxing au pair gig. Then you build a mini media enterprise. And now working with Mum's party planner."

A bashful smile grows on my lips.

"You're fearless," he adds.

I chuckle, but my tone turns stern as I press my chin deeper into my forearm. "Exactly. I'm really good at making you think I am."

"So what are Kat McLauren's deepest, darkest fears, then? Aliens? Angela Lavergne?"

I start to smile, then sigh. "That it doesn't work out," I mumble.

Jamie twists his torso to face me straight on. "The Soarers program?"

"That too."

He inhales slowly and trots his finger along the pool's edge. "Mc-Lauren Films?"

I don't say anything, just take a deep inhale, the chlorine thick in the air.

"And why wouldn't it work out?" Jamie asks.

"Well, I'm not Steven Spielberg. Or Octavia Butler. Or Jane Austen."

"No, you're not." He turns toward me.

"Oh, thanks."

"You're not supposed to be. You're Kat McLauren. That's all you ever have to be."

The ripples of the lapsing water are reflected in his emerald eyes. Those same eyes that pierce me to the core.

"You owe it to yourself to start somewhere," he finishes.

My nostrils flare and I grip the cement edge before he can offer any more advice that he won't walk the walk himself.

"And what? Take a leap of fucking faith? And what am I supposed to do with that?" I push myself out of the pool and wrap myself in a towel before charging out the nearest door.

In my rush, I knock my folded shirt into a damp puddle on the tile. But I leave it and march onto the backyard patio to cool my rage.

I close my eyelids, not even close to tired, but confused, frustrated, and torn. Sighing through my nose, I turn to see Jamie joining me on the porch swing. He's brought a bottle of champagne. No glasses. It's that kind of night.

He hands me the chilled green bottle of my good old friends Moët and Chandon. It weighs heavy in my palm.

"Count of three," Jamie says, his thumbs pressed with mine on the bottle's cork.

"One, two . . ."

Pop!

"Woo," Jamie exclaims softly as cool bubbly foam runs down the bottle and around our hands. He hands me his button-up, and we drink in silence, admiring the moonlit view of Monte Carlo. My focus lands on the labyrinth of hedges outlined in front of us.

"I'm sorry," I begin to say, but Jamie waves his hand.

"You don't have to apologize. I'm the one who should be . . . I didn't mean to upset you."

"It's not your fault. You were just my punching bag." I take a sip and press the bottle against my chest, the thoughts that've been swirling in my head over the summer are ready to erupt. "I think I might've just wasted half my life trying to get something I don't even know if I want anymore."

The hopelessness seeps into my words.

"Couldn't have been a complete waste."

An appreciative smile tries to tug at the corner of my mouth, but it fizzles out. We sit, admiring the view.

I'd never imagined, not from my first encounter with Jamie Chessley, that we'd be here now.

Him on the verge of earning a Michelin star, and me running the Riviera's most profitable travel magazine—with Manon's help, of course—even after the crapshoot reception that accompanied the first publication.

I take a swig of the sweet, bubbly drink. I've been hogging it, Jamie's barely had any. The bottle is half empty, and the buzz is coming in hot. Jamie's words have hypnotized me, and he's not done yet.

"So what if you give up the Soarers? Would you regret it if you didn't?" The moonlight gleams in his eyes. "You're not leaving something to chance by being yourself."

My voice is depleted and raw. "That's the thing though. If I just *be* myself, I'll be a stranger to everyone I've ever known. I'm Kat McLauren, full steam ahead to being a corporate big shot in the travel industry. I've been spouting that line since I was in the sixth grade. No one knows Kat McLauren, filmmaker."

Jamie's eyes soften, and he mutters, "Like how no one knows the real Jamie Chessley. Pastry chef and . . ." He casts his gaze to the sky.

"We're more alike than I'd realized," I say.

He scrunches his brow, and I go on.

"We both have dreams and visions, but both care too much about what other people think about them. As much as we'd like to deny it, it paralyzes us."

I stare into his gentle green eyes, and his closed lips curl into a smile.

"I think you might be right," Jamie says. "You hungry?"

—*—*—*—

THANK YOU, CREATORS of this world, for planting the idea of twenty-four-hour McDonald's drive-thrus in the minds of humanity. And not just any Mickey D's. The bougie European kind. Which, when enjoyed while slightly intoxicated, is an out-of-this-world experience.

Since Jamie didn't really drink any of the champagne, he drives us to the nearest joint. Our hair, drying like hay, reeks of chlorine, but all my attention goes to the electric signage listing familiar menu items like Le Big Mac and Le Filet-O-Fish.

Out of pure stupor, I hit his forearm in shock and point to the menu board.

I'll admit, maybe I don't go to McDonald's enough back in the States to know the menu backward and forward, but I'm like eighty-seven percent positive we don't have a KitKat McFlurry!

"Hey!" Jamie laughs. The car in front of us releases their brakes, and we cruise closer to the lit-up sign.

As he rolls down the window, a chirpy voice greets us from the speaker box.

"Bienvenue, je vous écoute," they say so fast, I'm shocked I even caught it.

"Ready?" Jamie asks.

"Oh, merde."

He snorts but contains himself as he relays his order. When it's my turn, Jamie waits for me to tell him my choices, but I have other plans. I unbuckle my seat and nearly clamber over the driver side, leaning my palms on his door. My chest is probably two inches from his nose as I poke my head out the window.

"Bonjour!" I shout at a little black speaker.

Jamie's snickers get louder, only making mine more delirious. The cars behind us probably think we're two lunatics.

"Bonjour, s'il vous plaît. Je suis, em, no. I want . . . Je veux . . . le Charolais." I point at the sandwich on the screen. "Et les Deluxe Potatoes. Ooh! Et La Sauce Curry. Et Le McPancakes, s'il vous plaît."

That last one was an impulse decision, but am I gonna say no to two pancakes sandwiching a layer of chocolate cream? I think not.

Jamie talks in between explosive laughter. "Don't forget your Mc . . ."

"OH! Et Le KitKat McFlurry! S'il vous plaît!"

The worker reads our order back, and I nod, but I'm not even listening.

Anything sounds good right about now.

By the tone of their voice when they tell us to pull forward, I can only guess the massive eye roll they're making.

Jamie tries suppressing his chuckle. "Never seen anyone so flabbergasted by a burger with cabbage and spicy ranch."

"I'm glad I was your first." I bat my eyes toward him, sending him into an uproar all over again.

"Good one, McLauren."

We're handed our food through the window. Here comes eye roll numbuh two! Pulling into the parking lot, we gorge on our feast for a few uninterrupted moments.

"What in Dieu's name is that?" I point to his circular ham and cheese toast sandwich.

"A Croque-monsieur," he says, taking a bite of half of it.

"Hmm." I scoop up some ice cream with one of my *potatoes deluxe*. Jamie lifts his brow. "What in Dieu's name are you doing?"

"You've never . . . ?"

I hand him a crispy potato wedge that's more like a home fry from an American diner—McDonald's, please bring this to the US—and Jamie hesitantly dips it into my McFlurry.

Wow, I might have to use that as an innuendo if I ever write a steamy romance screenplay.

His face contorts from apprehension to surprised delight after the first bite.

"Good?"

"Merde. Yeah."

We plow through the rest until we're fully satisfied. It's amazing how much my hunger disappears when I've got eleven hundred things on my plate.

Now that the champagne has almost burned itself entirely off, I still don't feel tired.

"Who would have thought you and I would be here now," I say, taking a sip of water.

"I know. I thought I'd never see you again after that picnic on your first day."

"Oh?" I turn my torso to face him.

"With Manon's hijinks alone, I figured you'd be packing the next morning. But that was before I knew *the* Kat McLauren."

"And what do you know about *the* Kat McLauren?" I press.

His gaze goes soft, and silence invades the front seats, only interrupted by the bumbling song on the radio.

"That you're a no bullshit badass."

Heat crawls along my neck and cascades in my blushing cheeks.

"Can I ask . . . you're clearly not some Don Juan girl-charmer, so why were you so willing to tell me about the Vigne when we first met?"

He lifts his head but doesn't make eye contact until the words leave his mouth. "There was something about you that made me feel like I could trust you, like I already knew you."

My breath gets shaky. We hold each other's gaze until Jamie has a moment of reckoning.

He turns the ignition and says, "I want to show you something."

Despite my persistence in questioning our next stop on this midnight road trip, Jamie keeps quiet. The road signs say we're heading straight for Èze, so I figure it's back to the villa we go until he blows right past the exit.

Instead, Jamie jolts us onto an unpaved downhill driveway. Brambles cocoon us, blocking the site. Then it comes into frame. Manon's hiding place and the highlight of Solange's gossip piece: the chateau. Its recently scrubbed, creamy stone finish basks in the moonlight, and a newly appointed fountainhead gurgles in the garden.

"We shouldn't be here," I say, twisting my neck over my shoulders. Though there aren't signs of other people, the last thing I need now is to get caught breaking and entering. Especially at the place whose owners I'm supposed to be writing a "welcoming" exposé on. That wouldn't end well for Solange either.

"It's all right. I know the owner."

"You do?"

"Oui." He winks and gets out of the car. We make our way to the entrance. Once dilapidated, the stone steps have been polished and the cracks filled in. The buyer even took care to add a few plant pots spilling out ferns and vibrant irises that seem to glow in the night's darkened light. Jamie types in the key code to the added electrical feature at the wide wooden doors. Inside, the crumbling brick walls have been patched and painted, and a gorgeously polished hickory staircase welcomes us to explore further.

"Wow." I crane my neck to admire the wood beams across the ceiling, effusing its rustic modernity. "This is incredible."

Jamie drinks in my admiration. "I'm glad you like it." He looks away, but I settle my focus on him. And it hits me.

"This is yours, isn't it?"

His silence confirms it.

Craptastic. And *I'm* gonna be the one to out him to the public and, more importantly, his parents? Of course not.

I consider bolting before I learn any more details, but my own curiosity overtakes me as he leads me from room to room. Some require a bit more paint, wall decor, and furniture. But on the whole, the three-story little castle is shaping up to be what I can imagine will be Èze's newest best kept secret.

Jamie confides the renovations he's undertaken with the goal to open an inn. He admits that he's rather enjoyed the restoration more than he anticipated.

"Is this your version of the Vigne?"

"Not exactly. People go there for the food and the views. I want people to come here to detach. To eat farm-to-table French cuisine. To explore the countryside. Sit in nature, be with it, be with each other."

"A retreat."

"Oui."

He explains why he's worked at the Vigne and London restaurants for ages: to sharpen his skills as a chef and to learn what guests crave, not just on the food side.

"So this is why you were so adamant about being my cameraman. To keep us far and away?"

"Well, I couldn't have the right lot of them three running 'round here when the contractors were nailing in the floorboards and chatting me up for blueprint approvals."

"Fair enough." I grin and trace my fingers along the polished banister. "You're lucky I've been pushing off that gossip article for Solange. Not that I'd rat you out. Seriously, I wouldn't. I won't."

"I know." He looks over his shoulder and casts a warm smile.

As we continue up the stairs, I ask, "When do you plan to tell your parents?"

"When it's done."

I scrunch my brow, and he continues.

"A win in their book is clear-cut uphill profit. There's no space for the in-between."

"Then did your mother consider her fashion line a failure up until she made her first million?"

"Not a failure, just a milestone not worth harping on when her end goal would blow that out of the water."

"So you'll just keep them in the dark—"

"Until I triple my investment," Jamie finishes.

He leads me to a little library on the second floor. Overtop a tapestry rug, blue velvet sofa chairs surround a grand fireplace. Floor-to-ceiling windows give the illusion that we're standing in one big gazebo.

"This is my favorite spot," he says. But I've stopped listening. My mind is abuzz with what-ifs until Jamie brings me back to the present. "What is it?"

"So what if you triple your investments and they still don't get it? What'll you do then?"

"You mean, what if they're physically incapable of acknowledging their son as a success outside of the inherited world of Chessley Enterprises?" He shakes his head. "I don't know."

He lights a match in the fireplace, and the logs crackle to life.

"I'm sorry, I didn't mean to go there. I just know what it's like to chase approval."

"No, you're right though. There's a good sixty-percent chance they'll call this a well-done hobby project and move on to asking when I'm gonna get my life started."

"I don't believe it when people say that dissenting opinions don't bother them."

Jamie looks at me, intrigued and surprised.

"Really," I press. "It's like how every commencement speech always ends with the line 'follow your passion,' but we know full well that the second we actually do, we're branded as nonsensical risk-takers because we opt out of the"—I use air quotes—"*safe* option."

"You've given this some thought, huh?"

"You think?" I say with a soft exhale through my nose.

"So how do we do it? How do we say eff it and c'est la vie?" he asks.

"I'll let you know when I've figured it out," I add.

"If Estelle were here—" Jamie starts, and I can't help but jump in.

"She'd tell us to screw the patriarchy."

"And get our heads out of our arses. If it's worth giving up, we probably would have already done so by now."

Our boiling cynicism slowly dries as we watch the flames dance. Jamie drops some dried twigs on the glowing logs. I glance toward my backpack and pull out a package tied in brown paper and string.

"Here," I say to Jamie, handing him the gift.

"What's this?"

"Something for a no bullshit badass in training." We exchange smiles before he tears the wrapper. The intrigue in his face drains and trades places with unwavering stillness.

"Where did you find this?" His voice is raw. He palms the Epictetus volume's worn leather binding.

"Saint-Tropez."

Jamie bites his lip, flicking through the pages, before sending his gaze in my direction. He stands abruptly and grabs one of the few books along the mantle.

"And this . . . is for you. Saw it at Solange's shop when we hid in there from Mum."

He hands me a book titled "The Cinema of Agnès Varda: Resistance and Eclecticism."

"She pioneered the New Wave of filmmaking. Got started with this experimental approach and created documentaries for social commentary. Basically invented her own style," Jamie says. "I may have read a few pages. But you get the point. She didn't have an end goal, just a north star."

Shock layers over my fascination.

"But that was months ago. You didn't know about my—"

"I went back for it. And to every thrift store in Nice until Solange conveniently remembered the one she donated it to."

My eyes meet his.

"Jamie. You didn't have to—"

"And *you* didn't have to do this." He holds up the book I gifted him. "Look at us, a pair of bookworms who don't know how else to express our feelings."

My body stills. Did he say what I think he just did?

I can't look away from his green irises shimmering in the firelight. Heat radiates off my chest. My fingers dig into the rug as I feel our bodies moving closer.

I can't tell who leans in first.

He takes my face in his palms, and I wrap my arms around his neck.

Nothing else captivates me more at this moment than his warm lips firmly pressed against mine. The room is warm from the fire, but it's cooler than the embers swimming through me. He moves his hands down around my waist and pulls me in. My chest melts against his. He's grown out his beard stubble. It's coarse and gruff against my bare skin. His tongue teases at the seam of my mouth, and I open up to let him in. The warmth of his palm melts my shoulders as his hand travels underneath my shirt, tracing his fingers along my lower back. My stomach flutters with delight.

A loud whack outside the window stops our movements, stirring my eyes open. For all I know it could've been a snapping branch, but it's enough to snap me out of my daze and back to the harsh reality of our situation.

No one's in the house but us. Still, I frantically untangle myself from his grasp.

"Jamie . . . I-I have to go. We can't . . ."

Another snap draws Jamie's attention to the windows where we're surely on full display to any onlooker who might be traipsing around the olive groves at Angela's request.

"Kat, wait," he says and holds up a hand.

It's too late. I've already swung my bag over my shoulder and started on my beeline back to the villa. I can't risk getting back in his car and having anyone see us together like that.

"Kat!"

It takes everything in me not to turn around, but I fight every urge as I race down the staircase and out the front door. The night has chilled considerably since we left, but my body still burns. Running through the muddy groves back to the villa, there's abundant glee coursing through my veins, and it helps to quiet the agony of now knowing the chateau's owner and that I'll have to keep the secret tightly sealed from Solange. I helplessly giggle, brushing past fluffy branches, recounting that most luxurious kiss.

Slowing my sprint, I catch my breath in the crisp air.

Damien. What am I going to tell Damien? Am I going to tell him? I don't owe him anything, sure. But withholding the truth is still a lie. What am I going to do? I can't just throw away the safe space we've built together because I have the hots for Jamie, even though the feelings aren't solely physical anymore.

"Et merde," I say to myself and toss the debacle to the back of my brain. I'll deal with it later. When the moonlight hides behind encroaching clouds, I use my phone's flashlight to lead the way back to the villa where not a single light is on. Removing my shoes before getting to the terrace so as to avoid any soily tracks, I tiptoe through the door nearest the kitchen.

Back in the solace of my own room, I take a look at myself in the mirror. My capris are covered in dirt from the shins down. Though my hair has dried since the night swim, I realize I'm still wearing Jamie's button-up. I press the collar to my nose and inhale. Either I'm still a little tipsy or I'm catching all the feels. (Cue the Twice song.) But I don't care.

I lavish in the night's events, scrubbing my feet in the bidet I thought I'd never touch before collapsing on the mattress and avoiding all consequential details till tomorrow.

CHAPTER TWENTY-SEVEN

*N*othing. Absolutely nothing can steal me from my comforter cocoon.

Except for a warm, wet stream south of my bikini line. It gushes out, and I jump up, hoping I didn't just sully the ecru sheets as I propel out of bed.

Seriously, Aunt Flo!

After months of ghosting me—like she normally does when my stress levels spike or when I'm traveling—*now* she decides to show up. I guess she gave me fair warning with those hormone blitzes this past week. Fortunately, I have a few old pads stuffed in my toiletry bag, flattened to paper's thickness. Knowing I'll have to grab more, I quickly get ready and praise Sylvie for agreeing to prepare the kids' breakfast while I run to the local *pharmacie*.

Something I'll miss about this place when I leave in a few weeks is how crisply quiet the mornings are. A handful of locals scuff their feet along cobblestone to grab their family's tear-and-share baguette and mull over café au laits with friends. Shop owners wedge their doors open, waving to one another in routinely amicable glee.

A small green cross hanging inside the pharmacy's window blinks alive, and I head in. As I start navigating the narrow aisles stocked with medications and personal care items, a woman in a lab coat yawns and asks if I'm looking for anything in particular. It hits me that I haven't a clue what the French word for tampon is, and I'm not about to make hand gestures that I'll live to regret.

"Uh . . . Tam . . . Tam . . ."

The pharmacist looks at me boredly.

A cramp pangs my side, and I give up searching for the translation.

"Tampon," I exclaim in the most obvious American accent. Just as I do so, the bell dings above the entrance. I snap my head over to see Emi muffling a laugh.

"Ah, tampon," the pharmacist says with a nod, leading me down the second aisle.

Tam-po(n). Really, Kat.

I peruse a selection of foreign brands, but my focus remains on my peripheral vision. Emi chats with the woman before grabbing some skin cream and strolling my way.

"Bonjour," she says politely.

"Emi." My face is strained, my voice desperate. "Look, I shouldn't have brought you to the school. I didn't mean to pressure you—"

"I'm glad you did. I didn't go to university just to keep my childhood job at the Cave."

"Have you told your parents?"

Emi nods confidently. "Oui. It's taken me years to do it, but I'm tired of holding myself back. She knows I'm ready to move on. It's time."

"How'd she take it?"

"Better than I thought. At first she didn't say anything, just kind of looked at me like a ghost. But only because she hasn't hired extra staff before and doesn't know how to post a job opening online." Emi's eyes go to crescents as she giggles. "I'm taking a teaching position in Paris next year. In the meantime, I'll occupy myself at that primary school in Nice and maybe dip my toes in Teachers Without Borders during the school breaks."

"Très bien, Em. That's amazing."

I sigh with a relieved grin, and she gives me one big bear hug.

"I need to tell you something too," I say to Emi after we pay at the register. All the way back to the Chessley house, I relay my night with Jamie. Then about my skyrocketing feelings for him and Damien. And my angst over the imminent party—knowing it's my last hurdle to jump over before finally getting into Young Soarers.

"You're not surprised about Jamie?" I ask Emi, whose expression hardly changes when I tell her.

"Kat, he hasn't taken his eyes off of you since you first came to Èze."

My cheeks flush with heat.

"So what does this mean for you two?" Emi asks as we round the tall cypress trees lining the stone wall to the Chessley villa.

"That it ends here," I claim, though my stomach turns as I hear myself speak the words. I've decided. I won't give up a chance with Damien. Besides, even if I indulged the idea of being with Jamie after my au pairing is up, who's to say Angela wouldn't seek revenge on my reputation for "stealing her son."

When Emi and I make our way through the kitchen, both of us comment on the silence in the house. Normally, a boxing match would be breaking out over the last pain au chocolat.

On the terrace, Sylvie rests her feet on an ottoman and sips a large cup of tea. She relays that Angela and Nick took the kids to breakfast at the tennis club and that I'm more than welcome to join. Emi comes along, knowing she's always invited. I can't imagine Jamie would willingly show up to such a prolonged outing with his family with no easy escape route. And when we arrive at the Monte Carlo Country Club, my suspicions are confirmed. Emi and I join Nick, Angela, and the kids in the sea of white umbrella tables. The club's terrace, nestled along the cliffs of Monaco, overlooks a plethora of tennis courts, swimming pools, and the glistening ocean just a few kilometers in the distance.

Milo insists that I sandwich myself between him and Josie. I didn't know what to expect seeing Angela face-to-face after Jamie and I had our little rendezvous. If there was a photographer on our tail last night, they must not have caught anything proof worthy of Jamie's and my entanglement to show to Angela. Because if there were, I'd be back in Boston by now.

Under a wide-brimmed, creaseless sunhat, Angela stares as I take a seat. She doesn't blink once nor does she glance down at the grapefruit she's so gracefully scooping out.

Thankfully, Emi incidentally comes to my rescue from Angela's bone-chilling yet searing gaze. She points to the two empty chairs at the end of the table. "Est-ce que quelqu'un d'autre vient?" she asks Angela.

I myself wonder if someone else plans to join. Before Angela can answer, Jamie shuffles past the maze of wicker chairs to our table.

"Désolé," he says and gives his mother a kiss on the cheek.

My fingers scrunch up my white sundress at the knees as he shuffles behind my chair.

"Pas de problème," Nick says, waving his hand and setting down his copy of *Conseils*.

Jamie takes his seat next to Josie. Our eyes fall on each other, but we both tear them away.

"Jamie," Angela says, flicking her napkin over her lap. "Your car wasn't at the house this morning. Where did you come from?"

Jamie swigs a sip of water.

"I spent the night somewhere else."

True.

Angela daggers her eyes to me until she lowers her tensed shoulders. She raises her brow at Jamie, waiting for him to expound, but she can't help herself.

"You went to the vineyard, didn't you? Getting drunk with strangers all over again."

He shrugs. "Not strangers," he mumbles into his glass.

Warmth races through me.

"Mon amour," Angela says to him. "When will enough be enough?"

Jamie holds a grave stare with his mother until the waiter interrupts to take our orders.

Angela lists an assortment of items for us to share.

Nick removes his tennis jacket and rests it on the empty chair beside Jamie.

"Uh-uh." Angela waves a finger. "That's for our guest."

Nick, apparently having not been clued into any details on the matter, scrunches his brow.

"And there she is," Angela says, waving to someone behind me.

Probably Estelle or Marie is my guess. Until I hear the voice.

"Angela, comment ça va!" Vivian says. She greets us all with a double-cheek kiss.

"Kat," she says to me. "So nice to see you again. We keep running into each other everywhere, don't we?" Her lip-glossed grin is as amiable as ever.

"Oh?" Angela asks, gesturing for Vivian to take her seat next to Jamie.

Vivian gestures to Emi and I. "We three found each other at the same bookstore in Saint-Tropez."

"Quelle coïncidence," Nick says matter-of-factly with a grin.

Vivian points to me. "This one is a smart cookie," she says. Her French accent makes English even sound attractive.

"Likes to read philosophy," Vivian adds, draping her pristine white blazer over her shoulders.

Jamie's eyes freeze on his glass of juice, his neutral expression tensing. I take a mouthful of orange juice to avoid answering any follow-up questions.

"Really?" Angela tears apart a croissant, layer by layer. "Give us a quote then, Kat."

My jaw clenches. Merde-y merde merde.

"Don't explain your philosophy. Embody it," Jamie says as he pops a grape into his mouth. "Epictetus."

Manon grunts. "That sounds like a flesh-eating virus."

Angela laughs. "That's right, Jamie. You took a few university courses in philosophy."

"You remember?" Jamie says.

"Of course. Vivian, please enjoy." Angela gestures to the assortment of breakfast items spread over the glass table.

"Merci beaucoup," Vivian responds, scooping some chopped apples onto her plate.

Angela traces the rim of her empty coffee cup, glancing around the terrace. "Où est le serveur?"

"I'll go find him," I say without a second thought. We may be outdoors, but I need to get some air from all this.

Inside the lounge, I rest my forearms on the bar's granite countertop, trying to put my feelings at bay.

"Hey," Jamie says, walking up to me.

My eyes dart around the room filled with club members dressed to play a tennis match. Any one of them could be Angela's or Nick's friends ready to spill the details of our conversation. I grab his wrist, pulling him around the corner and down a narrow staircase that leads to a red-carpeted billiards room.

We pause halfway down the wooden steps.

"Kat, what happened last night? Did I do something?"

"Would you please stop?" I beg, scanning my feet on the narrow stairs.

He scrunches his brow and motions closer. "Kat—"

"No, Jamie. No. I can't do this. The secrets and the rules and the hiding. The back and forth. I'm sick of it."

Tears well in my eyes, but I don't dare break my gaze with his.

"I'm tired of hiding too, Kat. I tried my best to hold back, but I can't anymore. I won't. Look, summer's almost over, and in a week, my mother won't be your boss." Jamie takes my hand in his. "What's stopping—"

"Your mother doesn't want us together. To her, I'm your biggest distraction."

"Yeah. From a career that I've never even wanted."

"Well, she still has an impact on the career I've been after for over a decade. I need the best reference I can get. And that means I can't . . . we can't . . . not now. Not ever." I glance down, a weight sinking in my stomach.

Jamie's cheekbones hollow out.

"You're chasing her good word for a dream you're barely hanging on to," he asserts.

"What the fuck are you talking about?"

"The Young Soarers, Kat. You don't want it. You've said it yourself."

I cross my arms. "No, I haven't." My chest rises and falls with deep, aggravated breaths.

His green eyes pour into mine.

"Not in so many words," he mumbles and glances to the side.

I've lost track of what and to whom I've shared my evolving opinion around the Young Soarers. What were random, cryptic comments to Jamie, Emi, and Damien and what were my own epiphanies.

Sucking in my cheeks, I squint at him. "You're one to talk. Telling me to follow my real dreams, yet you're eons away from being transparent about yours."

"That's different. You're clearly on to something with *Conseils*. You've proved you can do it, the writing and filming. But you won't see it for yourself. And you're so resistant to changing your direction now, still focused on the Young Soarers."

"Look. Magazines aren't movies," I interject tersely, shoving away the little voice inside my head that highlights the miniature documentaries we've filmed for *Conseils*.

"It's the principle of it. You made something out of pure passion and spark."

I inhale sharply. Jamie leans closer, his sun-kissed locks framing his jawline.

"Just because I keep my plans a secret, and for good reason I may add, what does that have to do with you? Even if I told the world about my chateau today, would you still keep your true dream on the backburner?"

Maybe he's right. Still, I purse my lips and straighten my spine. Nodding my head toward the terrace, I divert the conversation.

"Why doesn't she know about the Vigne? If you're so close, how come she's not clued in?"

He scrunches his brow. "What. Viv? I love her like a sister, but she can't keep a secret to save her life."

"You know, you're pretty haughty for giving *me* career advice when you can't even take it yourself. That little 'own up to your truth' spiel sounds a bit like bullshit to me."

Gulping, I wrap my hand around the railing. Only a few inches separate our mouths. His cologne is thick and cozy as ever, and I am just as susceptible to falling prey.

But I turn my head.

"Jamie, please. It can't happen," I state firmly. "This"—I gesture between us—"can't happen."

Jamie sighs and bows his head, surrendering. "You're right."

Oof. It doesn't feel good to hear him say it too.

I push myself back and cross my arms. His eyes search mine, carrying the same tender gentility he had last night and the first day I met him.

"Kat." His voice goes soft.

A cloud of warmth diffuses around us, but my better judgment cools me off.

I drop his hand and ascend the stairs, breathing out any remaining tingles in my stomach. Eventually, he follows behind, and we spend the rest of breakfast without speaking a word to each other unless it's in regard to passing the pastry basket.

Angela carries on about how she's adding a few more people to the guest list, that I'm to make sure their invitations get express-mailed by tonight, and to enlist Vivian for assistance because of her accumulated experience in supporting Lavergne company functions in the past. I'm only half listening as I agree, peeling my eyes away from the table and setting my sight on the tennis courts below.

CHAPTER TWENTY-EIGHT

*T*wo nights ago, the Lavergne vineyard carried an alluring magic in its emptiness. Tonight, sparkly-dressed attendees will populate the candlelit grounds, sipping special reserve rosé and nibbling fine culinary creations while models saunter around in immaculately curated outfits that take inspiration from airline uniforms. Angela's party planner extraordinaire, Cécile, knows how to throw a proper shindig for multimillionaires. The day of the party, she had delegated me to chaperone the decorators and caterers, making sure everything they put out meets Angela's specific requirements.

Everything's nearly ready. The stringed quintet, the event staff, and the saddled horses that'll carry guests from the car park up the carriage road. Howie had even insisted that the Vigne cater the event. He must've been wildly impressed by his meal there a few weeks back.

The sun is about to set, a lavender and orange hue coating the sky.

Emi and I help with setup, assembling carnation bouquets to adorn the tables overlooking the vineyards.

"Pass me some string," she says, pointing to the spool I'm toying around my fingers. "Tout va bien?" she asks, tilting her head.

"All good," I assure her. If "all good" accounts for 1) not getting a response letter or even a text from Damien, though he's surely back in town 2) debating how I'll explain to Solange that I won't be writing her supposedly-friendly-yet-rather-scandalous article, now knowing Jamie to be the local chateau's new owner. Sure. It's all good.

"Excited to see your mère?" Emi asks.

I nod, picturing Mom noshing on a homemade turkey sandwich at the airport gate. A grin brims on my lips. As much as we don't see eye to eye when it comes to career and lifestyle, I'm ecstatic for her to visit me in my final week in Èze.

"I invited her to the party, but her flight may be delayed coming in."

"Oh, too bad she won't be here for the announcement."

And in light of such a fruitful collaboration, Howie and Angela thought it most fitting to announce the new class of Young Soarers tonight. In fact, the top thirty-five finalists make up most of the names on the extended guest list. And being the ambitious, hungry applicants they are, not one denied the offer to be flown in overnight. Well, one did. But only because I'm already here.

When the last table is set and electric lotuses float in the garden pool, a few violins commence their warm-up prelude, and waiters take direction from the galley kitchen. Emi and I hurry to a private room in the vineyard's manor to don our gowns and apply fresh faces of makeup.

Guests have begun trickling in by the time we finish. I take a peek out the window to see nearly a hundred people already strolling the grounds, enjoying hors d'oeuvres, and taking group photos in the soft twilight backdrop.

"This is it," I say to Emi, interlacing my elbow in hers.

"Minou, c'était un plaisir."

It's been more than a pleasure. It's been the breath of fresh air I didn't even know I needed.

"I'm just glad I got to dress up this time," Emi adds, sashaying in her lacy lilac gown as we click our heels down the stony hallway and onto the lawn where Antoine and Marie greet us with full glasses of bubbly.

"They like this one, eh?" Marie says, eyeing the guests guzzling down the champagne. "We'll have to stock more at the Cave. Remember that, Emi."

Emi swiftly swerves her attention to a server circulating through the crowd and carting a silver platter of tiny bread thins with tapenade piped on top. She excuses herself just as Howie, sporting his branded Continental ascot, approaches Emi's parents and me with arms wide open.

"Miss Kat," he exclaims and shakes his head in astonished delight. "My, what a summer you've had. I've never seen a Chessley au pair accomplish what you have in just a few months."

"They grow up so fast," Antoine kids, his eyes going to crescent slits.

Marie rolls her eyes playfully and escorts her husband away when Howie asks to speak to me privately.

"You've done a lot for this family, you know. Hell, for Èze."

"I'm glad to have helped."

"Well, I hope that dirtbag—pardon my language—will right bugger off now."

I scrunch my brow, but Howie doesn't notice as he swigs a hefty gulp of brandy.

"Shouldn't be like this. Not fair to Nick to lose his entire career over some silly headlines."

"Mr. Gupta, excuse me, but I'm not—"

"Well." Jamie steps up to my left and hands me a glass of champagne. "How about a drink then."

Damn, I almost forgot how nicely he cleans up. His black satin blazer complements his tanned skin.

Rein it in, Kat. Before I get the chance to ask Howie what the heck he meant by his comment, Angela struts over, swinging her floor-length chiffon scarf across her collarbone and seizing my attention.

"Kat. Your help is . . . commendable. Cécile thanks you. And so do I," she says with only an ounce of reluctance.

I lower my head bashfully, and catch Jamie tossing me a smile.

Angela clears her throat. "Jamie, go say hello to the Blanchets." She points to a dinner table where an older couple nurses their gin and tonics, while beside them Vivian lavishes doe-eyed young men in conversation. Jamie scowls at his mother with a squabble in his eye until Angela repeats his name with reignited firmness.

After Jamie reluctantly departs, a waiter walks by with a tray of Jamie's wild mushroom vol au vents, bite-sized puff pastry cups filled with a creamy white wine and garlic sauce. Angela and I sample the hors d'oeuvre.

"Now that's what I call *un morceau de paradis*," Angela says, wiping her mouth in delight and pointing to the appetizer.

I lift my brow, a warmth growing in my heart. If only Jamie had heard her say it.

Moments after, Howie escorts Angela to the microphone stand on the lawn to introduce the models.

Coordinated with a lively piece from the quintet, a line of men and women decked out in Lavergne's newest collection stride across the lawn. Spotlights sprinkled along the grass provide a serpentine path for them to follow.

I have to admit, Angela really surprised me with a mix of models of various weights and heights. Even her designs are fresh. Like the cherry pant suit one woman sports. Or the black evening gown featuring gilded pilot stripes on the wrists. Howie made sure his ascot came through on a couple of the ensembles too. Guests gawk and point at the dresses, skirts, and suits, and I make a mental note to have a fair batch of food set aside for the models to feast on at the end of the party.

"Excuse me." A woman taps on my shoulder. Her English accent makes me wonder if she's a colleague or a Chessley relative. "Bonjour. Kat, right?"

I nod skeptically.

"Hi," she says, outstretching her hand. "Lottie Cho-Hayworth. I'm one of Nick's old colleagues."

"Ms. Cho. Hi. It's wonderful to meet you."

"Mr. Chessley over there, " Lottie points to Jamie, who's nodding along to Vivian's rave reviews on the salmon puffs, "says you may be exploring a career in the film industry. I'm a professor at London Film School and a producer at BBC Studios."

My toes clench at the same time that my stomach does. I scratch the back of my neck and pull my hand down to hide the glistening sweat glazing my palm and fingers. Wow, a real person in the film industry. In the flesh. And *talking* to *me*.

"I-I, um . . . I don't know what he's told you but, um . . ." I laugh nervously to stall.

"He says you have a long-standing, spirited interest and that you're hungry to apply it."

Well, I guess that is true.

"I've read your magazine and seen your docu-shorts online. You've got a great eye from the looks of it." Lottie shuffles around in her purse and hands me a business card. "Let's stay in touch. I have assistant roles opening up all the time."

I graciously take the card with a dropped jaw that refuses to reset itself.

"Seriously, Kat. Think about it." Lottie pats the back of my hand and makes her way to the bar, leaving me to a moment of peace where I can devour a few appetizers while hyper-analyzing the smooth card-stock between my fingers. Biting my lip, I find myself searching the lawn for Jamie.

I tempt the idea of wandering to the indoor pool in the back of the manor, figuring he might use that as a private escape as well. But as I take a few steps along the gravel walkway, Emi comes rushing up to me.

"Minou," she says, nearly out of breath, and grabs my wrists. "Solange printed the next *Conseils*."

"What? I haven't turned in . . ."

My forehead strains, and I heave a sigh. Something clenching in my throat holds back any words. I won't do this to Jamie. I won't reveal his secret.

"What did she tell you?"

Emi continues on. "Nothing much, except that she's taken care of it. Whatever it is."

The color drains from my face. I navigate the crowd with my gaze, searching for Jamie. He stands beside the tower of champagne glasses. His eyes are already latched on to me. I've got to tell him that whatever Solange put in there, I had nothing to do with it. Maybe she knows it's him.

Maybe she managed to acquire local real estate documents and found out Jamie's ownership of the chateau. Whatever she wrote, I've got to warn him before word spreads like wildfire.

"Em," I say, gently squeezing her elbow. "I'll be back."

I excusez-moi my way through the crowd, but when I meet Jamie, he beats me to it.

"Kat, I want to tell you something, okay?"

"No, Jamie. *I* need to tell you some—"

Jamie's face freezes when he sees someone approaching me from behind. A hand grazes the back of my shoulder. I know that cologne. But it's lathered on so thick, it burns my nostrils.

"Damien," I whisper, still facing Jamie.

I spin around to see Damien's slicked-back hair and charming dimpled grin. Jittery nerves charge through my abdomen and into my throat.

After more than a month of waiting, our reunion seemed like it would never transpire. Now that it's happening, it almost feels like an illusion.

He holds up my arms and clicks his tongue. "Wow. Radiant." His raspy French accent had only been a distant memory until now. "Puis-je dire que tu es absolument stupéfiante."

"Must be something in the water," Jamie mumbles. I furrow my brow at him, trying to recollect why that's so familiar.

"Will you excuse us?" Damien asks Jamie, taking my hand.

I glance at Jamie, and our eyes meet.

"Jamie, wait here. I'll only be a minute." Maybe two. I feel his gaze burning a hole in the back of my head as Damien escorts me toward the lawn's perimeter. At first, I think he wants to take in the view, but he keeps leading me past the manor and into the circular lab-yrinth of hedges to the west of the indoor pool. I bite my lip, glancing at the natural smolder his face always seems to make. He hides those piercing gray eyes behind thick lashes. My stomach is in knots, though I can't decipher why. Perhaps our minds have found safety with each other through the letters, and now our bodies have to catch up.

"I waited all summer for this," he says, draping an arm around my shoulder.

A smile tugs at the corners of my mouth. "Really?" I stop in my tracks in the gravel path. "Damien, wait. I need some answers, okay?"

"To what?" His chuckle is lighthearted but serious.

"You never got back to me when I asked to meet up this week."

Confusion spreads across his freshly shaven face.

"Did you not get this week's letter?"

He straightens his velvet blazer. "What letter?"

"C'mon. Be serious." His silence sets my imagination running wild. "The letters we've been exchanging all summer? You *have* been getting them, right?"

"Kat, what are you talking about?"

My throat goes dry as the blood drains from my face. I press a sweaty palm to my forehead, scanning the pebbly ground, trying to surmise a possible explanation.

I mumble, "How is this possible?"

Who had I been writing all summer? Who had I been sharing so many secrets with? If not Damien then . . .

Maybe there's something in the water.

The second I gasp in realization, Damien steps closer and looks longingly into my eyes.

"Hey, what do you say we just forget the party, huh? Let's have some fun." He lifts his dark brows and firmly presses his hand on my lower back, herding me closer to his body.

I shove him away. "No!"

"Quel est ton problème?" He raises his voice.

"What made you think it was okay to just—" But I leave it there. My vexation at being objectified pales in comparison to the betrayal surging through me right now. *He's* been lying to me. Not Damien. No. Damien only wanted to get in my pants. This rage is Jamie's doing.

I part ways with Damien in the rubble of our fallout, leaving him to spit out French curses that I'm fortunate not to be fluent in.

Storming back to the manor, I hear Howie's voice echoing through the speakers peppered around the property as he gives a five-minute warning for the Young Soarers ceremony. Just as I turn the corner back to the party, Jamie steps in front of me, scanning my face.

"What did he do?"

I scoff sharply. "What did *he* do?" I shake my head, reciting a line from our correspondence. "'Something in the water?'"

Every muscle in his face tenses as his cheeks hollow out.

"Were you just making fun of me? This was all a joke, wasn't it?" I press. "Why did I ever think you gave a damn about me. Seriously, Jamie, what did you expect would happen when he came back?"

"I was trying to tell you," he says.

"Not hard enough," I exclaim. Some partygoers turn their heads, catching on to our conversation, so I lower my voice. "Do me a favor, go jump in the ocean and stay there for a while. Oh and when you get back, don't talk to me." A pang carves itself in my stomach as I utter the words and turn away from him. The cellos crescendo as I abandon him for the crowd gathering near the microphone stand.

Tears coat my eyes, but I'll be damned if I let one fall over this.

"Kat," Angela hisses.

What now?

"Viens avec moi," she says, tugging my wrist.

"But—" I point to the makeshift stage, illuminated in red, blue, and white lights.

"C'est urgent."

Great, she's probably firing me. I bet she found out about the kiss with Jamie from her spies.

I spin my head around the property. Okay, where's the helicopter to fly me out of sight or the human-sized slingshot to fling me across France?

Nestled inside a lush row of grape vines and at least a hundred feet away from wandering attendees, Angela has gathered Nick, Jamie, and myself. Nick's face is the most frigid I've ever seen it, his thin frame hunched over with arms tucked behind his back. Jamie is just as cold, a taciturn attitude rolling off of him in waves.

"What is said here will *not* go beyond these vines, eh?" Angela whips her index finger around.

I swallow hard and inhale a grapey waft. A glass of that rosé would be nice right about now.

Nick clears his throat. "Someone has been watching us this summer."

Oh, you mean the secret spy Angela let loose on me to make sure I didn't make out with your son? Oops, too late.

But Nick goes another direction. "Some of Chessley Enterprise's rather bitter competition figured the only way to squash us was to take the underhanded route," he says, trading weight on his heels.

I lift my brows, still unclear of where he's going with this. Jamie mirrors my shock.

"They hired a private investigator to spy on us, the family. Wanted to find some," he pauses to shrug his shoulders, "inflammatory details. Anything they could use to ruin our reputation, sully our name. They followed all of us looking for any meager scrap."

"What," Jamie interjects, "so you'd lose the Netherlands deal?"

Nick bows his head, his silence confirming Jamie's question.

A weight sinks in my stomach. No wonder Nick had been so anxious about putting his *happy* family on display.

"I knew it," I mumble, rather in relief that my suspicions of being tailed aren't contrived.

"So you saw them," Nick says.

"I thought it was you two," I admit, glancing between Angela and Nick. "Checking up on me, making sure I didn't . . ." My gaze goes straight to Jamie, whose head is bowed as he scuffs his shoe in the dirt.

Angela rolls her eyes. "I wouldn't be so petty."

Oh, you wouldn't?

Jamie brushes his hand over his slicked-back hair. "Dad, how could you not tell me? Or Kat?"

"I insisted that it remained between your father and myself," Angela asserts. "And I couldn't run the risk of having our new au pair quit within the week, not after the last few summers. That would be evidence enough that the stability of our family was compromised. And Nico's competitors would outlandishly brand him as having an unstable foundation at home that would only bleed into his business."

I stuff my arms across my chest and trail my focus to the vines at my side. Trying to decipher what was true and what was pretend this summer would only leave me with a throbbing headache.

"We asked them to meet us here," Nick states, causing Jamie's head to snap up.

"Quoi?" Jamie asks. "Them as in . . . How do you know who they are?"

Nick explains that after no reputation-tarnishing news, his competitors dropped the investigator's services. But the spy contacted him, requesting a private deal in return for their silence on any details they may uncover now or in the future. It's like preemptive blackmail.

"Dad," Jamie argues. "I know you're trying to protect us, but if those competing firms find out you made a deal under the table, they'll accuse you of corruption. And whoever the investigator is, what if he takes this all back as evidence that you paid to save your name. He could be testing you."

I watch Angela lifting her long nose to the sky. Her height gives an advantage of peering around the vines for the expected detective.

And here I was thinking this whole summer that Angela was investigating me. But this reveal does confirm that I indeed wasn't hallucinating at seeing cameras following my almost every move this summer. Whichever competing company hired the spy on the Chessleys must've been desperate to find some dirt since they felt the need to tail the au pair too.

Nick goes on. "Whoever it is, I couldn't give a rat's ass if this is all a test. So what, then I'll be slandered for protecting my family from outlandish abuses. And if our partners have a problem with that, they know the door. At least I'll go down the honorable way."

"Trust me," someone says in a heavy French accent. Full branches block his face, but a particular cologne reaches my nose. No. "If this deal promises any good, I'll make sure the Chessleys are seen as angels."

Damien rounds the corner at the end of the row. Jamie instantly clenches his fists. A gasp shoots through Angela, and a shudder reverberates down my spine.

The olive skin and thick eyelashes that once lured me in are no longer charming. Instead, I see him for who he truly is: a slimeball.

This was just another well-paying gig to him. As if he's not already swimming in dough. Well, ka-friggin'-ching.

"Je sais, Monsieur Chessley, that you are sure to make a reasonable offer." Damien presses his fingertips together.

"How much do you want?" Nick asks.

"No more than we agreed," Angela reminds her husband.

Jamie shakes his head, trying to convince his father to take another route. But Nick has made up his mind.

My tongue is sour from the last sip of bubbly I'd taken only ten minutes ago. I harden my stare on Damien, the Frenchman who entranced me with his devilish charm and suave manners. I move my gaze to Jamie.

Anger flushes through me. His betrayal of trust, pretending to be Damien in all those letters, fogs up my brain.

While Damien and Nick haggle, Angela taps my forearm.

"You're not off the hook yet, Kat," she whispers in my ear and lifts up the most recent copy of *Conseils*.

"Where did you get that?" I ask.

Jamie's gaze wanders from the negotiations to us.

"Not a word is to be written about this family or this investigation. Est-ce clair?"

"What makes you think I'd wr—"

Angela flicks to the page displaying a wide shot of Jamie's chateau.

"Seeing that she's having you do things like this." She smacks the page titled "Les nouveaux propriétaires."

Jamie's jaw drops as his eyes lock on the photo.

"Jamie," my voice croaks. My head is spinning. "I didn't . . . I promise I didn't . . ."

"Didn't what?" Angela presses.

Nick and Damien pause the negotiations at Angela's raised voice. Jamie lets out a heavy exhale, wiping his hand across his face.

"Merde. Cat's outta the bag now, isn't it," he grumbles.

"Quoi? Did *you* buy that dump?" Damien asks, pointing to the article.

"Of course he didn't," Nick assures, but Jamie's cold silence suggests otherwise.

Angela's raised brow matches Nick's.

"Why are you so surprised?" Jamie asks his mother.

"Your name isn't in here." Angela holds up the magazine. Instantly, Jamie's fiery eyes soften toward mine.

"Now," Damien says, wagging his finger like someone made a fascinating point. "*That* sounds like a good deal."

"What do you mean?" Nick asks.

"Money is nice, but property, that's something worth fighting for. And I got a nice look at it the other night. Charming place. Jamie, Kat, don't you agree?" A devilish grin plays on Damien's lips. My eyes widen, and my palms go clammy. There *was* a photographer that night Jamie and I kissed. And it was Damien!

Before Angela presses on his snide comment, Damien clasps his hands behind his back, taking a step toward Jamie. "I'll take it for a hundred euros."

Jamie paid eight hundred times that. Ten years of savings, gone.

"It's not for sale," Jamie says, taking a step closer to Damien. Their heights are nearly identical.

Damien shrugs. I want to tell him to wipe the smug smirk off his face.

Cracking his knuckles, Damien sighs. "Suit yourself. But I'm afraid that's my last and final offer."

Jamie curses at Damien a few times.

"Jamie, no," I press. "You can't sell the chateau." Jamie looks at me, holding me in his gaze for a few seconds.

Angela examines the article's photographs of the chateau. Tears well above her lower lash line. "Pourquoi as-tu gardé ça secret, Jamie?"

Jamie runs his hands through his hair, loosening the low bun.

"I'm waiting," Damien says impatiently.

"Jamie, you don't have to do this," Nick urges.

Exhaling slowly, dejection lingers in Jamie's voice as he says, "You know what's at stake if I don't. You've spent half your life going for this Netherlands deal. I won't let him take that away from you."

Jamie eyes a proud Damien.

"He'll ruin everything you've worked for. And it's not just your reputation and mine. It'll be on Manon, Josie, and Milo when they're grown. The Chessley name won't be worth shit."

Nick sighs, but Jamie points at the magazine in Angela's firm grip.

"I know what you want to say about that. That it was a crap choice, and I threw my savings away. I know you want to say it."

Flaring his nostrils, Nick protests. "No, I don't."

"Were you ever going to tell us?" Angela interjects, her eyes softening in a way I haven't seen all summer.

"Does it matter now?" Jamie turns his palms up. "I know what you'd have said if I told you right from the start. You know what you'd have said."

Nick steps closer to Jamie. "We just don't want to see you making mistakes."

Jamie scoffs and shakes his head. "My fucking intuition doesn't make mistakes, all right? And screw it, while we're on it, you know what else?" His voice is fiery and getting louder with every word. "You don't have to like the choices I make, but that's the point. The fallacy is believing you ever had control over my life. Yes of course you want the best for your kids, but can you try and fathom the idea that what's best for us might not be what you had in mind?"

Simultaneously, Nick's and Angela's shoulders sink. Angela mutters to herself, "How did our family become so broken? Suis-je vraiment un échec d'une mère?"

Even with my gripes against her, seeing Angela so afraid that she might've corroded her own family relationships makes my heart sink.

Jamie calms himself. Turning to Damien, he raises his hand, waiting for Damien to shake it.

"It's a deal. I'll have the key to you tomorrow," Jamie says without a drop of emotion.

"Bon choix." Damien's lips curl into a devious smile.

"Jamie," I mumble. His eyes are somber.

Damien walks closer to me. "I should have asked for you too," he says, leaning in closer than I'd ever like him to be. "Gift wrapped." He winks.

Angela's arm comes out of nowhere and hurls a stinging slap across Damien's cheek.

"Agh," he cries, rubbing the spot. When he removes his hand, a throbbing red palm shape paints his skin.

Angela throws her scarf over her neck and broadens her shoulders, stepping beside me. "Quitte cette maison tout de suite," she tells Damien in a tone so deep, it makes my gut spin. "Et ne reviens pas. Jamais."

"I'd do what she says and get the hell out of here," I say firmly.

Damien still can't help himself, shooting us a leery smile before sauntering out of the vineyard. Not four seconds of silence pass before Howie's voice booms again from the party.

Hands on his hips, Jamie sighs, tilting his head toward the sky. Angela presses two fingers to her lips in trepidation, hesitating to reach for her son's arm. I sneak a glance at the chateau article in the newest *Conseils* that Solange had written.

Howie's voice bellows through the speakers across the lawn once more, inviting guests to the stage area for the Young Soarers reveal. Flooded with frustration, betrayal, and some guilt of my own, I hurry myself back and try to soak in the moment without my worries berating my brain.

Was Jamie putting on a show for the investigator? Is that why he was so nice to me? So caring? Was he planning on using the letters as proof of "good character"? The ideas running through my head are relentless, but they lack validity. No matter the circumstance, I'm not going to let this summer's mess ruin something I've been working toward for a decade. The lies and secrets of the past few months would suffocate me if I try to digest them now.

Emi finds me in the crowd and wraps her hand around mine. "Here we go," she says with a big smile.

Manon, Milo, and Josie gather at my right, noshing on a plate full of raspberry, white chocolate, and blueberry macarons.

Howie stands proudly on the stone patio "stage." Fifteen blue, white, and red balloons float beside him. His voice rings out through the microphone. "I would like to ask all of our candidates to gather at the front."

Emi pats me on my back as I nudge my way from the rear of the crowd until I'm side by side with thirty-four other hopefuls. I wonder if they've been as obsessed as I've been for too many years to be proud of.

Howie disperses a sealed notecard with our names labeled on the front. He instructs us not to open them until his signal.

"Our advisory board has deliberated for many hours and would like to thank each of our finalists for the outpouring of effort. If we could induct you all, we would."

I see Jamie approach the crowd in the corner of my eye.

"On my go," Howie continues. "You will open your cards together. Is everyone ready?"

A few murmurs ripple around our group.

"Everyone else, are you ready?" Howie bellows. Whistles and claps return his question. "All right, all right. Freya," he says to a young woman on the switchboard. "Can we dim the lights?"

When the crowd has settled, Howie begins his countdown.

"Three . . ." His pauses draw out a lengthy tenure. "Two . . ."

Hurry up!

"One!"

Tape tears ripple around me, followed by excited gasps, unfiltered yelps, and dejected sighs. The smile on my face doesn't move an inch as I read my card. My stomach drops.

"We regret to inform you . . ."

This can't be right.

I did everything. I got the grades, the internships, the references. I flew to friggin' France to au pair for one of Europe's most elite families. Launched a damn travel magazine. Became buddy-buddy with Howie Gupta.

How did this happen?

"Ladies and gentlemen, may I introduce Continental Air's twenty-fifth class of Young Soarers!"

The last of the confetti cannons explode in tandem with the spotlights radiating every inch of the patio. I watch fifteen qualified new graduates take their place on stage while the crowd roars with applause and cheers. This time, the tears stream out, and I don't bother to shove them back in. I pick up the bottom of my dirt-soaked dress, high-tailing it into the manor. My vision's completely blurred by the salty droplets.

I hear my name called behind me more than once and by a smattering of voices, but at this point, it doesn't matter. My feet pull me to the familiar and a wave of chlorine invades my stuffy nostrils. Dropping to the cement floor, I dunk my feet, heels and all, straight into the pool.

The reflection ripples across the surface. A young woman stares back. She stands confidently, with her head held high and her shoulders back, her sun-kissed skin complemented nicely by the champagne sequins glittering on the gown she wears.

She's not the same person who stepped off the red-eye from Boston's Logan airport. *She* wouldn't have been so self-assured or relaxed in a dress like this.

I catch my breath as my sobs subsist. A door behind me creaks open. I'm torn on whether I actually need human support or if I've expended all the words I can speak tonight. Estelle takes a seat beside me, following my lead and thrusting her tie-dye sandals into the water. She tugs my shoulder to hers, and we rest our heads on each other's, drinking in the needed calm until someone else appears in the doorway.

Mom.

CHAPTER TWENTY-NINE

I haven't cried as much as I did last night since my parents divorced when I was ten. All the makeup in the world won't hide the residual raw nose and puffy eyes.

And as much as I'd rather see Jamie stick his head in twenty feet of cow manure for feigning Damien's letters and lying to me all summer, *I'd* be lying if I said it wouldn't bug me to leave here with him thinking the worst of me—that I'd considered selling him out. Still, he's not off the hook yet. Why *did* he continue with the letters for so long? Cheap entertainment? No, I know his character isn't *that* shitty. He's not Damien. Regardless, Jamie's certainly no Prince Charming. And that kiss? To me, it was magic. But for him, was it just as special?

For one of the first times yet, I'm grateful to Angela for dissolving my remaining au pair duties to be with Mom for the rest of the week. I'm still raw after last night's party. When I get to her room at the Monte Carlo Marriott, Mom swings open the door. Her face is as Mom-like as ever. Her fluffy brown hair layered at the shoulders. The rosy Calvin Klein perfume spritzed from the tip of her Lands' End tee to the bottom of her khaki capris. She pulls me in for a bear hug, pressing the back of my head into her shoulder as I let loose a howling cry.

We sit out on the balcony, and she listens to my outpouring of details from the summer. I omit some of the steamy moments between Jamie and me, alluding to a fortified connection now broken. It's new territory for me to discuss romantic inklings with Mom. But the *c'est la vie* mantra has truly wedged itself into my life.

I sprinkle in the latest events. For starters, I've already initiated the Plan B I never anticipated needing: the MBA program at my undergrad alma mater. It'd check the next box and give me some time to reevaluate career next steps.

And I won't have to worry about running into Jamie again. Apparently, after he surrendered the chateau to Damien, he agreed to join Nick as a full-time partner in Chessley Enterprises as they expand into the American real estate market. They'll be in morning-to-evening meetings all week. I doubt I'll see him before my departing flight in a few days.

I mull over countless ruminations. Would things be different if I had stuck to my guns and refused to write the fussy, intrusive chateau article in *Conseils*? Or maybe if I'd been a bit more vigilant with Damien? Maybe if I'd seen him as the dirtbag who just wanted to get some action of his own *and* cast me as the Chessleys' sleazy nanny, tainting their family name. If I could've seen through the spell, then *I* could've been the one to out *him* as a seedy private detective willing to blackmail anyone to get his way.

When I've cried out all the tears left in my body, I blow my nose and give Mom the chance to say something.

"Kat, hon. This isn't the end," Mom says, patting my knee.

Really? Because nothing has gone to plan this summer. Not Damien. Not *Conseils*. And most definitely not Young Soarers.

"You're a smart cookie. So what if the Young Soarers said no to you? A thousand other companies are out there and will say yes."

I shake my head and peer over the balcony at the sparkling blue sea.

"I'm just sick of it. I'm absolutely fucking sick of trying to impress the fuck out of people just to end up at rock fucking bottom."

"You can't be perfect all the time."

"Yeah? Doesn't feel like that," I mumble, shooting her a look.

"Did I ever give you that impression?"

I close my eyelids and stand at the railing, scraping my fingers across the polished cream stone. "Whenever I talk about any career outside the realm of school or even Young Soarers, you don't say anything. How the hell am I supposed to read that?" My voice starts to raise, but I bring it back down.

Mom inhales deeply and stands next to me. "I'm sorry it came across that way. I thought it's what you wanted. What you always talked about."

"Well, I knew you couldn't exactly give a thumbs-up to anything else if it didn't have the same weekly paycheck as the Soarers."

Mom sighs, bowing her head.

After my parents' divorce, Mom raised me on her own. I suppose prudence hardwired itself into her brain, and it vicariously trickled down, training me to see the illusory security of living paycheck to paycheck.

"It'd be so easy for me to blame you and everyone else. All the teachers, guidance counselors, even my friends. Part of me wants to," I admit, my throat tightening. I exhale and look out at the ocean. "But it wouldn't be fair. It's no one's fault, really. We all fell under the same spell. I guess it's just part of life, to figure out what identity you really want and give up the rest that doesn't fit." Which means I have to give myself some grace to move in a new direction.

Before I even hit puberty, and without consciously realizing, I'd fooled myself into thinking I'd be securing my future by assuming someone else's approach to life: a gig in corporate America. It may be their first step, but it doesn't have to be mine. It's the greatest paradox. A job that dangles "security" over my head, yet keeps me barricaded from my true calling. So the question remains, am I willing to crack the cocoon and spread my wings?

"I want you to be happy," Mom adds, wrapping her hand around my waist. "We all have different lives to live. It's taken me more than a few decades to realize that."

"And that I'm gonna do things differently than you would," I affirm.

She sucks in a breath and nods. I rest my head on her shoulder, gazing at the harbor. The headache that was my future starts to wane, and I hug her tightly.

"You are one special woman, Kat. And I'm proud to call you my daughter. Live life for you. Not for me. Not for anyone else," she says gingerly, rubbing my back.

When we pull away from each other, both of us have freshly moist eyes.

"Did you finish that MBA application yet?"

My shoulders slump. "No."

"Good. Delete it. It's obviously keeping you from something more important to you."

I pull her in for another hug and whisper my thanks.

— ✳ — ✳ — ✳ —

WE WRAP UP our breakfast on the patio before heading to Èze. I take Mom up and around nearly every café and shop in the village in her hunt for souvenir magnets. We stop at the Cave where Emi is just about to head out the door. I wave and call out her name.

Emi skips to meet us on the cobblestone street, tugging the strap of a packed canvas tote bag on her shoulder.

"You must be Maman McLauren," Emi says to Mom, giving her a double bise on the cheeks.

Mom giggles and concedes.

"See, Mom, you're getting Frencher by the minute," I joke before nodding to Emi, who's wearing a modest cardigan and pencil skirt. "Où vas-tu?"

"I'm going to school." Emi winks and straightens her spine, barely suppressing the enormous grin sneaking onto her face. "*Les enfants* aren't going to teach themselves," she quips.

Emi leans in closer, dropping her voice to just above a whisper.

"Apparemment, ma mère says," she looks over at Marie helping a customer inside the wine shop, "Jamie's quitting the Vigne for good. He came in for his last pickup this morning. So he really is a full-time Chessley Enterprise employee. I never thought I'd see it happen."

"Do Angela and Nick know about his time at the Vigne now?"

"Je ne sais pas." Emi shrugs. "They aren't speaking."

"How's that? Aren't he and Nick partners now?"

"Maybe so. But Jamie won't talk about anything if it's not the Chessley business. He won't even answer ma mère's questions. Says it's not worth bringing up," Emi explains.

Mom tilts her head. "I'd probably avoid it too if I just left a Michelin kitchen and gave up my renovated chateau. Such a shame. He's got a good heart, that one," she says. "Well at least he won't have to deal with those property taxes, probably exorbitant given its age."

I stuff my arms across my chest and fixate on her first point. "He's no saint," I grumble.

"I didn't say he was."

"Did you not listen to any of what I told you about the letters?"

"Of course. But trust me, Kat. No man nowadays would commit to writing a love letter every week if he didn't actually care. And nothing in relationships is ever black and white."

I roll my eyes. "They weren't love letters. They weren't real."

"They read like they were," Emi butts in.

"Besides, I knew he was a good one ever since he started sending me—" Mom stops herself, but I insist that she continues. "Oh well.

He asked me not to tell because you were so nervous about it at the beginning. Jamie's been sending me every copy of the *Conseils*—is that how you say it? Probably cost him a fortune to ship those overseas every week."

My mouth gapes open, and Emi presses a hand to her chest.

"Oh, comme c'est précieux."

"His intentions with you were in the right place. Just the execution . . ." Mom shrugs and holds her palm out. "But you know. Men."

"Hommes," Emi says at the same time.

Leaving Emi to get on her way, Mom and I tick off the places we still need to stop by on our tour: my favorite crêperie in Nice, the Cours Saleya market, and a nature walk on the north end of Èze. As much as I try to ground myself in the moment, Jamie lingers in my mind all the way into the late afternoon when I retreat to the Chessley villa to pack my bags while Mom takes her jet-lagged cat nap. There's a hollowness in my stomach as I take my clothes out of the boudoir drawers and fill my suitcase once again.

Buzz. Buzz. Buzz.

It's a text from Angela.

Meet me at L'atelier Lavergne. Her company's fashion studio in Nice.

—≫ — ≫ — ≫

IT'S BEEN ALMOST three months since I stepped foot onto French soil and the first time I've walked within half a mile of Angela's office. Only a few hundred yards from the coastline, it's situated on a rather calm pedestrian-only street, seconds away from the hustle and bustle of beach-going traffic. The road boasts a refined chic feel. Smoothed obsidian ground tiles, jet-black lampposts, creaseless awnings overhanging shop windows. While Angela's workshop is on the second floor, the storefront before me on the street is one of the Lavergne Designs boutiques. Chanel and Louis Vuitton are only a couple of her elite neighbors. Inside, the air conditioning cools the back sweat forming from the August heat. I tug my backpack over my shoulder, striding past clothing racks specially curated to hang only a few complete outfits. Fine satin, immaculate threadwork, and clean lines are Angela's hallmarks.

An assistant greets me and takes me upstairs to an office space in complete disarray. The hot, sticky summer air sweeps through the space. On one side of the room, design sketches coat the knotty hardwoods.

On the other is an immaculately neat desk and a wide-open window where Angela stands in a stretchy cobalt dress, her striking auburn hair frizzy and missing its regular shine and her makeup nearly melting off her face. I've never seen her so disheveled.

When she turns around and sees me, the assistant has already fled. Then, Angela Lavergne does one thing I've rarely seen her do, let alone in my presence. She laughs.

"Oh, Kat. Quel été nous avons eu."

I lean my chest back, unsure of how to respond.

"Definitely not the summer I expected," I say, taking the seat she gestures to.

Angela sits as well in the chair beside me. She wipes the gleaming sweat off her upper lip with a silk handkerchief. "I want you to know I appreciate everything you've done to support our family this summer. And I apologize if my manner toward you was rather"—she bobs her head side to side—"coarse."

I shrug and sigh. "C'est bon. You were just trying to protect your family, to keep it intact."

"I assumed, wrongly, that if you and Jamie got close, I'd never see him again, that he'd throw away his responsibilities to the family. But the truth is, in the past few months, I've seen more of my son than I have in three years. And he's never looked happier," she admits with a pleased smile. "I have nothing against you," Angela emphasizes.

"In fact, I'm in awe of your courage, of all the responsibilities you've assumed this summer. You executed each with such gravitas, and I respect people like that."

My cheeks go a touch red, and I can't help the burgeoning smile spreading over my face.

Is this really Angela Lavergne speaking?

"And I'm sorry about the Young Soarers program. I'll have you know I had a long conversation with Howie. As you Américains say, I let him have it." She clicks her tongue and shakes her head. "He should have known that knowing him personally would've disqualified your admission."

Again, is this Angela Lavergne?

"Merci, Angela. This means a lot to me. Really. And I hope everything turns out okay with your family after that whole mess with Damien."

A gentle smile tugs at her lips, her lipstick cracking.

"That's another reason why I asked you here," Angela says, crossing her arms. "That Damien might think he can get away with his little stunt, but I won't have it. My Jamie will not lose everything he's worked for."

Her softening eyes and maternal protectiveness warms my heart. Someone shuffles in behind the sitting area. The corresponding voice pipes in with, "Oui. He's hurt too many people already."

I turn around to see Vivian standing tall and composed. Her face is stern. She takes a seat next to Angela and me.

"Why? What else did he do?" I ask her.

Vivian toys with the handle of her faux snakeskin purse. "Remember the guy I told you and Emi about in Saint-Tropez?"

"The . . . connard?" I quickly glance at Angela, but she's not bothered by my French cursing. Given her eyebrow raise and nod, I'd say she's actually impressed.

"Oui," Vivian confirms. "C'était Damien."

"What?" I scrunch my brow.

Funny. Jamie painted himself as some womanizing half-drunk jackass to shield his entrepreneurial pursuits from his parents, but it's been Damien all along who qualifies for such a title.

All the befuddling assumptions I'd made about Jamie this summer have turned out so outlandishly off base. Relief and hope course through me, but it evaporates in seconds. Yeah, like *he and I* have a future.

Angela stands up from her chair. "Now, let's get to work."

We discuss the various methods of getting Damien to willingly or forcibly forfeit the chateau back to Jamie. Some approaches are softer than others. With Angela's wealth of knowledge in the French business world, she hatches a well thought through plan. I'm guessing she's been drumming this up all day, given the legal statutes she recites by memory and the key piece of information that would send Damien running for the Alps if we go public with it.

"Jamie deserves that chateau," Angela says, her lip quivering. "C'est son rêve. And he's worked so hard for it." She tosses her head side to side. "Je ne peux toujours pas y croire."

"Can't believe what, Angela?" I ask, tilting my head.

"That he's been working at that restaurant in town all these summers."

"You know?"

"He just told us this week," Vivian says.

Angela sighs. "I should've known. He spent more time in the kitchen than his playroom as a toddler." She straightens her spine. "My son deserves what he's sacrificed for. Are we all set on the plan?"

Vivian and I share a smile.

"Bien," Angela says with an encouraging clap. "Faisons-le."

CHAPTER THIRTY

*H*e's more than twenty minutes late. From what little I actually know of him, this only reads as typical Damien. I've asked him to meet me at La Jolie Plage beach bar in Cannes, west of Nice and bordering Saint-Tropez. Little does he know, I brought Vivian too. She takes a seat a few stools down and wears a wide-brimmed sun hat that covers most of her face.

Damien had given me a follow on Instagram after the other night's party, invalidating what the letters indicated about him keeping off social media. Makes sense why nothing came back when I searched for Damien de Dandeneau, given that this one features Dam Emmanuel. I scrolled through his timeline, finding numerous pics of him chugging Sidecars and Singapore Slings and clinging to half-naked women at this bar alone.

There I was for nearly two months thinking a distance of 500 miles separated us. Huh. More like fifteen. And that was when he or one of his cronies weren't spying on us for dirt on the Chessleys. It gives me the creeps, and now, so does his voice and gelled-back hair, which he undoubtedly applied in excess today.

"Kat!" Damien waves from across the packed beach bar. A leftover plate of oysters sits in a tub of dirty dishes behind the counter. But it does a fantastic job of covering up his suffocating cologne. He goes in for a double bise, and I hold my hand up.

"Non, merci," I say, leaning back.

He bounces his wrist on the counter and clicks his tongue. The pounding club music is not at all my cup of tea, especially not in broad daylight.

"Kat, I hope we can be friends. Why else did you ask me to come here, eh?"

"Well, I want to see if you have any intention of actually keeping the chateau you stole—I mean bought."

Damien orders a rum and coke and presses his back against the counter's rim.

"I mean this with complete respect. But why do you care?" he asks.

"Because, he doesn't deserve this."

"Jamie." Damien scoffs and tosses in an eye roll. "Don't tell me you're in *love* with him."

"I'm not telling you anything." I squint at him. "*You* don't deserve to know."

Damien slugs his drink. "Well I'm not giving it back."

"Okay." My voice lightens to an inquisitive tone. "Just out of curiosity, are you planning on selling or keeping it?"

He shrugs, adjusting his Rolex. "Don't know yet. Pourquoi?"

I stir the lime in my seltzer. "Oh, it's just impressive."

Damien takes another long sip and wrinkles his brow at me.

"I can only imagine how hard it'd be to sell it again. Took fifteen years for the last owners to get someone like Jamie to make an offer," I add. "I guess if you want to speed up the process, you can finish up the renovations if you're willing to dish out a good chunk of change."

Damien furrows his brow as he scans the ground before puffing up his chest. "Well maybe I'll just keep it then," he says smugly.

"That's really honorable too. Willing to pay those added historic site taxes to the town."

Thank you, Angela, for the intel.

It's obviously the first time Damien's hearing about this, given his deer-in-the-headlights, unblinking reaction. I hold back my grin.

"I see what you're trying to do," Damien says.

"Oh?" I tilt my head and take a sip of water.

He presses his glass on the counter, the condensation dribbling down the sides. "It's not gonna work."

"Well, that's too bad. But I guess that leaves us with our only other option."

"Quoi?"

I square my torso toward his. "Have you ever taken a tour of the Lavergne vineyard? The grounds manager is a real stickler for producing the best crop." I don't give him time to answer. "And apparently, he's adamant about keeping rodents out of the grapevines." My voice goes up a few playful octaves. "Did you know he even keeps little cameras hidden in every row to see if they turn up again?"

Damien's face goes pale. A smirk plays across my face.

None of us had known this vital clue before. The vineyard manager had let it slip in his latest conversation with Angela just days after the party when he was assessing the latest footage and watched the group of us in a hushed quarrel between the grapevine trellises.

"We could erase the recording. Your demeanor was rather impolite and not very businessman-like. All that blackmail." I slowly stir my seltzer with the straw. "Or maybe la police would like to see it too, hmm?"

Damien finishes his drink and curses to himself.

"C'est de la merde. It's not worth it." Fishing for something in his pocket, he whacks an aluminum key on the counter in front of me. "He can have it. But only if you all promise not to release that footage, okay?"

I lift my brows. Did that really just work?

Because Angela already gave her approval for me to make the deal on her behalf, I nod and say, "Bien."

Damien's anxious self-concern evaporates quickly, as he wipes his palms on his linen pants. "I like seeing you like this," he says smugly, leaning on the counter space in front of me. "I always thought your eyes were blue?"

Noted. The man before me most definitely didn't write a single letter this summer.

Damien can't help but give me one last flirtatious grin and asks me to enjoy dinner with him this evening. Figuring he can tempt me with steak at the Ritz, he's close to dangling his investigative service paycheck in my face.

"Thank you very much. But I'd rather not regurgitate my mushroom risotto." I scrunch my nose into a forced smile and take the key. Turning to my right, I call out, "Vivian? Ready?"

Stupor fills Damien's eyes as he and I watch Vivian strut toward us looking absolutely glowing in her lacy white sundress.

"More than ready," Vivian concedes and gives a forced grin to Damien, whose cheeks are hollowed out in embarrassment. He rushes away. Looking over our shoulders just before the exit, we watch Damien bash right into a waiter who had zipped behind him carrying a plate of escargots. The cooked snails fall into his button-up shirt, staining his clothes and chest in garlicky slug juice.

Vivian and I interlock elbows and leave Damien to clean up his mess in the sea of partiers.

CHAPTER THIRTY-ONE

*V*ivian and I go our separate ways in downtown Nice when we return from La Jolie Plage. She has a picnic date with a woman she met in Saint-Tropez. And I've got to get a move on to the Chessley villa.

On the bus back to Èze, I twirl the metal key as giddily as a kid in a candy shop, and rest my head on the window. I know I'll miss it. I hug my backpack tight and pull out my journal, reminiscing on the documented memories via bullet points, ticket stubs, and polaroids. The transfixing coast kissing the shoreline. Laughing uncontrollably as Emi teaches me the French "R." Helping Josie pick out her outfit while Milo and Manon wrestle downstairs. Writing and filming for *Conseils*. Sharing chance luxurious moments with Jamie.

My phone dings, and I'm reminded that I completely forgot to message Angela that our "squash Damien" plan had worked. When I lift my phone, it reveals missed calls and piles of texts from Angela, Estelle, and Jamie.

My phone must have lost connection passing through the mountainous highways from Antibes.

Estelle's latest all-caps message doesn't startle me at first. It's how she types all of her texts. But after reading it in entirety, I promptly ask the bus driver to let me off here at the Saint-Jean-Cap-Ferrat peninsula, knowing he'll tell me it's not on this line.

"We're already here though!" I want to scream. But I just stick with the excessive pleading until he pumps the brakes, much to his and the other passengers' annoyance.

I call Estelle, cursing myself until she answers on the last ring and maneuvering down the terra-cotta sidewalk amid blood-orange and turquoise buildings sandwiched together.

"Estelle!" I dodge hanging flowerpots as I navigate through a winding seaside street. In the distance, Èze's mountains cast dominant shadows over this snug harbor. Strange how I've watched this peninsula through almost every sunrise and sunset up at the villa, but this is the first time I'm actually seeing it from ground level. "Which boat are they?" I say into the phone, stretching my neck toward the shipyard lined with yachts, sailboats, and ferries.

Tourists coming and going without a sense of direction dwell at the dock's entrance, where cafés and pizza places have set up shop, adding to the foot traffic.

"We're at the end of the dock. A long sailboat with a navy-blue stripe. *Le joug* is its name," Estelle chimes back. Wind chops through our connection, even though we're less than 500 feet apart. But I spot them and scurry my way through hordes of people.

Estelle explains that Nick and Jamie were called to a can't-miss goodwill trip to meet and greet the owners of an Italian hotel franchise they just acquired. They're headed to Genoa to start their four-week, seven-city journey across the neighboring country.

And I have to see Jamie. I have to thank him. For championing my dreams even when I didn't. For connecting me to Lottie at the party. For actually giving a damn. He's been so adamant that even if he couldn't have his dream, that I have mine. But that's not how this works. He's just as worthy of his goals too. I can't let him tie his joy to my journey.

That's his to own.

So I *have* to give him the key he's owed. It's up to him what he'll do with it.

"Pardon," I grunt, almost taking a nosedive into the bay as I avoid a woman rolling her suitcase across my open-toed shoe.

"Kat!" Milo runs toward me. I tousle his blond hair growing back to the moppy style he had when I first met him. Lifting him up in a mama-bear hug, I carry him over to the group of Chessleys giving stiff shoulder pats.

Jamie turns around and pulls his sunglasses off, his eyes glued to mine. He's pulled his hair into one of those tight low buns and wears a white polo shirt and slim black plaid trousers.

"You didn't answer," he says softly.

"No connection," I respond, putting Milo down but never breaking my gaze with Jamie.

From inside the yacht bobbing next to us, someone shouts a hello.

"Good old Howie's captaining us to Italy," Jamie explains.

"You're really going?" I examine the two-story ship.

Jamie's mouth gapes open, while Angela beats him to the punch.

"He insists that he won't have it any other way," she declares.

"Well I don't really have any other choice," Jamie says begrudgingly.

Angela and Nick share a concerned glance. I lock eyes with Angela, who's visage is filled with anxious hope. I'm about to pull the key out of my bag when Howie honks the horn from the control room on the top deck and gives a wave.

"And that's our cue," Jamie says, giving his younger siblings quick hugs, then hoisting his bags onto the boat, all while trying to mask those melancholy green eyes.

"Wait," I say, hopping up the yacht steps and grasping his forearm. "Before you go. Tell me the truth. Do you honestly believe if you do this, that you'll have no regrets?"

Milo, Josie, and Manon have followed me, but they race up to the second floor to try on PFDs.

"I'll never regret helping my family," Jamie says, looking at his parents standing on the dock.

Angela presses a hand to her cheek.

"If you had the chance to get it back, would you?" I ask.

"I'm full out of chances, Kat."

I swing my bag around my torso. "What if I said you had one more?"

Jamie's expression trades between intrigue and confusion.

Pulling a fist out of my backpack, I unravel my fingers, letting the silver key glisten in the sun. Angela covers her mouth, muffling her gasp.

"You did it," she whispers from the dock.

Jamie points to the key but steps back. "Where did you get that? How did . . .?"

I take two steps closer to him, my palm still outstretched. "You deserve the chance to give it a chance."

Angela, Nick, and Estelle watch his reaction like hawks. Manon listens in, leaning over the sundeck's railing.

Jamie hovers his hand over the key in mine but takes my fingers and reshapes his fist.

"I can't."

A loud thump thuds behind us. Angela's face contorts as she drops Nick's suitcase on the dock's wooden planks.

"So that's it, eh? The universe brings you *une chance* and you're not going to take it?"

"Maman," Jamie starts. "I can't do that to Dad or the company. I can't just up and leave when they're counting on me to take it over."

"Your father can take care of his business. Tu es responsable de ta propre vie."

Jamie shakes his head. "I don't get it. How did you . . ." His eyes trail to the key still in my hand.

Angela and I share a quick smile.

"A story for another time," I say and hold my open palm toward Jamie again. "So?"

Jamie pulls back. Something between a laugh and a scoff tumbles out of my mouth.

"Yes or no. Make a choice, Jamie. You've been like this all summer."

He gives a snarky yet curious grin. "Like what?"

"Oh. Come on. Hot, cold, here, there. One second it's like you're my best friend, the next you can't wait to push me an arm's length away. For once, I wish you'd be a little decisive, if not about me then about this," I say, holding the key closer to him.

Encircling the boat, a family of seagulls caw, and a salty breeze sweeps across the harbor, sending the yacht bobbing left to right.

"That is if you care," I can't help but add.

Jamie shakes his head, ruffling his hand through his hair, loosening the low bun.

"You think I don't care? Kat, I've been crazy about you since the second I saw you. And sure, at first I was just trying to keep Mum from thinking there was something between us."

I sink into his emerald irises, butterflies racing through my stomach. The chitter-chatter over the docks has dulled as passersby shift their attention to us.

"I saw myself falling for you, and that bloody effin' terrified me. I just kept thinking, what if I mess it up like every other relationship in my life?" He pauses to look at his parents on the docks. Nick's arm is wrapped tightly around Angela's shoulder. Jamie returns his eyes to me. "Because who says I won't drive away the best person that's walked into my life."

My throat clenches, and tears pool above my lash line. A cheeky smile spreads under my nose. I take his hand as I say, "What happened to c'est la vie?"

Jamie lets out a soft laugh through his nose.

"Isn't giving it a go, into the unknown, better than the regret of never trying?"

We hold each other in our sights, until Howie honks the yacht horn again.

"Go on, kiss her already!" he hollers.

Smiles push through our cheeks as our lips meld together. The whistles and cheers spread from the immediate group to the travelers swarming the length of the dock, Nick and Angela included. My nerves can only take so much, and Jamie and I eventually separate, but lingering warmth courses through my body.

"Kat," Jamie says, unraveling my fist and clasping the key. "Merci."

"I expect the Friends and Family discount," Nick shouts with a pleased smile.

"You're really all right with this?"

Angela, Nick, and Estelle join us on the yacht.

"Of course. We want you to. After all, you are a Lavergne . . . and a Chessley," Angela says, softly clasping Jamie's forearm. "Tu es un entrepreneur. And we wouldn't change one thing about it. We never wanted you to throw your life away, all that ambition inside you. But it's clear you wouldn't do that with this chateau."

"Roger that, son," Nick affirms. "I for one couldn't live with myself if I were responsible for stifling my son's endeavors. We've all got our own legacies to leave."

"Then I'll make sure to put some pints on ice in your room, Dad."

Jamie pulls his mom and dad in for the deepest hug the three of them have probably ever shared. Estelle pats me on the back, sharing in my delight.

Howie thumps down the spiral stairs at the rear of the boat and requests me on board for a moment. Jamie nudges his head in his direction, and I give him a cheeky grin.

I take a seat on the cushioned benches toward the stern. Howie leans back.

"You," he says, wagging his finger. "You, Miss Kat. I haven't forgotten about you. Oh no."

He takes my hand and starts shaking it ferociously. My vision board snippet comes to life, and the blush sitting in my cheeks doesn't fade.

"I know Young Soarers didn't work out. And truthfully, had I known you would've been disqualified for your closeness to me, I wouldn't have been so encouraging. But you know how office politics go."

I twiddle my fingers. "It's all right. Really. There are other paths." A giddiness spurts within me as I consider options that I hadn't deigned to take seriously before this summer.

"That's what I wanted to talk to you about."

My head snaps up.

"You've proven yourself to be no faint heart when it comes to immense responsibility." He continues on listing my work on *Conseils* in tandem with au pairing for three kids. "With, let's be honest, assertive parents," he says in a hush, but I can feel Angela squinting at us. "All this to say, I'm well-acquainted with many of the Ritz-Carlton executives, and I'm sending your resume and my personal recommendation along to the recruitment team. They're hiring junior marketing analysts at their corporate headquarters, and given your academic experience, I'm certain they'll take you in a heartbeat."

My stomach tenses.

"Really?"

Howie uses ferocious hand gestures to explain the job duties, but my inner voice eventually drowns him out. It's definitely not what the Young Soarers would be doing. On paper, it's better. A five-year program that'll lead straight to a managerial role and a six-figure salary. Part of me thinks someone's about to give my elbow a pinch and I'll wake up at any moment. I look over my shoulder at Jamie, who gives a delighted smile. The face of someone who's about to charge full steam ahead on a dream. I bring my focus back to Howie.

Am I really going to say what I think I am?

CHAPTER THIRTY-TWO

*T*here's something bewitching about the salty sea air and
plentiful flora enveloping the Côte d'Azur. So enchanting
that it stirs me from the cat nap I committed to in the passenger seat. Sunshine cascades over every inch of my body as the wind
courses through my hair on each curvaceous turn we take along the
cliffside road.

"Ah," I sigh. "Feels good to be back."

It's nearing the end of May, meaning tourist season is just around
the corner, leaving a few weeks of relative calm to dwindle around the
streets from Èze to Marseille.

"Just make sure to look under the bed sheets," Jamie says, wearing
a smirk. "Baa baa."

"Ha-ha-haaaa." I tousle his free-flowing hair and stroke the back
of his neck. Jamie keeps one hand at twelve o'clock as we interlace our
fingers resting on my thigh. My Canon camera sits at the ready in my
lap.

A white rectangular sign points us toward Èze up the hill. Butterflies race through me as I drink in the pent-up anticipation. It's
been almost a year since I first arrived at the Chessley villa and since
Jamie started the chateau's renovations. After he regained ownership

last summer, he split his time between Èze—managing construction and preparing for the grand opening—and London—connecting with investors for the venture that sprouted from the initial endeavor. It turns out that sustainable tourism and property renovations caught his attention early on, prompting him to start Le Voyageur Durable. He's got his eye on a few worn-down cottages in Italy and Spain that he's hoping to acquire and polish up for property managers to run with the help of local chefs specializing in the regions' cuisines.

His parents, having never really dabbled in the tourism space, didn't have strong opinions for or against it. But that didn't stop them from booking a weekend stay for the grand opening even if their villa sits only a mile away.

Jamie's godfather, Howie, commended him for it too, saying it was the new wave of the industry, encouraging visitors to participate in preserving the local cultures and terrain. For the Èze chateau, that included solar panels, artisanal decorations, and partnerships with vineyards, perfumeries, and dairy farms that'll allow guests to participate in an afternoon of contribution.

Plus, the crowning name isn't too shabby.

Château de Rêves. Chateau of Dreams.

Rounding a curve, the Saint-Jean-Cap-Ferrat peninsula slides into view, and I prop myself over the side of the cherry-red door to record the dramatic perspective.

Less than a year into my master's at London Film School and the internship with Lottie at BBC, I'm one thousand percent certain it was the right choice to turn down the position Howie recommended me for at Ritz-Carlton. How do I know? Easy. If I was laboring away at Ritz-Carlton, I wouldn't have met Lottie's son, a VP at one of the largest London-based production studios specializing in documentaries. Now he's helping finance my own project: *La Joie d'Èze*. Outside the meticulously manicured ten-year corporate career plan, serendipity has a bit more room to run wild. Who would've thought? Some may call it spontaneity. I call it intuition. Plus, it's a boon to see the rest of the Chessley group for afternoon teas and movie nights at their dwelling in the Cambridge suburbs.

"Nous sommes arrivés," Jamie says, pulling the car into park at the base of the village.

We trek through the cobblestone streets, arm in arm, hitting up the supermarket to grab some food for our afternoon adventure. Later, we're headed to the first annual villa dinner of the summer, where I'll finally get to reunite with Emi in person so she can tell me how the school year finished. Hour-long phone calls every few weeks don't do the stories justice.

Jamie goes off collecting berries and cured meats while I mosey along the refrigerated aisles. I pick out a camembert rind, and goose-bumps crawl over my skin from the chilled air. A raspy, yet gentle voice calls my name. I turn my head and see Solange waving from the yogurt section.

The last time I saw her, I'd turned in my final article and footage roundup for *Conseils* before heading back to Boston in August, politely thanking her for the opportunity. But I still held a grudge for the unscrupulous tactics she wanted me to employ.

She's changed her fuchsia lipstick to a more approachable and flattering mauve, though still lacquered on in ten layers.

"Bonjour," I say as we greet each other with cheek kisses. "Comment ça va?"

"Bien, Kat. Et toi?"

"Bien." My smile is genuine.

"Quelle année," she exclaims.

What a year it's been indeed. We get to chatting about the goings-on in our lives, our undertakings, and our summer plans. She tells me her customer base has skyrocketed, even in the winter months. She partnered with local businesses that sponsored *Conseils* to offer discounted specialty packages only bookable through her travel agency.

The most popular pack économique includes a tasting at the Lavergne Winery, entrance to the lavender farm an hour north of Cannes, and a discount at a botanical cosmetics store in Èze.

"Are you still publishing the magazine?"

"I've had a few interns from the Université in Toulon take some assignments in the offseason. There's a large journalisme program. But you are always welcome to contribute, you know." Solange winks at me.

"I'd like that."

I'd be lying if I said I hadn't thought about *Conseils* this year. I do miss it. And Jamie's international ventures have inspired ideas I never knew had been floating in my subconscious, like how *Conseils* doesn't have to be isolated to the French Riviera.

Solange walks with me to the checkout counter and expresses her gratitude at least six more times. "If there is anything I can do to repay you," she says, "you let me know."

"You do not owe me anything. Really." My tone turns lighthearted. "But you wouldn't happen to know anyone with two Twice tickets they don't plan on using, do you?"

She tilts her head and points her finger in the air. "En fait, my niece was supposed to go next month with her daughter in Paris, but her summer camp begins the same week."

"Tu veux rire." I drop my jaw.

Solange shakes her head. "No joke."

I can't help but pull Solange in for a tight hug. We part ways with a plan to rendezvous for cafés au lait this week, and Jamie and I head out for the rest of our day's journey.

We cruise Èze's coastline. Only a smattering of beachgoers drink in the sunshine, leaving pristine stretches of sparkling sand uninhabited. We park in front of a swanky yet relaxed beach bar that reminds me of the one I visited in Saint-Tropez with Emi. But we take our grub and towels and make our way up the inclined street to the base of a steep trail. Spindly shrubs and fluffy squat trees shroud either side of the narrow path until we reach the flat granite landing. Before us on the horizon are miles of opaque waters punctuated only by outward juts in the verdant terrain. In front of steep mountain edges, vibrant dwellings and terra-cotta roofs occupy much of the coastline.

A gust of wind swirls around us, and Jamie takes a few steps toward the edge of the rock landing. Twenty feet below is an equally deep cove without much of a current. It's a popular place for cliff jumping. My heart's pace picks up, and I can hear it pounding in my chest as we strip to our bathing suits. Jamie nods and holds out his hand. I take it.

There's this French quote from Jacques-Yves Cousteau, oceanic adventurer:

"L'avenir est entre les mains de ceux qui explorent."

The future is in the hands of those who explore.

Now it's Jamie and I who stand at the helm of our ships, one hand on the wheel, another on the sails. Full steam ahead, not shackled to every treasure we'll collect or every memory we'll make. But trusting our inner compasses, our visions on the horizon. Finding joy in the journey itself. And every so often, we drop the anchor, purvey the waters, and dive right in.

Jamie and I share a quick glance. The excitement in his eyes matches the adrenaline coursing through my entire body. He gives my hand a squeeze.

We shout in unison, "Trois. Deux. Un!"

Our feet leap from the cliff. And we're airborne.

ACKNOWLEDGMENTS

We often hear the saying "It's the journey, not the destination." And in my most recent life experience, this has proven to be true. Cherishing each precious present moment in the here and now. And as of late, I feel that what makes the adventure so much more special is the company along for the ride.

With that, I wholeheartedly thank the special people in my life who have blessed my path. It's your kind words, unconditional love, earnest support, willingness to share a laugh or lend an ear that reminds me how fortunate I am to share moments and memories with you. Thank you for supporting my authenticity, my passions, and my evolving journey. Calling special thanks to Clara, Jill, Malthe, Mom, Dad, Aidan, Claire, Lara, Stephanie, and Jessie.

And thank you to the CamCat Books team for your outstanding support in bringing this book to life!

ABOUT THE AUTHOR

Maia Correll is a native Rhode Islander and Bryant University graduate, with degrees in International Business and Spanish. An avid traveler, cook, and yogi, she seeks adventure in all areas of life. When she's not involved in any of her hobbies, she can be found at the beach, on a hike, at the nearest metaphysical shop, or scouring Pinterest for recipes and DIYs. As an author and screenwriter, she's focused on empowering, inspiring, and entertaining, primarily within the realms of contemporary sci-fi/fantasy and commercial fiction for Middle Grade through Adult audiences.

If you enjoyed
Maia Correll's *Dare to Au Pair*,
please consider leaving a review
to help our authors.

And check out another great read from CamCat:
Haleigh Wenger's
Managing the Matthews.

CHAPTER ONE

Kell

*B*eing the manager for a trio of hot celebrity brothers sounds amazing until you're the one thing standing in the way of their sleep.

Between the three of them—Ash, Jonah, and Ryan—I don't get days off. Someone always ends up needing to be on set at 8 a.m. sharp, no matter the day. Never mind that wake-up calls are most definitely not in my job description.

Today, I have the unparalleled pleasure of knocking loudly on Ash Matthew's bedroom door, waiting outside of it for an appropriate amount of time, and then beating on the door some more. It's a blast. "Ashley! I know you're in there! You have a photoshoot in fifteen! Fifteen min-utes!"

There's not a single sound from inside his room.

When yelling doesn't work, I pull my cell phone from my purse and call him over and over and over. He doesn't answer. Instead, a banging sound comes from inside his bedroom, and the door swings open.

Ash looks me over through half-open eyes and then flops back onto the enormous California King in the center of his room. I toss my phone back into the bag on my arm and follow him in.

"I don't have work today," he says, his words obscured by the pillow he's planted his face into. His dark brown hair splays out to the sides, curling slightly at the ends. I tried to talk him into a haircut a few months ago, but it turns out he was right. Annoying, but right, that the longer hair suits him.

I put a hand on my hip. "You do have work."

Despite the text I received at 2 a.m. letting me know that he didn't think he'd make it in, I'm not letting Ash off this easily. As his manager, it's my job to keep on top of him about these kinds of things.

He grumbles something else unintelligible into his pillow. I sigh and lower myself to his bed, swaying slightly at the too-soft mattress underneath me. "You're contracted. The movie is almost done. Just promo and then you're off the hook for this one. And, come on, it wasn't that bad. From what I saw of it, there were some really funny scenes."

Ash lifts his head and glares at me, daring me to keep going with the lie. "I want out. I don't want to be the romance guy anymore. Not for movies like this."

"What if I promise to buy you pizza afterward?"

He scoffs. "Bribery doesn't work on me anymore. I can buy my own pizza."

I nudge his foot with my hand, but he swats at me. "It's not gonna happen. I'm not doing the photoshoot."

The dejection in his voice hits me, stalling me for a quick second. It sounds like he needs a vacation.

I'll have to check his calendar. Ash and I were friends in college, and when he told me that he was going into acting, it felt like fate: platonic, career-oriented fate.

I was nearly done with my public relations degree and had a healthy obsession with Hollywood. He got cast in a handful of quirky indie films, one of them took off, and he's scored half a dozen romantic comedy roles since then.

But lately, something has shifted, and more and more often I find myself here, trying to talk him into putting on pants and getting his ass to work. Things were simpler before fame.

I flip open my phone and scroll through the online calendar while I talk. "I don't know what to tell you, Ash. Ryan does action movies, you do romantic comedies, and Jonah does sports. I can put feelers out for more serious auditions, but for now—you signed the contract. You have to finish this out."

"You'll tell people I'm looking for different stuff?" He arches an eyebrow. He rolls to sitting and leans forward to balance on the edge of the bed. His gray eyes, just the tiniest tinge of blue at the edges, study me.

None of the producers we work with will be very happy with me, but I'll let them know. I'm not going to make him lose himself over movies he hates. When we first decided to work together, we agreed: friendship before business. It may not be a motto that works for everyone, but it's always served us well.

"Fine." He winces. "But I already told them I'm pulling out. I can't go to any more promos for this. It's humiliating."

I'm too late. "You already told them? You're supposed to leave the communicating to me. I could have . . ." I trail off at the look on his face.

Whatever. It's just one more Matthew mess to clean up.

"Don't worry about it. I'll deal with it." I fake an unaffected shrug as I smooth one hand over his crumpled bed sheets. I bend to pick up a stray protein bar wrapper on the floor near my feet. There's no point in getting mad when I can get the other thing I came here for: information. "Tell me about last night. How did it go?"

"You should have been there."

I arch an eyebrow, smelling a tragedy. There's something about the way he says it: You *should have* been there, because it is my job to know, after all. "What? What happened?"

Ash runs a hand over his face, messing up his hair even further. It only adds to his sex appeal, and I make a mental note to get him a new set of headshots featuring this longer, messier hairstyle. It'll kill with the casting directors, even the new ones he's looking to pursue.

He groans. "It's bad. You shouldn't hear it from me."

I almost stomp my foot with impatience. If it's as bad as his voice makes it sound, I'm surprised I haven't heard it already, no matter the early hour. "I need to hear it, period. I don't care who it comes from at this point. I'm here now, so spill." With every emergency comes a seemingly never-ending cycle of damage control, and if I've learned anything in the past five years of managing the brothers, it's that the sooner I start on fixing their mistakes, the better.

"Talk to Ryan." Ash finally meets my eyes, and I see something there I don't expect. Is that . . . pity?

Ryan's name kicks my chest into double-time, and I slap a palm over my sternum. Great. Just, honestly, great. Sure, I suspected that he was involved the moment Ash said something, but to have it confirmed sets my stomach on edge.

I grit my teeth. "Ash. Please. You're killing me here."

"We were out at the bar last night. After the fan meet and greet, remember?"

I nod. I remember because I was the one who facilitated the entire thing. Except, thanks to a major guilt trip on my parents' part, I couldn't be there. Instead, I spent the day with my GI doctor and the night hosting my visiting-from-out-of-town parents before they caught a late flight. I was forced to listen to Mom bemoan that fact that I work too much for the hundredth time.

"Ryan spent all night with this one fangirl. She was sitting in his lap, and they were all over each other. Out of nowhere, he proposed. It was bizarre. I've never seen him act like that. I don't even think he'd had that many drinks. It was like he pulled a diamond ring from thin air."

I flinch but cover it as I stand. Maybe we can work out a deal if Ryan agrees to let her keep the ring. I lick my lips and half turn, nodding. "Thanks for the heads up. I'll go find the girl and take care of this. We probably should keep Ryan away from fans for the next few weeks, or they'll all be expecting proposals."

Ryan has done worse, like the bloody bar fight he got into with a fan's husband last month. I'm not supposed to get my feelings hurt about him going out and doing things like this. Still, as his manager, it's a nuisance.

But as just me, Kell, it feels like a betrayal.

Ash doesn't laugh at my dumb attempt at humor. The space between his eyebrows furrows, forming a sharp V. "I doubt they will. Now that, you know, he's engaged and all."

The room freezes around us. "What do you mean?"

Ash gives his head a slow shake. "I told you. He proposed to this girl at the thing last night. Which means . . . Ryan is engaged. He says they're getting married. Having an actual wedding. The whole big thing. He seems serious for once."

"Serious about some woman? Who even is she?" My body flushes hot and then cold as a mixture of emotions hits me at once. I stutter, but nothing comes out. I'm completely out of words.

"Just some fan who he's been out with a few times. I don't think anyone saw this coming."

A hysterical laugh nearly chokes out of me. "This is ridiculous. Ryan wouldn't . . . Ryan's not . . ."

"I'm sorry, Kell." Ash's voice is soft but out of focus. "I don't know what he's thinking. But yeah, it seems real."

"How could it be real?" Somehow, I find the doorknob, and I prop myself up on it with one hand. I thought that this was another one of Ryan's stunts. He does over-the-top public displays and then sends me in to clean up the ensuing chaos. None of the tabloid-worthy escapades are real, though. Not wedding-planning real.

The floor spins beneath me as I try to gather my thoughts because this can't be happening. Ryan getting engaged without so much as a heads up is a PR nightmare, but I will deal with it because I have no other choice.

Normally, I can deal with anything. But with Ryan, things are different, and there's no way I'm letting him do this without having a serious conversation for once. Given our history, it's way overdue.

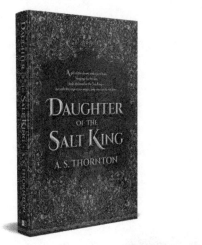
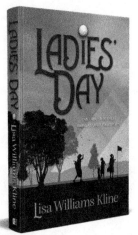

CamCat
Books

VISIT US ONLINE FOR MORE BOOKS TO LIVE IN:
CAMCATBOOKS.COM

SIGN UP FOR CAMCAT'S FICTION NEWSLETTER FOR
COVER REVEALS, EBOOK DEALS, AND MORE EXCLUSIVE CONTENT.

CamCatBooks   @CamCatBooks   @CamCat_Books   @CamCatBooks